For Lauren and Pancake

The Black Lotus

Act I
The Criminal

1

Saturday, the 31st of December, 9:32 p.m.

The soothing falsetto of Patti LaBelle filtered through the earpiece resting in Pierre Pelletier's right ear in between short bursts of radio static and jarring scratches of talk radio. However, tonight there was no time to enjoy her sweet crooning.

"Remy, can you hear me?" Pierre called in a harsh whisper, trying to press the earpiece into a position to minimize the interference.

He was perched high above the ground, balancing on the branch of an old oak tree, wearing a black turtleneck with the sleeves rolled up and matching black pants. On top of his golden brown, curly mop of hair he had a black knit ski mask that was resting there, rolled up. The white trainers that he was wearing were a stark contrast to the rest of his ensemble. His soft, azure eyes twinkled in the moonlight as the old oak's branch bowed beneath him and swayed subtly in the crisp, evening breeze.

Static.

"Remy! Come in, Remy." Pierre repeated, pressing the earpiece deeper into his ear.

Voulez-vous coucher avec moi ce soir?

"Not now, Mademoiselle LaBelle!" Pierre grunted to himself. He pressed the earpiece into the darkest recesses of his ear. "Remy, are you there?"

On today's program...static...Voulez-vous...static...The New Year's... static...Eve...static...avec moi ce soir...static...MURDER...static.

The earpiece replied ominously. Pierre recoiled at the final word which seemed to pierce through, destined for him. It had been spoken so suddenly, that he wasn't even sure that it had been real.

"Earth to Remy," Pierre tried, somewhat nervously. He tried to shake it off and calm his nerves. It wasn't normally like him to get apprehensive before a mission, but something about tonight seemed foreboding. "Can you hear me?"

"Pierre?" His companion's voice finally returned through the static frantically. He seemed short of breath. "Come in, Pierre!"

1

"Ah, Remy, so nice of you to join me," Pierre said as he rolled his eyes. Biting sarcasm usually calmed Pierre's nerves. "What are you doing over there?"

"Apologies, Pierre, we must be experiencing some radio interference."

"You don't say," Pierre replied. "And here I thought that you were playing your old Patti LaBelle records again. I thought that I told you once already, there's no place for her, *or* them on this mission."

"Very funny, Pierre," Remy answered with feigned laughter. "I've left my records at home, you know that."

"I thought it was pretty funny," Pierre said and shrugged.

His anxiety had faded away. He lifted the expensive pair of night vision binoculars that he had picked up for just the occasion to his eyes and surveyed the scene in front of him.

"Are you in position yet?" Remy asked.

"Not quite," Pierre replied. He lowered the binoculars once again. "I was waiting for my IT expert to get his act together."

"Well, what are you waiting for now?"

"The right moment…"

Pierre sat motionless for a moment on top of the branch of the oak tree. He slipped the binoculars into his back pocket and lowered the ski mask onto his face.

"Showtime," he muttered.

In the next instant, he suddenly leapt backwards off the branch, narrowly grabbing it on the way down with one gloved hand. He placed his feet firmly on the branch below and then began his descent down the tree. Pierre moved swiftly, scaling down its limbs. His feet engaged the tree dexterously, almost like extra hands, and his fluid and limber motion resembled that of a chimpanzee.

On the last branch, which rested some five meters above the ground, the neck strap of the binoculars, that were dangling from his back pocket, accidentally caught one of the limbs and fell to the ground. Before Pierre could stop himself, he landed on the ground next, more precisely, directly on top of the fallen binoculars, with a loud *crack*.

"What was that?" Remy's voice cried through the earpiece.

Pierre picked up the shattered remains of this year's Christmas present to himself and fought back real, grown man tears. He would have been even more upset if he had actually paid for the binoculars.

"Nothing," he answered and dropped the crumpled plastic back onto the ground. They were the first casualty that they would encounter on the mission, but they wouldn't be the last.

"Are you in position?" Remy repeated.

"Give me another second, Remy," Pierre answered, growing agitated at his partner's impatience. "I don't tell you how to do *your* job."

"Yes, you do," Remy reminded him. "All of the time."

Pierre waved off Remy's comment and then took off running across the lawn. He ran from under the brush of the first oak tree to a position that was concealed behind a second, and equally as old, oak. He peeked out across the empty street toward the large eighteenth century stone wall that rested on the other side of the road in front of him. Everything was deathly still.

"Alright, Remy," he whispered. "I'm in position."

"It's about time," Remy responded.

Pierre scoffed.

"Do you want me to run you through the plan again?" Remy asked. "We've only got one shot at this."

"I think that I know the plan already, Remy. We've been over it hundreds of times in the last two weeks. I think that I'll have nightmares about it for the rest of my life."

"Which might not be very long if you're caught," Remy replied. "Remember, you only have a *twenty* second window to make it over the wall and safely into the bushes on the other side before the cameras swing back around again and you'll be caught *dead* in their line of sight."

"Piece of cake," Pierre said and rubbed his hands together gluttonously.

"I've got the live feed from the cameras pulled up here, just like we planned," Remy said. "If you're spotted, you can bet that I won't be sticking around to see what plays out. I have a wife and two kids at home."

Pierre rolled his eyes.

"Some friend you are," he mumbled.

"We're not friends," Remy reminded him. "This is strictly business."

That would explain why these two men didn't even know each other's last names. However, that was okay, because those were the terms that they had agreed upon when they had first worked together six years ago. Besides, Pierre had never considered Remy much of a friend anyways.

"Can't you just disable the cameras or something?" Pierre asked.

"The feed is almost certainly being monitored from the inside," Remy said. "Disabling the cameras would arouse too much suspicion. This is the plan that we've worked on and we're following through with it."

"Easy for you to say," Pierre mumbled. After all, Remy wasn't the one who was taking the risk here.

"Do you see me?" Remy asked.

Pierre glanced over his shoulder and saw the flashing lights of his companion's white panel van parked just down the street.

"I see you," Pierre answered harshly and waved for him to stop. "How about a little subtlety? Are you trying to get us caught?"

"Is your watch set?" Remy asked.

Pierre rolled his eyes once more.

"What are you, my mother?" He asked. "Yes, my watch is set."

"Remember," Remy began. "You have *twenty* seconds. Not twenty-one, not twenty-two, *twenty*. Two-zero."

"Are we going to do this or not?" Pierre asked.

"On my signal," Remy said and then was silent.

Pierre glanced across the street as he waited for his companion's signal. Everything was unusually still. Pierre felt a bead of sweat form under his messy curls pressed up against the ski mask and it tickled his forehead as it rolled down. He steadily eyed the stone wall in front of him. It was certainly a marvel of eighteenth-century architecture that Pierre could appreciate, in fact—

"Now!" Remy called.

Pierre clicked the button on his watch and then darted out from his position across the street. With the dexterity of an experienced acrobat, he leapt onto the stone wall and hoisted himself up. He turned his body and sat there, facing the street, with his legs dangling from the wall. He lifted the watch to his face which read that only five seconds had passed. He gave a big yawn and then waved down the street towards Remy's white van.

"Now you're just showing off," Remy said, shifting his eyes quickly between watching Pierre through the van's windshield and the camera feed.

Pierre quickly flipped himself off the wall and landed safely in the bushes on the other side.

"What did I tell you?" He asked. "Piece of cake."

"Oh, so you have the necklace already?" Remy asked sarcastically. To which he was met with radio silence. This had been the easy part of the plan, after all. The next part would prove more difficult. "I didn't think so, keep that hot air balloon you call a head strapped to your shoulders."

"Hot air balloon," Pierre mumbled and peeked out of the shrubbery.

From his position, Pierre could see guests still arriving through the front gates of the château that rested beyond the stone wall. The Chinese Ambassador, Zhao Zhu, was just escorting his wife out of their limosine. In front of them was the Russian Ambassador, Yuri Yachnitch and his wife strolling down the imperial red carpet. Others were just arriving behind them. Beautiful women were dressed in brilliant evening gowns that shimmered in the moonlight and the men were clad in dashing tuxedos. Security for the event was leading all the guests past the tremendous stone lion statues that loomed over the long stone staircase and inside the château.

"Remind me again why we aren't attending this soirée?" Pierre asked.

"Because we're robbing it," Remy answered coolly. "Eyes on the prize, Pierre."

"That's right," Pierre replied and turned his attention back towards the side of the château that he was facing.

Directly in front of him, along the terra-cotta brick wall was a gutter that ran all the way from the ground to the roof, passing by three floors of windows along the way. The first-floor window was ablaze with light and activity. It was like a window into a world that Pierre longed for, a New Year's Eve soirée for only the incredibly wealthy and influential. One that *he* would have never belonged. He stared in through the window and pretended that someday he could until a large man stood in front of it and blocked his view.

Pierre's eyes followed the gutter up past the next two windows. The second floor was moderately aglow, probably only filtering up from the gathering below. The third-floor window was completely dark, and Pierre could make out nothing on the other side of it. This was his point of entry.

"Remember," Remy's voice called Pierre back to reality. "*Twenty* seconds."

"Yes, I remember," Pierre answered, exasperated. "Not twenty-one, not twenty-two."

"On my signal," Remy repeated.

Everything around Pierre felt unusually still again, except for the cool, light breeze which trickled through the bushes and sent goosebumps across Pierre's bare arms. He certainly wasn't nervous anymore, nervous wasn't Pierre's style anyways. But still, he couldn't shake the creeping suspicion that something was off, something that he couldn't quite place. It was almost as if—

"Now!" Remy cried out.

Without another moment's hesitation, Pierre darted across the lawn and leapt up the side of the building, grasping the shaft of the gutter with his hands and the tips of his shoes. He began to shimmy his way up towards the third-story window.

About halfway up, and without warning, Pierre heard a distinct grinding sound of metal against metal. He felt a sudden shift of the gutter and he froze in his tracks.

"That can't be good," Remy said as the sound of the grinding metal screeched in through his own earpiece.

5

The section of gutter that Pierre found himself on unhinged from the rest and began to slip backwards. Pierre made a desperate lunge toward the next section of gutter above that was still attached to the wall and managed to grab it in one hand.

As he hung there, about ten meters off the ground, the separated section of gutter grinded against the other and then came to rest, blatantly protruding from the side of the wall. Anybody with eyes would be able to see that something was amiss. Anybody without eyes would probably be able to tell the same for that matter.

Running on pure instinct, Pierre reached his other hand up to stabilize himself and pressed his feet firmly against the brick facade of the château. He then released the gutter from one hand and extended this hand toward the separated section of gutter. He was barely able to graze it with his fingertips.

"Hurry!" Remy called out as the camera feed on his screen began circling around once more. However, his eyes quickly shifted back through the windshield at the action scene that was unfolding in front of him. It was as if he were yelling at a movie screen. If his stomach wasn't in a knot, he probably would have wished that he had some popcorn to go with it.

Pierre extended his arm with one last desperate push and finally grabbed the separated section of gutter in his hand, pulling it back into place against the wall. He scrambled his way up the rest of the wall until he reached the window. When he peered in, he nearly tumbled off the gutter in surprise with what he saw. There, staring back at him through the window, were the piercing, hazel eyes of a woman.

2

Saturday, the 31st of December, 9:44 p.m.

The woman on the other side of the window stared at Pierre until a smug grin spread across her face. In the next second, she hoisted the window up.

"Well, well, well," she began. "If it isn't the infamous Pierre Pelletier."

With no time for pleasantries, Pierre rolled in through the window and she quickly slammed it closed behind him.

Remy pumped his fist emphatically as the third-floor window passed through the camera feed just as the window had closed.

"Phew," he said, wiping a streak of nervous sweat from his brow. "We did it, Pierre!"

Pierre laid sprawled out on the ground, struggling to catch his breath.

"What do you mean we?" He gasped.

The woman clicked a button on the side of her watch.

"Nineteen seconds," she said. "Personal best. But I bet I could have done it in eighteen."

"We're not supposed to use last names," Pierre reminded her, still trying to catch his breath. "But I'm glad that you were here to see that, Colette."

He yanked the ski mask from his head and let his sweaty curls bounce freely.

"By the way," he continued. "May I say how lovely you look tonight in your sparkling, scarlet evening gown?"

He reached out his hand to his old, childhood friend to help him up from the carpeted floor.

"You may not," Colette answered and swept her long, brunette and perfectly curled hair to the side, refusing to reach down for him. She crossed her arms defiantly. "Do you have my earpiece?"

Pierre reached into his pocket and dug around through the lint until he finally found it. They had decided, almost at the last second, that Colette wouldn't wear her own earpiece inside. Security was a lot tighter than they had initially expected and they feared that the entire mission could be compromised if her earpiece had been detected.

Pierre held out the earpiece to her and Colette reached out to grab it from his hand but instead, he grabbed her forearm and pulled himself to his feet.

"I greatly appreciate it, Mademoiselle," Pierre said and then moved past her, slapping the earpiece victoriously into her open palm.

She rolled her eyes and fitted it into her ear.

"I hate to break up this touching reunion," Remy said. "But do I have to remind you that we have a mission to do?"

Pierre glanced around the study. The walls and the shelves were littered with photographs, all of which contained one thing in common; the rather large figure that was Bastien Boutrel. Pierre recognized him from all the tabloids that filled the kiosks on the streets around his apartment.

The Boutrel's were one of France's wealthiest families. The château, of course, belonged to them. That was, after all, the reason that Pierre was there to begin with that evening. If, for some reason, you didn't know that the château belonged to the Boutrels, it was certainly obvious from the number of photographs that Bastien Boutrel kept of himself along the walls of his study. If, for some reason, you didn't know that Boutrel was an egomaniac, this was certainly obvious for the same reason.

There were a few photos of Boutrel smiling with important dignitaries, a handful of him forcing a smile with his wife, Beatrice Boutrel, in which his eyes seemed to be pleading, "help me," and even more photographs of Boutrel smiling proudly with his mistress, Lucile Lebas, who certainly gave him *plenty* of reasons to smile. Two of them came to Pierre's mind immediately.

As his eyes perused the photographs, Pierre couldn't decide which was bigger, Boutrel's head or his ego. What he could decide was that the only thing that he hated more than Boutrel's stupid smile was the stupid mustache that it rested under.

"Pierre!" Colette called out in a harsh whisper. "The safe!"

Pierre broke from his daydream and turned to her. She had placed a large, painted portrait of Boutrel and his prize-winning poodle onto the floor and behind it rested a large safe, carved out into a niche in the wall. Pierre walked over to it and closed his eyes. He then placed his ear up against the cold metal, as if he were trying to hear something on the other side of the safe door. Colette knew that Pierre's methods were rather unorthodox but methodical. She had learned a long time ago not to question it and just to let him work in silence.

"So," Pierre began, suddenly breaking the silence that he usually required. "How's your date going?"

"It's not a date, Pierre," Colette reminded him.

"Looks like a date to me," Pierre said, juvenilely.

"We've been over this, Pierre, it's part of the mission. He had an invite to the soirée; we needed a man on the inside—"

"Are you going to sleep with him?" Pierre interrupted.

"It's not a date, it's part of the mission!" Colette cried out before regaining her composure. "Besides, that's none of your business."

"Speaking of the mission," Remy interrupted. "Can we please get back to that?"

Pierre's ear was still pressed against the exterior of the safe.

"Are you sure that you can handle this?" Colette asked.

"I don't tell you how to do your job," Pierre said.

"Yes, you do," she reminded him. "All of the time."

Pierre held up a finger to his lips and shushed her. Colette's face became flush red.

"Colette," Remy began. "Are you at your post?"

Colette made her way to the door and gave one last look at Pierre. His head was pressed against the metal safe and his right hand was stroking its smooth exterior. She let out an exasperated sigh and then left the room, taking her assigned post just outside.

"I'm in position," she whispered as she kept an eye over the third floor bannister on the New Year's Eve soirée downstairs. "How's it going in there, Pierre?"

"In order to crack the safe," Pierre began. "I have to first *become* the safe."

"We're doomed," she mumbled under her breath.

Pierre ignored her. His fingers passed through every groove and every notch of the safe's front surface, caressing each like the curves of a beautiful woman. Then, he began to run his fingers gently along the sides of it. On the face of the safe was a digital passcode monitor requiring a six-digit sequence to be input.

"German steel, craftsmanship is methodical, every groove is intentional. Obviously, manufactured by the Germans as well," he said, admiring the safe in front of him with his hands before finally opening his eyes. "It's a Doettling."

"No kidding," Colette whispered. "It says *Doettling* in big bold letters across the front. Is that good or bad?"

"Only two people in the world know how to open these," Pierre said. "It's virtually uncrackable."

"Great, so you can't do it?" Remy asked.

"I didn't say that," Pierre answered and glanced around the room. "These things are tamper proof. Even the slightest amount of pressure and *poof*."

"Poof?" Remy repeated.

"It'll clam up tighter than a prude oyster at a Sunday service," Pierre finished. "The only way to reset it is from the inside."

"So, the mission's over," Colette whispered frankly.

Pierre wasn't ready to give up quite yet. He continued glancing around at Boutrel's study, trying to uncover the potential secrets that it held.

"Not necessarily," he said, distractedly as he turned his attention back to the digital passcode entry of the safe. "I'll just have to guess the passcode."

"Guess the passcode?!" Colette roared so harshly into the speaker that the earpiece screeched, and Pierre winced in pain. Colette quickly checked herself and glanced down nervously at the soirée to make sure that she hadn't been heard. Nobody seemed phased by her sudden outburst.

"That's what I said," Pierre replied as he rubbed his ear. "Boutrel is just as stupid as anybody else, maybe even more so. I'm sure that his passcode won't be too difficult to guess."

He glanced around the room again at the pictures that hung from every corner. Boutrel had a look of pompous superiority with his hand clasping the hands of foreign dignitaries in several photos. In other photos, he had a look of utter dissatisfaction—almost as if he were being held hostage—with his arm barely touching his wife. Then there were the photos of his mistress. In them he was wearing a smug, arrogant grin and had his arm around her hourglass figure, pulling her close. They far outnumbered any of the other photographs. Then, it hit Pierre all at once with the force of a ton of bricks.

"The mistress, Lucile Lebas!" He shouted excitedly and turned back to the passcode interface. She was, after all, the thing that he was most proud to have in his possession.

"Keep your voice down," Colette whispered harshly. "I can hear you shouting through the door."

"You think the numbers of the passcode spell out *Lucile*?" Remy asked, as Pierre began typing. "Hold on, Pierre, let's think about this! If you're not right about it, then you're going to be *poof*!"

"Not her name," Pierre said. "The passcode is his mistress' measurements! 90…60…90!"

He punched the measurements of the hourglass figure in centimeters into the keypad emphatically as Remy tried, in vain, to talk some sense into him and remind him to think this through.

When he punched in the final number, he was rewarded with a loud clunking noise and a beaming red light along the digital passcode interface. It was not the kind of clunking noise that you might expect to hear when a safe had been unlocked. It *was* the kind of clunking noise that you might expect to hear when a safe had clammed up tighter than a prude oyster at a Sunday service.

"Uh oh," Pierre said with a frown.

"Uh oh?" Colette repeated.

"What do you mean, uh oh?" Remy demanded. "Tell me that you didn't just type in your stupid passcode and that it didn't work."

"Okay," Pierre said. "I didn't just type in my stupid passcode and it didn't work."

"Pierre!" Remy roared angrily. "You absolute idiot! Of all the stupid people that I have ever encountered, you are by far the absolute stupidest…"

He continued his tirade against Pierre, holding nothing back, as Pierre tried to calm him.

"Just a minor setback," Pierre insisted.

"Minor setback?!" Remy repeated, irate.

"Pierre," Colette interrupted, her voice suddenly becoming gravely serious. "I hear someone coming up the stairs."

Pierre began to chuckle madly to himself.

"What's so funny, you imbecile?!" Remy shouted and then continued his tirade, throwing in a slurry of other insulting names. "You've sabotaged the whole operation!"

"You've got to have faith, Remy," Pierre said calmly and reached into his back pocket and pulled out a small crowbar.

"Please tell me that you have a plan, Pierre?" Remy pleaded.

"Of course, I have a plan," Pierre said. "I just like to build suspense. You see, those Germans are crafty little bastards, but the Doettling safes have one major flaw."

He placed the crowbar into a gap between the back of the safe door on the hinge and the wall.

"While it might seem foolish for a thief to lock the safe further," he continued as he jimmied the crowbar in place. "In this case, it's the only way to break into it."

"What are you blabbering about?" Remy asked.

"Pierre!" Colette called. "Someone is *definitely* coming this way, you've got to get out of there, *now*!"

"You see," Pierre continued calmly. "By activating the locking mechanism of the safe, it shifts the distribution of the weight of the safe itself. Thereby, shifting the center of gravity of the safe door…"

He pulled at the end of the crowbar that was protruding from the gap of the safe door.

"I can't stay here any longer," Colette said. "I'm compromised."

"Exposing one of its most vulnerable areas," Pierre continued. "And…"

The hinge suddenly snapped and swung the door open backwards.

"Voila!" Pierre finished, expecting bewildered admiration from his companions but instead being met with a rush of static through his earpiece. "I said that only two people in the world could open these safes, I never said that I wasn't one of them." He was met with only static again. "Guys?"

"You've got it?" Remy called wildly; his voice nearly indistinguishable from the static.

Pierre pulled at the rest of the door which grinded against the side that was still locked in place and then he paused for a moment.

"Just to be sure…" he said and reached behind the safe door. There was a switch on the interior surface that he flipped. Doing so reset the digital passcode interface. He turned his attention back to it and punched in the combination 94-60-90. The locking mechanism deactivated with an audible click and a green light as the safe door became completely detached and fell unceremoniously to the floor.

"What was that?" Remy called.

"Oh, I unlocked it," Pierre answered casually.

"Tell me that you didn't know the passcode the whole time," Remy asked.

"A magician never reveals his secrets," Pierre said. "But anybody with eyes could tell that she was a 94."

"Get the necklace and get out," Remy said. "Colette, status?"

Pierre's mind began to drift to the untold treasures that awaited him as he gazed into the safe's dark confines. His palms became clammy. There was only a single treasure within, but one that would more than suffice.

"Come to papa," he said and reached his hands into it, pulling out a sparkling diamond necklace set with a brilliant sapphire at the center. "The Han Sapphire," he marveled as he held the necklace up to the light that peeked in from the window. The sapphire centerpiece twinkled in the moonlight. "Much more sparkly in person," he admired with lust in his eyes. "And lighter too."

He lifted it up and down a few times in his palms and then shrugged. For a moment, he was entranced by it.

"Pierre," Remy called through more static. "Pierre, are you there?"

"Ah, yes," Pierre began again, slipping the necklace carefully into his pocket. "I almost forgot."

He reached into his other pocket and pulled out a black origami lotus flower that he had produced for just the occasion. He placed the black lotus flower into the safe right where the necklace had been.

"Pierre?" Remy called. "*static*...Did you leave...*static*...the flower?"

"I know that you said it was stupid before," Pierre replied. "But where's your sense of style, Remy?"

The signal coming in became less and less clear until Pierre's ear was flooded with a rush of static.

"Remy?" Pierre called.

Voulez-vous coucher avec moi ce soir?

"Ugh," Pierre groaned. "Not now, Mademoiselle LaBelle! How is this song still on anyways? Is this the only song that they play? What station is this?"

Pierre didn't receive any answers to these burning questions. Instead, all that he heard was a rush of static that flooded the earpiece. Outside, he could barely make out the sound of voices coming from beyond the door to the study and drawing ever closer.

"Colette?" Pierre tried. "Colette, are you there?!"

The knob on the door began to jiggle and then twist open.

"That can't be good," he muttered.

3

Sunday, the 1st of January, 8:48 a.m.

Detective Matthieu Martin of the Toulouse Police Department, Homicide Unit, woke up Sunday morning with a ringing in his ears like the bells of Notre Dame and a pounding headache.

He tried to open his eyes through the crusts that had formed but the morning sun that poured through the window burned into them and he was forced to close them again with a loud groan.

Matthieu had slept like the dead the night before. To be honest, when he woke up, he was a bit surprised that he had been able to wake up at all and that he *wasn't* dead.

For a moment, he didn't even remember his own name or where he was, but the funny thing about it was that he didn't much care. He only knew one thing for certain—he never wanted to see another glass of wine again. Although, the stench still lingered on his breath.

The pager on his nightstand began to buzz incessantly and he rolled over and flung his half-asleep arm towards it. There was a picture frame there that had already been laid face down and he inadvertently knocked it onto the floor, shattering the glass.

He slowly opened one eye and peered at the digits on the pager, which he instantly recognized, even in his drunken haze, as the number for the Toulouse Crime Scene Unit and he groaned again.

He contemplated either screaming into his pillow or making a break for the window and throwing himself through it. He elected for neither, instead shifting his body robotically to the edge of his bed and knocking three wine bottles off the bed and onto the ground in the process. He vaguely remembered at some point last night switching from the wine glass to drinking directly from the bottle. He slid into his slippers and then shuffled himself into the bathroom.

Matthieu didn't think that he could possibly look as bad as he felt. When he looked in the bathroom mirror, he could see just how wrong he was. He looked worse. *Much* worse. His beard had overgrown, and his lips were stained blood red. His greying hair was a disheveled mess. He wiped his lips, combed down his hair as best he could, then gave himself a quick, dry shave and neglected to brush his teeth. Then, he got dressed in his white collared shirt and began to knot one of his favorite pink ties when he suddenly remembered that this was the same tie that Genevieve had given him for their last anniversary and he frowned.

He took the tie off and crumpled it up into a ball, then threw that tie ball into the corner of the room. On the bright side, at least he wouldn't have to look forward to another tie this year. He grabbed out one of his other black ties and tied it around his neck in front of the mirror. At first, the tie slid through the knot too easily and began choking him. He reached to loosen it, but instead, something possessed him to tighten it and he did so, tighter and tighter until it felt almost like a noose. He wondered briefly if the strength of the tie would be enough to hang himself before finally regaining his senses and loosening it.

"Things can only get better," he reminded himself, reciting the mantra that the office psychologist had recommended that he practice every day in the mirror before his administrative leave.

He slipped on his black leather shoes and was strapping on the gun holster which would have normally held his issued pistol, the Chief had taken it away from him for obvious reasons, when his pager buzzed again on the nightstand.

"Alright, alright," he said, and he grabbed the pager and clipped it onto his belt. Then, he threw his tweed jacket over the rest of his ensemble. "I'm coming."

He began to move towards the bedroom door which led to the living room when the broken glass from the shattered picture frame crunched under his gait. He thought to himself, *I'll get that later*, but then decided that he probably wouldn't care then either.

In the living room, there were a plethora of other photos that had been laid face down and the walls were completely bare. There were spots where other picture frames had once hung, but they had been recently taken down as well, exposing the hideous yellow paint underneath. As much as Matthieu tried to fight it, this place was full of memories and one in particular came to mind as he stood in the living room doorway.

It was an argument that he and Genevieve had had years ago, shortly after they had bought the house. She insisted that the paint color she wanted for the living room was chartreuse, Matthieu argued that it was yellow. Genevieve had to explain to him that chartreuse was a shade of yellow. Either way, it didn't really matter to Matthieu what it was called. The fact was that it was still a disgusting color. Nevertheless, Genevieve could be a convincing woman and Matthieu could never refuse her. So, the walls had remained chartreuse for the last twenty plus years. Maybe that argument had been the start of it all going wrong.

Matthieu shook himself free from the memory and put his head down as he continued toward the front door. He stopped just before the door and reached for his car keys that were in the wooden bowl on the entryway table before an upright photo on the table caught his attention.

It was a photo of Genevieve with her arms lovingly around his neck that was taken at their engagement dinner many years ago now. She was wearing her favorite, red dress. He was wearing a blazer and matching tie. Genevieve had worked hard to maintain virtually the same physique and Matthieu thought that she could probably still fit her slim figure into the dress. As he looked down at himself, the depressing realization struck him that there was no way he could fit into the same blazer. Not without a girdle, anyways. He frowned and turned his attention back to the photo. Genevieve's long, straight, hazelnut hair was draped across his shoulder. Their faces were pressed against one another so closely that the two appeared to blur into one being, even if only for a moment in time. If ever love could have been captured in an image, *this* was that image.

"Forgot one," he said coldly as he tipped the photo face down.

He slipped his dark peacoat on over his tweed jacket and then made his way out of the door and to his blue Renault which was parked just outside. His phone buzzed in his pocket with the address of the crime scene.

Matthieu arrived at the famous Château de Boutrel and parked his blue Renault on the street, accidentally riding it up onto the curb where he carelessly left it. Yellow crime scene tape spanned the large stone wall around the château which provided a natural border to keep unwanted visitors out. But not *all* unwanted visitors, as would become evident from the events of the night before.

The pink terra-cotta bricks of the château were truly a sight to behold and a marvel of eighteenth-century French architecture in the light of the morning sun, but their beauty was lost on Detective Matthieu.

He exited his car and gave a nod to the officer guarding the entry to the crime scene. Her eyes warmed to greet him in a nauseatingly fake, sympathetic way. He thought for a moment that it would have elicited the same reaction from her if he had told her that his dog had just died. Matthieu tried to hide a mildly amused grin at his own morbid sense of humor. He grunted at her and crawled under the yellow tape and onto the scene where he was promptly greeted by the Department's forensics expert, Simone St. Clair.

She was a rather short young woman, with a blonde ponytail and a button nose that had always reminded Matthieu of what it would look like if a mouse suddenly had become human. Matthieu was almost positive that Simone St. Clair had gotten smaller in his absence.

"Welcome back, Detective, and Happy New Year!" Simone began, cheerily. Her greeting felt more like an assault. "You look…well."

Matthieu grumbled something incomprehensible and stormed right past her. He was never one for engaging in the casual nuances of small talk, but especially not today.

Simone followed close behind.

"How was your vacation, Detective?" she asked.

He turned and looked at her without saying a word. He didn't need to, the way that he looked pretty much summed up how his "vacation" went. Simone had noticed the bags under his eyes from almost across the lawn and from a distance she wasn't sure if it was the Detective or a vampire that had been approaching the crime scene because of his pasty white skin. This could have probably been attributed to the fact that he hadn't left the house in the last four weeks. Up close, she noticed, he looked even worse.

Matthieu turned away from her once more and began walking up the stone steps to the door. He frowned at the large, stone lion statues that guarded the staircase.

"Detective!" Simone cried out again right before he had entered the château.

"Yes, Simone?" Matthieu asked, growing increasingly more annoyed.

"I wouldn't go in there yet if I were you," she said hesitantly.

Matthieu stared at her for a moment.

"Well then," he began. "What would *you* do if you were me?"

"We could start with the exterior of the building," Simone offered. "It's a beautiful day after all. The sun is shining, the birds are chirping…" She couldn't help but notice the expression on Matthieu's face didn't change in the slightest. "We could check for prints?"

"Well, if I were me, which I am, I would first find out why I was called here in the first place *before* I started diving in and searching for clues. Does that sound good to you?" Matthieu answered with a halfhearted wink and turned away from her again.

"Detective!" Simone cried out once more, but in vain.

Matthieu ignored her and pushed open the large double doors of the château, leaving a worried Simone St. Clair behind him, nervously biting at her fingernails.

When he first entered in through the doors, he found himself in an open foyer. A large glass chandelier hung from the center of the room and a twin staircase, which had been painted gold, sat across from him on the other side of the room. The staircase wrapped around the walls and met on the second floor. The steps of the twin staircase were lined with a bright red carpet and along the walls were colorful painted portraits of people who were completely naked, sprawled out into various poses. There were more exposed butt-cheeks in this room than Matthieu had ever seen in one place. Except, of course, for that murder at the men's bathhouse.

To each his own, Matthieu thought to himself.

The next thing Detective Matthieu noticed was that the château was littered with police officers this morning, more than any other scene he had ever been to. In his haze, he tried to make sense of it all. Only two explanations came to mind—option one, Bastien Boutrel, the wealthy philanthropist, had decided to exploit his vast wealth and influence and buy the entire Toulouse Police Department to do his bidding, or option B, something dastardly had occurred here last night. Matthieu tried not to think too hard about it, but he didn't have to try too hard because he still had a nice buzz going. It was a good thing that he wasn't being paid by the thought, because his mind was still curled up in the fetal position in his bed.

He made his way up the right side of the twin staircase, as most of the officers were congregated on the second floor. As he approached them and they noticed him, he noticed the expressions on their faces change from boredom, to surprise, then to sheer terror. For many of them, it was as if they were looking at a ghost.

"Good morning, Detective," Detective Thomas Thibodeau, the much younger partner of Detective Matthieu stammered hesitantly. Thomas reminded Matthieu a lot of himself as a young man and for this reason, he had always despised him.

For starters, they had the same dark, jet black hair. Although, Matthieu's hair had greyed considerably, especially during these last four weeks. Thomas was also very enthusiastic and full of life. Matthieu had been that way too when he was fresh out of the academy, but those days were long gone. The similarities ended there. Thomas was slightly taller and a little more built than Matthieu, but Thomas was an emotional cupcake. Matthieu would obviously never tell him this, but he had always secretly admired Thomas. This made him despise him even more. Thomas reminded him of the person who he used to be, and that, of course, reminded Matthieu that his best days were most certainly behind him.

"Good morning, Thomas," Matthieu answered robotically without looking at him. He stormed right past him into a crowd of more officers gathered at the steps to the third floor of the château.

"Detective," Thomas began and jumped in front of him, impeding him from progressing any further.

"What is it, Thomas?" Matthieu asked, growing more and more irritated with each passing second that he was standing there.

Thomas fumbled for words.

"Maybe we could start with the exterior of the building," he finally offered.

Matthieu grunted and pushed him aside, continuing up the staircase to the third floor. The officers that lined the stairs cleared a path. It was almost as if Matthieu had some sort of horrible disease that the officers were afraid they might catch if they contacted him.

"Maybe we could check the scene for prints," Thomas continued, following Matthieu and trying to dissuade him from reaching the third floor. "Or we could just go for a nice stroll and catch up. It's a lovely day after all. Speaking of which, how have you been? How was your vacation?"

Matthieu ignored his partner. When he reached the top of the staircase, he heard the familiar sound of a camera snapping in a room to his left and followed it. He pushed past a few more officers and entered the study of Bastien Boutrel.

"Ah, Martin, so good of you to join us," said a shrill voice which sent a shiver up Matthieu's spine. Detective Matthieu recognized it immediately as the voice of a cold-hearted witch and he knew all at once why everyone had been trying to keep him out of this room.

"Genevieve?" He stammered, immediately sobering up. "What the hell are you doing here?!"

Genevieve Gereaux, formerly Matthieu, the recent ex-wife of Detective Matthieu, stood in front of the remains of a safe which had clearly been recently broken into. The door had been ripped from the hinges and rested on the floor, next to a painting of Boutrel and his prize-winning poodle.

Genevieve was wearing a stiff, gray pantsuit. Her hazelnut hair was much shorter than Matthieu remembered. She was a slender woman, but her face seemed to have withered with age even more so since the last time he had seen her, four weeks ago now. When Matthieu had turned 50, he had bought himself the blue Renault. Genevieve had called it his mid-life crisis. Ironically, when she turned 50 just four weeks ago, she also had a mid-life crisis, of sorts, but instead of buying a car, she filed for divorce.

She motioned for the crime scene photographer to snap a picture of the inside of the safe. Genevieve gave her ex-husband a smug half smile of satisfaction at his reaction to her presence.

"There's been a break-in," she answered nonchalantly.

As slowly and as inconspicuously as they could, the rest of the officers began clearing out of the study, hoping to not get caught in the crossfire of the inevitable ex-lover's quarrel that was about to turn sour.

"A break-in?" Matthieu stuttered in disbelief. He couldn't take his eyes off her, it was as if he was staring at the devil himself. He probably would have preferred the devil to Genevieve.

"That's what I said," Genevieve answered and then changed her tone as the smug grin spread across her face again. "You know what," she continued. "I'm actually glad that you came, but I'm almost done here anyways." She motioned to the crime scene photographer and grinned widely from ear to ear. "Get a picture of this," she said and pointed to her ex-husband. "I want a photo of the first time I've finished before him."

There was an audible groan from the unfortunate officers still in the room that hadn't been able to exit fast enough at the obvious sexual innuendo. The crime scene photographer snapped a picture of a furious Matthieu.

"What the hell are you doing here?" Matthieu repeated through gritted teeth.

"This is *my* crime scene," she answered. "There's been a theft, and a rather expensive one at that."

"Then what the hell am I doing here?" Matthieu asked.

"I believe that you're here for him," Genevieve answered and pointed to the corpse of Bastien Boutrel which was sprawled out, face down on the floor of the study. His body was cold, pale and stiff. Boutrel looked nearly as bad as Matthieu.

4

Sunday, the 1st of January, 9:31 a.m.

When the crime scene photographer had finished detailing every aspect of the scene as it was, Detective Matthieu flipped over the body of Bastien Boutrel to examine the anterior side.

Once he did so, the cause of death couldn't be more excruciatingly obvious if it had stabbed the Detective right in the chest. It hadn't, of course, stabbed Matthieu in the chest, but it had done so to the late Bastien Boutrel. There was a large dagger protruding from his chest that had pierced him right through the heart with so much force that it had nearly come back out through the other side.

"Well," Thomas began eagerly. "It's fairly obvious that the victim was standing right in front of this open coat closet when the assailant stabbed him." He made a swift stabbing motion with his arm. "Boutrel must have staggered back up against this shelf, knocking down this photograph of his mistress," he retrieved a broken picture frame from the floor. "And then fallen forward onto his face, plunging the dagger even deeper into him."

Matthieu didn't know when exactly Thomas had decided that *he* was the lead detective, but he surmised that Thomas had given the role to himself sometime during Matthieu's absence. Matthieu relished the opportunity that he had been presented to make a fool out of his inexperienced partner and re-establish his own dominance by teaching him a valuable lesson—never make an obvious statement at a crime scene to sound intelligent.

"Brilliant detective work, Thomas," Matthieu began. Thomas smiled but was soon about to meet the back side of the compliment he had just been handed. "Truly, none of us here had deducted that already. Here I was, working on the theory that Boutrel must have stumbled on the carpet and impaled himself on the blade of a dagger which, for some unknown reason, was resting upright in this very spot on the floor."

Thomas' face became bright red and Matthieu tried to hide a smug grin.

"Get a picture of this," Matthieu motioned to the crime scene photographer.

He turned his attention next to a display case on Boutrel's desk. The case contained a variety of daggers with intricate wooden handles. However, one of the displays was empty.

"It looks like this is where the murderer took the dagger from," Matthieu said. "Our killer didn't intend to kill Monsieur Boutrel, but they must have done so in the heat of the moment. The murder was, therefore, a crime of passion…and *that* is how you make a deduction, Detective Thomas."

"Forensics shows that there is very little blood except for in a pool directly under the victim," Simone St. Clair noted. "The killer stabbed him straight through the heart, but then the dagger acted almost like a cork to seal in the blood. Only when Boutrel fell to the ground did the dagger dislodge and some blood trickled out from his wound, onto the white of his tuxedo and onto the floor. Obviously, we have our murder weapon. What do you think the odds are that our killer left any prints?"

"Highly unlikely," Genevieve interrupted.

Matthieu glanced over at her with a snarl.

"I'd venture to guess that you won't find a single print in this château that belongs to the killer," Genevieve concluded.

"Why don't you leave the details of the homicide to the *homicide* detectives," Matthieu said. "You can focus on your little art theft or whatever it is that you were doing."

"If you think that the theft and the murder are two separate occurrences than you're even worse off than you look. I mean, for God sakes, Martin, you look like Boutrel's poodle chewed you up and crapped you back out, then it chewed you up again and *spit* you out!"

"That's Detective Matthieu," he answered bitterly, ignoring the bit about the poodle.

"Well, *Detective Matthieu*," she continued sarcastically. "If you haven't figured it out already, our two crimes are connected and we're going to have to work together to solve this."

Matthieu gritted his teeth.

"Luckily for you, I already have our prime suspect," Genevieve declared proudly.

Matthieu stared intently at her.

"Don't keep us all in the dark then if you've already figured it out, Nancy Drew," he said. Genevieve's ego recoiled for a moment at the demeaning insult. Her ex-husband had used it often enough during arguments to disparage her career and it stung every time, but this time, she recovered quickly enough.

She regained her composure and held up a small, black piece of paper that had been folded into the shape of a flower in her gloved hand.

"Is that supposed to be some sort of art project that you've been working on?" Matthieu scoffed, unamused. "Truly, it's lovely. Now, if you'll excuse us, the *real* Detectives need to get back to work. If you and your little Art Crime and Thefts Division want to play detective, do so somewhere else."

"Don't you recognize this, Martin?" Genevieve teased. "This is the signature of one of the most notorious art thieves in all of Europe."

"If they're so famous, then why have I never heard of them?" Matthieu retorted.

"The *Black Lotus*," Thomas interrupted in bewilderment. His wide eyes were focused on the flower in Genevieve's palm.

"Good boy, Thomas," Genevieve replied with a smile that made Thomas blush and Detective Matthieu flush with rage.

"How about before we jump to conclusions, we get all of the facts of the case together," Matthieu said coldly.

"The facts of the case are quite simply this, Martin," Genevieve began. Matthieu was gritting his teeth so hard that it was nothing short of a miracle that he didn't displace his own jaw. "There was a break in last night. The thief was able to crack into the safe here and liberate the treasures held within its confines. They must have been discovered while doing so by Bastien Boutrel, the owner of the treasures, and so the thief killed him in a desperate attempt to cover their tracks."

"That's speculation," Matthieu said. "Not facts."

"Must have been some hell of a treasure to kill a man for," Thomas said, buying every word.

"Oh, it was Thomas," Genevieve replied. "Haven't any of you been reading the papers as of late?"

The crowd in the room had thinned out to just Thomas, Simone, Matthieu, Genevieve and the unfortunate crime scene photographer. None of them responded.

"Martin?" Genevieve asked. "Have you been too busy these last few weeks to pick up a newspaper?"

Matthieu felt the sting of her comment, like salt in an open wound, when he remembered back to the pile of four weeks' worth of newspapers that were scattered around his front lawn when he left the house this morning. A cold chill passed over him. At first, he suspected that it was from Genevieve's icy heart. When he turned, he noticed the open window of the study where a cool draft was entering through. He walked over to the window and grunted as he shut it.

"If you had," she continued. "You would all know that Monsieur Boutrel had just come into possession of a very rare piece of Chinese jewelry, the Han Sapphire necklace."

"So, he purchased a small gemstone," Matthieu replied, unamused.

"A small gemstone," Genevieve repeated as she scoffed. "Do you know how much he paid for that small gemstone?"

"A couple of thousand euros?" Matthieu guessed.

"Try €60 million," Genevieve declared.

Matthieu's jaw dropped.

"I'd kill a man for that," Simone St. Clair said.

Genevieve grinned at her victory.

"That's sixty with six zeros after it, Martin," she said.

5

Saturday, the 31st of December, 9:52 p.m.

Pierre Pelletier stood there like a deer in headlights, a deer that had a €60 million Chinese necklace in its pocket, as the doorknob to the study of Bastien Boutrel began to slowly but assuredly twist open.

The first thought that occurred to Pierre was that he would have to kill this poor, unfortunate soul. In the next instant, he knew exactly how he was going to do it.

On Boutrel's desk, there was a display case filled with daggers that had intricate wooden handles and sharp enough blades to do the trick. Pierre was going to grab one of them and plunge it directly into the heart of the intruder. Even Pierre could appreciate the irony of referring to *this* person as an intruder.

He reached down for the display case with grave determination but suddenly froze.

Pierre had never killed anyone, or even anything, in his life. In fact, the sight of blood made him woozy. Even the thought of blood made him woozy. Even thinking about the thought of blood made him woozy. Besides, what if he missed the intruder's heart and failed to kill them? Then he was going to have a lot of explaining to do. Even if he was able to successfully kill the intruder, he would surely faint right next to them at the first sight of blood. Little good that would do him for a clean getaway. The police would find him passed out right next to the body as soon as somebody came looking for them.

The second thought that occurred to Pierre was that if he wasn't going to kill the intruder, he'd better find a place to hide. He had to hope that the intruder coming in didn't notice that the safe had been broken into or, if they did notice, that they would leave the room to get help long enough for Pierre to make his escape. Either way, they would both hopefully be making it out of this alive.

Without another moment to lose, Pierre turned to his left and noticed the only other door in the room. It was just to the left of a shelf which housed a shrine of framed pictures of Boutrel and his mistress.

Pierre ran to the door and pulled it open, praying that it was a coat closet that would be large enough where he could wiggle his way into it and hide there until his intruder had left. Fortunately for him, it *was* a coat closet that was large enough for him to fit into. Unfortunately for him, someone was already using the coat closet as a hiding place.

In his surprise, Pierre went to let out a scream, but nothing came out, from his mouth, that is. What came out of the closet was the body of Bastien Boutrel, which fell lifelessly out of the coat closet, right on top of Pierre, and the two toppled to the ground. The impact from the fall displaced a photograph of Boutrel and his mistress from the shelf and shattered the glass frame on the carpet.

The door of the study creaked open, flooding the room with light. Pierre was out of time. The intruder poked their head inside.

"Well, this isn't the restroom," a man with a thick British accent said casually as he scanned around the room before finally settling his eyes on Pierre with the body of Bastien Boutrel sprawled out on top of him. "Oh! I'm terribly sorry, gents," the man stuttered and closed the door as quickly as he could. "The French are such a strange people," Pierre could hear him mumble to himself as he walked away.

Pierre fainted.

For some reason, a memory slipped back in from his subconscious and Pierre was transported back in time to his early childhood.

Pierre had had a tumultuous upbringing. At a very young age, he was a sickly boy. When he was hospitalized, doctors thought that he would never recover. Obviously, he did, to an extent, and blossomed into the criminal that he was today.

Pierre's mother always blamed his later rambunctiousness on this early traumatic experience. He was a difficult child and when he became a little older, he began to display his criminal tendencies, or "sticky fingers" as his mother called them. It was almost as if he was born to steal.

The particular memory that Pierre was brought back to in his unconscious state occurred when he was just eight years old. His curly mop of golden-brown hair nearly covered his eyes. His brother, Phillipe, was a few years younger than him. Phillipe was just like a miniature version of Pierre with an even shaggier mop of hair. Pierre was always involving Phillipe in whatever new little schemes he had cooked up. This occasion was no different.

The job was simple, the target—the pearl necklace that their mother kept in her jewelry box, the one that had belonged to her own mother and that she only wore on special occasions. However, ever since their father had passed, special occasions were few and far between. If everything went according to plan, they could pull off the heist and their mother would never suspect a thing.

On Pierre's signal, Phillipe tripped over a corner of the living room carpet and came down hard on his knee. Pierre always admired his brother's dedication to the mission.

With their mother's attention occupied, Pierre slipped past them and crept upstairs and into his mother's room. His eyes immediately landed on the old, wooden jewelry box that rested on her dresser.

Pierre picked the lock of the jewelry box with a simple technique that one of the older kids at school had shown him. He had practiced the technique for weeks in preparation for the heist until he had become a master locksmith.

Everything was going just as they had planned it, but there was a slight problem. As it would turn out, Phillipe was a little *too* dedicated to the mission and had landed on the ground harder than he had intended. When he landed, he had scraped his knee and blood began trickling out from the fresh scrape. Their mother decided that he would need a bandage and left his side for a moment, despite Phillipe's desperate cries to keep her there. This wouldn't have been a problem except that their mother kept the bandages in a drawer of the same dresser that the jewelry box rested on. She was headed straight for Pierre.

When the lock finally clicked open, Pierre opened the jewelry box and gazed at the magnificent necklaces, earrings and brooches that were contained within its wooden borders. Lust filled his eyes. He never stopped to wonder how a single mother raising a family on the cusp of poverty could afford such pieces. He finally came back to his senses and he was wise to avoid falling into their pitfalls.

For one reason, his mother often wore these other pieces and she would have noticed if they went missing. For another reason, all the other pieces were worthless because they were all fakes. The pearl necklace was the only thing contained within the jewelry box that was worth anything. They were her mother's pearls and before she passed, she had left them to her. So, Pierre dug down to the bottom of the box, where he found the pearl necklace that she rarely wore kept in a separate compartment. He pulled it from the box and held it in his palms, he couldn't take his eyes away from it. That's when he heard his brother's wails grow louder and his mother's footsteps on the stairs.

As quickly as he could, he replaced the necklace with a counterfeit pearl necklace that was made of plastic. The fake was close enough to the real thing and Pierre figured that he could get away with it since she never wore the pearls anymore anyways. She was about halfway up the stairs now; Pierre was nearly out of time. He quickly replaced the rest of the contents of the box *exactly* as they had been. Pierre was always very attentive to details like this. She was on the last step now; he was out of time and there was nowhere left for him to run. So, instead, he dove underneath the bed and held his breath. His mother entered the room but stopped in the doorway. Pierre felt a lump form in his throat—*did she sense that something was amiss?*

She continued walking again and then her feet stopped in front of the bed, no more than a couple of centimeters from Pierre's face. She stood there for a moment. Pierre suddenly felt very aware of every subtle twitch that his body made, and he was frozen stiff. He thought his muscles might give out when finally, she turned her attention back to the dresser where she retrieved a bandage from the drawer and then returned to his brother downstairs.

Pierre expelled his breath in a sigh of relief and crawled out from under the bed. Phillipe's cries had dulled to a whimper as their mother put the bandage across his knee and continued to console him. Pierre came downstairs and winked at Phillipe, then gave him a sly thumbs up.

With the perfectly executed heist behind him, Pierre went to his bedroom to admire his new treasure. It wasn't more than an hour later that his mother had discovered the counterfeit necklace and confronted Pierre about it. He was spanked savagely.

25

Pierre always thought that they had pulled off the heist flawlessly and the thought of what had gone wrong would haunt him for years to come. It just didn't make any sense. There was no reason why she would have noticed that the necklace was a counterfeit because she wouldn't have even been looking for the necklace in the first place. Unless, of course, she knew that Pierre had stolen it. Did he forget to put back a piece exactly as it had been? Did she know the whole time that he was under the bed? Had he left some sort of trace? Was his mother some sort of clairvoyant? It wasn't until years later that his mother would reveal to him the one painfully obvious mistake he had made that had buried him…

Speaking of buried, Pierre finally came to his senses sometime later and realized he was still buried under the dead body of Bastien Boutrel with a dagger plunged into his chest. Boutrel's chest, thankfully, not his own.

"Ew, ew, ew," Pierre exclaimed as he squirmed his way out from under the large, dead man and then stood there, staring down at the body. "That *really* can't be good."

Without another moment's hesitation, he made a desperate break for the very window that he had come in from with the help of Colette when a singular thought stopped him, *Colette.*

He glanced at the door that he had last seen her disappear behind. Then, he glanced down at the dead body of Boutrel, sprawled out on the floor.

Every man for himself, he thought. *That includes women too.*

Besides, Colette was fully capable of taking care of herself. At least that's what Pierre would tell himself to help him sleep that night. To rationalize his decision even further, he remembered the last thing that he had heard from her through the earpiece. She had abandoned her position, and Pierre in the room, to save herself. Regardless, no matter how much he tried to rationalize it, Pierre didn't think he would be able to sleep much that night with the image of Boutrel's lifeless corpse burned into his brain.

Pierre could hear voices coming from outside of the room once more and decided that it was time to go. He turned back to the window and propped it open. Then, he slid down the line of the gutter, darted across the lawn and scaled the large stone wall before landing with a heavy foot on the sidewalk along the other side.

He quickly turned and began running in the direction that Remy's van had been—the key word here being *had*. When he got to the spot on the street where the van had been parked, it was completely vacant. Remy was nowhere to be found.

"Some friend he is," Pierre mumbled.

However, his mother's words now echoed in his ears. They were the same words that she had used to explain how he had been found out all those years ago, and they were surprisingly still applicable now, "there's no honor among thieves."

Pierre couldn't be mad at Remy. After all, he was guilty of the same thing himself. However, he was mad anyways.

Pierre looked around to make sure that nobody had seen him, or at the very least, make sure that nobody was after him, and then, the infamous *Black Lotus* disappeared into the night.

6

Saturday, the 31st of December, 10:02 p.m.

Pierre took off on foot towards the direction of his apartment, trying to blend into the crowd of people along the Rue Saint-Rome just in case he had been followed, but still careful to avoid all the street cameras. The lights on the street were blinding and the colors of the buildings and storefronts around him swirled around in his head like a toilet bowl. He felt like everyone that he passed by on the street could see the guilt written all over his face, and he couldn't shake the paranoid suspicion that everyone around him was an undercover police officer. No matter how inconspicuous he tried to look, he could tell—*they all knew what he had done.*

He ducked into one of the dark alleyways, gave one last paranoid look behind him and then ducked into his apartment building.

Pierre ran up the stairs and down the long, carpeted hallway until he reached the thick, grotesquely green, metal door with the bronze placard of apartment 2B. He fumbled for his keys in his pocket, still glancing over his shoulder every other second. Finally, with a shaky hand, he was able to insert the key into the lock and he forced open the door before slamming it shut behind him. He leaned up against it to catch his breath.

He stood there with his back up against the door for some time, playing back the entire scene in his head before he realized that his hand was cramping because he was clenching it into a fist so tightly. He looked down and realized that the entire time he had been running and leaned up against the door, he had been grasping the Han Sapphire necklace tightly in his pocket.

With his clammy hand, Pierre grabbed the necklace out of his pocket and tossed it carelessly on the dining room table. He began pacing back and forth nervously but could tell that he was starting to lose it. The colors of the room were a blur around him, and the ground seemed to teeter back and forth, like he was on a sailboat. He reached back into the same pocket and pulled out his prepaid burner phone.

He flipped it open and stared at the blank screen for a moment, then closed it immediately and ran into the kitchen.

There, he began digging frantically through the drawers for the small, yellow Post-it note with the unsaved number that he had written down to get into contact with Remy.

Any time that they had contact with one another, Pierre only used the burner phone to call him. Afterwards, he deleted any trace of their communications. As far as any physical evidence or phone records could tell, Remy and Pierre may as well have been perfect strangers.

Pierre was smart. He always purchased burner phones from a different kiosk so that he wouldn't be recognized, and he always paid cash. On this night, he had kept his other cell phone, his work phone, in a drawer of the table by the door. There was too much risk if it was found.

However, Pierre was also sometimes an idiot. Since he never saved Remy's number, the only way, therefore, that he had to contact Remy in case of a situation, not unlike this one, was in the form of a handwritten Post-it note somewhere in this mess of wires, old batteries and other Post-it notes, many of which contained Pierre's half-brained ideas for a crime novel that he had been "working on" for the last 10 years. It wasn't like Pierre could look him up in the phone book either, considering they hadn't shared last names.

Finding the Post-it note, therefore, would be like finding the hay in a needlestack, or better yet, finding a particular *needle* in a needlestack.

Nevertheless, he dug around in the drawers like a dope fiend searching for his last pill, or a panty thief digging around for—well, you get the idea. He threw the entire contents of the drawers onto the floor, along with all the dust that had collected there already.

When he finally found his fix, he held the Post-it note up to the light and then brought it back down to his face where he kissed it a few times in emphatic delight. He flipped open the burner phone again and dialed the number, hoping to give Remy a piece of his mind for abandoning him at the château. However, instead of Remy, he was greeted by the voice of a woman and nearly hung up the phone, mistaking it for Remy's wife.

The number you are trying to reach has been disconnected, the woman's voice said robotically.

Pierre pulled the phone away from his ear and stared at in dismay. He glanced down at the Post-it note in his hand and recited the numbers out loud.

"07 81 56 24 85," he said and carefully punched it into his phone before stopping himself. "No wait," he said. "Is that a 4 or a 9?"

He dialed the number again with a 9 instead and was greeted by the voice of another woman.

"Toulouse Police Department," the woman said.

Pierre dropped the phone frantically on the floor and scrambled for it before finally retrieving it and hanging up as quickly as he could.

"Of course, it is! Of course!" he mumbled spastically and then dialed the number again with a 4, this time more slowly and deliberately than the first. However, it was the same, robotic woman that answered.

The number that you are trying to reach has been disconnected, she repeated.

"That rat bastard," Pierre mumbled before trailing off.

He shuffled his way back into the dining room like a dead man walking and slumped down in the chair of the table across from the Han Sapphire necklace. Remy was supposed to link Pierre to the buyer of the necklace. Without him, Pierre wouldn't be able to sell this priceless artifact.

All at once, Pierre began to chuckle softly to himself, which soon emerged into full blown, nearly maniacal laughter.

The necklace certainly was priceless, he thought to himself comedically when he realized that he was now sitting across from the most valuable, and yet at the same time, most completely worthless piece of jewelry in the world. He may as well have just stolen the plastic pearl necklace that he tried to slip into his mother's jewelry box.

He continued laughing hysterically until there was a bang on the floor from the downstairs apartment and a deep voice yelled out, "shut the hell up, you lunatic!"

Pierre cleared his throat. He was fully convinced that he had completely lost his mind. He found himself alone in the uncomfortable silence of the room, a man on the very brink of unraveling, staring at the necklace which seemed almost for an instant to be smiling at him wickedly. It was a constant reminder of what had transpired that evening—*there was blood on his hands.*

Pierre sat back in his chair and tried to regain his composure as he played lawyer for a moment.

Even though he knew that he hadn't killed the man, who would believe him now? What would he say? *No, no, I was simply robbing Monsieur Boutrel, he was already dead when I arrived.* Believable. For God sakes, he had the dead man's prized possession sitting across from him on his own dining room table.

When all hope seemed lost, Pierre's inner defense mechanisms began to take over, as any person's would when they were faced with an impossible situation. He began to think of whatever he could to make himself feel better.

Sure, although it wasn't entirely plausible, it was nevertheless at least *possible* that Pierre had come across the necklace after the real perpetrator of the crime had killed Boutrel, stolen the necklace and then dumped it in the street somewhere. His ownership of the necklace didn't necessarily tie him to the murder. Hell, it maybe didn't even prove he was *in* the château that night. Pierre began to feel a little better until he remembered what *did* prove that he was in the château that night. Remy was right—*why did he have to leave that stupid flower?*

Pierre groaned. The church bells of la Basilique Saint-Sernin in the Toulouse town square chimed twelve times. It was midnight. Not far in the distance, he could hear the midnight train to Paris chugging away from the station.

Pierre spent the first hours of the New Year sitting at the table across from the necklace until the sun came up the next morning with only one thought on his mind. Bastien Boutrel had paid a great price for this necklace, €60 million to be exact. Before the sun came up that morning, Boutrel had paid the ultimate price.

Happy New Year, Bastien Boutrel.

7

Sunday, the 1st of January, 10:43 a.m.

After the scene had been fully swept and potential witness statements taken, the body of Bastien Boutrel was loaded into the back of an ambulance, but not without incident.

He was first lifted onto a stretcher in the third-floor study and then covered with a thin white sheet, king size. Boutrel was a bigger man. The only thing bigger than him physically was his ego. So, he spilled over the edges of the stretcher. The dagger in his chest was left in place and stuck out like the Eiffel Tower in the sheet itself, truly a grim sight to behold. Two of Toulouse's burliest officers wheeled the stretcher carefully down the first flight of stairs.

Downstairs, Matthieu was wrapping up initial interviews with the servants of the château. The last man he had to speak to was one Monsieur François Fouquet.

François was a handsome man, Matthieu wasn't afraid to admit that. His shaggy blonde hair radiated in the light of the chandelier in the foyer and his eyes sparkled like deep, blue oceans. Matthieu found himself strangely captivated by François. Besides his appearance, François was very forthcoming and helpful, Matthieu couldn't help but admire him.

"Just one last question," Matthieu began.

"Of course, Detective," François said. "Anything that I can do to assist."

"Can you describe how you felt about working for Boutrel?"

François hesitated.

"Boutrel was…a demanding man," he finally decided.

"Don't sugarcoat it," Matthieu said. "Let me hear how you truly feel about him."

"I was taught to never speak ill of the deceased," François began again. "But Monsieur Boutrel was an old, dirty, blowfish in a suit."

"A blowfish in a suit?" Matthieu repeated.

François extended his arms widely around his stomach and puffed out his cheeks. Obviously, he wasn't too fond of the man. His sentiments mirrored that of the other servants as well.

"Alright, Monsieur Fouquet," Matthieu began again as he jotted down François' exact words in his notepad.

He looked up at François but saw that his attention had shifted elsewhere. He turned to follow his gaze and saw that François had been distracted by the grim sight of Boutrel's stretcher turning at the base of the third-story staircase and continuing down the right side of the twin staircase on the second floor, passed the wall lined with butt-cheeks, where it finally landed in the large foyer.

Matthieu's eyes turned next to the strange sight of Boutrel's mistress, Lucile Lebas, burying her face and crying into the broad shoulders of Boutrel's wife, Beatrice Boutrel. Beatrice stood there stoically watching her husband's body pass. She herself had been the one who had discovered his body early this morning and had called the police. Genevieve was beside them, collecting their statements.

Matthieu would come to find that during her brief line of initial questioning, each of the women had told Genevieve that they assumed Boutrel had spent the night with the other. That was why they never suspected that anything was amiss until the body was found this morning.

Matthieu turned back to François.

"Alright, Monsieur Fouquet," he repeated. "Thank you for your assistance in the matter."

François nodded distractedly.

Matthieu rushed ahead of the stretcher and held the front double doors open for them. He continued down the staircase where he waited for them by the ambulance. He turned up the collar of his peacoat to shield his face from the wind, but mostly from the reporters that had gathered and were berating him with questions. Then, he struck up a cigarette.

The reporters filled in the area in front of the golden gate of the château and began circling the premises like a flock of vultures, looking for any way in. When they saw the covered body emerge, their cries for a quote from the Detective became even more incessant and they began jostling one another for position, trying to push their way inside. The officers at the front struggled to hold them back.

"Animals," Matthieu mumbled to himself and took a healthy drag from his cigarette as he shivered in the cold air.

As if in answer to the reporter's prayers, one of the officers pushing the body tripped on a chip in the staircase and accidentally bumped into the stretcher. The stretcher slowly tipped over and sent Bastien Boutrel out from under the sheet and tumbling down the long staircase. The scene became eerily quiet as his limp body ricocheted off each individual step. The body finally landed uncovered on the pavement below, right beside the Detective whose mouth was now nearly as wide as his eyes. He stood there, mortified.

The reporters roared back to life wildly and began ferociously snapping their cameras like a pack of hungry wolves that had just been given a slab of meat on a silver platter.

The officers that were escorting the body watched helplessly as Boutrel had tumbled down the stairs, watching in disbelief as it had collided with every step. When they finally came to their senses, they rushed to the bottom of the staircase and quickly threw a cover over the body.

Matthieu's jaw was still on the floor when the ambulance drove off, sirens roaring. The lit cigarette in between his fingers dwindled to its last embers.

"That's going to make a great headline in tomorrow's papers," Genevieve said as she casually strolled by him, a smug half grin spread across her face. "I thought you quit smoking?"

"I did," Matthieu answered, his senses coming back. "It's a disgusting habit."

He took one last drag of the cigarette stump and then flicked the butt on the ground.

She was right, of course. Later that day and into tomorrow, nearly every news agency in France would lead with the story. On the front page, they would plaster the photo of the dumbstruck Detective staring in bewilderment at the uncovered body of Bastien Boutrel like, well, like a man that had just seen a corpse tumble down a flight of twenty stone steps and land face up in front of him.

Thomas and Detective Matthieu rode together in Matthieu's blue Renault, following the course of the ambulance and nearly running over several overzealous reporters in the process.

Matthieu usually had a strict "no talking" policy in his car, but today, he was going to make an exception to the rule. For once, Thomas may have had some useful information for him.

"Alright, Thomas," he began. "Who's this *Black Lotus* that you seem to be so infatuated by?"

"You've truly never heard of him?" Thomas asked, amazed.

"Of course, I have, but let's pretend for a moment that I haven't," Matthieu answered. "How would you describe him to someone like that?"

"Well," Thomas began. "They'd have to have either been living under a rock or be a complete ignoramus."

Matthieu scowled.

"He's only the greatest art thief in all of France!" Thomas exclaimed excitedly with a twinkle in his eye. "Possibly even the world!"

"Alright, Thomas," Matthieu began. "Don't get too excited. Save me the fan fiction version and just give me a name."

Thomas chuckled until he noticed the stone-serious look on his partner's face.

"Oh," he said. "You're serious."

"Of course, I'm serious," Matthieu replied. "How do you expect me to arrest him if I don't have his name?"

"Well, that's just it, Monsieur," Thomas began. "Nobody knows his name. He's a ghost."

"Nobody knows his name," Matthieu mumbled under his breath mockingly and shook his head. "Tell me then, Thomas," he continued. "What makes this 'ghost' the greatest art thief in all of the land? Tell me why you've devoted so many valuable pages of your diary to him."

"Have you heard of the now infamous heist of the Museum of Modern Art in Paris?" Thomas asked.

"Let's pretend, again, for a moment that I haven't," Matthieu said. "Enlighten me."

"It was all over the papers six years ago. Someone broke into a third-story skylight of the Museum of Modern Art in Paris. No alarms were tripped, not a sound was made. The security guards on duty had no idea anyone was even there. One security guard claimed that he saw a ghost moving through the museum's hallways."

Although he would never admit it, Matthieu was intrigued and he was listening intently. For once, something that Thomas was saying had piqued his curiosity.

"Of course, it must have been a real person," Thomas said. "Anyways, the cameras at the museum were all on a rotating loop and every time they panned back around, another painting was missing. However, the thief was never caught on camera. Supposedly, the thief made several trips into and out of the third-story skylight. When all was said and done, he had taken *five* paintings in all. There was a Léger, a Modigliani, a Picasso, a Braque, and a Matisse."

"Are these friends of yours?" Matthieu interrupted.

"I beg your pardon?" Thomas asked.

"The names you just said," Matthieu began. "Are these your friends?"

"These are famous artists, Monsieur," Thomas replied, slightly dumbfounded at his uncultured partner. "You've truly never heard of Picasso?"

"Ah, of course, Pistachio," Matthieu answered. "I thought you said something else. Anyways, please, continue."

"Right, anyways, the total estimated value of the pieces was conservatively appraised at around €100 million."

"Then what happened?" Matthieu asked, trying, but failing, to hide his interest.

"Nothing, Monsieur."

"Nothing?"

"Yes, nothing."

"Didn't they ever find him or the paintings?"

"They both vanished without a trace," Thomas said. "Like a ghost." Thomas shook his head and continued. "The only trail he left behind was a single piece of evidence, the black lotus flower."

Matthieu sat on everything he had just been presented for a moment as they approached a steady red traffic light.

"Six years ago, you say?" Matthieu asked. "If it is him, I wonder why he's decided to resurface."

"And why he decided to *kill* this time," Thomas added.

8

Sunday, the 1st of January, 10:59 a.m.

The simple answer as to why Pierre Pelletier had decided to resurface was that he was flat broke. There was really nothing more to it than that. As for the accusation of the latter, Pierre, of course, truly had nothing to do with the death of Bastien Boutrel. However, he was tangled in the web, nonetheless. Especially after leaving behind his signature flower.

However, the now infamous heist of the Museum of Modern Art in Paris wasn't Pierre's first venture into criminal activity. It just happened to be his most notable.

Pierre always enjoyed petty crime—small break-ins and jewelry thefts. He considered himself a Robin Hood of sorts. Namely, he enjoyed stealing from the rich and giving to the needy, the needy of course being himself. Throughout his early 20s, he struggled to maintain a regular job. So, he had resorted to a life of petty crime in order to support himself.

He was 31 now, and not much had changed. While he was managing to hold down a stable job, it wasn't the most lucrative position, and it certainly didn't give him the adrenaline rush that his body craved. So, he still subsidized his income and his thirst for that thrill with small crimes now and again to support himself.

The heist of the Museum of Modern Art was his big break, and it was the first time he had employed his signature, the black lotus origami flower. He hadn't originally intended to do so, but it was too impressive of a feat to *not* claim credit for.

The black lotus flower held a strange significance for Pierre, even as a child.

Pierre had first become introduced to the black lotus flower while walking home from school one day. He and his old friend, Colette, used to walk home together through the cemetery when one day, he saw the flower resting on top of a tombstone.

He snatched it and kept it until it withered away. Still, Pierre could never get the lotus flower out of his mind. He would often find himself distracted, even in school where he would be mindlessly folding paper in the back of the classroom into the shape of the flower. He was mesmerized by its beauty. It was only natural that this would serve later as a signature for his crimes.

The story of the museum heist blew up in the media and the French public became enamored by the mysterious thief. Strangely, the *Black Lotus* was made out to be some sort of hero, rather than a villain.

As for how Pierre had managed to blow through €100 million in a matter of six years, the answer to that question was quite simple as well—hookers and blow. Just kidding, you see, Pierre never *had* €100 million. He only made a mere couple hundred thousand euros in return for his part in the greatest art heist in the history of France, possibly even the world, as Thomas had so eloquently put it.

Pierre had first been contracted through Remy. He thought Pierre would be perfect for the job because he was working at the Museum of Modern Art, at the time, and Remy needed an inside man. Remy had been hired by a mysterious art dealer who offered Pierre €150 thousand to pull off the heist. However, the dealer was only interested in one piece that was being held at the museum, a Matisse painting called, *La Pastorale.*

On that fateful night, the plan was for Pierre to use his own key to open the front door and make a late-night visit into the museum. He had been studying the patterns of the security cameras for weeks, but the whole thing just didn't seem dramatic enough for him.

At the last minute, he changed the plan, much to the displeasure of Remy. Instead of the front door, Pierre decided that he was going to enter through the third-story skylight. When Pierre had broken in through the window and had recovered the Matisse in under two minutes, he was completely undetected and totally unsatisfied. He became even more emboldened and decided to make *four* more trips through the window, returning with another valuable painting for himself each time. Remy was livid and pleaded desperately each time for him to stop.

Upon completion of his fifth trip, Pierre stole a piece of black paper from a drawer of the security desk at the museum, a feat that Pierre was almost even more proud of. He folded it into the shape of his black lotus flower and left it on the security desk. Just like that, the legend was born.

Remy sold the Matisse to the dealer and Pierre was left in a similar predicament as he found himself in now. You see, once a piece of art has been tagged as stolen, it's nearly impossible to sell it legitimately, if at all. No buyer in their right mind would purchase such a high-risk item since its resale value is practically nonexistent, except in small, dark circles of the art world. Without a connection to these circles, in Pierre's possession, the paintings were now virtually worthless.

Remy eventually reached out to Pierre and told him that the mysterious art dealer was willing to buy the pieces if Pierre still had them on hand, but at a much-reduced price. By that point, the utilities company had turned off the heat in Pierre's apartment and he was debating burning the paintings for warmth. The dealer knew that Pierre couldn't unload the paintings and he graciously still offered him €50 thousand for the set, probably because he felt bad that Pierre had gone through the trouble.

The growing popularity and mysterious shroud over the identity of the *Black Lotus* made the value of the paintings skyrocket on the black market, unbeknownst to Pierre. The mysterious dealer netted a profit of nearly €200 million and the paintings vanished from the face of the earth without a trace. Pierre had done all the footwork and came away with a measly €200 thousand, which he had easily blown through in six years to support his gambling addiction. When you're an adrenaline junkie like Pierre, you take your kicks anyway that you can get them.

As Pierre remembered back to every decision that he had ever made in his life, he was filled with regret. He remained seated at the dining room table across from the necklace which seemed to be mocking him with its brilliant beauty.

He had been contracted for the Han Sapphire necklace through Remy again. Although Remy had been exasperated working with Pierre, he couldn't deny the fact that Pierre was good, *very* good. However, right now for Pierre, the problem was that he had no way to get in contact with Remy, and certainly no way to get into contact with the buyer.

He had made a few attempts to reach Colette. Fortunately, the number that he had for her was still connected, and he had left a few, frantic voicemails, but to this point she hadn't returned any of his calls. It was like they were teenagers all over again; she rarely returned his calls then either.

Pierre suddenly heard a police siren whining outside and his stomach sank. He got up slowly from the rickety chair at his dining room table and walked over to the window. The curtains were drawn and only a sliver of morning sun was bleeding in through them.

Pierre pulled the curtains back, only slightly, and peered a cautious eye outside. He expected to see the entire Toulouse police force forming a blockade around his apartment building. Instead, he only saw a single police car, an unmarked blue Renault with a blue light attached to the top, trailing an ambulance. The two vehicles blazed down the street behind his apartment.

He breathed a sigh of relief. He knew where the vehicles were coming from, and probably where they were going. At the very least they weren't coming for him next. Not yet, anyways. Pierre shuddered at the thought. He knew he wouldn't do well in prison; he was far too pretty.

The events of the night before replayed like a bad dream. Every time he played them back in his mind, it was as if he could see them happening to someone else. His mind began to disassociate, and his paranoia was beginning to settle as he finally closed his eyes. However, he was transported once more to the scene where he watched it all unfold like an out-of-body experience.

The heist itself had been flawless. He had crept in through the window, avoiding detection and was positive that he hadn't left a single fingerprint at the scene. The safe had been cracked without a hitch. Pierre tried to skip over the next part, fast forwarding through the incident where Boutrel had fallen on top of him. The intruder, the man with the British accent, had seen him in the room, but it was so dark in there that there really was no way that he could have seen Pierre's face or would be able to identify him after the fact. Besides, the intruder was probably intoxicated from the soirée downstairs and had no idea what it was that he had seen anyways. Pierre decided that he was in the clear for this incident.

The next thing Pierre remembered, he was squirming out from under the body of Bastien Boutrel and making a break for the window. He slid down the gutter and scaled the fence, landing safely on the other side. Nobody had seen him, and nobody had followed him. In all respects, it was a clean getaway, he assured himself.

He had run back through the Rue Saint-Rome and disguised himself among the crowd. Pierre was quite familiar with this area and he knew the locations of all the cameras, there was no way that they could have—

Suddenly, Pierre's eyes shot open.

The cameras, he realized and then sealed his eyes and rewound the scene in his head. He ran through the Rue Saint-Rome, all the way back to the Château de Boutrel and leapt over the fence. He ran across the lawn and slid up the gutter to the window before the eyes of the out-of-body observer recognized the château's security cameras, pointing directly at Pierre.

9

Sunday, the 1st of January, 11:18 a.m.

The ambulance drivers lifted Bastien Boutrel off the stretcher and slapped his body down on a steel slab at the morgue like a cut of raw beef.

Detective Matthieu and Thomas followed him in.

"I always hate coming in here," Thomas whispered to Matthieu, glancing around at the closed drawers that lined the walls. It was like a shady motel for dead people, and it would have a few more reservations before the week was over. "Gives me the creeps."

The medical examiner, Dr. Amber Aveline, stretched a latex glove over her hand and nodded at it in satisfaction.

"Alright," she began. "What do we have here?"

Matthieu glanced at the man with the dagger in his chest.

"A man with a dagger in his chest," he said.

Dr. Aveline raised a curious eyebrow at the Detective.

"Obviously," she replied callously.

She lifted the surgical mask up to her face and pulled the dagger out of Boutrel's chest which complied with a terrible suctioning noise. She placed the dagger on the table next to her.

"Our murder weapon," she offered, as if she was the first to figure this out.

Thomas' gaze was locked in horror at the sight in front of him.

Next, Dr. Aveline ripped the gaping hole in Boutrel's tuxedo open further and dove two of her fingers into the open wound. The noise that accompanied it was a bit like the sound of cooked pasta being mixed around. She dug around for a bit, as if she had dropped something down there and was desperate to find it.

Thomas gagged and turned away.

Dr. Aveline finally pulled her hand out and then made a note in the pad she kept to her side, not even bothering to take off the latex glove. The glove smeared a thick clot of blood onto the page of the notepad.

"What did you write there?" Matthieu asked.

Dr. Aveline glanced up at him and he cleared his throat nervously. The doctor could always be an intimidating woman.

"You'll have to wait for the full report, Detective," she answered coldly and then turned her attention back to the body. She immediately began tearing the clothes off of it enthusiastically.

"Usually you've got to buy them dinner first," Matthieu mumbled with a smug grin.

The thought of dinner made Thomas nearly lose his breakfast.

"Why's he all purple?" Matthieu asked when the body had been completely stripped. Boutrel's stomach looked heavily bruised.

"Dependent lividity," Dr. Aveline said. "It's when all of the blood in the body settles. Usually observable two hours postmortem. This pattern suggests that Boutrel was face down shortly after he died."

"No kidding," Matthieu mumbled.

Dr. Aveline shot him a glance.

She grabbed a scalpel blade and made a midline incision in Boutrel's abdomen.

"What are you looking for?" Matthieu asked.

Dr. Aveline froze about halfway through her incision and looked up at Matthieu, obviously irritated.

"You'll have to wait for the full report, Detective," she repeated and then continued her incision, just as Thomas had regained the courage to look.

"You know what," Thomas decided upon seeing the man being split open in front of him. "I think I'm going to go wait outside."

Dr. Aveline stopped again.

"I think that's a great idea," she said. "Take your partner with you."

Matthieu nodded and began to follow Thomas out before turning around once more to the medical examiner.

"When can we expect that full report?" he asked.

"When it's finished," she answered, elbow deep now in the corpse. "The initial report anyways. Toxicology should take a little longer."

"I don't think we'll need a toxicology report," Matthieu said before giving Boutrel one last look and then turning towards the exit. "I'm pretty sure he was stabbed."

Matthieu and Thomas exited the room, leaving behind Dr. Aveline who by now had managed to get nearly her entire shoulder inside of Boutrel. Matthieu thought with mild amusement that she might be trying to squeeze her entire body in there to settle in for the rest of the winter.

Upstairs, Genevieve had made herself comfortable in the conference room and smiled through the plate-glass windows that spanned from the floor to the ceiling when she saw Matthieu coming up the stairs. Matthieu tried to avoid eye contact.

The other conference room upstairs was darkened except for the glow from the TV. A team had already begun watching through the security footage recovered at the château from the night before.

Detective Matthieu made his way to his desk cubicle but caught the eye of the Chief along the way who was trying to perform his favorite magic trick, a rather nifty one at that. He could make a Detective appear in his office by wiggling a single finger.

Matthieu changed course and ducked into the office of Chief Jean-Claude Jaubert. In his absence, Matthieu was almost positive that the bald spot on the Chief's head had grown considerably and his thin mustache was speckled with even more white.

"Matthieu," the Chief began. "Please, close the door and have a seat."

He motioned to the Detective to sit in one of the chairs at the desk across from him. Matthieu did as he was instructed and closed the door behind him before taking a seat. The Chief immediately stood up, almost simultaneously as Matthieu sat down, and turned to admire the bust of himself on the shelf behind him. His bald spot *had* certainly grown and cast a mean glare from the lighting above.

"I expect you had a productive four weeks off," the Chief said as he polished the chrome bust of himself with the back of his forearm. Surprisingly, his own head was shinier.

Matthieu thought about how he had tipped nearly every photo in the house down and then laid in bed with the lights off, curled up with a bottle of wine, only getting up to retrieve a new bottle from the cellar or heat up a microwave pizza.

"Very," he answered.

"Good," the Chief replied and turned back around to face him. "Listen, I know this is difficult for you. It being so fresh and all. But you know, the two of you are going to have to work together on this case."

"When can I get my gun back?" Matthieu asked.

The Chief scoffed before he realized this was a completely serious question.

"Not until you pass the psychological evaluation," he answered.

"Great, so you want me to see that quack psychiatrist again?"

"She's not a quack, Matthieu," the Chief replied. "I've actually been seeing her as well and she's done wonders for my blood pressure."

"I'm not going into a room with Genevieve without protection," Matthieu replied.

The Chief sighed.

"Then take Thomas with you," he said. "She's the best we've got in the Art Crime and Thefts Division. You were the best homicide detective in the city. She's got a good lead. I need you both on this and I need you to play nice."

"*Were?*" Matthieu repeated.

"Are," the Chief corrected with a grumble. "You *are* the best homicide detective in the city."

"As for this lead," Matthieu added. "This *Black Lotus* character. I'm not entirely convinced. What do we have to go off of besides this silly flower?"

"Isn't that what I'm paying you to figure out?" The Chief asked.

"Right," Matthieu answered. "But anyways, I've got a hunch. I suspect that it may have been an inside job. I interviewed a handful of the servants of the house. They all had a few choice words about the guy. None of them complimentary." Matthieu flipped open his notepad and began reading from it. "Cheapskate, old bastard, one of them, François Fouquet, called him an old, dirty, blowfish in a suit, whatever that means. I guess everyone really does hate their boss."

The Chief, aka, Matthieu's boss, raised a questioning eyebrow at the Detective before interrupting him.

"We're going to brief on this in the conference room in a few hours," he said. "You can share your ideas there. We've got a long day ahead of us and I can already feel my blood pressure rising. I'm going to heed the doctor's orders and take some time for myself."

"So, you want me to go?" Matthieu asked.

The Chief nodded and began rubbing his temples.

Matthieu stood up and retired from the Chief's office. He knew they had a long day ahead and he was dreading it.

10

Sunday, the 1st of January, 3:02 p.m.

"The *Black Lotus*," Genevieve began, pausing for dramatic effect. "Is believed to be a member of the Chinese crime syndicate, the *Viper Triad*. Their influence is believed to be primarily in Hong Kong, but they have tentacles that extend all throughout Asia and Europe."

Detective Matthieu stood beside her at a safe arm's length distance away. He could still smell the unsolicited scent of her perfume penetrating into his nostrils. As much as he tried to despise it, it was the same perfume that she always wore and it took him back to the first time that they met, many, many years ago.

He was 25, in his second year on the police force. She was 24, just starting as a clerk upstairs. Matthieu had gone into the breakroom where the Chief and his much fuller head of hair had bought doughnuts for the station that morning.

Genevieve was standing beside the box of doughnuts, leaning up against the counter and chatting with one of the Detectives from the Art Crime and Thefts Division. The scent of the doughnuts was intoxicating, but the scent of her perfume was even more so.

The Detective from the Art Crime and Thefts Division left the breakroom, leaving the two young adults completely alone.

Matthieu reached his hand out for the last glazed doughnut and at the same moment, Genevieve turned and reached her hand out for the same one. Her hand rested on top of his and their eyes met. It was like, for a moment in time, that these two souls had been intertwined. There was something so simple and yet so profound in that second before they both pulled their hands away sheepishly.

Matthieu scratched the back of his head and blushed.

"You take it," he insisted.

A single strand of her hazelnut hair had danced in front of her face, and she brushed it aside, behind her ear.

"No, you," she said, also blushing.

"Really, I insist," Matthieu said.

His insistence was followed by a brief silence between them. It wasn't an uncomfortable silence by any means. It felt like they were the only two people that existed on the planet. In the next moment, they began sucking face, right there in the breakroom of the police station.

"I love your odor," Matthieu said when he finally came up for air. The back of his hair was sticking up from where she had run her hands through it.

"My what?" She asked when she came up, slightly offended.

"Your odor," Matthieu repeated before clarifying. "Your perfume."

"Oh," she said and then pulled his lips right back to hers.

Their relationship had continued just as passionately as it had begun for the next 24 years, until it had ended abruptly just four weeks ago. Matthieu now stood next to her in the conference room, inhaling those same toxic fumes and he tried not to gag. When he thought back, maybe the spark had dwindled a bit, but Matthieu had thought that it was still there. In fact—

"What do you think about this, Martin?" Genevieve intruded upon his thoughts.

Matthieu suddenly broke from his daydream and turned to her. His eyes were glazed over and disoriented. He hadn't been paying the slightest bit of attention to the briefing.

He wondered whether he should answer her question as specifically as possible, but decided instead to answer vaguely, while still trying to disagree with every word that she said.

"No, I don't think that's the case at all," he said defiantly.

"That doesn't at all answer the question that I asked you," Genevieve replied. "But I'm glad to see you're still with us."

Matthieu cleared his throat.

"This was found underneath a tree across from the crime scene," she said as she grabbed an evidence bag which contained broken shards of plastic. "I asked you what you think it is."

"What did everyone else say already?" Matthieu asked sheepishly.

Genevieve rolled her eyes.

"Like I was saying," she began again, placing the shards of broken plastic back down on the table in front of her.

Matthieu's mind began to drift once more. She had won this round, Genevieve—1, Matthieu—0.

"The lotus flower has a lot of symbolism in Chinese culture and religion. The white lotus symbolizes purity and life, while its counterpart, the black lotus symbolizes rebellion and *death*."

Thomas raised his hand.

"But the *Black Lotus* crimes are completely victimless," Thomas suggested. "He didn't kill anyone throughout the course of the heist of the Museum of Modern Art."

"I'm sure that will provide great comfort to Boutrel's grieving widow," Genevieve answered. "There's nothing to suggest that this criminal wasn't capable of murder. For all we know, he slipped up and was caught, panicked this time and killed Boutrel by mistake. The newspapers made him out to be some sort of public hero, larger than life, like some sort of infallible deity, but he's only human after all."

Thomas scribbled down every word that she said furiously in his journal, or diary, as Matthieu had called it. Matthieu pictured Thomas scribbling the *Black Lotus*' name on the paper and then encircling it with hearts.

"As for the Han Sapphire necklace," Genevieve began once more. "We don't know terribly much about it, just the value that it was purchased for at €60 million."

There was an audible gasp from the other officers in attendance and they began to whisper among themselves.

"The black market value could be much higher," Genevieve continued. "I've made arrangements to bring in an expert on Chinese antiquities. Maybe by shedding some light on the Han Sapphire's origins, hopefully it can give us some sort of lead as to the *Black Lotus*' identity."

Matthieu scoffed under his breath. He thought that *she* was supposed to be the expert.

"Something funny?" Genevieve asked, hoping to embarrass her ex-husband again.

Matthieu felt the spotlight on him once more and cleared his throat.

"We should still consider pursuing other leads as well," he declared with such determination that even *he* was surprised by the tone of the words that had exited his mouth.

"Well, well, well," Genevieve began. "Would you look who suddenly recovered his manhood from my coin purse? I must admit, Matthieu, I'm not used to this much enthusiasm from you. Usually, you just lay there."

The entire mood of the room suddenly shifted dramatically at the innuendo. Officers squirmed uncomfortably in their chairs. It was as if everyone present had just remembered that they had somewhere else very important that they were supposed to be. Anywhere was better than caught in between the inevitable ex-lover's quarrel once again.

The Chief stood up from his chair and cleared his throat.

"Alright," he said to the group of officers before the conference room turned into a circus. "That's all for now. You're dismissed."

Before he could even finish getting the words out, the entire conference room was cleared out without leaving a trace behind. They had, fortunately, been spared this time.

"You two," the Chief motioned to Matthieu and Genevieve. He was performing his favorite magic trick once more. This time, with a wiggle of his finger, *two* detectives appeared in his office.

"Do either of you want to explain what *that* was in there?" The Chief asked, clearly irate.

"He's trying to undermine my entire investigation!" Genevieve proclaimed.

"Undermine?" Matthieu repeated. "I was simply suggesting that we keep all of our leads open. Don't base the premise of the investigation contingent upon one individual and then fit all the facts to suit that person. Especially someone as infamous as the *Black Lotus*."

"Up until five minutes ago, you'd never even heard of the *Black Lotus*," Genevieve sneered.

"Enough!" The Chief demanded and slammed his fists down on his desk.

Genevieve and Matthieu's bickering came to a screeching halt. The bald spot on Chief Jaubert's head looked like a red balloon and the vein that split his forehead into two equally large portions looked as if it was ready to burst. Matthieu decided that he would duck for cover behind Genevieve if it did.

"Now," the Chief began again calmly, practicing the meditative breathing technique that the office psychologist had taught him. "My blood pressure is too high for this nonsense. If you two are going to act like children, then I'm going to treat you like children. Is that what you want?"

"No, Monsieur," Matthieu answered.

"I think the question was rhetorical, you imbecile," Genevieve mumbled.

The Chief shot her an angry look.

"He started it," she said.

"I don't care who started it!" The Chief roared. He tried breathing meditatively again but he was shaking with rage. "Now, one at a time," the Chief continued slowly. "What other leads are you referring to, Matthieu?"

"I've been doing this for a long time," Matthieu reminded him. "A crime like this is usually committed by someone close to the victim. I think we should look closer at the wife, or the mistress."

"I already interviewed both of them and they gave me everything they knew," Genevieve said. "Parading them around here like criminals would be bad publicity for the Department."

"Bad publicity for the Department?" Matthieu repeated. "They might know more than they're letting on. If they're capable of murder, I'm sure they're capable of lying."

"Meanwhile, you just want to ignore the obvious trail staring you right in your stupid face, Martin?" Genevieve interrupted. "That's your problem. You're so stubborn that you can never let me be right."

"Let you be right?" Matthieu repeated. "Is that what you think this is about?" She wasn't too far off.

"Are you just going to repeat everything that I say?" Genevieve sneered.

"That does it!" The Chief roared and rose angrily from his seat. "You two need a time out. Both of you, in the corner!"

"In the corner?" Genevieve asked.

"In the corner!" The Chief shouted.

Genevieve and Matthieu cowered away and scrambled to a corner of the Chief's office.

"Not the same corner, you idiots," the Chief said. "Different corners!"

Genevieve and Matthieu scrambled to opposite corners of the room when suddenly, there was a faint knock at the door.

"What is it?!" The Chief barked.

The door slowly opened, and Simone St. Clair poked her mouse-like, button nose into the Chief's office. Genevieve and Matthieu were standing in opposite corners of the room, motionless, with their faces nearly pressing up against the wall.

"The medical examiner's report is complete," Simone squeaked nervously. "Dr. Aveline wanted me to bring it up to you immediately."

"Excellent, Simone," the Chief said, trying once more to calm himself. "Bring it here."

Simone placed the folder of the autopsy report on his desk and then scurried as quickly as she could out of the room.

"I want you both to stand there and think about what you've done," the Chief said to Genevieve and Matthieu as he picked up the folder and began scanning through the documents.

Matthieu tried to sneak a peek at Genevieve who was also trying to sneak a peek at him. The two made eye contact and then turned away from each other stubbornly.

Finally, the Chief spoke. More of a grunt at first.

"Hmph," he began. "Turns out you might both be right."

The Chief slapped the file down on his desk and Genevieve and Matthieu turned to face him.

"Bastien Boutrel was poisoned."

11

Sunday, the 1st of January, 11:06 a.m.

Pierre remained seated at the dining room table, engaged in an intense staring contest with the Han Sapphire necklace. There were two main things on his mind. The first was the cameras that had seen him, obviously that was bad. The second was Colette. The last time that he had seen her in that sparkling scarlet evening gown, she looked equal parts beautiful and fierce. He hoped sarcastically that the rest of her date went as well as it had appeared to be going while Pierre remained here, alone and in a desperate position. At any moment, he expected something to give from his current predicament. Finally, it did.

The cell phone on the table buzzed and Pierre reached over and grabbed it. The caller ID informed him that the call was blocked. He answered it regardless.

"Hello?" Pierre called hesitantly.

"Pierre, is that you?"

"Colette," Pierre began, instantly recognizing the voice on the other end. It was almost as if he had thought the call into existence. "Thank God it's you."

"Pierre, I saw in the papers," she began, hesitantly. Her voice was barely above a whisper. "You killed Boutrel?!"

"What?" Pierre stammered. "No, I didn't do it. He was already dead when I got there. All I did was open the closet door and he fell out on top of me—"

"Pierre," Colette interrupted. "Would you listen to yourself?"

He did have to admit that his story sounded absolutely ridiculous.

"But, it's the truth!" He insisted. "Colette, you've got to help me here."

Colette was silent.

"Do you have the necklace, Pierre?" she finally asked.

"Of course I have the necklace," he said. "What kind of amateur do you take me for?"

She was silent once again.

"I'll be in touch, Pierre," she finally said.

"What does that mean?"

Before he received an answer, the line was dead and he was alone again, staring at the necklace.

She had to believe him, she just had to. There was no way that she could think that Pierre was capable of a thing like this. They'd known each other since they were kids and even used to walk home together every day after school, through the graveyard where Pierre would disrespectfully practice parkour on the tombstones in a feeble attempt to impress her. Sure, Pierre had always had that disrespectful streak, but *murder*?! That was entirely out of his repertoire.

As much as he tried to convince himself, he had to admit that things didn't look good for him. His skin felt hot and uncomfortable. Pierre needed to get out of there now, and he knew unfortunately exactly where he had to go. He needed to get his grubby little hands on the château's security tapes.

So, Pierre grabbed a black baseball cap from his closet and a pair of big rimmed black aviator sunglasses that nearly covered his entire face. He also grabbed a scarf that he wrapped around the bottom half of his face. He looked fittingly like someone that had just committed a robbery. Ironically enough, these were all things that he had previously stolen.

Pierre grabbed the burner phone off the table and put it in his pocket, just in case one of his accomplices tried to contact him again. He hoped that the next call would be Remy. Then, he went over to the table by the front door and reached into the drawer for his work cell phone, if for some reason he needed that one too.

There was still one more thing that he had to do. He walked into his bedroom and pulled open the window across from his bed which led to the fire escape. He grabbed the small milk saucer that he had left out there for the stray cats in the neighborhood. Pierre had taken a liking to them and since he had spent many years in the same harsh streets, he could empathize with their plight. He filled the saucer to the brim with what remained of the milk in his refrigerator and returned it to the fire escape before heading towards the front door of his apartment.

He pulled open the door before giving one last look to the necklace he had left on the dining room table.

In his delusion, he thought for a moment that he heard the necklace cry out with the voice of a woman, "*Pierre, take me with you!*"

He shook his head but could not resist its beckoning call.

"I'm losing it," he mumbled. He went back and grabbed the necklace from the table, stuffing it into his pocket next to the burner phone before finally exiting the apartment building.

Pierre emerged outside and the chilly winter air struck him in the face. He was grateful that he had stolen the scarf, it would be more than a fashion accessory today.

———————

To his surprise, there was no police blockade that had surrounded his building, no guns pointed directly at his face. Pierre shuddered at the thought.

He never liked guns, using them or when they were pointed at his face. He always said that they lacked finesse.

He glanced down both ends of the alleyway his apartment building was situated in and he started walking with purpose. The path was all too familiar, and he knew exactly where it was going to lead him, right back to the Château de Boutrel.

The perpetrator always returns to the scene of the crime, he thought to himself. Only this wasn't a case where he needed the adrenaline rush from returning to the scene. No, he had a plan. The security tapes, those were his ticket out of this.

Although the path to the château was familiar, the Rue Saint-Rome was much different than the night before. There were no large crowds to blend into, which made evading the cameras slightly more difficult, but certainly not impossible.

Before long, Pierre found himself at the scene of the crime. Only this time, it was much different than it had been just over twelve hours ago. Pierre's heart sank.

The wall that surrounded the château that he had scaled so effortlessly the night before was now surrounded by yellow crime scene tape and dark clouds loomed ominously overhead. Police cars littered the scene and reporters were desperately trying to get inside. At his apartment, Pierre assumed that the police would probably have the scene locked down by now, but he hoped there would still be some way to retrieve those tapes. However, now it seemed impossible.

Pierre became absorbed.

There were a few security cameras mounted along the exterior of the building. However, there was only a lone security camera on the side of the château that he had scaled the night before. He fixed his gaze on it.

It was an older model of security camera, and one of the cheapest of its time at that.

Pierre and company had only had two weeks to prepare for the heist, which isn't much time to prepare for such a sensitive mission. While they were focused on the movement of the cameras, they hadn't given as much attention to the quality of the cameras. Pierre was now realizing that the quality of this brand of camera wasn't that good. These cameras were more of a crime deterrent than anything else. Boutrel must have settled on such a cheap brand of camera because he had decided that they weren't entirely necessary.

Boutrel always kept a large security presence on retainer. That, along with the large stone wall around the château and the towering golden gate at the front would be more than enough to keep unwanted visitors out, except for Pierre, of course.

Nevertheless, being caught on the cameras at any point during the mission wasn't an ideal situation. However, being caught on the way in would have been a lot worse than being caught on the way out. On the way in, he might not have had enough time to break into the safe if someone on the inside was monitoring the feed. On the way out, it would have resulted in a grainy visual of him fleeing across the lawn.

Still, he would have preferred to have the security tapes to erase any of his involvement whatsoever. That was when he thought up another, much bolder plan to recover them.

He was lost in thought when his work phone began vibrating in his pocket. It startled him at first, but he grabbed it out and glanced down at the caller ID. At that moment, he knew exactly how to put his new plan into action.

12

Sunday, the 1st of January, 3:31 p.m.

"Poisoned?!" Matthieu stammered. "But Boutrel was stabbed!"

"It would appear that Boutrel was poisoned *before* he was stabbed," the Chief answered. "The stabbing was what killed him, but it looks like he had something called *Gu* in his system. Says here it's ancient Chinese poison."

"I knew it was the Chinese!" Genevieve said.

"Hold on," Matthieu interjected. "All this proves is that there were *multiple* people that wanted Boutrel dead."

"Isn't it possible that the same person that poisoned him also stabbed him?" Genevieve suggested.

"Why would someone go through the trouble of poisoning him if they were just going to stab him anyways?" Matthieu asked.

"Maybe the blade of the dagger was dipped in poison, entered his system that way," Genevieve offered. "That way it would ensure that he was dead, even if the stabbing failed to do the trick."

"No," the Chief interrupted. "Traces of the poison were found in his digestive tract. The poisoning and the stabbing were two separate occurrences."

"Maybe the perpetrator couldn't wait long enough for the poison to take effect, so he had to speed up the process a little," Genevieve suggested. Matthieu was enjoying watching her squirm to defend her argument.

"We're looking at multiple people that wanted him dead," he said definitively.

"Why would so many people want to kill a humanitarian such as Boutrel?" The Chief wondered aloud. "At a fundraiser for orphaned puppies no less!"

"Fundraiser for orphaned puppies?" Matthieu repeated.

The Chief waved his hand.

"That's what the event was about," he said. "Well, besides ringing in the New Year, of course. The Boutrel's were raising money for the Toulouse Rescue Society. It was a whole thing."

"How did you figure that out already?" Matthieu asked.

"Well, I was there, of course," the Chief declared.

"Wait a minute, you were there?" Matthieu asked, surprised.

"Of course, I was there," the Chief answered proudly. "Everyone who is anyone was invited!"

"I wasn't invited," Matthieu stated plainly.

"Oh," the Chief said and then began to stutter. "Weren't you invited? Genevieve, did you know that he wasn't invited?"

Genevieve shrugged.

"Let me guess, *you* were invited too, Genevieve?" Matthieu cried. "Was I the only person in the whole town who wasn't invited?"

"Your invitation must have gotten lost in the mail," Genevieve said. "You know how that goes."

"Besides," the Chief began again. "It wasn't *that* big of an event. More of a gathering really. Just a few close, personal friends. Boutrel was a good friend of the Toulouse Police Department."

Suddenly, Thomas and another officer pushed their way into the Chief's office, all smiles.

"That was some soirée last night, eh Chief?" Thomas began before his eyes met his partner's.

The Chief cleared his throat uncomfortably and signaled for Thomas to leave.

"We'll come back," Thomas said, sensing the awkward tension as he backed out of the office, closing the door quietly behind him.

"Thomas was invited?!" Matthieu shouted.

"He wasn't invited, per say," the Chief defended. "He was only there for security purposes."

"Well, he should be commended for a fine job," Matthieu said.

The Chief began rubbing uncomfortably at the back of his neck and Genevieve glanced down at her watch, like she remembered somewhere else she was supposed to be.

"Oh, I see what's going on here," Matthieu said, coming to a sudden realization. "Boutrel was a 'good friend' of the Toulouse Police Department? Is that why we're working this case so hard? How much does he donate at the annual police gala? Is that it? Thomas was 'security for the event,' is that because Boutrel bought us out?"

"That's enough, Matthieu," the Chief warned sternly.

"Just tell me why we're investing so many of our resources on this case. It's because of the money, isn't it? We don't want the money to stop coming in from Boutrel's widow?"

"It's because a man was brutally murdered last night," the Chief interrupted.

Matthieu cleared his throat and took a step back. For a moment in his excitement, he did forget about that one minor detail.

"You're right, you're right," Matthieu replied. "...But Thomas was invited? Really?"

"Enough," the Chief demanded. "Besides, this case has become the top priority, but it's not the only case that we're working. Not that I have to answer to you, Matthieu. Genevieve, where are you on that jewelry store robbery from three weeks ago?"

"We hit a dead end," Genevieve said.

Matthieu scoffed and Genevieve threw him a wicked glance.

"Maybe you should figure out how to handle one case before you start taking on another," Matthieu snarked.

"Well, some of us don't need to be coddled because we're too emotionally fragile to be able to handle one case assignment at a time, Martin," Genevieve replied coldly.

Matthieu shrunk away. She was right, after all. This was a big case, but it was Matthieu's only case. The Chief was babying him.

"Stop it!" the Chief begged. He cleared his throat. "Keep on it Genevieve. I'm not surprised that you hit a snag in that investigation. It was certainly a strange one. I mean, what kind of jewel thieves rob a jewelry store but don't steal any jewels?"

"They didn't steal any jewels?" Matthieu asked.

"Just one of their machines," the Chief said. "Anyways, we're not here to talk about that. I need to know that you two will be able to work together on this, do I make myself clear?"

"Crystal," Genevieve answered.

"First thing's first," Matthieu began. "Before I do anything, I'm going to need to see that guest list."

"Ugh," the Chief groaned. "Let it go, Matthieu! It doesn't matter who was invited and who wasn't!"

"It's not about that," Matthieu assured him. "Someone on that list could be our killer, or *killers*."

"Right," the Chief said. "Don't worry about that guest list, I'll take care of that. I want you two to follow all the trails we've been presented so far and for the love of God, try to do it peacefully and without anymore sexual innuendos."

They were interrupted again by a knock on the Chief's door and Simone St. Clair poked her button nose in once more.

"We've got something you should all see," she squeaked.

The Chief made his way to the door before giving Matthieu and Genevieve one last look, pleading with them to cooperate.

The two made eye contact with one another. Genevieve stuck her tongue out at her ex-husband tauntingly.

"Oh, that's real mature," Matthieu mumbled and the two followed the Chief out of his office and onto the floor of the police station.

———————

Simone had run ahead. She was standing in the doorway of the darkened conference room and was waving at them all. They followed her into the room.

"What's this all about, Simone?" Genevieve asked.

"We've got him on camera," Simone answered.

"Who?" Matthieu asked.

"The *Black Lotus*," she replied.

Matthieu felt his heart sink into his stomach. He would be damned if he was going to let Genevieve be right.

The Chief, Genevieve and Matthieu made their way into the room and took a seat in the folding chairs across from the TV. The video was paused and on the screen was a dark, pixelated image of a mysterious figure on the lawn of the château.

"What am I looking at here?" Matthieu asked.

"Ladies and gentlemen," Simone declared. "I present to you, the *Black Lotus*!"

She gestured her hand proudly toward the screen.

"It's him!" Genevieve cried.

Matthieu stuttered.

"Sacre bleu!" the Chief exclaimed excitedly.

"In the next frame," Simone continued and fast-forwarded the tape. "He's gone."

"Like a ghost," Genevieve said.

"Now everyone just hold on a second," Matthieu tried.

53

"If you look here," Simone continued, ignoring him. "The third-story window is wide open."

Matthieu remembered absentmindedly closing the open window at the crime scene.

"It's not that way in the previous frame," Simone said. "The time stamp in the corner of the screen is consistent with the time of death from the medical examiner's report."

"This is insane," Matthieu tried, unwilling to accept that Genevieve was correct.

"I hate to bring the excitement level in the room down," the Chief began. "But there's no way we could possibly pull an ID from that picture."

"Not yet," Simone said. "There's something else though," she continued and ejected the security tape. She replaced it with another, identical tape. "The cameras at the château are incredibly outdated. They work off of VHS tapes and the tapes themselves can only hold an hour's worth of film. The tape showing the figure begins at 9:35 p.m. and the previous one ends right before that."

Matthieu was crushed and the words she was saying only sounded like a jumble of nonsense.

"It's a preliminary viewing of course," she continued. "But we've scanned all of the tapes from this angle hours prior to the mystery figure's appearance. We see the figure leaving in the frame I just showed you, but we never see the figure entering in any of the other tapes. Do you know what that means?"

Matthieu immediately regained himself and his fingers began tingling with excitement. Of course, he knew what that meant. It meant that he was right, but more importantly, Genevieve was wrong.

"Our mysterious figure, the murderer, was *at* the soirée!" He declared excitedly.

"Bingo!" Simone replied. "Gold star for Detective Matthieu!"

Matthieu pumped his fist in excitement. He had won this round. Genevieve—1, Matthieu—1. Genevieve seemed deflated.

"Why don't we try to reign down some of the enthusiasm," the Chief said. "Let's keep it professional. The man is still dead."

Matthieu cleared his throat uncomfortably as the Chief stood up from his chair.

"Brilliant work, Simone," he said. "You made it seem like you thought we might be able to get an ID off that image. What do you think about getting it down to the lab, seeing if they can't enhance the picture? I also want to keep reviewing the other tapes, make sure that we're absolutely certain that the culprit didn't enter the château the same way that he exited, or maybe from another vantage point."

"I'll get on it right away, Chief," Simone answered with a salute. Her right eye began rapidly twitching on its own.

"How long have you been watching these tapes, Simone?" the Chief asked.

"About four hours," she informed him.

"Maybe get someone *else* to watch the tapes for a bit," the Chief suggested. "You should try to get some rest in the breakroom."

"Aye aye, Captain," Simone replied with another salute.

"I'll take the tape down to the lab," Genevieve said and snatched the security tape from Simone's hands. "I'll put the fear of God into them to get it done as quickly as possible."

Matthieu didn't doubt that she could.

Simone marched out of the room. Her back leg seemed to drag a bit behind her as she did so.

"Alright, Matthieu," the Chief said. "Looks like you were right about one thing. I'll get you that guest list. Tell me, where do you want to go from here?"

"I want to interview the wife and the mistress," Matthieu answered.

"Alright," the Chief replied. "We'll get them in here right away."

The Chief turned and walked away. Matthieu turned to Genevieve who was mulling the tape over in her hands. He stuck his tongue out at her. Genevieve shook her head angrily and stormed out, but not before shoving Matthieu to the side.

Matthieu proceeded through the station floor with an arrogant grin plastered on his face and made his way to the sidewalk outside of the station. There, he lit up a cigarette and took a long, healthy drag. There was something on his mind that was bothering him, but he was almost too excited to let the thought through—it was that stupid flower.

The presence of that flower certainly suggested that the *Black Lotus* had been at the scene. If that figure in the image was the *Black Lotus*, as Genevieve surmised, then something was amiss. Maybe Matthieu had been right initially about trying to keep the two crimes separate.

When Thomas was rambling on about the heist of the Museum of Modern Art in Paris, Matthieu remembered him saying that the thief was able to enter the museum *five* times to retrieve the paintings. Not once was he caught on camera. If this was the same thief, and he was there that night to steal the necklace, now, there he was, front and center on the château's security tapes. It all just seemed a little too convenient.

If it really was him, then maybe something spooked him, Matthieu wondered. *Made him careless… killing someone could certainly do that.*

Matthieu tried to dismiss the thought with a long puff of his cigarette. He refused to believe in the involvement of a criminal parading around leaving flowers behind him everywhere that he went. He stared at a fresh scratch on his blue Renault that was parked on the curb outside and he frowned.

"Excuse me, sir!" A voice called out to him, breaking him from his trance.

Matthieu turned to look.

Just down the sidewalk, a man was approaching him. The man was dressed in all black with a baseball cap, large sunglasses that nearly covered his whole face and a black scarf.

"I'm here to see the Chief of police," Pierre Pelletier said.

13

Sunday, the 1st of January, 3:58 p.m.

"Who are you supposed to be," Matthieu began. "Fabien Corbineau?"

"I'm afraid I don't know who that is," Pierre replied.

"Really?" Matthieu asked, scanning Pierre's all black ensemble up and down. "He's a famous male model in France."

Pierre stared back at Matthieu blankly.

"Vogue? L'Officiel? Krave?" Matthieu tried.

"Are these friends of yours?" Pierre asked.

"No," Matthieu responded. "These are men's fashion magazines."

Pierre pulled his glasses down a bit and raised a curious eyebrow at the Detective. He scanned him from head to toe.

"What do you know about men's fashion?" Pierre asked.

Matthieu could feel his jaw tighten.

"What business do you have with the Chief of police?" He demanded, annoyed.

"None of *your* business," Pierre replied.

"Oh," Matthieu said. "So, you're a smart guy, are you?"

"Better than being a *dumb* guy, wouldn't you say?" Pierre retorted and raised an eyebrow again at the Detective.

Matthieu had to restrain himself from reaching out and strangling Pierre. His neck looked particularly strangleable today, especially in that scarf.

"What's your name, smart guy?" Matthieu asked.

"Pierre Pelletier," Pierre answered without hesitation. "It might do you well to remember it."

"So," Matthieu began calmly, but his face was red with rage. "You want to see the Chief of police?"

"You have a world-class memory, Monsieur," Pierre mocked. He was trying his hardest to suppress his smile. He was enjoying this. "Like that of an elephant." His eyes glanced down at the Detective's gut which had grown considerably since his days at the academy.

"How about I lead you to him in cuffs?" Matthieu threatened and pulled out the handcuffs that he had linked to his waistline.

"That won't be necessary," Pierre said. "I haven't done anything wrong." *That you know of.* "Like I said," he continued. "I simply have business with the Chief of police."

"I heard you the first time," Matthieu said. "You want to see him so badly? Fine! I'll take you to him."

Matthieu threw the cigarette down and stomped it out with the heel of his shoe.

"You should really think about quitting," Pierre said. "It's a disgusting habit."

Matthieu grabbed the handle of the front door of the Toulouse Police Department and nearly ripped it off its hinges. He motioned angrily for Pierre to go inside.

Pierre began walking through the door but stopped and eyed the Detective once more.

"If you want to know something about men's fashion, lose the tie," Pierre said. "And unbutton that top button. And also lose the tweed jacket, who do you think you are, a tenured University history professor?"

Matthieu looked down at himself and gritted his teeth.

"On second thought," Pierre decided. "Just burn the whole thing."

Pierre grinned and then proceeded into the building. He stopped in the front hall so that Matthieu could escort him in further.

Matthieu indignantly led Pierre up the stairs to the second floor of the building where Genevieve was there to greet them at the steps. Her eyes suddenly lit up.

"Pierre!" She shouted excitedly and went over to the man Matthieu had just met.

"You know this clown?" Matthieu asked.

Genevieve and Pierre locked arms and then kissed each other cordially, once on each cheek. Just a moment ago, Matthieu didn't think he could detest this man anymore, he was wrong.

"Of course, I know him," Genevieve said. "He's my Chinese antiquities expert. I called him just this morning to consult on the case!"

She turned back to Pierre.

"I see that you've met Detective Matthieu," she said. "Sorry about that. I promise we're not all like him."

"What's that supposed to mean?" Matthieu asked.

Pierre and Genevieve giggled like school children.

"When you called this morning, Genevieve," Pierre began. "I have to admit that I was pleasantly surprised. It was horribly dreadful business that I read about in the paper today, but any chance I get to be in the same room as a beautiful woman such as yourself, I consider a treat."

Genevieve blushed at Pierre, who was always the charmer. Matthieu blushed with rage.

"Speaking of the paper," Pierre continued and turned to Matthieu. "I thought that you looked familiar." He reached into his back pocket and pulled out a folded up late edition of the newspaper, *Le Figaro*. He unfolded it and presented it to Matthieu. There on the cover was the photo of Matthieu standing stupefied over the body of Bastien Boutrel. "Any chance I could get an autograph?"

Matthieu stared down at the photo in Pierre's hands and his brain began to short circuit.

"Maybe later, then," Pierre said after a few moments where Matthieu was frozen in place. He thought for a moment that he had broken him.

"Please, Pierre," Genevieve interrupted. "Follow me. I'll show you where you can set up."

"Tootles," Pierre said and waved back at Matthieu.

Matthieu's entire body was shaking with rage. He stormed off to the restroom, mumbling obscenities to himself.

Genevieve led Pierre into the conference room. When she turned to the side, the Chief was performing his favorite magic trick once again and she rolled her eyes.

"Make yourself comfortable," she said to Pierre and then closed the door behind him to join the Chief in his office.

Pierre was left alone in the conference room. The table was littered with evidence bags, his evidence. It was like a trail of breadcrumbs that ended directly at him.

The air vent in the room high on the wall behind him roared to life. Hot, dry air burst from the vent as he picked up one of the bags which contained shards of broken plastic. He had to fight back real tears when he recognized the plastic as the destroyed remains of the Christmas gift he had gotten himself that year, his expensive night vision binoculars.

Genevieve appeared in the Chief's office and closed the door behind her.

"Where's Matthieu?" The Chief asked.

"The last time I saw him I believe he was on his way to cry in the restroom," she answered.

"Not again," the Chief mumbled and then yelled out to Thomas who was seated in his cubicle on the station floor. "Thomas!" He shouted. Thomas nearly fell out of his chair.

"Yes, Chief?" Thomas called back.

"When you see Matthieu, send him in," the Chief said.

Thomas felt a wave of relief that *he* hadn't been called into the office.

A few moments later, Matthieu appeared in the Chief's office, completing the final act of the Chief's trick. Matthieu's eyes were bloodshot and his cheeks were tearstained. There was something else that was different about him that the Chief tried to place.

"Nice of you to join us, Matthieu," he said before pausing and focusing his attention in on the Detective. "Wait a minute, weren't you wearing a tie before?"

Matthieu had removed his tie and let loose the first two buttons on his collared shirt, following Pierre's advice.

"No, Monsieur," he answered and took a seat in the chair beside Genevieve.

"Anyways," the Chief began again. "Matthieu, I'm speaking to you directly. Are you hearing me?"

Matthieu sniffled once and nodded.

"Monsieur Pelletier is a guest here. I want you to treat him as such, is that understood?"

"Yes, Monsieur," Matthieu grumbled.

"Good," the Chief said. "Then in the meantime, you'll be responsible for Monsieur Pelletier while he is our guest."

Matthieu's eyes widened.

"But, Monsieur—" he tried.

"The only *butt* that I want to see," the Chief interrupted. "Is yours getting Monsieur Pelletier anything that he wants or needs!"

Matthieu sat there in shock and a smug grin spread across Genevieve's face.

"Who the hell does this guy think that he is anyways, this *Pierre*?" Matthieu said. The name was bitter on his tongue. "Why have we included him into our investigation?"

"He doesn't know the full details of the investigation, Matthieu," the Chief assured him. "Besides, we bring in civilians all the time to consult on cases."

"He's one of my many connections to the art world," Genevieve interrupted. "He's currently the head curator of the Chinese exhibit at the Museum de Toulouse and before that, he was the curator of the Museum of Modern Art in Paris. And he happens to be a close, *personal* friend. He knows everything that there is to know about Chinese art and culture."

"Well, isn't that lovely for him," Matthieu grumbled. "You two seem to be pretty comfortable with one another. Don't think I didn't notice you getting lost in each other's eyes."

"It's a strictly professional relationship, Martin," Genevieve said. "But his soft, azure eyes certainly aren't hard to look at."

"Azure?" Matthieu asked. "His eyes are blue."

"Azure is a shade of blue, Martin."

"Then why not just say that?" Matthieu cried. "Say that they're blue, not azure!"

Genevieve rolled her eyes.

"Did we tell him the details of the murder?" Matthieu asked.

"We didn't have to," the Chief reminded him and began typing on his computer. "The whole country knows about *that* already." He turned the screen to face Matthieu and there on the front page of the website for *Le Monde* was an image of Boutrel standing wide eyed next to the uncovered body of Bastien Boutrel.

"That thing's everywhere," Matthieu mumbled before stammering, "that wasn't my fault."

Genevieve smirked.

"It doesn't matter whose fault it was. The point here is that Monsieur Pelletier is consulting on the case and you are to get him anything that he needs," the Chief said.

"But, Monsieur, I—" Matthieu protested before he was interrupted once more.

"I mean it, Matthieu," the Chief interrupted. "*Anything* that he needs."

Matthieu wasn't entirely comfortable with what he thought the Chief might be implying, but he nodded his head all the same, even if only to get him to stop talking.

"He's preparing a briefing on the Han Sapphire as we speak," Genevieve added. "He'll be presenting that momentarily. Hopefully he can shed some light on the Chinese influence that seems to heavily surround this crime."

"Brilliant," the Chief responded. "As for your request, Matthieu. I put in a word with a contact at the château to get us that guest list from last night. I also spoke with Mademoiselle Lebas and Madame Boutrel who should be on their way over."

Matthieu began to grow excited again. This was *his* time to shine and prove Genevieve wrong, Pierre too for that matter.

"Was there anything else?" The Chief asked.

"Not at the moment," Matthieu answered, trying to hide his excitement.

"Good," the Chief said. "Now, why don't you take some time to get to know your new companion, Matthieu?"

"The two of you will probably be spending a *lot* of time together," Genevieve said. Her lips curled into a smirk.

Matthieu grimaced and stood up. He walked out of the room and poked his head into the conference room where Pierre was typing away on a PowerPoint program on one of the police laptops.

"Can I get you anything?" Matthieu asked in between his tightly clenched teeth forced into a horrific smile.

Pierre looked up from the laptop.

"I'd love a chai latte," he said with a smile.

"We have coffee in the breakroom," Matthieu replied.

"Yes," Pierre said. "But I'd like a chai latte."

Matthieu stared at him and Pierre stared back. Matthieu thought about rubbing the smug grin off of his face, with his fist. Genevieve brushed by Matthieu and into the conference room.

"*Anything he wants*," she whispered to her ex-husband and then smiled and sat in the chair right next to Pierre. She looked back at Matthieu and then moved the seat closer to Pierre.

Matthieu felt like his head was about to explode. Before he screamed, he left the station and went to get Pierre his chai latte.

14

Sunday, the 1st of January, 5:02 p.m.

Matthieu didn't even know what a chai latte *was*, let alone where to find one.

After exploring nearly every cafe along the Rue Saint-Rome, he finally found a small cafe called, Deux Point Zero, which sold them at an exorbitant price. He purchased one and brought it back to the station, slurring a litany of obscenities towards Pierre along the way.

"Here's your latte," he said and threw it down in front of Pierre.

Pierre looked up at Matthieu with the same smug grin that he had on earlier. Once again, Matthieu had to restrain himself from physically wiping it off.

"Two sugars, extra foam?" Pierre asked.

"You didn't say anything about any of that," Matthieu stuttered. His right eye had begun to twitch as he passed a glance between Pierre and Genevieve. Both were grinning from ear to ear.

Pierre leaned back in his chair and laughed heartily.

"Lighten up, Detective," he said. "I'm just messing with you."

Matthieu thought that he might have a conniption as he left the room.

"So," Pierre began casually once he and Genevieve were alone. "There were probably security cameras at the château, no?"

"There were," Genevieve replied.

"Did they find anything on them?"

"Nothing useful," Genevieve said. "Although, there did appear to be someone fleeing the scene."

Crap, Pierre thought.

"But nobody breaking in," Genevieve continued. "Matthieu is convinced that it supports his theory that the thief was a guest at the soirée and not some sort of intruder."

Pierre let out a subtle sigh of relief.

"Did they see the person's face on the tapes?"

Although the answer to this question was obvious, Pierre still felt like he needed to ask it anyways. If they had his face on camera, he wouldn't have been called in as a consultant, he would have been a suspect.

"Fortunately for them, no," Genevieve said. "But, we sent them down to the lab to try to enhance the image."

Double crap.

"How long does that usually take?" Pierre asked nervously.

She shrugged.

"If it works at all, it usually takes several hours," she said mindlessly.

"If it works at all?"

"Image enhancement technology is pretty poor," she said. "There's no guarantee that we get anything from it other than a blurry face. That's what usually happens."

Hallelujah, Pierre thought. His plan to try to recover the tapes from the police station seemed like a wash, but it didn't seem to matter. However, with that out of the way, he still wasn't ready to leave just yet. He had thought of another plan and this was too good of an opportunity to pass up.

"How's your presentation coming?" Matthieu interrupted in between his tightly clenched, horrifying attempt at a smile.

"Nearly finished," Pierre said as he dragged over the last picture onto a slide. "And…voila!"

"It's a masterpiece!" Genevieve declared. Matthieu couldn't help but notice that she was swooning—and why not? Pierre was certainly a handsome and charismatic young man, three adjectives that Matthieu despised most about him.

The Chief and other members of the Toulouse Police Department slowly filed into the conference room. Many of them were annoyed. Pierre's presentation was the only thing that now stood between them and a shift change.

Thomas took a seat right next to Matthieu and Genevieve sat right up front and waved flirtatiously at Pierre. Thomas noticed his partner's bright red forehead and could tell that he was fuming. So, he slid over a seat, just in case Matthieu's head exploded.

Pierre dimmed the lights and then clicked a key on the laptop keyboard. The slide show opened with a big bold font that spelled out "Pierre Pelletier Productions."

"Oh, brother," Matthieu mumbled to himself.

Genevieve turned back and shushed him.

The next slide that Pierre turned to contained an image of the Han Sapphire necklace. The light from the projector lit up the eyes of nearly every officer in the room. Pierre could see the lust in every one of them. The necklace seemed to have a strange effect on people.

"The Han Sapphire," Pierre began, pausing briefly for dramatic effect and then flipping the presentation to the next slide. A portrait of an old Chinese man with a long, drooping mustache rested on the screen.

"Passed down through generations of emperors during the Han Dynasty in what is considered by many to be the golden age of Chinese history."

"Should we be taking notes?" Thomas whispered to Matthieu.

Genevieve turned around again and stared directly at her ex-husband.

"Be quiet," she warned with a harsh whisper.

"But that was Thomas—" Matthieu tried to defend himself before realizing it was a lost cause.

Pierre turned to the next slide which contained a geographical map of China.

"The Sapphire was lost for centuries after the subsequent collapse of the empire and the civil war that ensued between the three feuding states."

He flipped to the next slide which contained a recently taken photograph of Bastien Boutrel. Boutrel had a wide smile on his face under the stupid mustache that Pierre detested. He was holding up the necklace in his right hand. His left hand was around the hourglass figure of his mistress, Lucile Lebas. An outside observer probably would be unable to tell which he was more proud of having.

Noticeably absent from the photo, Matthieu thought to himself, Boutrel's wife, Beatrice, and Matthieu's prime suspect nombre un.

"The Sapphire was recently discovered, along with a whole trove of valuables, embedded in a diamond necklace buried in a field in Hong Kong," Pierre continued. "It was subsequently restored and purchased at auction by Monsieur Bastien Boutrel for a sum of €60 million."

Pierre slipped his hand into his pocket and began fiddling around with the very same necklace that was presumably now stolen. It gave him a thrill knowing that he possessed it, the best part was that he was hiding it right under their stupid noses. Of course, this wasn't why Pierre had come to the police station in the first place—for a cheap thrill. He had his reasons and, hopefully, a plan.

He flipped the slide show to the next slide which had the word, "Fin," in a fancy scripted font. Then, he walked over and flipped the lights back on.

"That's it?" Matthieu asked in disbelief.

"I didn't have very long to prepare, Monsieur," Pierre said. "But that's the jist of it, yes."

"What about the poison?" Matthieu asked. "What about the symbolism of the black lotus flower? What about any details of the case for that matter?"

"What about the *Viper Triad*?" Thomas asked.

Now, there was a name that Pierre hadn't heard in a while—the infamous *Viper Triad*. He remembered when the papers had claimed an affiliation between himself and the group, which he denounced in subsequent anonymous letters to the police. Pierre had inserted himself into that investigation, just as he found himself doing now. He just couldn't help himself. Nevertheless, Pierre wasn't affiliated with the organization. Gang affiliation was too messy, although the *Viper Triad* probably would have given him a cool, gang nickname, but Pierre didn't think it was worth the trouble.

"You didn't tell us anything that we didn't already know," Matthieu said. "Except for a lot of nonsense about some fairy tale from ancient China."

Genevieve turned back once more and stared daggers at her ex-husband. If looks could kill, Matthieu would have been the next victim in the case.

"Well," Pierre began, sensing his opportunity. "I didn't expect to open this up to a Q&A, but what would you like to know?"

"What do you know about *Gu*?" Matthieu asked.

"That's nasty stuff," Pierre assured him. "I wouldn't go messing around with that if I were you."

"What do you know about it?" Matthieu repeated.

"What does this have to do with the Han Sapphire?" Pierre asked.

They had kept Pierre largely in the dark when it came to the details of the case. *This* was the reason that Pierre had decided to stick around. It was to find out how much they knew. He wasn't as interested in clearing his name and making sure that there was justice for Boutrel's death. He was more interested in keeping his own name out of the investigation. What better way to do that than by inserting himself directly into it? If the police were going to get information out of Pierre, then he was going to get information out of the police. Boutrel was found with a dagger in his chest, why was the Detective suddenly so interested in ancient Chinese poison?

"That's not important for you to know," Matthieu answered.

The fact alone that he had mentioned it meant that it was important for Pierre to know. After all, he was *heavily* involved in this case, whether the Detective knew it or not.

"All I know is the traditional sense of it," Pierre said. "The legends and folklore."

"Great, more fairy tales," Matthieu grumbled. "Go on."

"Well, in traditional Chinese culture," Pierre began. "*Gu* was believed to be used in certain religious practices. Monks in ancient times would put several venomous species, such as snakes, centipedes and spiders, together in some sort of closed container. Then, they would agitate the creatures, encouraging them to consume one another in a battle royale to the death. The species that emerged victorious presumably had the venom of all the other species in a highly concentrated amount coursing through its veins. This was then extracted and used for various, sinister purposes. Just the smallest trace amount of the stuff could take down an elephant."

"What about an antidote?" Genevieve asked.

"No, I said an elephant," Pierre repeated.

Matthieu rolled his eyes and then spelled out his next word carefully.

"An-ti-dote," he said.

"Oh," Pierre replied and then shook his head. "Death is excruciatingly painful because the poison is slow acting. Hypothetically, this would allow for ample time to procure the antidote, but unfortunately there isn't one. At least none that I've ever heard of."

"So," Matthieu began. "What does this poison have to do with the *Viper Triad*?"

Pierre shrugged.

"You tell me, Detective," he answered as he locked eyes with Matthieu. "They're both Chinese, I suppose."

Pierre could almost visualize the cobwebs breaking down as the rusty gears in Matthieu's head slowly began to turn.

"Any other questions?" Pierre asked. More like information for himself to use.

The Chief stood up after a moment of silence.

"We'd like you to stay aboard here for the time being as a consultant," he said. "In case anything comes up that we would need clarification on. Genevieve was right, this case has a very heavy Chinese influence surrounding it and you seem to be the man to go to about these things."

Pierre had intended to stick around anyway, whether or not he had been invited. It was too good of an opportunity to pass up. Now, he could know everything that they knew, maybe even *before* they knew it. The first item on his list of things to know, why was Matthieu so interested in *Gu*?

"It would be my pleasure, Chief Jaubert," Pierre answered with the faintest hint of a sly smile. "I thank you for your hospitality."

Pierre watched as the Chief tucked a manilla folder under his arm. The number 1593 was plastered down the side in color coded tape, presumably the case file number. He and the other officers began to filter out of the room. Those who would be going home after the shift change moved hastily while those whose shifts were just starting moved sluggishly. They knew that they had a long night ahead of them.

"Interesting stuff," Matthieu said to Pierre when it was just the two of them alone in the room. "How did a museum curator come to learn so much about Chinese poisons?"

Pierre could sense the obvious suspicion in his voice.

"Books, Detective," he answered.

The Detective stared at him as he nodded his head. They were nearly face to face. So close, Pierre could smell the stale odor of alcohol on his breath. Pierre felt a cold shiver pass over him as he stared into the Detective's dead eyes. For a moment, it felt almost as if Matthieu could read his mind.

Matthieu suddenly broke from his trance with a sly smile.

"I'm glad you're going to be sticking around," he said. "It'll be good to have a fresh face around here."

Pierre swallowed hard. That vaguely felt like a threat.

"And who knows," Matthieu continued. "You may be spending a lot more time in here than you bargained for."

That *definitely* felt like a threat.

Just then, Thomas knocked on the conference room door, interrupting the tense exchange between the two men.

"They're here," Thomas said to his partner.

Matthieu kept his gaze fixed on Pierre and then winked at him before finally turning away and heading for the door.

"Oh, Detective," Pierre fumbled, trying to regain his control over Matthieu and get in the last word. "I notice that you took my advice."

He pointed down to his own shirt collar. Matthieu looked down at his own unbuttoned shirt and his jaw seemed to clench tightly on its own accord. It took everything he had not to lunge at Pierre. He was keeping score with his ex-wife already, but if he were keeping score with Pierre, Pierre would have won this round.

He slammed the door shut behind him and then made his way out onto the floor of the station.

Just coming up the stairs of the station was Lucile Lebas, crying inconsolably into the shoulder of Beatrice Boutrel as Genevieve escorted them inside. Both women were cloaked in black.

15

Sunday, the 1st of January, 5:43 p.m.

Beatrice Boutrel, suspect nombre un, sat at the interrogation room table as Detective Matthieu entered the room.

She was dressed in a subtle, black dress with large pearl earrings. Her lips were stained with dark, red lipstick left over from the night before. Beatrice was an older woman now, but Matthieu could tell she had been an attractive woman in her heyday. Her face was stoic, very stoic for a woman whose husband had just been found murdered in their own home less than twelve hours earlier. As to not form a foregone conclusion, Matthieu reminded himself that everyone grieves in their own way.

"I'm glad he's dead," Beatrice suddenly proclaimed before Matthieu even had a chance to sit down.

Matthieu nearly tripped over his own feet in surprise. He just barely caught the back of the interrogation room chair to support himself upright. He cleared his throat and took a seat across from her.

"Do you want to elaborate on that?" He asked, scribbling something down in his notepad.

"I'm glad he's dead," she repeated. "But I didn't kill him."

"Do you know who may have wanted to kill him?" Matthieu asked, calmly.

"That little witch in the other room," Beatrice answered, coldly.

"Mademoiselle Lebas?"

Matthieu remembered how he had seen Lucile Lebas crying into Beatrice's shoulders earlier in the morning and even when they had walked together into the station just moments before. Was it all just an act?

"Let me guess," Beatrice continued. "She probably told you that she thought he spent the night with me last night?"

"Yes, Madame Boutrel," Matthieu replied, flipping back in his notepad to the witness statements that Genevieve had taken earlier at the crime scene. "That's exactly what she said."

Beatrice Boutrel scoffed.

"Bastien and I haven't spent the night in the same bed in five years," she said, holding up her hand to extend all five of her fingers. Matthieu noticed the tan line around her ring finger, presumably where her wedding ring had rested. She seemed to be moving on rather quickly. "Ever since he met that bimbo."

"You all live together in the château?" Matthieu asked.

"That's correct."

"I see, Madame Boutrel," Matthieu replied. "And how does that whole situation make you feel?"

"How does it make me feel?" Beatrice repeated. Matthieu had to admit that his interrogation skills were a bit rusty. "How would you feel if your wife was sleeping with another man in *your* house? I already told you that I'm glad he's dead!"

Matthieu had thought about that exact scenario, quite a lot actually. He wondered if Genevieve leaving him had something to do with her finding another lover. Whatever the case, at least she had the decency to not do it in the house they shared together. Or maybe she had? He tried to shake off the thought and return to the matter at hand.

"Right," he began again as he cleared his throat. "Of course, of course. So, I take it that the state of your marriage was—"

"In shambles," Beatrice finished for him. "The only reason we remained married was to keep up appearances. That and the fact that I didn't have a prenup."

"A prenup?"

"I should have listened to my father, God rest his soul," Beatrice said. "But yes, in the event of an annulment, Bastien would have been entitled to half of our fortune. Well, my parent's fortune. *My* fortune."

"I see," Matthieu said as he scribbled furiously.

"But I did everything I had to in order to keep the old bastard happy," Beatrice assured him. "Between his weekly allowance and allowing his mistress to live under our roof, I don't see what else I could have done!"

"Of course, you did," Matthieu said. "Speaking of Mademoiselle Lebas, did you notice her acting suspiciously at all last night?"

"I notice her acting suspiciously *every* night," Beatrice said.

"In what way?"

"I'll tell you one thing, she wasn't with Bastien out of love."

"What do you mean?" Matthieu asked.

"Do you want me to spell it out for you?" Beatrice replied. "She was out for his money, *my* money."

"I'll give you that one," Matthieu said. Lucile Lebas was nearly half of Boutrel's age and was almost certainly in it for the money. Matthieu and all of France had already presumed the same thing.

"And to think," Beatrice continued, seemingly grumbling to herself. "The bastard had the audacity to put her into the will!"

"I beg your pardon?" Matthieu asked.

"Just the other day," she continued again. "He had his will altered. In the case of his death, she would collect all of his inheritance. Half of *my* money!"

"When did you say he had this will altered?"

"Thursday," Beatrice answered, curtly. She was fuming but Matthieu didn't want her to stop talking.

"Madame Boutrel," Matthieu began once more.

"Please," she interrupted and then took a deep breath to regain her composure. "Call me Beatrice."

"Beatrice, when was the last time that you saw your husband last night?"

"I barely saw him at all last night," she answered.

"Did you see him go off to bed with Mademoiselle Lebas?"

Beatrice shook her head.

"Do you know of anyone who may have wanted to hurt a…humanitarian," Matthieu decided, remembering back to the phrasing the Chief had used. "Such as your husband?"

Beatrice scoffed.

"Did I say something wrong?" Matthieu asked.

"Have you ever seen a fox that gets caught in a bear trap?"

"I don't believe I have," Matthieu answered.

"Well, I have," Beatrice answered. "Bastien used to hunt them for sport. It's a terribly gruesome thing. A fox will gnaw off its own arm to escape, slowing them down enough for that lard, Bastien, to come in for the final blow. He wasn't exactly the humanitarian that everyone believed he was."

"Oh no?" Matthieu asked. "Please, go on."

"He didn't think I knew what was going on, but I did," Beatrice declared, she seemed completely derailed now. "All I'm saying is that you might want to take a close look at some of his offshore accounts," she said. "Some of the money in those accounts may have been coming in through *other* means, if you catch my drift."

"Interesting," Matthieu replied, encouraging her to continue.

"If it comes down to it, maybe you can take that dirty money out of the witch's share."

"I can assure you, Beatrice, if Mademoiselle Lebas had something to do with your husband's murder, she won't see a cent."

"Good," Beatrice said. She sat back in the chair with her arms crossed. She had just divulged nearly everything that she had to offer, every little detail of their marriage that tabloid reporters would have killed for. Yet, she looked strangely comfortable.

"Beatrice," Matthieu began again, struck with a sudden idea to possibly catch her off guard and elicit an impulse reaction from her. "What do you know about *Gu*?"

"Who?" Beatrice asked. Her facial expression held steady.

"No," Matthieu replied. "*Gu*."

"What?"

"Never mind," Matthieu answered.

Beatrice's facial expression did not reflect the slightest hint of recognition or surprise at the mention of the poison. Either she had no knowledge of it, or she was just *that* cold blooded. A third option was that she had no knowledge of it, but she *was* the one that had stabbed her husband. Matthieu's head was beginning to reel from the possibilities.

"Was there anything else that you wanted to tell me?" Matthieu asked.

"Just that I'm sure it was that little witch in the next room," Beatrice began. "You're a smart man, Detective. Don't fall victim to her lies."

"I'll be sure to heed your warning," Matthieu said and rose from his chair. "Can we get you anything while you're waiting in here?"

"Chai latte," Beatrice replied.

Matthieu nearly stumbled over his own feet again.

"We'll get right on that," he answered and then made his way out of the room.

Thomas was standing on the other side of the two-way mirror when his partner exited.

"Do you still think it was her?" He asked, enthusiastically.

"I'm not sure, Thomas," Matthieu answered. He peered through the mirror at Beatrice Boutrel just in time to watch her pick something from her teeth callously.

"Surely it *must* have been Lucile Lebas," Thomas insisted. "She wormed her way into the will and then killed Monsieur Boutrel to cash in! She had all of the motive!"

"I would say that Beatrice Boutrel had a significant amount of motive as well," Matthieu said. "You see, Thomas, there are two types of guilty suspects in the interrogation room. There's the type that clam up and refuse to say anything. Then, there's the type that are very forthcoming, quick to tell you exactly what you want to hear."

"What motive did Beatrice Boutrel have to kill her husband?" Thomas asked. "You heard it yourself, just *three* days ago, he altered his will to give half of the inheritance to his mistress. Less than 72 hours later, he turns up dead. That screams Lucile Lebas to me."

"I still think she had plenty of motive," Matthieu replied. "Remember her story of the fox and the bear trap?"

"What about it?"

"A nice tale to paint her husband as a heartless bastard but try to look past that for a moment and think of it like a metaphor, Thomas. Beatrice was the fox; her marriage was the bear trap. A fox gnaws off its arm to escape, Beatrice kills off her husband. He was dead weight to Beatrice just as the arm is dead weight to the fox."

"I still don't get it," Thomas replied. "Now half of her fortune will go to Lucile."

"Not if she makes it look like Lucile was involved in Boutrel's murder," Matthieu reminded him. "Which is the direction that she's obviously trying to lead us."

Thomas thought for a moment.

"Wouldn't it make more sense to just kill Lucile?"

Matthieu shook his head.

"Too messy," he said. "Especially if she wants them both to go down. But we'll keep an open mind, see what Mademoiselle Lebas has to say for herself. By the way, what are you still doing here, Thomas?"

"What do you mean?"

"You heard the woman, chai latte!" Matthieu ordered. "Now!"

Thomas scrambled around for a moment before fleeing the hallway outside of the interrogation room. The door to the hallway screeched open and then closed behind him. Matthieu continued to stare in through the window at Beatrice Boutrel.

16

Sunday, the 1st of January, 5:34 p.m.

While his babysitter, Detective Matthieu had his hands full with the interrogations of the two women in the life of Bastien Boutrel, Pierre decided that now would be a good time to do some investigating of his own.

Up until now, the police had only let Pierre see what they *wanted* him to see, but Pierre still had many unanswered questions about the progress that the investigation had made. He needed to stay one step ahead of them if he was going to come out of this unscathed. The most pressing question at the forefront of his mind, why had Matthieu developed a sudden interest in ancient Chinese poison? He was almost positive that it wasn't a recreational interest.

He *needed* to see that case file.

Pierre glanced out through the large, plate-glass windows of the conference room. The room was beginning to feel like his very own prison cell. There were no outside windows, so his only view was through the plate-glass windows, facing the floor of the Toulouse Police Station and roughly two dozen police officers. He didn't plan on being cooped up here much longer. As he glanced through the window, most of the officers were seated at their cubicles, buried in stacks of paperwork. They would be far too busy to notice if he slipped away.

So, he opened the door and slipped away.

Pierre remembered seeing Chief Jaubert walk past the conference room window in the direction to Pierre's left with the manilla folder under his arm, the one with the number 1593 taped down the side, the case file. When the Chief returned from that direction, there was no manilla folder under his arm. Pierre decided to start his investigation by going left. Nobody stopped him.

He came upon a long hallway and proceeded down it. At the other end of the hallway, just in the corner on the ceiling was a camera that looked like it covered the entire surface area of the hallway. Pierre would have to be careful, there was nobody on his side to monitor the camera feed this time.

Two of Toulouse's burliest officers strolled around the corner at the end of the hallway, discussing something. Pierre smiled up at them as inconspicuously as he could.

Just act like you belong here, he thought. *They won't question it if you just act like you're supposed to be down here.*

The officers walked past him but then one of them suddenly stopped.

"Hey," he began. "Are you supposed to be down here?"

Pierre hesitated for a moment. He thought about trying to take down both officers in one swift blow, but the security camera would make that a little tricky. Besides, who was he kidding anyways? He couldn't take down a man who was one quarter of the size of the man in front of him. He opted for a much more casual approach.

"Yes," he answered.

"Oh," the officer replied. "Okay."

With that, the two officers continued along their way down the hallway.

Pierre let out a sigh of relief and continued in the other direction, careful not to make any sudden movements or arouse any suspicion on camera.

Just to his left, a little bit further down the hallway, Pierre noticed a door with a small window that read, "File Room," in white sticker letters.

This must be the place, he thought to himself.

He casually slowed his gait and looked up at the camera in the corner of the hallway. Its glass eye was fixed right on him. He bent down to tie his shoelace when he heard two more officers coming his way from around the corner.

Pierre stood up and moved himself against the wall, closer towards the door of the file room to allow them to pass. Once in position there, Pierre subtly gave the door handle a jiggle.

Locked. Of course, it was.

The officers had nearly passed him when one of them suddenly turned to him.

"Are you supposed to be down here?" He asked.

"Yes," Pierre replied with more confidence this time.

"Oh," the officer said. "Okay."

With that, the officers proceeded on their way.

Pierre glanced at the locked file room door just for a moment and stored the image away in his mind before continuing on his own way down the hallway. If he lingered around the file room door for too long, it would certainly arouse suspicion.

He conjured up the image as he walked. The first thing he had noticed was that there didn't seem to be a lock on the door. Even if he wanted to pick it, there was nothing to pick. The second thing that he had noticed was a small, black box that rested on the side of the door with a glowing red light on the top.

He remembered seeing the ID cards that every officer in the building carried around their necks or clipped to their belts. They were the reason that they had known he wasn't supposed to be down here, and he knew that the lock on the door must be some sort of key card unlocking mechanism. Remy might have been able to disarm the mechanism long enough to get in, but Remy wasn't here. Pierre would need to think of another way inside.

He was lost in thought, trying to think of a solution to the locked door problem in front of him and he didn't even notice Genevieve coming around the corner of the hallway. Genevieve's eyes were glued to her phone and the two walked right into each other.

"Oh," Pierre exclaimed. "I'm terribly sorry! I need to watch where I'm going."

"No, no," she insisted, straightening the edges of her pantsuit. "I wasn't looking either. Stupid phones, I tell you."

Pierre came to a tense moment of realization. He hoped Genevieve would just continue on her way and skip the obvious question.

"Wait a minute," Genevieve began suspiciously. "You're not supposed to be down here, Pierre. What are you doing here?"

"Yes," Pierre answered instinctively before back tracking. "I mean, I was looking for the restroom. I must have gotten turned around a little."

Genevieve stared back at him with the eyes of a seasoned Detective. The eyes that could spot a liar from the other side of a crowded room. She searched every little wrinkle of his face for some hint of deceit. Pierre was sure that his face was covered in it. His forced, nervous smile was beginning to hurt his cheeks and he thought it might give way at any second.

Pierre thought again for a moment that he would have to kill her. A quick blow to the head would probably do the trick. Pierre shuddered at the thought. Although this woman was quite smaller than him, he still didn't think he could take her. Fortunately, the feeling of impending doom faded when Genevieve finally returned his smile.

"Come with me," she said. "I'll lead you to the restroom."

She led Pierre back down the hallway, past the locked file room door. The ID badge on the lanyard swayed tauntingly around her neck. Pierre had the sudden urge to grab it and open the door, but he wisely fought the urge. It would be too messy; the camera would see everything. He needed to come up with another way in.

She led Pierre back through the station floor and down another hallway before she stopped in front of the men's restroom.

"Well," she began. "Here we are!"

"Here we are!" Pierre repeated with nervous laughter.

"Alright," she said, trying to fill the awkward silence between them. "Well, if you're not out of there in five minutes, I'm coming in after you!"

She winked at him.

Pierre cringed and backed his way through the restroom door, still laughing nervously. He had the sudden urge to wash his hands. The door closed behind him.

Alright, he thought to himself once inside, *you need to start thinking about what you need to do now.*

The blinding fluorescent lights off the white walls caught Pierre's attention first. The second thing that caught his attention was the odor. It *reeked* of a strong ammonia smell that burned the inside of Pierre's nostrils. He attributed it to the poor ventilation as his eyes caught the air vent on the wall above the third stall. The air vent was identical to the one that Pierre had seen in the conference room.

He walked over to the sink in front of the mirror and splashed water in his face. He was tired, but this was no time to rest.

When he wiped his face dry with a paper towel, he looked at himself in the mirror, but his eyes were drawn once again to the air vent above the third stall.

The file room was located in the center of the building, much like the conference room that had become Pierre's very own prison cell. There were probably no outside windows in that file room, just like there were no outside windows in the conference room. Therefore, the only way air could be moved in or out of those rooms was the air ventilation system. This meant that if Pierre climbed through the vents in the restroom, they should theoretically branch out everywhere that he needed to go.

Pierre turned and glanced up at the air vent which looked almost too narrow for any person to crawl through, but he really didn't have any other options.

"Ugh," he groaned. "Why does it always have to be air ducts?"

Pierre made his way into the third stall of the restroom and locked the stall door behind him, he was going to be in there for a while. He stared up at the air vent on the wall. It looked even more narrow up close.

He positioned himself so that he was standing on the toilet, legs spread above the bowl and he reached up for the grate in front of the vent. Fortunately, it wasn't bolted down. So, Pierre just had to lift it up and slide it off the groove and, *voila*, it was off.

He set the grate down on the floor beside the toilet and then hoisted himself up so that he could see inside.

Pierre scanned the metal edges of the tunnel of the air duct in front of him. He felt a steady stream of warm air coming from the vent. The inside was dark and it was narrow, but when he felt his hand in, it seemed to widen a little bit deeper into it. He would just need to squeeze himself through the narrowest portion of it at the entrance and then he thought he would be able to fit comfortably, or as comfortably as one could fit in an air shaft.

He had already lost enough time trying to hatch a plan as it was, and he feared that Genevieve would be true to her word and come in after him. So, without another moment to lose, Pierre hoisted himself up by his fingertips and put his head into the duct. His neck followed, and then his shoulders. Before long, he was waist deep in the air duct. That's when he became stuck.

The large buckle of his belt was jammed on something and for a moment, he regretted having ever stolen the thing. Pierre tried with brute force to pull himself through, but it was no use, he was helplessly stuck. He tried once more and could feel the buckle give a little. Optimistic, he pulled with all his might and it gave a little more. He stopped for a moment to catch his breath and regain all his strength when the restroom door swung open. What followed were footsteps on the tile floor and then the distinct sound of a person whistling. Pierre froze.

Thomas entered the restroom, whistling to himself as he walked over to the urinal.

Pierre was still waist deep in the air duct, his legs dangling behind him in the air high above the ground. He was a sitting duck. A bead of sweat dripped down from his curls.

Finally, Thomas flushed the urinal. He paused for a minute at the sink and looked at himself in the mirror and smiled. Just above his head were the dangling legs of Pierre, holding deathly still.

"You've got this today, Thomas," he said encouragingly to himself. "Just keep your head up, your eyes open and be ready for anything."

He winked at himself in the mirror and then turned and walked away.

Pierre heard the door to the restroom swing open and then close. He was alone once again.

"He didn't even wash his hands," he mumbled in disgust before turning back to his dire circumstances. The next person that came into the restroom could be Genevieve. If she caught him, this was an impossible position to talk himself out of.

Pierre strained with all his might. The belt buckle on his waist suddenly snapped and he shot through the smooth metal of the air duct before hitting his head on the other side.

He was right, at least, the air duct did widen. It wasn't much, but it was enough that he had some room to wiggle around. The next thing that he noticed was that the air duct was like a sauna.

He reached his hand out into the open space to his right and then turned his body and began crawling through the tunnel of the air duct.

A little bit ahead of him, he saw a faint light that was pouring through another vent. When he finally reached it, he tried to get a glimpse of what was on the other side.

There in the room was Simone St. Clair, staring at the TV screen. She was clicking the buttons of the remote like a woman that had been hypnotized. Pierre didn't know her, but she scared him.

He continued along until he reached another vent and peered inside. It was the empty conference room that had been set up as his temporary office.

The next room he came across was the Chief's office. The Chief was sitting in his office chair, with a half-eaten box of chocolates and a box of tissues at the ready. The lights were dimmed and he was watching his favorite romantic comedy. He was, "taking time for himself," as the office psychologist had recommended. Although, this probably wasn't what she had in mind.

The next vent that Pierre reached was the vent to the first interrogation room. There, he could see Detective Matthieu and the widowed wife of Bastien Boutrel, Beatrice sitting across from him.

"And how does that whole situation make you feel?" Matthieu asked.

"How does that make me feel?" Beatrice repeated and then trailed off.

"Idiot," Pierre mumbled and continued down the air shaft.

The next vent that he reached he almost didn't see but it scraped up against his arm. The inside of the room was completely dark except for a faint light pouring in from the window on the door. There were white sticker letters on the window that read, "mooR eliF."

"Moor Elif," Pierre read as his brain processed this information. "The file room!" He shouted before remembering this was supposed to be a covert operation.

He placed his fingers through the vent and carefully lifted it up before setting it down on a shelf which was just below the vent. He then squeezed his way out through the opening, where he landed on the floor on the other side in a cloud of dust. There were faint voices coming from the other side of the door as he tried to refrain from coughing.

The faint light pouring in through the window illuminated the shelves behind him. They were all lined with identical manilla folders, all of them labelled with color-coded stickers that spelled out a number.

1593, Pierre reminded himself of the number that he had seen on the folder under Chief Jaubert's arm.

He fingered his way through the thousands of files on the shelf before he finally found the one that he was looking for, 1593. He pulled it down from the shelf and opened it, holding it out to the light so that he could read it.

The first thing he saw was a photograph of Bastien Boutrel, who had been dissected open. Pierre dry heaved violently and quickly turned the page over. The next document in the folder was the autopsy report.

"Come to papa," Pierre said, as if this were some sort of elaborate heist that was just reaching its stunning conclusion.

He scanned the document and read fragments of it aloud to himself.

"Cause of death was a stab wound through the left ventricle," Pierre read. Just as he had suspected. He assumed ventricle was a police term for heart. To be fair, he was kind of right. He turned the page and read on. "Dependent lividity suggests the victim was face down shortly after death." That one was over his head. "Toxicology report. The victim was found with a lethal dose of *Gu*, a rare poison found in traditional Chinese culture, in his digestive tract?"

Pierre reread the last line to make certain that he had read it correctly and then put the folder down.

"Must have been one hell of a soirée," he mumbled. "But why would someone poison him and then stab him?"

Truth be told, he was utterly stumped.

17

Sunday, the 1st of January, 5:55 p.m.

Unlike Beatrice Boutrel, there was nothing subtle about Mademoiselle Lucile Lebas, the mistress of the recently deceased Bastien Boutrel.

She wore a skintight black dress with a plunging neckline, and she had a massive pair of hoop earrings that, much like her blonde hair that ran like fields of sunflowers, hung down to her shoulders. She was dressed as if she would be attending another dinner soirée after this, not mourning the loss of her lover. Nevertheless, her face was stained with tears.

Detective Matthieu entered the room and sat down across from her.

"Is this going to take long?" Lucile asked innocently. "I have a soirée to attend tonight in remembrance of Bastien."

Just as he had suspected.

"That depends," he replied, trying to make himself comfortable in the interrogation room chair. "On what you tell me."

"It was that old witch in the other room," Lucile said, bitterly. "Let me guess," she began again. Her tone was much different from the innocent girl that she had been portraying just a moment ago. "She probably told you that he *always* spends the night with me and that they haven't had a night together in five years."

She held up her hand and extended all five of her fingers.

"Well, yes, Mademoiselle Lebas," Matthieu said as he flipped through the pages in his notepad. "That's exactly what she said. Almost word for word."

Lucile scoffed.

"I wonder how long she's been planning to use that one," she said.

"So, you're saying it isn't true?" Matthieu asked.

"No," Lucile answered. "It's true. Would you want to spend a night with that old hag?"

Matthieu considered. He had been lonely since Genevieve left.

"Now," Lucile continued, breaking the Detective from his daydream. "I'm not a handsome and smart detective such as yourself, Monsieur, but her grieving widow routine seems a little transparent, wouldn't you agree?"

Matthieu tried to conceal the fact that he was blushing. He cleared his throat.

"Would you say that the two of you get along well?" He asked.

"Like a snake and a mongoose," Lucile answered.

What's with all the animal analogies, he thought to himself as he began to wonder which of these women was the mongoose and which was the *poisonous* snake.

"Why do you think you didn't get along?" Matthieu asked.

Lucile made a gesture to her own figure.

"Look at me," she proclaimed proudly. "She couldn't handle playing second fiddle to someone like this. She was jealous."

Matthieu realized that Lucile didn't need another boost to her ego, so he changed the subject.

"Did you and Monsieur Boutrel spend last night together?" He asked.

Lucile hesitated, almost as if she had been stumped by the simple question.

"No," she finally admitted.

"No?" Matthieu repeated, slightly taken aback. "I thought you spent every night with him."

"He spends every night in my bed, yes," Lucile replied.

Matthieu could read between the lines.

"But not with you?"

"Not exactly," Lucile answered. Matthieu could tell that she was hiding something, trying to weave her way in between her own lies.

"I'm a bit confused," he began again. "How can he spend the night in your bed, but not with you?"

The color in Lucile's face seemed to drain and a look of panic overcame her.

"Bastien drinks," she answered. "Like a fish."

"Go on," Matthieu urged her.

"He often stumbles into the room late at night and passes out in the bed beside me."

"In your bed?" Matthieu asked. "And you're intimate?"

"In my bed, yes," Lucile said. "Intimate, not usually. With his predilection to drinking, he has trouble performing if you catch my drift."

"So, you end up sleeping beside him?"

"Not for the *whole* night," Lucile answered with a sheepish smile.

"Where do you go, Mademoiselle Lebas? If you're not in your own bed."

"Into the bed of François Fouquet," she admitted shyly.

"François Fouquet," Matthieu repeated. He flipped through the pages of his notepad. "Ah, yes, I believe he was the one that referred to Boutrel as a dirty, old blowfish in a suit. He was a servant of the château?"

"And my lover," Lucile added. "He can vouch for my whereabouts last night."

Matthieu was not terribly surprised by this revelation. Mistresses who are only around for the money usually have a second lover. This confirmed at least one suspicion that Beatrice Boutrel had. The rest was still up in the air.

"Did anyone in the house suspect that the two of you were having an affair?" Matthieu asked.

"We were careful."

"And obviously you told us earlier that Boutrel must have spent the night with his wife because you didn't want to tell us about the affair that you were having?"

"Exactly," Lucile replied with a sweet smile and a flirtatious wink. "Hopefully we can just keep that little secret between us?"

"Unfortunately, you know that I can't do that, Mademoiselle," Matthieu replied. The smile on her face faded quickly to a frown. Matthieu suspected that she was quite the actress. "Anyways," he continued. "Tell me about last night. When was the last time that you did see Monsieur Boutrel?"

"The last time that I saw him last night," Lucile said, thinking back. "He was drunk, of course. He was engaged in a heated exchange with some foreign dignitary."

"Do you know this dignitary's name?"

"He was British," Lucile answered hesitantly. "Worthingham, or Worthington maybe? He was a Baron of some sort, I remember that. He made everyone call him, 'The Baron.'"

"Then what happened?"

"François stole me away," she answered dreamily.

"He stole you away?"

"Yes," she replied. "He took me to his bedroom in the guest house outside where we made passionate love and then fell asleep in each other's arms."

"Do you remember what time that was?"

"Around 9:30, maybe?"

Matthieu was sure that François would corroborate Lucile's alibi. It was somewhat strange François hadn't mentioned the affair earlier, but not so if he wanted to keep it under wraps. There was, however, another reason why François would remain so tight-lipped even though he had appeared to be so forthcoming when Matthieu had interviewed him this morning. He was starting to wonder if the two of them had been in on it together. Maybe one had poisoned him, but the poison was taking too long to take effect, so the other stabbed him through the heart when the poor old bastard had refused to die.

"I see," Matthieu said. "And you never saw Monsieur Boutrel again that night?"

She shook her head.

Matthieu decided to change the subject again.

"Can you tell me about the recent alterations to Monsieur Boutrel's will?" He asked.

"Of course, she would tell you about that," Lucile answered, coldly. "I deserve every bit of that money, just as much as she does!"

"Forgive me for asking this," Matthieu interrupted. "But why do you deserve it?"

"I had to put up with Bastien for the last five years," Lucile replied. "My golden years, wasted away on him!"

"I'd say with a percentage of an inheritance that large, your golden years are just beginning," Matthieu said. "Or maybe these are your *sapphire* years?"

Lucile's face suddenly contorted, and she bared down into the Detective's eyes. Her sweetness suddenly became horribly bitter. Only one other woman had ever had this effect on Matthieu.

"What are you implying?" Lucile asked, more of a demand than a question.

"How do you feel about *Gu*, Mademoiselle Lebas?" Matthieu asked suddenly, hoping to catch her off guard.

"Who?" Lucile asked.

"No, *Gu*."

"What?"

"Never mind," Matthieu replied.

There was no change in facial expression from Lucile at the mention of the poison either. Lucile sat back in the interrogation room chair and crossed her arms.

"I just have a couple more questions and then you're free to go, Mademoiselle," Matthieu assured her.

"I'm probably already late, so get on with it," Lucile replied.

"Do you know anything about Monsieur Boutrel's offshore accounts?"

"I don't even know what that means."

"Foreign bank accounts," Matthieu explained.

"Why would Bastien need a foreign bank account?" Lucile spat.

"Sometimes they're used to evade taxes or hide finances from one's own government," Matthieu said. She didn't flinch. The way she answered suggested that she truly didn't know about any of these accounts. "I just have one more question."

"Be my guest, *Detective*," Lucile said, spitefully.

"Do you know of anyone that would have had any motive to hurt Monsieur Boutrel?"

"Other than the old witch in the other room?" Lucile asked. "No."

"Alright, Mademoiselle Lebas," Matthieu said. "Sit tight, we'll get you out of here shortly."

He rose from his chair and headed toward the exit. Lucile was staring at the corner of the interrogation room, disgusted. She refused to even look at him.

When he exited the interrogation room, the Chief was standing on the other side of the two-way mirror.

"I've got your guest list," he said, holding up a handful of papers. "We can discuss this in my office, follow me."

Matthieu grabbed the papers from him and scanned the names, then flipped through the pages as they walked.

"There's got to be ten pages of names here!" Matthieu said. "I thought you said this was a small gathering?"

The Chief cleared his throat.

"While you were talking in there, I found something interesting," he said, trying to change the subject. He grabbed the guest list from Matthieu's hands and scanned his own eyes down the list of names. "There," he finally said, settling on one name and pointing to it. "Baron William Worthington, *the* Baron, perhaps?"

Matthieu looked at the name resting under the Chief's finger.

"I'd like to have a word with him before he leaves France," Matthieu said.

"I'll see if we can get into contact with his people," the Chief replied and pushed open the door to the interrogation room hallway. The door complied with a deafening screech. Both men winced in pain from the harsh sound.

"Got to get that thing fixed," the Chief mumbled.

"I'll say," Matthieu remarked as he rubbed his ears and then turned his attention back to the papers. "You know what name you wouldn't find on this list?" He asked as he continued to scan through the other pages.

"Matthieu, listen," the Chief began. "I'm sorry that you weren't invited. It was nothing personal, it was just that—"

"*Staff* at the soirée," Matthieu interrupted. "Namely, François Fouquet. Did you know that the blowfish is a poisonous fish if cooked incorrectly, Chief?"

"I did not know that but thank you."

"I'd like to have a word or two with François as well," Matthieu decided. "If he's still around, that is. Maybe we can see if blowfish was on the menu for the evening."

"Then I'll get them both in here right away," the Chief replied.

18

Sunday, the 1st of January, 5:53 p.m.

"Poison," Pierre repeated. "Why would someone poison somebody and then stab them?"

Pierre didn't know that the police were having the same problem with this conundrum. Obviously, Detective Matthieu had his hands full with the widow and the mistress, but he had also shown suspicion towards Pierre. Either way, the real threat was Genevieve.

She was obsessed with the *Black Lotus*. Pierre decided that maybe it was in his best interest after all to solve the murder himself. Maybe, instead of taking the wrap for both crimes, he could figure out some way to pin both crimes on the *actual* murderer. Nobody knew of his involvement with the case anyways. He could solve the murder, sell the necklace and live happily ever after. He did know details that the police couldn't know about the case, and he couldn't very well tell them without implicating himself. So, the more that he thought about it, the more he realized that he was the best man for the job. As he read through the case file, he tried his best to play Detective Pierre Pelletier.

"The same person wouldn't poison Boutrel and then stab him. That doesn't make any sense. There must have been *two* murder attempts on the same night," he reasoned. "Or, if there *was* only one killer, maybe they wanted to make it look like there were two murder attempts, a sleight of hand, of sorts."

Pierre knew all about sleight of hand. Long ago, someone had once said to him that the difference between a good thief and a great thief was how well they could steal their audience's attention and then deceive them using nothing more than sleight of hand or misdirection. A good thief could steal something from you, but a great thief could make it disappear. A great thief, in a sense, was like a magician. Pierre could usually spot the misdirection of another "magician" from the back row of a packed house. It was easy, if you knew where to look. As a child, Pierre would always read up on the great thieves and most infamous heists, constantly learning from their successes but learning even more from their mistakes. However, *murder* was a completely different kind of magic, black magic. It was a realm that Pierre had never slipped into before. Getting away with murder also involved misdirection, but the sleight of hand was harder for Pierre to follow. His head was beginning to reel. Every time he thought up an explanation, three more presented themselves. The possibilities were seemingly endless.

"Where does someone even get the idea to use *Gu*?" Pierre wondered aloud.

Suddenly, there were voices outside of the file room door in the hallway. Pierre quickly decided that he had learned all that he could from the file on Boutrel. He knew everything that the police knew, and none of it pointed to him. Rightfully so, he thought, because he hadn't done it.

He put the case file back on the shelf in the exact location that he had taken it from. Then, he straightened every other folder exactly as they had been before, he was always very attentive to details like these. Finally, he grasped at the ledge of the air vent and pulled himself through it. He passed through relatively easily without the hindrance of his belt buckle and he turned around and put the grate from the air vent back into place.

In the next second, the door to the file room opened. Genevieve came into the room and grabbed case file 1593.

"Too close," Pierre mumbled to himself, but he was secretly enjoying every second of this. The close calls were even more thrilling.

He travelled back down the tunnel of the air duct, back towards the restroom. He first passed by the interrogation room where Beatrice Boutrel now sat alone, callously picking something out from under her fingernails. Her eyes were bone dry, which Pierre thought, with the mind of a detective, was quite suspicious.

The Chief's office was completely empty, as was the temporary office which Pierre had been given in the conference room.

Simone St. Clair was still in a trance, staring at the TV screen. She still scared Pierre.

Pierre found his way next to the vent of the men's restroom, peered out to make sure it was still empty, and then pulled himself out through the vent and onto the safety of the floor once again. He put the grating back into place and then emerged from the stall.

"Piece of cake," he said to himself as he brushed his hands together satisfactorily.

The hallway just outside was empty and Pierre began walking back towards the conference room. His mind was still racing with possibilities. He didn't even notice Simone St. Clair rush out of the conference room until she brushed by him and collided hard with his shoulder. Pierre recoiled in pain and grabbed his shoulder, but Simone was completely unphased. She didn't even stop to apologize. In the pale saffron lighting of the station floor, Pierre could see that her ponytail had fallen out, leaving her hair in a disheveled mess and he thought that she resembled someone who had just emerged from a cave.

What's gotten into her? Pierre wondered. He decided that he had maybe better follow her to find out. After all, he was the new lead detective on the case.

She stopped in front of the door to the Chief's office and then pushed her way in, interrupting Matthieu and the Chief who were discussing something in hushed whispers.

Pierre could only make out the words, "guest list," and then something about Lucile Lebas and her lover before the door to the Chief's office slammed shut in his face. Still, what they were saying suggested that the police were still focused on someone that had been *at* the soirée, which of course, Pierre had not been. He was in the clear, or so he thought.

Through the crack in the door, Pierre could barely make out what was said next.

"Jesus, Simone," the Chief said, startled as Simone rushed towards them. "What is it?"

"The tapes," she said. "I found something on one of the other security tapes that you need to see, Detective. We were wrong, the killer *wasn't* at the soirée. Or, at least, they weren't invited."

Pierre felt a pit in his stomach. What else had he done wrong?

19

Sunday, the 1st of January, 6:11 p.m.

Detective Matthieu followed Simone out of the interrogation room hallway and towards the conference room where the poor woman had locked herself away for the last eight hours.

Pierre tried to act casually, as if he *weren't* just standing by the door to the Chief's office and he wasn't just eavesdropping on everything that they were just saying. Matthieu gave him a suspicious look when he brushed passed, but he was fortunately too engaged to stop and ask Pierre what he was doing there. His mind was flooded with the new possibilities and the bitter idea that they all seemed to suggest, Genevieve was right. He disappeared with Simone into the conference room.

Chief Jaubert remained in his office to make some calls and line up a few more interrogations. Still playing detective, Pierre assumed that it had something to do with Lucile's lover and the guest list, not necessarily in that order.

Pierre glanced around to make sure nobody was looking at him and then crept over to the conference room door, trying to make it seem as if he wasn't trying to listen in. Pierre may have been a criminal mastermind, but when it came to obvious things like this, he was a bit of a simpleton. Besides, his morbid curiosity had gotten the better of him. What did Simone find on those tapes?

Pierre had done something wrong, he had made a mistake, but he couldn't, for the life of him, figure out what it could have been as he racked his brain. It was his mother's jewelry box all over again.

Matthieu took a seat inside the conference room across from the TV screen. Simone had placed her laptop computer on the desk in front of him and then went over and turned off all the lights in the room.

"Alright, Simone," Matthieu began, hesitantly. He wasn't overly enthusiastic about what she could have found. "What have you got for me?"

Simone whirled around wildly. Both of her eyes were twitching uncontrollably, independent of one another. Her hair was a frizzled mess. Although he had never seen one before, Matthieu thought that in the dark she resembled some sort of barely human, cave-dwelling creature.

"This," she said and presented the screen to him. It was a closeup—and very pixelated shot from the security camera that faced the side brick wall of the château.

"What am I looking at here?" Matthieu asked, squinting.

"The side wall of the château!" Simone declared proudly.

"The side wall of the château?" Pierre mumbled under his breath. He was beginning to think that this woman had almost certainly lost her mind. Then, in the next instant, his mind drifted to the sudden realization of the possible significance of the image.

"I have isolated these two images," Simone said, pulling up two images side by side on her laptop computer on the desk in front of Matthieu.

Matthieu studied the pictures like a game of spot the difference.

"These two images were taken at two separate time points," Simone said. "They were on the tape that was filmed in the hour before the tape with the mysterious figure that I showed you earlier. The images in front of you were taken twenty seconds apart from one another."

"Twenty seconds apart," Matthieu repeated mindlessly. He was still trying to spot the difference.

"Twenty seconds apart," Pierre mumbled the all too familiar phrase.

"Exactly," Simone replied. "You see, the surveillance cameras around the château are all on rotating views. Every twenty seconds, they complete a full 360-degree rotation and will end up back in the same vantage point that they started."

"Every twenty seconds," Matthieu repeated, his eyes shifting wildly between the two images.

"Not twenty-two," Pierre mumbled. "Not twenty-one."

Simone eyed the Detective with a hopeful look of expectation. His eyes suddenly lit up with realization.

"The white pixels," he said, and pointed to a collection of white pixels on the screen. "They're in a slightly different position in the second image than they are in the first."

"The gutter!" Simone replied excitedly.

"The gutter?" Matthieu repeated.

"The gutter," Pierre groaned under his breath, another breadcrumb that he had left behind.

"I'm still missing the point," Matthieu said. "You said you found something that proves that the killer wasn't *at* the soirée." *And even more unbelievable, that proves Genevieve's theory correct.*

"The perpetrator *scaled* the gutter," Simone said.

"Scaled the gutter?" Matthieu repeated.

"Yes," Simone replied. "Look at this."

She traced her hand along the white pixels of the gutter, almost to the roof of the château.

"This third-story window," she continued. "Is the window to Boutrel's study. It's the same window where the previous security footage that we found showed a shadowy figure leaving from earlier. The gutter passes *directly* beside it. Our perpetrator must have scaled the gutter and entered the study through the window. The weight of the intruder must have skewed the gutter slightly, resulting in this!"

That was a gross oversimplification of what happened, Pierre thought as he remembered back to the dramatic action sequence the way that he remembered it. He was beginning to wonder now if he had overstayed his welcome here and he thought that this would be a good opportunity for him to leave. He glanced at the sea of officers around him. He was like a minnow in a pool of sharks.

Matthieu contemplated this information for a moment as Simone stared at him excitedly.

"Come on now," he finally said. "You're telling me that our perpetrator scaled that gutter in under twenty seconds and climbed through the third-story window? Nobody could have done that, nobody except—"

"The *Black Lotus*," Simone finished for him. "I believe that the thief must have somehow timed the angle of the cameras. He scaled the wall, broke in through the window, in under twenty seconds, stole the Han Sapphire necklace, killed Boutrel and then escaped from the same window!"

Yep, time to go, Pierre thought. Although they still didn't have his face, this was all beginning to hit a little too close to what had actually happened. He nearly made a break for the door until what Matthieu said next stopped him in his tracks.

"I don't buy it," Matthieu grumbled. For once, Pierre viewed the Detective's stubbornness favorably.

"But it's all there!" Simone insisted.

Matthieu couldn't deny that something was amiss. The gutter in the second image had shifted over no more than a couple of centimeters, but it was certainly noticeable, a subtle consequence of Pierre nearly collapsing the gutter as he climbed it the night before.

Pierre listened intently through the door.

Matthieu shook his head.

"Something still isn't adding up," he said. "Why would the thief time the cameras so precisely on his entrance and then ignore them so carelessly when he left?"

You're a genius, Pierre thought as he pumped his fist. He never thought he would find himself rooting for the Detective, and yet, here he was. He could almost kiss the man right now.

"On top of that," Matthieu continued. "I examined that open window myself. You could only open that window from the *inside*."

Thank God for Colette, Pierre thought.

"But what about the gutter?" Simone asked.

"I suppose it doesn't really matter," Matthieu replied. "If someone scaled the gutter or if they didn't. I don't believe in this *Black Lotus* fairy tale that everyone seems to be so enamored with, but even if he was real, the simple fact remains that someone would have needed to be on the inside to open that window. My theory still stands."

"But Detective—" Simone tried.

"Besides that," Matthieu continued, rising from his chair. "It all just seems too personal. Someone on the inside of that soirée killed Boutrel and stole the Han Sapphire necklace. It wasn't some mysterious figure. We find that necklace and we find our killer."

Pierre couldn't help but chuckle.

"The necklace that's already right under your big, stupid nose, Detective," he mumbled to himself with a sly smile.

He reached his hand into his pocket to feel the precious corners of the jewel in his grasp, the most valuable and yet most worthless stone in the world. The only problem was, when he reached into his pocket, there was nothing there. The Han Sapphire necklace was gone.

20

Sunday, the 1st of January, 6:24 p.m.

"Pierre!" Genevieve called out.

Pierre was nearly elbow deep in his pocket, praying that the missing necklace would somehow miraculously reappear, like this was all a part of some sort of elaborate magic trick. Genevieve had snuck up behind him and startled him as he was listening in through the door at Matthieu and Simone.

"Hmm, yes? Pierre called out as casually as he could, his voice cracked. Pierre turned to face her.

"I was looking all over for you," she said. "You were in that restroom for forever! I was afraid that you may have fallen in!"

Pierre laughed nervously.

"I...have a condition," he decided.

Genevieve eyed him curiously.

"Anyways, here I am!" Pierre declared. "You found me!"

"Here you are," Genevieve said. She continued to look him over suspiciously. "Anyways, I was hoping you could help me piece together some information. In the conference room?"

"About what?" Pierre asked.

"On the connection between the *Black Lotus* and the *Viper Triad*."

Pierre *really* didn't have time for that but what else was he supposed to say, "I would love to help you. Really, Genevieve, I would. But, you see, I have another pressing matter that I must urgently attend to. You see, the necklace that I stole worth nearly €60 million is now lost somewhere in this very police station. I must recover it and then get the *hell* out of here before you all figure out that it was *me* that stole the necklace and then possibly hold *me* responsible for the murder of its proprietor!"

That was everything that Pierre wanted to say, but instead, he said, "Yes."

Genevieve led Pierre back into the conference room and the two of them sat down next to each other, across from the police laptop on the desk.

"So," Genevieve began, pulling out her laptop. "The *Black Lotus*."

"Mhmm," Pierre mumbled nervously. His mind was entirely preoccupied by a more pressing matter at hand. Had he dropped the necklace in the air duct? Had he dropped it in the file room? Had he dropped it in the restroom? Had he dropped it on the floor somewhere?

Pierre didn't have the answer to any of those questions. That's the funny thing about losing something, you don't know where you left it. He tried to do what his mother had always suggested whenever he or his brother had misplaced something. He tried to retrace his steps by thinking back to the last moment he remembered having the necklace. His memory was clouded as scattered images of the necklace, sprinkled with images of Boutrel's lifeless body, emerged through the dense fog in his mind. The only thing that Pierre was certain of was that if he didn't find the necklace soon, it would be gone forever.

"Pierre?" Genevieve called out to him.

"Hmm?" He grunted.

"The heist of the Museum of Modern Art in Paris," she said. "That's what we were talking about. Is everything okay? You look like you've seen a ghost."

Pierre tried to shake some sense back into his head.

"I don't believe in ghosts," he said and inched his chair closer to the table. On the screen on the laptop were all the crime scene photographs of his biggest heist up until last night. It was like he was reliving all of his Greatest Hits.

"Right," Genevieve answered and turned her attention back to the computer, scrolling down the images.

Much like the heist the previous evening, physical evidence at the Museum of Modern Art crime scene was severely lacking. Most of the images were of the spaces on the walls where the paintings had been stolen from.

"You were working that day, correct? Do you remember any suspicious activity from earlier in that day six years ago?" Genevieve continued. "Or anything out of the ordinary?"

The only thing suspicious that day would have been him. Pierre remembered paying particular attention to the security cameras at the museum that day. Then he remembered Remy's instructions to evade them as he pulled up the live feed from his surveillance van. How could he also forget the infuriated look on Remy's face every time Pierre had made another trip back into the museum and returned with another valuable painting, both the paintings and the look on his face were priceless.

"Nothing," Pierre answered.

"Hmm," Genevieve grunted as she studied the photos. "We always suspected it was an inside job, someone with detailed knowledge of the security systems. But, all of the security people checked out."

"Right," Pierre answered, his mind was casually drifting off again.

"Then of course there was the flower," Genevieve said. "Maybe that was just to throw us off track..."

"It's a mystery," Pierre replied.

"Of course," Genevieve continued. "The *Viper Triad* could have had a connection on the inside."

The name brought Pierre back to reality.

"Why did the police immediately suspect an affiliation with the *Viper Triad*?" He asked.

"The black lotus flower, of course," Genevieve answered. "As I was just saying. It all just seemed very... Chinese-y..."

Pierre couldn't decide if that comment was racist or not. He began to drift again.

"It was the sole piece of evidence recovered from the scene," she continued. "Maybe it was a ghost after all," she scoffed. "Anyways, the reason we suspected the *Viper Triad's* involvement was because they've been linked to many different art related crimes all throughout France. Theft of valuable pieces, forgery and even murder."

"Interesting," Pierre said, not really listening in the least bit.

"Personally, I've dealt with a lot of their cases and they always share one thing in common," Genevieve hinted and then paused.

"Hmm, what's that?" Pierre asked finally, entirely disinterested.

"High risk, high reward."

During the presentation, Pierre suddenly remembered. That was the last time that he had felt the Sapphire in his pocket.

"Pierre?" Genevieve called. "I'm saying very dramatic things over here, but you seem like you're somewhere else. What's the matter with you?"

Pierre stumbled back to reality.

"I was just thinking about how maybe it was the wife or the mistress after all," Pierre suggested. "I don't think that the *Viper Triad* had anything to do with this. Besides, didn't this *Black Lotus* character denounce any involvement with them in letters to the police?"

Genevieve frowned. Pierre realized quickly that he may have said too much. The letters were written by the *Black Lotus* and sent directly to the police. Their existence was never released to the press. Therefore, there was no reason why he should have knowledge of them, except, of course, because he *was* the *Black Lotus*. He hoped that Genevieve wouldn't make the connection. Fortunately, she didn't seem to.

"That's why you're not a detective," she said with a bitter coldness that chilled Pierre to his core. "Besides, isn't that just what someone who *was* affiliated with them would want you to believe?"

Pierre considered this.

"All I'm saying," he began again. "Was that the *Black Lotus* never killed anyone during the heist of the Museum of Modern Art. What makes you so sure that he would do so now? What if he was just in the wrong place at the wrong time?"

"As I said before, the *Viper Triad* has been linked to numerous murders," Genevieve answered. Her eyes were fixed on Pierre's.

"Yeah," Pierre said. "But that's not his style."

"What do you know about his style?"

Pierre cleared his throat and looked away from Genevieve's accusatory eyes.

"Anyways," he continued as nonchalantly as he could. "Who was it that found the body?"

Genevieve finally broke off her death stare.

"I don't know if I'm at liberty to discuss that," she said.

Pierre got another idea.

"Come on," he tried. "Who am I going to tell?"

He moved his chair closer to her.

"Maybe we can help each other out with this investigation," Pierre implied seductively and moved even closer still. "You scratch my back, I scratch yours…"

"I think we might be able to work something out," Genevieve answered with a grin. "I don't see what difference it makes anyways if you know. The wife found the body early this morning."

"Hmm," Pierre grunted. "The wife…"

Genevieve nodded.

"I don't know whether to call her, 'that poor woman' or 'that lucky woman,'" she said. "She must have opened the coat closet door and the old bastard just plopped right out." She slapped her hand down on the table to simulate Boutrel's lifeless body flopping out of the closet.

"I can't even begin to imagine," Pierre replied.

Only, he could imagine it, very vividly, in fact, and he didn't appreciate the way that Genevieve casually used the word "plopped" to explain such a dramatically horrific event as Pierre remembered it.

"Anyways," Genevieve continued and moved closer to him still. Any closer and she would have been on his lap.

By this point, Pierre felt like he had squeezed all the useful information out of her already. But, he had to keep playing along, at least until he found the prime opportunity to get away and find the necklace. It was at that moment when Genevieve slipped her hand on Pierre's thigh.

"Yahtzee!" Pierre exclaimed, suddenly pushing his chair back. The chair screeched on the linoleum floor as he stood up awkwardly. "I need to use the restroom!"

"Again?" Genevieve asked. "But you just went!"

"It's my condition," Pierre said in a raised tone of voice, almost as if he were shouting.

"Okay," Genevieve said, puzzled. "Do you need me to show you where it is again?"

"That's okay!" Pierre assured her. "I'll be right back!"

He pushed through the wooden door of the conference room and rushed down the hallway to the restroom.

Once inside, he leaned up against the sink and stared at himself in the mirror. Behind him on the wall, he could see the vent of the air duct.

It's got to be in there somewhere, he thought, but he knew it would be too risky to go now. There wasn't enough time. Genevieve was almost certainly growing suspicious of him. He could sense it. If he was gone too long again, she would come after them. He just needed to keep her under his control a little longer. After all, he was the most handsome man in the station, and he knew it. He just had to use that to his advantage. She was still in his pocket. Although, he would have much rather preferred that it was the necklace in his pocket.

He nodded his head in the mirror with a self-reassuring grin and then made his way back out of the restroom. He just had to play his cards right until he could find the right time to slip away from Genevieve.

He turned the corner of the hallway distractedly and bumped right into a man on the other side. The two went tumbling to the ground. Pierre laid on top of the man for a moment as the two of them rubbed their heads.

"Pierre!" He heard Genevieve shout from down the hallway. "Are you okay?"

She rushed over to help him off the man.

"You need to watch where you're going, Monsieur," the man said as the two stood up.

"You walked into me!" Pierre assured him.

When he looked up at the man, Pierre suddenly realized with horror that he was no longer the most handsome man in the station. The man reminded Pierre a lot of himself, only better in every way. He was taller, more muscular, more handsome, and his blue eyes and shaggy blonde hair sparkled, even in the dull lighting of the police station.

"And who might you be?" Genevieve asked. Pierre couldn't help but notice that she seemed *very* intrigued.

"François Fouquet," the man answered. "It might do you well to remember it."

Pierre's control was slipping.

21

Sunday, the 1st of January, 6:40 p.m.

Not only was François Fouquet just a better all-around version of Pierre, but, as Matthieu would soon come to find out, he was almost twice as arrogant, which Matthieu didn't even think was possible. He would soon come to find that this François, the *real* François, was a much different François than the one he had met during his initial interviews of the servants at the château. Of course, that could easily be explained by the fact that François had been trying to hide something from him. The only reason he had at first appeared so helpful and forthcoming was maybe to keep his affair with Lucile a secret.

François was sitting at the interrogation table completely disinterested when Matthieu took a seat across from him. If he was being honest, Matthieu was surprised to be sitting across from François at all. He was almost positive that François would have been long gone by now if he was involved in

Boutrel's death. Then again, maybe there was something keeping him here. Matthieu intended to find out.

"It's good to see you again, Monsieur Fouquet," Matthieu began cordially.

"Let's speed this along," François replied, much less cordially as he glanced at his wristwatch. "I've got places to go and people to see."

I'm sure you do, Matthieu thought suspiciously. This was definitely not the same François. He seemed much less warm and inviting, a far cry from how he had seemed earlier when he had won Matthieu's admiration.

"That's a nice watch you've got there," Matthieu said, admiring the gold band on François' wrist.

"Tag Heuer," François answered indifferently. "Would probably cost you two years' salary. Can I ask what this is about?"

"Two years?" Matthieu repeated. "How does a servant afford something like that?"

"Savings," François answered without missing a beat. "Did you call me in today to compliment my attire?"

"Must pay pretty well," Matthieu replied, ignoring François' latter comment. "I may need to rethink my own line of work."

"Well," François began with a slick coolness that made Matthieu both despise and admire him. "Boutrel isn't currently accepting applications."

"You asked what this was about," Matthieu continued. "But I presume you already know why we called you in to talk again."

"It couldn't possibly have anything to do with my employer's untimely death, could it, Detective?"

"It could, believe it or not," Matthieu replied. "The old... blowfish in a suit, I believe were your exact words."

"Dirty, old blowfish in a suit," François corrected him.

"Right," Matthieu replied. "How long have you been employed under Monsieur Boutrel?"

"A little under a year," François answered.

"How would you describe him as an employer?"

François shrugged his shoulders.

"I'm going to stick to my original sentiment," he decided.

"Would you say that you hated your boss?"

"Everyone hates their boss," he replied.

François was right. Nearly every servant in that house had nothing but negative things to say about Boutrel. Usually when someone dies, people remember the better things about them, maybe these were Boutrel's better qualities. This line of questioning to establish a motive was getting Matthieu nowhere, and he knew it. He would need to try something else, and he thought he may have had the solution.

"We know about your relationship with Lucile Lebas, Monsieur Fouquet," Matthieu said suddenly, hoping to catch François off guard.

Maybe *she* was what was keeping François from leaving. Maybe they were in on the scheme together and were waiting to cash in on her inheritance before they could both flee together. The puzzle was beginning to fit together.

"It's pronounced, *Fouquet*," François replied without hesitation.

"That's what I said, isn't it?"

François shook his head and rolled his eyes.

"You said, *Fouquet*," he said. "It's, *Fouquet*."

"Fouquet," Matthieu tried again.

"*Fouquet*," François corrected once more.

"François," Matthieu began again. "Can I call you François?"

"No," François answered.

"I guess it doesn't bother you that we know about your affair?"

"For God sakes, Detective," François began. He was cool, calm and collected but beginning to grow slightly annoyed. He immediately calmed himself and a devilish grin spread across his face. "This is France. Everyone is involved in some affair or another. Lucile was Boutrel's affair. Are you married Detective?"

"We're not here for me," Matthieu stuttered.

"A sore subject I see," François said. "Based on the tan line around your ring finger, I'd say that you *were* married. Recently separated? Was your wife having an affair?"

"We're here to talk about you and Boutrel," Matthieu declared. He tucked his hands under the interrogation room table, out of sight.

The grin spread wider on François' face. He knew that he had crawled under the Detective's skin and he intended to stay there.

"I suppose what you said is true," François continued. "I was Lucile's 'affair' if you want to call it that, just as Lucile was Boutrel's. The only difference is perspective."

"A valid point," Matthieu decided, trying to regain his footing. He was beginning to think that he had underestimated François. "You seem to be a smart guy," he continued. "Maybe we can play a little game?"

"Is that why you called me here today, Detective?" François asked. He placed his elbows on the rusty table in front of him and stared into the eyes of the Detective.

Matthieu nearly found himself lost in the vast, deep blue oceans he was staring back into. He presumed that any woman that found herself lost in these oceans could get swept up in the waves and feel like she was the only girl in the world. For a moment, Matthieu even felt like *he* was the only girl in the world.

"You wanted to play a game," François continued. "What did you have in mind? Twister? Connect Four, perhaps?"

"How about a little role reversal," Matthieu answered.

"Ah, role play," François replied. "I didn't take you for the type, Detective. I've heard that Boutrel himself was *heavily* into role play."

"What makes you say that?"

"He was always pretending to be a decent human being," François answered. "When really, he was nothing but a *roach* wearing a human suit."

"That's an interesting observation," Matthieu said, slightly disturbed by the analogy. "But really, put yourself in my place for a minute. What are you thinking right now if you're me? What are you feeling?"

François studied the Detective up and down for a moment.

"Probably sadness," he answered. "A tinge of regret sprinkled with a healthy dose of self-loathing. The fact that you've unbuttoned the top two buttons of your shirt screams to me that you're going through some sort of mid-life crisis and the bags under your eyes suggest that you've spent many of the past few nights crying. Ah, interesting…"

"What's interesting?"

"Let me guess. Here I was thinking that you found out about your wife's affair and that you broke things off. It would appear to be the other way around though, no? Did your wife get bored with you and split? Am I close?"

"I meant what I was thinking about the case," Matthieu replied. His voice cracked as he fought back tears. He would never admit just how right François was.

"That depends, Detective," François answered. "I don't have all of the information in front of me."

"What more information do you want?"

"I don't know everything that you already know about me."

"Is there something worth knowing?" Matthieu asked. "Maybe something that you're hiding?"

"Is there something that *you're* hiding?" François challenged.

The two were locking eyes from across the table.

"I'm confused," Matthieu finally said. "Are we still role playing?"

François scoffed.

"And here I thought I'd found a worthy opponent," he said.

Matthieu collected his thoughts but it seemed as if François had turned his mind to mush.

"I know that Lucile had just recently become a key player in Monsieur Boutrel's will," Matthieu said.

"Are you being me right now?" François asked. "Or are you, being you?"

"No," Matthieu said, annoyed at François' lack of acknowledgement for what Matthieu had figured out already. "We're done with the role reversal. I'm telling you what *I* know now."

"Is this going to take much longer, Detective?" François asked. "I've got dinner plans."

"Are you sure there isn't a train that you need to catch?"

"Why would there be a train that I need to catch?" François asked. "Where would I be going?"

Matthieu continued.

"*I* know that you and Lucile were having an affair," he said. "And *I* know that Lucile stands to inherit a *lot* of money for the death of Monsieur Boutrel."

"So?" François interrupted. "What does that have to do with me?"

"I believe the Americans have a phrase for a relationship such as yours."

"Americans," François scoffed. "*Pew*!" He spit on the floor of the interrogation room.

"They'd call you a regular Bonnie and Clyde," Matthieu said.

"I'm afraid I'm not familiar with the reference."

Matthieu shook his head. This line of questioning wasn't seeming to go anywhere either.

"Can you confirm your whereabouts around 9:30 p.m. last night?" He asked outright.

François smirked.

"I was a little *preoccupied* around 9:30 p.m., if you know what I'm saying, Detective," he answered with a wink.

"Let's pretend I don't know what you're saying," Matthieu replied. "Why don't you spell it out for me."

"I was with Lucile."

"And Boutrel?"

"No, just Lucile."

Matthieu sighed frustratedly and then amended the question.

"Where was Boutrel?" He asked.

"How the hell should I know where Boutrel was?"

"Do you remember the last time that you saw Monsieur Boutrel last night?"

"I was serving drinks last night; I didn't realize I was in charge of babysitting as well."

"Maybe you should have been more concerned about his whereabouts," Matthieu replied. "Seeing as you stand to gain quite a bit from his death."

François focused his eyes on the Detective.

"What are you suggesting?" He asked.

"I'm suggesting that you had something to do with Boutrel's murder," Matthieu finally declared, not caring to mince words any longer. He was clearly engaged in a heated exchange of words that he was on the losing end of.

François scoffed again.

"You really think that I had something to do with this?" He asked. "I never stabbed Boutrel."

Matthieu suddenly froze.

"I never said that he was stabbed," he replied. He had nabbed François helplessly in his trap. Only, François didn't react like he was trapped. In fact, he remained the same as he had been—cool, calm and collected.

"You didn't have to," François laughed. "I can read the newspaper, Detective."

As much as he tried to forget, Matthieu believed that the image of himself standing over the body of Bastien Boutrel with a dagger plunged into his chest would be his legacy. That image was splashed over every news publication in France by now.

François began to chuckle.

"You know, you had the same look on your face in that photograph that you do now, Detective," he said. "Did you really think that it would be that simple? That I would conveniently suggest something to you that only the killer could know? You've been watching too much TV, Monsieur—"

Role reversal again, Matthieu thought. Now, *he* was the helpless one. François wasn't wrong either. Matthieu had spent the last four weeks watching far too much TV and for a moment, he did honestly believe it would be that simple.

Matthieu cleared his throat. It was a good thing that he wasn't keeping score with François either, because he had been bested once again. He began to feel a strong sense of self-pity and defeat, when he had a sudden idea.

"How do you feel about *Gu?*" He suddenly sprang.

It was virtually undetectable, but Matthieu was almost positive that he had noticed the most subtle twitch of surprise in François' beautifully stoic face.

"About what?" François asked, refusing to break eye contact with the Detective. "I'm afraid I don't know what that is."

Are you sure about that? Matthieu wondered as he studied him.

"Just one more question," Matthieu said. "What are you planning on doing now that your employer is deceased?"

François shrugged.

"I'm sure finding work won't be too difficult," he answered. "Now, can I go?"

Matthieu stared intently at François. As much as he wanted to arrest him, there wasn't much to go on. Besides, he didn't want to let on that he was suspicious of him, or it might convince François to flee. François knew more than he was letting on, but Matthieu couldn't prove it yet.

"You're free to go," he finally said.

François stood up, not nearly as collected as he had been when he arrived, Matthieu noted. He headed toward the door when Matthieu added one more thing.

"Just don't go too far," he said. "We may have more questions for you."

François scoffed and then left Matthieu alone. He left the interrogation room hallway and headed toward the stairs. Matthieu could hear the door screech closed behind him.

Pierre was back in the conference room with Genevieve, still trying to play into her desires, but remaining just far enough out of reach to fend off her advances. They both watched as François passed by the conference room in front of them.

"Who does that guy think that he is anyways?" Pierre mumbled.

"Why, he's the secret lover of Lucile Lebas," Genevieve replied. Pierre could almost see the ardor in her eyes.

François rounded the corner and headed towards the stairs that led to the exit.

Good riddance, Pierre thought.

Nearly as soon as the tip of François' beautiful blonde hair disappeared down the staircase, it was replaced by a head of flat grey hair that belonged to none other than Baron William Worthington.

He was an older man, in his mid-70s, dressed regally in a crimson coat with gold tassels that adorned the shoulders. He was escorted by two of his security advisors.

Worthington was otherwise nondescript and would have been completely unmemorable to Pierre except for two key things. The first, was the thick mustache that rested above his upper lip. It reminded Pierre of Boutrel's stupid mustache and the equally stupid smile that rested under it.

Pierre realized that he already subconsciously hated this man, even before he had the opportunity to meet him.

The second key thing, more of a realization, occurred when Pierre first heard the Baron's voice float into the conference room with his immediately recognizable, thick, British accent. Pierre realized that he had, in fact, already had the opportunity to meet Baron William Worthington. It was last night, as Boutrel's body lay on top of him and the words that he had heard the Baron mumble echoed in Pierre's ears—

"The French are such a strange people."

22

Sunday, the 1st of January 7:00 p.m.

A third realization naturally followed the first two; Pierre had most definitely worn out his welcome. He needed to get out of there, now, and not a second later.

However, Genevieve was as persistent as ever. It seemed like she was determined to not let Pierre out of her sights again. She was like a moth to a flame. Pierre quickly realized that he would never be able to escape with her on his case, no pun intended. On top of everything else, the Han Sapphire necklace was still lost somewhere, in the police station, of all places. Pierre wasn't ready to leave it behind just yet. It could be the key to unraveling this whole mystery, or at the very least, provide a substantial payday when this was all said and done.

Detective Matthieu had emerged from the interrogation room shortly after François and had followed his path with a watchful eye. He had a feeling that he hadn't seen the last of François in this case, at least he didn't intend this to be their last meeting. However, that was all contingent on whether François decided to stick around. Matthieu believed that he would.

Matthieu stopped by the Chief's office momentarily to give him a full rundown of the interrogation when Baron William Worthington had arrived. When he exited the Chief's office, he saw the Baron's flashy ensemble from across the room. The Baron was wandering around aimlessly. He looked lost and confused. Matthieu went over to greet him.

Pierre watched from over Genevieve's shoulder as the two men grasped hands and shook. Worthington's eyes shifted over Matthieu's shoulder and into the conference room where Pierre detected the slightest hint of recognition before ducking behind Genevieve. Fortunately, Genevieve was too busy blabbering on to notice Pierre's sudden alarm.

Matthieu led the Baron to his cubicle and then gestured to him to make himself comfortable in the chair across from his desk.

"Can I get you anything?" Matthieu asked. *If he says a chai latte, I'm going to scream.*

"No, no, that won't be necessary," Worthington answered. "Hopefully this won't take long. It's quite late after all."

"Of course not," Matthieu assured him. "This isn't a formal interrogation. Just think of it more as a...casual conversation. I just have a few questions about last night. You're not a suspect or anything." Matthieu chuckled to ease the tension. *Yet*, he thought to himself.

"Of course, of course," the Baron replied, chuckling along with the Detective. "Anything I can do to help."

Before Matthieu sat in the chair across from him, he turned around and opened the door to the conference room.

"The Chief would like to see you both," Matthieu said to Pierre and Genevieve.

Pierre glanced nervously out through the window at Worthington who was sitting right within the direct line of sight of the Chief's office.

"What, now?" Pierre asked in disbelief.

"No, how does sometime in February work for you?"

"February's good," Pierre replied.

"Now!" Matthieu demanded. "You idiot."

"Come on, Pierre," Genevieve said, scowling at her ex-husband and rising from her seat. "We'll take a quick break and come back to this."

Pierre eyed the Baron cautiously.

"We've been making some great progress," he insisted. In truth, he had stopped paying attention long ago. "I would hate to disrupt our pace."

"We can come back to this," Genevieve assured him.

Matthieu was looking at Pierre suspiciously again.

Pierre cleared his throat and stood up.

"You're right," he said. "I'm just too excited to solve this thing."

Matthieu scoffed.

"You two aren't going to solve anything in here," he said. "You're looking in the wrong place."

"We'll see about that," Genevieve declared as she brushed past him.

Pierre brushed past him as well but didn't say anything. His gaze was locked on the Baron.

"No smart remark this time from the smartest guy in the room?" Matthieu asked.

Pierre didn't even hear that Matthieu was talking to him. He was frozen just outside of the doorway and his face suddenly became deathly pale.

"Hello?" Matthieu called. He knocked his knuckles against Pierre's head. "Is anybody home?"

Matthieu chuckled to himself.

Worthington had grabbed a coffee mug off Matthieu's desk and was turning it over in his hands. The mug read, "World's Best Detective." He must have felt Pierre staring at him because he looked up to meet his gaze.

Pierre quickly looked away when Worthington glanced up at him and began finally walking again. His legs were wobbly beneath his body, but he moved forward toward the Chief's office, trying his best to hide his face.

"You there," Worthington called out to Pierre in his heavy, British accent.

Pierre pretended not to hear him. This felt like the beginning of the end.

"Excuse me," Worthington tried again, louder this time.

Pierre tried to brush him off again but nearly everyone in the station had stopped what they were doing and were looking straight at Pierre.

"Pelletier!" Matthieu called.

Pierre turned to look. Everything felt like it was in slow motion.

"The Baron is speaking to you."

Pierre craned his neck slowly toward Worthington like a ventriloquist doll that had just been brought to life until their eyes finally met.

"Don't I know you from somewhere?" Worthington asked suspiciously.

"I'm afraid you must have me mistaken for someone else," Pierre stammered. His fists clenched loosely into his sweaty palms, not that he was going to use these fists anyways.

"Are you sure?" Worthington asked, squinting his eyes to focus in on him. "You look so familiar."

"I get that a lot," Pierre replied with a nervous laugh. "I guess I just have one of those faces."

"Hmm," Worthington grunted. He was still studying Pierre intently, not ready to give it up just yet. "Perhaps," he finally said.

He turned his head away from Pierre and began conversing with his security advisors.

Pierre briskly walked away from the Baron.

That was too close, he thought to himself before joining Genevieve in the Chief's office.

Genevieve took a seat across from the Chief's desk, but Pierre stood by the door, unable to move.

"I just wanted to check on your progress," the Chief began before noticing Pierre's pale face and shaky legs. "Is everything alright with him?"

"I think so," Genevieve answered and shrugged.

"Take a seat, son," the Chief said. "You're making me uncomfortable."

Pierre waddled his way over to the seat at the desk across from him and then melted into it like the bundle of nerves that he was.

Genevieve began.

"We're almost certain that the *Black Lotus* has a connection to the *Viper Triad* in Hong Kong," she said.

"What's your working theory?" The Chief asked.

"We believe that he scaled the gutter seen in Simone's surveillance footage and climbed in through the window," she continued. "He broke into the safe and took the Han Sapphire necklace. Then, Boutrel must have entered the room. The *Black Lotus* killed him and then fled on foot."

"What about the… *Gu*?" The Chief asked, giving Pierre a look first before saying the word. Pierre was staring straight ahead.

"We believe that the perpetrator *may* have had a person on the inside," Genevieve answered. "They probably helped him climb in through the window, since it was only accessible from the inside. We believe this person might know everything that there is to know about the *Gu*. They might have slipped him a dose of it to try to knock Boutrel unconscious without realizing that they had given him a lethal dose. When it came down to it, the *Black Lotus* may have stabbed him unnecessarily."

"Interesting," the Chief said. "From the sounds of it, you and your husband are working a similar angle. I really wish you would just consider working together on this."

"Ex-husband," Genevieve corrected him swiftly.

"Right, what did I say?"

"Never mind," Genevieve replied. "The point is that Martin is in denial about the involvement, or even the existence of the *Black Lotus*. I believe that the whole ordeal was, in fact, cleverly orchestrated by the *Viper Triad*. I think someone on the inside of the soirée had a connection to the *Triad*. They let the *Black Lotus* in through the window and the rest followed."

So close, Pierre would have been thinking if he were paying attention.

"Do you have any other leads as to the identity of the individual who was inside, or this *Black Lotus* character himself?" The Chief asked.

Genevieve's eyes shifted subconsciously to Pierre, but she shook her head.

"Martin thinks that he's so clever," she said spitefully. "Well, I've been around a long time too. I've got plenty of contacts in the art world, plenty of informants. I can see if any of them may have heard any chatter about a heist going down. Maybe they even have information about our *Black Lotus*."

"You don't have to remind me about how long you've been here, Genevieve," the Chief began. "I'm well aware and I appreciate your dedication to the job. Just let me know if there's anything that you need from me, anybody that I can arrange for questioning and I'll see to it that they're here. I'm completely at your disposal. Do you have anything to add, Monsieur Pelletier?"

Pierre was still a little preoccupied with the thought that the necklace was still missing and that the only person who could potentially identify him from last night was sitting comfortably no more than ten meters from him.

"I think she summarized everything perfectly well," he said.

Genevieve glanced over at him and smiled.

"Good," the Chief decided. "Then I won't keep you any longer. Keep at it and let me know when you come up with something."

Genevieve nodded her head and stood up. Pierre slowly rose to his feet. His knees were still wobbly beneath him.

"Are you coming, Pierre?" Genevieve called from the door.

Pierre must have blacked out momentarily because he had no idea how she could have gotten there so quickly.

"Yep," he answered, his voice cracking.

He walked to the door and peered out. Matthieu was just sitting down to talk to Worthington when the Baron suddenly looked straight at Pierre and his eyes widened.

"I remember where I know you from!" Worthington shouted.

Pierre fainted.

23

Sunday, the 1st of January, 7:20 p.m.

When he came to, Pierre's head was resting in Thomas' lap and Genevieve was fanning him with air. His forehead felt cool and damp as he stared up at the dim lighting of the police station.

"Where am I?" He asked.

"You passed out, Pelletier," Matthieu answered.

Worthington's head rudely poked into view, obscuring the ceiling light.

"I remembered where I knew you from," he said.

Pierre suddenly remembered everything all at once. He felt as if he might pass out again. He almost didn't believe the words that Worthington said next.

"We shared a gondola on the London Eye!" Worthington proclaimed. "See, I never forget a face!"

"No, Monsieur," Pierre finally answered.

"Are you okay, Pierre?" Genevieve asked.

"In all my excitement, I just remembered that I haven't had anything to eat today," Pierre said.

"You poor thing," Genevieve remarked before turning to her ex-husband. "Martin, get the poor man something to eat!"

"Uh-uh," Matthieu replied. "He's your problem, not mine."

"I'm fine, I'm fine," Pierre insisted and tried to rise to his feet.

"Whoa, easy there, killer," Thomas said.

"What did you just call me?" Pierre asked. His legs were wobbling beneath him.

"What, killer?" Thomas asked. "It's just an expression."

"Are you sure?" Worthington interrupted. "You just look so familiar!"

"I just have one of those faces," Pierre repeated and pushed Thomas aside.

"I'm not so sure," Worthington said as he shook a finger at Pierre skeptically. "I'm going to get it, I swear. I have the memory of an elephant!"

Maybe a dead elephant, Pierre thought to himself as he wobbled back to the conference room. He was still woozy, but a wave of sweet relief passed over him.

"Anyways," Matthieu interrupted. "We were talking about Boutrel's soirée, Baron."

Genevieve brought Pierre a glass of cool water as well as a granola bar and rejoined him in the conference room while Matthieu and the Baron returned to the Detective's cubicle.

"Yes," Worthington continued. "The fundraiser for orphaned puppies."

"You were in the midst of telling me that this wasn't the *true* meaning for the gathering?" Matthieu asked.

"I was?" Worthington asked. "Ah, yes," he said as he tapped his fingers to his head. "Like a steel trap. Anyways, the real pretense for the soirée was to move the necklace."

"To move the necklace?" Matthieu repeated.

"Yes," Worthington replied. "Boutrel was looking for a buyer. Well, more specifically, choosing a buyer."

"But Monsieur Boutrel had just purchased the necklace himself," Matthieu stated curiously.

Worthington shook his head.

"Boutrel is more of a middleman when it comes to these things," he answered. "He finds the items through a private supplier and then he jacks up the price for an interested buyer."

"Okay, so, who was the buyer?"

"There had been an ongoing bidding war up until a few weeks ago," Worthington said. "The price became too steep for my own liking and I backed out."

"How steep?" Matthieu pressed.

"About €100 million steep."

"So, Boutrel was intent on selling the necklace for €100 million," Matthieu confirmed. "Who would have that kind of money to spend on jewelry?"

"It's not always about the worth of the piece," the Baron replied. "Often, when you have that much money, it's about having something that nobody else does. Lording it over them, in a sense. The amount of power that comes with is priceless."

"Give me a name," Matthieu insisted.

"The last I heard, the bidding war was between the Chinese Ambassador, Zhao Zhu, and the Russian Ambassador, Yuri Yachnitch," Worthington replied. "The soirée was an opportunity for everyone to meet face to face and make a final offer."

"Then why were you there?" Matthieu asked. "If you had already backed out?"

"For the free food," the Baron answered plainly. "No matter how wealthy you are, you should never pass up a free meal."

"Of course," Matthieu answered. "But that doesn't explain why someone saw you arguing with Boutrel shortly before his death."

Worthington's eyes fluttered.

"Are you accusing me of something, Detective?" he asked. His tone became defensive.

"Not at all," Matthieu assured him. "I just want to hear your side of events."

"Boutrel was a scoundrel, and he was heavily intoxicated, which wasn't odd. Everyone knew that he liked to partake in the drink. However, what was odd was that he would do so on a night like last night."

"What do you mean?" Matthieu asked.

"I've seen Boutrel drunk at many a soirée," Worthington answered. "But never when there was business involved."

"Interesting," Matthieu said.

"What's stranger still is that I only saw him with a single glass of wine all evening. Now, obviously, I couldn't be sure that it was the same glass, but I only ever saw him even take a couple of casual sips from it. Usually, Boutrel drank it by the liter."

"So, why did you think that he was heavily intoxicated?" Matthieu asked.

"He was slurring his words, bumbling around like a damned fool. He spilled wine on my lapel, which was the reason why I was arguing with him in the first place."

"Then what happened?"

"Well, he didn't stay long, he dashed off like a madman."

"Hm, do you have any idea who won the bidding war, Baron?"

"The last I heard, Zhu made the final offer at €100 million and Yachnitch graciously bowed out."

"It sounds like it was too steep for him as well," Matthieu replied. If Boutrel sold the necklace, then maybe the broken safe had been a red herring. He inquired further. "Anyways, when was the last time that you saw Monsieur Boutrel? Was it before or after he moved the necklace?"

Worthington chuckled.

"Boutrel didn't move the necklace that night, Detective," he replied. "So, I guess to answer your question, it would be before. The last I saw Boutrel was, regretfully, when he ran off. I was in the midst of declaring him a scoundrel in front of the whole soirée when he disappeared upstairs. I suppose that doesn't make me look very good for his murder."

"You would be right about that," Matthieu mumbled. "Do you remember anything else after he disappeared upstairs?"

Worthington closed his eyes and struggled to dredge up the memories.

"There was something else," he finally said. "There was a woman that followed him upstairs."

"There was?" Matthieu asked. "Who?"

"I never saw her face," Worthington recalled. "But I could never forget the way that the light played off of her sparkling, scarlet evening gown."

"It's not scarlet!" Matthieu suddenly erupted. "It's red, just say red!"

Matthieu's eruption quickly subsided and when he regained his composure, Worthington was staring at him with a frightened look on his face. Matthieu cleared his throat.

"I'm sorry," he said. "That wasn't for you, that was for someone else…"

He realized that he had let his anger towards Genevieve finally get the best of him and he unfairly unleashed it on Worthington.

"Are there any other details that you can remember about this mystery woman?" Matthieu asked.

Worthington shifted in his chair until he found a more comfortable position. He shook his head.

"One thing I did notice was that she moved like she was on a mission."

"A mission?" Matthieu repeated.

Worthington nodded.

Matthieu was still insistent that the *Black Lotus* character was a red herring, but, as much as he wanted to, he couldn't deny the mountain of evidence that was building in front of him. Still, even if the *Black Lotus* had been there that night, he would have needed an accomplice to help him in through the third-story window. Perhaps this mystery woman *was* that accomplice, or maybe even the murderer. If she killed Boutrel, maybe that had surprised the *Black Lotus* enough to make him become careless and flee back through the window, where he had been conveniently caught on the surveillance footage that Simone had seen. The presence of the *Black Lotus* was still a major "if" for Matthieu because he couldn't accept that Genevieve was right. Needless to say, this mystery woman was a significant person of interest and if Worthington had seen her at the soirée, that meant she was on the guest list.

"So, back to what we were saying before," Matthieu began again. "You're saying that Zhu doesn't have the necklace?"

"From what the papers are saying," Worthington began. "It's been stolen."

"That's what I've been hearing as well," Matthieu said. He was deep in thought, trying to connect the puzzle together. "Did Zhu find it odd that Boutrel disappeared that night *before* the exchange of the necklace?"

"I wouldn't imagine so, that would have been customary."

"How so?"

"Well, Zhu probably didn't even have the funds on him. The gathering was merely to establish a buyer. That's how Boutrel operates."

"Couldn't Zhu just wire the money to Boutrel?" Matthieu asked.

"Boutrel preferred to work with cash, he always preferred cash," Worthington replied. "Imagine carrying that much cash on you," he scoffed. "Preposterous! I'd never go anywhere with more than €5 million."

"Imagine that," Matthieu remarked sarcastically.

"Besides, like I said, Boutrel was drunk. I assumed, much like everyone else, that he wandered off somewhere and passed out."

"Either way," Matthieu began again. "I'll probably need to have a word with the two Ambassadors as well."

And track down this mystery woman, he thought to himself.

"Good luck with that, Detective," Worthington replied. "The two of them were on a plane this morning. Zhu for Hong Kong and Yachnitch for Moscow."

Matthieu was scribbling in his notepad but now suddenly stopped abruptly.

"Did you say, Hong Kong?" Matthieu asked, vaguely remembering something that Genevieve had been babbling about.

"Yes," Worthington answered. "What of it?"

"That's where the *Viper Triad* is based," Matthieu mumbled, more to himself than to the Baron. There was no way Genevieve could be right about this, but it was certainly heading that way.

"Detective?" Worthington tried.

"Do you have any idea when they'll be back?"

Worthington shrugged.

"I'm not their personal assistant, Detective."

"Right, of course," Matthieu said.

It was no matter. He would find out when they would be back soon enough. If they didn't plan on coming back, he would make them.

"Is there anything else that you can think of that was suspicious from last night?" he asked.

Worthington closed his eyes tightly and pressed his fingers to his head for a moment.

"Worthington?" Matthieu called after him.

The Baron's eyes suddenly shot open.

"Yes!" He proclaimed. "I had completely forgotten, but I *did*, in fact, see Boutrel again last night. You'll have to forgive me, Detective, my memory is not what it used to be."

The Baron's two security advisors both exchanged a glance with one another.

So much for the steel trap, Matthieu thought.

"I was searching for the restroom upstairs, after Boutrel had spilled his wine on my lapel, when I accidentally came across Boutrel, engaged with another man in his study."

"Engaged with another man?" Matthieu repeated curiously.

"I've never been one to judge," Worthington continued. "But it did strike me as odd. I didn't know that Boutrel was...*of* that persuasion."

"I'm confused," Matthieu said

"I walked in on Boutrel engaged physically with another man," Worthington reiterated.

"Do you know who this man was?"

"I'd never seen him before," Worthington replied. "It was so hard to see in there. He was wearing all black."

"And this was in the study?"

"In Boutrel's study, yes," Worthington replied.

"About what time do you think that this was?"

"Around 9:30, I believe," Worthington settled on. "9:30," Matthieu repeated, right around the estimated time of death. "Are you sure that Monsieur Boutrel was *alive* at that moment?"

"Are you suggesting that the man I saw was defiling a corpse?" Worthington asked, disgusted. "I knew that the French were a perverted people, but I had no idea that they were *that* perverted!"

"I'm not saying that at all," Matthieu began, slightly perturbed by the Baron's comments about the French. "I'm saying that I think that you may have stumbled upon our murderer."

Meanwhile, in the conference room, Pierre had completely settled down. He convinced himself again that the study was too dark to identify him and what's more, Worthington seemed to be going senile. Unfortunate for the Baron, but extremely fortunate for Pierre. There was virtually no way that he would be able to identify him. Still, Pierre didn't intend to stick around much longer. He just needed to find the necklace and then get the hell out of there.

Genevieve was mid-sentence when Pierre stood up.

"I have to use the restroom," he proclaimed.

"Your condition again?" Genevieve asked. "Do you remember where it is?"

"Of course," Pierre said.

He pushed open the conference room door with authority. Worthington suddenly looked up at him just as he was finishing his story with the Detective and his eyes widened once more.

"That's where I know you from!" He shouted.

Matthieu turned to face Pierre.

"*That's* the man that I saw!" Worthington proclaimed. "The murderer!"

Act II
The Fugitive

24

Sunday, the 1st of January, 10:03 p.m.

After the Baron's identification, Pierre was immediately tackled to the ground and piled on top of by at least a dozen officers before he even had a chance to defend himself. From there, he was led into the interrogation room by two of the Toulouse Police Department's burliest officers, a couple of real beefcakes. Nearly their entire hands fit around the width of his biceps. Pierre didn't know their names but decided that he was going to henceforth refer to them as Officer Beef and Officer Cake.

Detective Matthieu followed them into the interrogation room and ordered them to place Pierre in the chair. Pierre began to object but before he could say anything, Officer Beef and Cake pushed him forcefully downwards. They each grabbed one of his hands and held them out. Matthieu slapped down a pair of handcuffs around Pierre's wrists and then attached them to the metal cuff loops that were bolted down to the top of the table.

Matthieu locked the cuffs tight around Pierre's wrists and Pierre cried out, much to the delight of the Detective. This felt personal.

"Watch the merchandise," Pierre grunted.

Matthieu pinched the cuffs another click tighter around Pierre's wrists and grinned at him. Pierre winced in pain.

Matthieu then gave a nod to the two escorting officers and they all left the room, leaving Pierre alone in his stone prison to stew for the next couple of hours.

The only light in the room came from the lightbulb that was blinking incessantly overhead. After about twenty minutes, Pierre put his head down on the interrogation room table and slept soundly with visions of Colette dancing in his head.

"Wake up, idiot!" Suddenly broke Pierre from his pleasant slumber.

"Colette?" He mumbled as he sat up groggily. His face was damp from the puddle of drool that he had slept in.

"Good morning, sleepyhead," Matthieu teased. "*You* have got some explaining to do, smart guy."

Pierre finally remembered where he was. He tried to pull his hands back to defend himself from the Detective, but they wouldn't budge.

"How about loosening these up?" he asked, holding up his handcuffed wrists as high as he could.

Matthieu scoffed.

"I'll get right on that," he said. "Right after I bring you another chai latte."

He was holding a thick folder with the number 1594 in color coded stickers down the side. It wasn't the same number as Boutrel's case file, and Pierre wondered what was inside. He would find out soon enough.

Matthieu slapped the folder down on the table forcefully before taking a seat in the chair across from him.

"Scary," Pierre mumbled.

Matthieu opened the folder which had a large stack of papers in it that had been paperclipped together. He took the paperclip off aggressively and threw it down on the table in front of Pierre without breaking eye contact. The paperclip rattled across the table and landed just in front of the metal cuff loops.

"Is this supposed to be intimidating?" Pierre asked, unamused. "If you're the bad cop, where's the good cop? I'll talk to him."

"There is no *good* cop," Matthieu said.

"You can say that again," Pierre replied smartly. "Definitely no *good* cops in here."

Matthieu let out a booming laugh that startled Pierre.

"There's the smart guy," he said.

Pierre grinned victoriously at him.

"But," Matthieu continued. "You don't look so smart from over here."

"What's in the folder, Detective?" Pierre asked, moving past the banter. "Is that another Detective trick to make it look like you've got a whole folder of evidence mounted against me so that I'll tell you everything? I've seen police shows, Detective. I know that they usually make the suspect wait in the interrogation room for hours so that they start to panic. Then, you expect them to confess everything the minute you walk in the door. Is that what this is?"

Matthieu normally would have interrupted Pierre's rant. However, now he was going to let Pierre talk as much as he wanted to.

"Your experience isn't limited to just police shows," Matthieu said. "Seems like you've had your own run-ins with the law as well."

Pierre clammed up. Matthieu picked up the first piece of paper in the folder and began reading it.

"Pierre Pelletier, born 1988 in Paris, France to Pascal and Paulette Pelletier," he said. "Your father was gone, almost from the start, and your mother died when you were 18, leaving you without either parent. I'm sorry to hear that. But lucky you, dodged foster care by the skin of your teeth. Your only known living relative, a younger brother, Phillipe Pelletier, wasn't so lucky, then. He currently lives in Paris with his wife, Penelope. Do you get around to visiting them much?"

"Yeah, yeah, yeah," Pierre interrupted. "Why don't you save it for when you write my biography. For now, can you just get to the point?"

"Do you have somewhere else to be?" Matthieu asked.

"Not until midnight," Pierre answered. "So, let's make this quick."

"I'm afraid you're going to have to reschedule those plans," Matthieu said.

Pierre rolled his eyes.

"You've got a pretty decent arrest record in here," Matthieu stated, lifting the stack of papers and flipping through them before slamming them back down on the table once more. "I'll spare you the boring details, but I read through the whole thing. Mostly petty thefts, a few breaking and entering charges. Did your employer at the Museum of Modern Art know about these?"

He flashed Pierre a printout of his old mugshot. In it, Pierre was wearing a smug, toothless grin on his face. Pierre was still in high school when the photo had been taken and he couldn't have been older than 16.

"Was this taken before your mother passed?" Matthieu asked. "I'll bet she was proud of you."

"I was a minor," Pierre answered. "I thought those records were supposed to be expunged."

"Nothing is ever truly *expunged*, Pelletier," Matthieu answered. "And the fact that you were a minor doesn't mean anything to me. Once an offender, *always* an offender. Unfortunately, your file stops at around the time you became an adult. I'm sure your crimes didn't though."

Of course, he was right. Pierre had just grown smarter about not getting caught. He picked houses where he knew no one was home, stole things that he knew wouldn't be noticed or had someone on the outside surveilling the cameras.

Pierre remained silent.

"Did you kill Boutrel?" Matthieu demanded.

"No," Pierre replied.

"But you admit that you were in the château last night?"

"I never said that!"

"How did you do it?"

117

"Do what, Detective?"

"Get inside! Did you really scale that gutter?"

"I have no idea what you're talking about," Pierre answered, crossing his arms and shutting down.

"Don't play coy with me now, smart guy," Matthieu said. "We were just getting somewhere!"

Pierre was silent as Matthieu studied him intently.

"I don't really believe that you killed Boutrel," Matthieu finally continued.

"Oh really?" Pierre asked. "Because it sure seems like you do!"

He held up the handcuffs which were still tightly wrapped around his wrists.

Matthieu shook his head.

"I think that the murder was an inside job, you just got caught in the crosshairs," he said. "I think that you were there for reasons unrelated to the murder."

Matthieu flipped through the folder and pulled out an image of the crime scene. The door to the safe rested, unhinged, on the floor. He slid the photo in front of Pierre.

"I told you already," Pierre said. "I wasn't there."

"Well, I don't believe that," Matthieu replied.

"Well, it's the truth," Pierre assured him. The two locked eyes for a moment before Matthieu continued.

"Listen, Pelletier," he began. "I think that I'm the only friend that you've got in here."

"Oh, so we're friends now? My friends don't tie me down with handcuffs. Well, most of them…"

"Everyone else has already written you off as guilty. I think there's some shred of truth to your story. But you have to help me *see* it. I need something to go off."

Pierre genuinely considered this but decided to reject the kind offer. He shrugged.

"I'll tell you what I think," Matthieu continued. "I think that you *were* in the château that night. To steal the necklace. I think you might just be this Black Locust character that everyone seems to be so excited about."

"*Black Lotus*," Pierre corrected.

"So, you admit it?"

Pierre didn't flinch.

"I think there were three crimes committed last night. One, the attempted murder of Monsieur Bastien Boutrel. Two, the *actual* murder of Monsieur Bastien Boutrel and three, the theft of Monsieur Bastien Boutrel's priceless gemstone. I think that you were there for the latter and that maybe you saw something that you shouldn't have," Matthieu continued. "Something that could lead us to the *real* killer."

"The only thing I *saw* that night were the four walls of my apartment," Pierre replied.

"Come on," Matthieu said. "A good-looking guy like you? You expect me to believe you spent Saturday night, New Year's Eve, in your apartment, alone?"

"I never said that I was alone."

"Oh yeah?" Matthieu asked. "Then who were you with?"

"Colette," Pierre suddenly spouted without thinking.

"Colette," Matthieu repeated. He began sifting through the folder. "That's the name that you said when you woke up earlier. Does this Colette have a last name?"

"I don't know it," Pierre lied, trying to see what Matthieu was searching for.

Matthieu chuckled and then stopped on a page in the folder.

"Here she is," he declared. "Colette Couvrir. Is this her?"

He turned the image around to face Pierre. Pierre felt a flutter in his stomach when the piercing, hazel eyes of the dark-haired woman in the photo fell upon him.

"One of your few known associates," Matthieu continued. "Says here you were schoolmates. We've got no known address listed for her, maybe you could help us out with that?"

"It wasn't her," Pierre finally answered.

Matthieu tucked the paper away into the folder.

"I think you were together last night, but at the château, not your apartment," he said.

Pierre was silent.

"Was she, by chance, wearing a sparkling scarlet evening gown?"

Pierre's eyebrow raised subconsciously. She had, of course, been wearing such a gown. How could Matthieu possibly have known that? He cleared his throat and shifted in his chair. Matthieu waited for him to speak, but he said nothing.

"What did you do with the necklace, Pelletier?" Matthieu asked outright. "I'm sure you have it stashed somewhere. Of course, you wouldn't be stupid enough to bring it right to us, but you might be arrogant enough. Regardless, when we searched you, we didn't find anything. The next step is to search your current residence. Unfortunately, we don't have that either and we won't until we're able to contact your employer tomorrow. So, why don't we start there? Where are you living these days?"

"I don't know where your *stupid* necklace is," Pierre answered.

This might have been the one true thing that he had said all day. All he knew was that it was somewhere in the station.

"Did Boutrel walk in on you?" Matthieu asked. "That's what the theory is. I don't buy it, but is that the truth? Because, to be frank with you, Pelletier, you're looking pretty good for the murder right now. You know what they do to pretty guys like you in prison?"

Pierre *did* know because, like he said, he had watched a lot of police shows. He placed his head into his cuffed hands.

"I told you, I wasn't there!" He said as he banged his head a couple of times on the table in front of him in frustration before resting his forehead against it. "It's like I'm talking to a wall."

"You're *going* to be talking to a wall for the next 25 years if you don't start talking to *me*," Matthieu said.

Pierre lifted his head from the table.

"What makes you so sure that I was there?" He asked.

"Obviously, you've already met our star witness," Matthieu answered and gestured outside.

"The old man?" Pierre asked in disbelief. "That guy couldn't identify *himself* if he was looking in a mirror!"

"In any event," Matthieu continued. "It's just a matter of time before the forensics unit returns an enhanced image of the security footage from that night. Whose pretty little face do you think they're going to see on it?"

"Well, I'm guessing with that choice of adjectives," Pierre began. "It isn't yours."

"That's right, it isn't mine. It's *yours*, Monsieur Pelletier. And things won't look so good for you if you don't start cooperating."

"So, you want me to admit to something that I didn't do?" Pierre asked. "Excellent police work, Detective."

Matthieu scowled. He was getting nowhere with Pierre.

Just then, there was a knock on the two-way mirror and the Chief poked his head in through the door.

"Matthieu," he said. "Can I see you for a moment?"

"Looks like you need some more time to stew," Matthieu said as he rose from his seat. "I'll give you some time alone to think about what you want to say to me next. Think carefully though, Pelletier, this could be your *last* chance."

"My answers will be the same," Pierre said.

Matthieu closed the cover of the folder and slid it under his arm.

"We'll see how you feel in a few minutes," Matthieu replied and then moved towards the door before stopping and turning to Pierre once more. "Oh, and Monsieur Pelletier?"

"Hm?" Pierre asked.

"Which side is your good side?" Matthieu asked with a cocky smile. "I'm sure the news agencies will all want to know when you're dragged out of here for booking."

Pierre squinted his eyes and focused them in on the Detective.

"They're all good sides," he answered with a sly grin.

Matthieu rolled his eyes.

"Of course, they are."

25

Sunday, the 1st of January, 10:15 p.m.

"Do you mind telling me what was so important that it couldn't wait?" Matthieu demanded. "I was working him over in there!"

"Yeah," the Chief replied. "Working him over like a dead horse."

Matthieu was fuming.

"Well?" He asked. "You've got me now, what is it?"

"We've got a problem," the Chief said. "Come with me."

Matthieu followed the Chief angrily out of the interrogation room hallway. The door to the hallway shrieked closed behind them. They went into his office and Matthieu took a seat in the chair across from his desk.

"I got in touch with the Chinese Ambassador, Zhu's, people," the Chief began, slowly and deliberately to try to calm Matthieu down. He wanted him calm because there was no way to prepare him for the news that he was about to drop on him shortly. "He's going to be back in town in a week. Same story with the Russian Ambassador, Yachnitch. They've both agreed to meet with us then."

"A week?" Matthieu repeated in disbelief. "Tell them to get back here sooner, this is a high-profile murder investigation!"

"Alright, alright, lower your voice, Matthieu," the Chief said. "Are you sure you want to do this?"

"Do what?" Matthieu asked. "Follow up with a prominent lead in the investigation? You're damn right that's what I want to do!"

"I meant going after them as hard as you're proposing," the Chief replied. "These are foreign dignitaries we're talking about here. What makes you so sure that Zhu is so heavily involved in this anyways?"

"The Hong Kong connection," Matthieu answered. "The *Gu*, the *Viper Triad*, the Han Sapphire, hell, even the Black Locust!"

"*Black Lotus*," the Chief corrected.

"Whatever," Matthieu replied and continued his rant. "Everything seems to point back to China some way or another. I think that Zhu has something to do with this. At the very least, he *knows* something!"

"So, now you're on board with that connection?"

"I beg your pardon?"

"That's what Genevieve has been suggesting from the start."

Matthieu shook his head.

"Genevieve thinks that the thief and the killer are one in the same. I think that the thief was in the wrong place at the wrong time, possibly even set up!"

"Matthieu," the Chief interrupted sternly. "Are you familiar with Occam's Razor?"

"Is that a feminine hygiene company?"

The Chief stared at him blankly.

"No, Matthieu," he said. "In layman's terms, it basically states that between two explanations for any event, the simplest explanation is often the most correct. I think you've gotten yourself so wound up and dead set against anything that Genevieve has to suggest, that you've blinded yourself to the facts."

"Maybe I can try talking to the Baron again, maybe he saw something else last night."

"Oh, brother," the Chief interrupted. "That's the other thing. Pelletier was right about one thing after all."

"Right about what?" Matthieu demanded.

"Right about our star witness' testimony being shaky."

"Shaky? What do you mean?" Matthieu groaned.

"We presented him with a photo lineup of six people and asked him to identify the man that he saw last night. Do you know who he picked from that lineup?"

"Who?"

"You, Detective," the Chief said. "He pointed to a photograph of you."

Matthieu slapped his forehead.

"Maybe you want to start explaining where you were that night too," the Chief suggested.

"What about the security tape from the château?" Matthieu remembered. "Where are we on enhancing that image? If it shows Pierre, then we've got him!"

The Chief sighed again.

"That's the other thing," he said. "The idiot on duty in the lab tonight seems to have misplaced the tape somewhere. Until he finds it, we're screwed."

"You're kidding me," Matthieu whined in disbelief. "So, you're saying that we've got nothing on him?"

"It would appear that way for the time being," the Chief said. "Without a confession, we're dead in the water."

"I can get that confession out of him," Matthieu assured him. "I know that he was there last night, but I still don't think that he killed Boutrel."

The Chief hesitated. While everything he had revealed to Matthieu thus far had been bad, he still hadn't figured a way to deliver the worst news of all to him. So, he decided to do it quickly, like ripping off a bandage.

"I'm pulling you out of there," he declared suddenly. "I'm sending in Genevieve."

"You're joking."

"Does it look like I'm joking?"

"No, but you must be!"

The room began to spin around Matthieu's head.

"I'm not, Matthieu," the Chief said. "You're blind to the facts in front of you. You've let your bitterness cloud your judgment…"

The Chief continued to drone on, but his voice just sounded like a faint buzzing in Matthieu's ear. How could Matthieu have strayed so far? Was the Chief right? Worse yet, was Genevieve, right?

There was a knock on the door which brought Matthieu back to reality.

"I'm prepared to go in," came the words from his ex-wife. Each stung Matthieu like a bullet in his chest.

Matthieu turned around to face her with a pleading look. She had already taken everything else from him, his pride included. Thankfully, she had at least left him the house, but Matthieu would have burned it down to have his life back again. Genevieve looked down at him. He looked small to her and she almost felt a shred of pity for him before she finally turned away.

"Excellent," the Chief said, and rose from his chair. "There is one more thing. I can't have my two best detectives on opposing sides. Matthieu, either you're with us or against us, what do you say?"

Matthieu thought about it for a moment but realized this wasn't really a choice at all.

"With you," he decided.

The Chief held the door open for Matthieu and Matthieu walked through it.

"Good," he replied and then closed the door so quickly that it nearly collided with Matthieu's rear end.

Genevieve was waiting just outside with a smirk on her face. Thomas was waiting behind her. Matthieu shot him a look of betrayal, but Thomas couldn't even look at his partner.

26

Sunday, the 1st of January, 10:15 p.m.

When Matthieu left the interrogation room, he left Pierre alone, staring across from the reflection of himself in the two-way mirror. He was having a particularly good hair day today, but there was no time to linger on that. A moment later, he could hear the screeching creak of the door to the interrogation room hallway, someone was either coming or going through it.

In the corner of the room, he turned and noticed a camera with a steady red light that signified it was currently recording.

When he turned back to the two-way mirror, he noticed something else. Just above his head there was an air vent. He remembered using the same vent to peer down at Detective Matthieu trying to interrogate Beatrice Boutrel sitting in this very same seat, the key word here obviously being *trying*. As it turned out, the two-way mirror in the interrogation room wasn't just good for looking at himself.

However, Pierre still had a problem. Even if he could use the air vent to escape, he was still handcuffed to the table, and he couldn't very well take it with him. Hoisting the table through the air duct first and then climbing in after it wasn't going to work. Neither was climbing into the air duct himself first and then dragging the table along next. He needed to slip out of these handcuffs.

Pierre jingled the chains of the cuffs back and forth under the metal cuff loops.

They were sturdy, police issue. Back in the day, he and his brother, Phillipe used to play cops and robbers all the time. Pierre, of course, had always been the robber and he had made a knack of escaping from the plastic cuffs that they played with. However, the plastic cuffs obviously were much less sturdy than the real thing.

Pierre studied the cuffs that he was currently locked down by. They functioned on a teeth and groove system, just like the plastic cuffs. Theoretically, breaking out of these was basically the same concept as breaking out of the plastic cuffs.

124

When the cuffs lock in place, it's just a matter of the teeth locking into place along the grooves on the interior workings of the cuff. All he needed to do was slide something thin, but solid, in between the teeth and the grooves to disrupt them. Then, he just needed to click the cuffs another notch tighter and, voila! The thin object would press down on the grooves and push them out of the way. Then, the teeth could just move freely out and unlock the cuffs. It was a little like Boutrel's safe, when he thought about it. He had to lock the cuffs tighter before he could open them.

Now, Pierre just needed to find something thin, but solid to disrupt the teeth and grooves. Fortunately, Pierre had made a contingency plan.

He stuck his tongue out and the paperclip that he had been hiding in the corner of his mouth fell out and clinked along the table.

Throughout the course of Matthieu's rambling, when Pierre had placed his head down into his cuffed hands, he had slyly picked up the paperclip that Matthieu had thrown down threateningly in front of him. Pierre kept it tucked away safely in the back of his mouth, not because he had a lot of papers to file, but for an occasion just like this.

The only other problem was whether or not someone was watching him from the other side of the two-way mirror or monitoring the video recording from the camera in the corner of the room.

There was only one way to find out.

He sat there for a moment in the silent room, staring at the paperclip on the table. The only sound in the room was the sound of the chains of the handcuffs rubbing up against the metal cuff loops on the table.

Pierre looked at the mirror, then he looked back at the camera. Then, he picked up the paperclip.

If he was going to do this, he probably didn't have much time. Matthieu could come back at any minute and if Pierre wasn't out of here by then, he was in for a world of trouble. As it turned out, Matthieu was right about one thing, it was Pierre's *last* chance—to escape.

He took the paperclip in his left hand and slid it into the space between the teeth of the handcuffs and the grooves along the inside. He pushed it in as far as it could go until he felt the end of the paperclip up against the edge of the groove. Pierre tightened the cuff one more notch and let out a groan in pain. Matthieu had already put them on nearly as tight as they would go. Incredulously, when he released the pressure, it had *worked*. The cuff was unlocked.

Pierre chuckled and stared down at his free hand in disbelief. There was a dark ring around his wrist from where the cuffs had rested. He grabbed the paperclip in his right hand and set to work quickly on the left cuff. This was going to be a little trickier, since Pierre was naturally left-handed. On his first attempt, he dropped the paperclip and it pattered across the floor. The sound of it tinging off the stone floor echoed vibrantly throughout the interrogation room. In the next moment, he heard the screeching of the creaking door to the interrogation room hallway. Pierre had heard the same screeching shortly after Matthieu had left, meaning that he must have exited the hallway. Now, it meant that they were coming back for him.

Pierre reached out frantically, barely brushing the paperclip with his fingertips. At any second, they would be here. He reached out again, extending every centimeter of his wingspan and was just barely able to grasp it. He gripped the paperclip tightly and tried again, sliding it into place between the teeth and the groove as far as it could go. He tightened the cuffs another notch, just like the first, and the second handcuff came off without issue. Pierre rubbed his sore wrists, he was a free man, well, nearly. He wouldn't be for long if he stopped to celebrate. In the silence of the room, he could hear three pairs of footsteps in the hallway just outside.

Pierre took the chair and pushed it over to the wall right under the air vent.

"Why does it always have to be air ducts?" He mumbled to himself.

He climbed on top of the chair and reached up for the vent grate. Quickly, he lifted the grate up, unhitching it from the grooves. He was about to climb into the vent when he turned to the camera in the corner of the room with a smug grin.

"Make sure you get my good side, Detective," he called out.

———————

Genevieve led the party first through the interrogation room hallway doors and marched down the hallway with Thomas eagerly at her heels. Matthieu was slumped over in the defeat. His feet dragged as he walked.

"Watch and learn, Thomas," Genevieve said and cracked her knuckles.

They walked past the first interrogation room toward the second when Genevieve suddenly let out a gasp when she had reached the room's two-way mirror, Thomas shrieked excitedly. Matthieu looked up.

Thomas' eyes were nearly bulging from his head. Matthieu rushed over to see what the commotion was about and when he glanced through the mirror, he knew immediately what it was. The room was completely empty.

"Where is he?!" Genevieve demanded, frantically pacing from one interrogation room to the next.

"The *Black Lotus*," Thomas mumbled to himself dreamily with a twinkle in his eye.

Matthieu couldn't help it and he burst out into a fit of laughter.

27

Sunday, the 1st of January, 10:32 p.m.

It wasn't more than two seconds after Pierre had climbed into the duct and replaced the vent grate back to its original position that the party, led by Genevieve, turned to see the empty interrogation room.

Pierre could hear frantic screaming from the hallway, and it took everything in him to not burst out laughing.

"Where is he?!" Genevieve demanded.

Thomas was bumbling and stuttering over his words. It was as if Pierre was truly a ghost all along and had vanished from sight, leaving nothing behind but a tipped over chair and a pair of empty handcuffs. The room itself was surrounded by reinforced stone walls. The only point of exit seemed to be the interrogation room door. He never even considered the air vent where Pierre was currently sitting, trying to refrain from laughter.

"Set up a perimeter!" Genevieve cried. "Pierre has escaped!"

Thomas stood there in awe as Matthieu continued to laugh hysterically.

"Didn't either of you idiots hear me?!" Genevieve shouted. She grabbed the closest of them that she could, which happened to be Thomas, and shook him back to reality. "Do something!"

Thomas began circling frantically and then ran over and pulled the fire alarm, dousing the interrogation room hallway with sprinklers of water and splashing the blood red emergency lights along the walls.

"Do something else," Genevieve said, unenthused as the water poured down on her. Matthieu was doubled over from laughter and she turned to him. "I'm glad you're enjoying this!"

Her sharp tongue lashing brought the hysterics to an end and Matthieu regained his composure.

The three of them ran from the interrogation room hallway where the Chief had come out of his office and was waiting there for them on the other side of the door.

"What's going on?" He demanded. "Thomas! Did you pull the fire alarm again?"

"It's Pelletier," Genevieve began, winded. "He's escaped!"

"Escaped?" The Chief repeated. "How is that possible? Matthieu! Didn't you have somebody watching him?"

"*I* was the one watching him," Matthieu replied. "Remember? When you pulled me *out* of the interrogation?"

"Now he's missing!" Genevieve declared frantically. "Gone! In the wind!"

"Where did he go?" The Chief stammered.

"If I knew that, he wouldn't be missing!" Genevieve snapped over the roaring sirens of the fire alarm.

"Well, where was the last place you saw him?" The Chief asked.

"I didn't misplace my car keys," Genevieve replied. "This is a dangerous criminal that we're talking about here! We need to set up a perimeter. He can't have gotten too far. For all we know, he could still be in the building."

"I was only out of that room for maybe 15 minutes," Matthieu added.

"How far should we extend the radius?" The Chief asked.

"I don't know," Genevieve said. "I'm not the expert on this stuff."

She turned frantically to her ex-husband for an answer. Matthieu felt a smug bit of satisfaction.

"Five blocks should be enough," he decided.

The Chief ran back into his office and called the dispatch to send all available units to establish the five-block perimeter around the station with orders that no one was to get in or out.

Meanwhile, in the air duct, when the emergency lights switched on, it blanketed the station in a dark crimson, which made it much more difficult for Pierre to see than it had been in there already.

Pierre already didn't know how to get out of here, but he realized that staying put wasn't going to get him anywhere. So, he picked a direction and began crawling.

The duct became pitch-black very quickly until Pierre could see a faint red light pouring in through a vent in the distance. He continued toward the light until he finally reached it and then peered into the room to orient himself.

Pierre looked out through the glass window on the door to the room. Officers were running back and forth frantically in the hallway beyond it. Pierre's eyes shifted focus from beyond the window to the window itself and he immediately recognized the white stickers that lined the inside of the window.

"Moor Elif," Pierre read, the file room.

A voice suddenly piped up, seemingly from nowhere, while the fire alarm continued to roar. It was the voice of a woman.

"*You were just going to leave me?*" The voice cried out. It was the same voice that he had imagined once before, begging him not to leave her behind at his apartment. It was the voice of the Han Sapphire necklace, beckoning him.

"Dammit," Pierre mumbled. He unhinged the vent grate and climbed into the room. He wasn't ready to leave her just yet.

28

Sunday, the 1st of January, 10:41 p.m.

Pierre landed on the floor with the feather-light feet of a career cat burglar. The file room was much darker than it had been the last time he was here. The dark crimson emergency lighting spilled through the door window and onto the floor. Outside, Pierre could hear the shouts of officers and the clanging of their uniforms and utility belts as they ran past.

He knew that he had to make this quick and just hoped that the necklace was in this room and not lost somewhere in the air ducts.

"*You're getting warmer, Pierre,*" the voice of the Han Sapphire necklace called from the darkness.

Pierre dropped to his knees and began feeling his way around the carpeted floor.

"Come on, come on," he mumbled. "Where are you?"

His eyes caught a glimmer of something in the crimson light, just in front of the shelf that contained all the case files.

He crawled over to it and snatched it up.

"The necklace!" He cried out as he held it up in satisfaction and then brought it down to his face and kissed it. He almost felt like he could cry.

"*Oh, Pierre!*" The necklace called. "*I was so afraid that I'd lost you!*"

"Me too, mon cher," Pierre answered. "But it's okay! We can finally be together now."

"*Oh, Pierre, you're my hero!*"

Pierre heard a couple more officers' heels hit the linoleum floor hallway just outside of the room and one of them shouted, "I think he went this way!" He realized that he would have to unfortunately cut this touching reunion short.

He slipped the necklace back into his pocket and then hoisted himself back up into the air duct where he continued until he reached a split in the duct system.

"What do you think?" Pierre asked.

"*I don't care, Pierre,*" the necklace answered. "*As long as we're together!*"

Pierre shook his head.

"You're no help," he said and went left.

Pierre couldn't even see his own hands in front of his face as they felt their way along the cool, metal ducts.

Without warning, the floor of the duct suddenly dropped off sharply. Pierre tumbled down and smacked his face on the metal, one level below.

"Ow," he grunted and then reached his hand into his pocket to make sure that the necklace hadn't slipped out again.

"*Still here, mon amour*," the necklace assured him.

Pierre rubbed his sore forehead and then continued forward. Off in the distance, he could see another air vent where faint crimson light was filtering in. Following the lights had worked out well for him so far, so he proceeded to it. As he continued along, he could still hear frantic footsteps, only now, they were coming from above him.

As he approached the faint crimson light, he noticed hot steam also pouring in through the vent. Pierre tried to wave it away and look out. There were large shadows, cast from huge metal beasts that spewed steam, dancing menacingly along the bare stone walls in this room. He was in the boiler room.

He lifted the vent grate off and hopped out to have a look around. There were no officers down here. In fact, there appeared at first glance to be no one at all.

A voice suddenly called out to Pierre from the dark. It was a real voice, not that of an inanimate object. However, Pierre was beginning to find it difficult to distinguish between the two.

"You there!" The voice called.

Pierre turned around, startled, and there behind him was an older man wearing a pair of dark coveralls with a name tag that read, Emile, and under that it said, Foreman.

"Me?" Pierre stammered.

"No, the guy behind you," Emile said.

Pierre turned to look behind himself.

"Yes, you!" Emile said. "What are you, deaf?"

"No, Monsieur," Pierre sputtered out.

"Did you hear the fire alarm, genius?"

"Of course."

The blaring siren was hard to miss.

"That means we're supposed to evacuate," Emile said. "I *don't* need another citation on my hands. Now, let's get those scrawny little legs in gear and get out of here."

"Right," Pierre replied. "Of course."

Emile led Pierre down a long hallway, passed a row of huge metal beasts, which Pierre now realized were boilers, and through a back door. There, Pierre found himself in an open lot surrounded by a handful of other men wearing coveralls.

"Is that everyone in there, Emile?" One of the other men asked.

"Let me get a head count," Emile said and began counting off the men.

"Hey, what do you think they're doing in there, Emile?" one of the men asked.

"Probably just another drill," Emile replied frustratedly. "Hold still."

"Whatever," the man said. "As long as we're still getting paid."

There was a murmur of agreement from the other men in the group.

"Wait a minute," Emile insisted. "Ugh, I lost count. Now I have to start over…"

Pierre slowly began to creep away from the crowd of men, which wasn't too difficult. Before long, he was out of sight and taking off down the street and into the night.

———————

A couple of blocks later, he came upon the familiar turn which would lead onto the Rue Saint-Rome, just about a block from his apartment building. He didn't know where else to go and at least the police didn't know where he lived yet, but it was only a matter of time before they did. He knew that he wouldn't be able to stay there forever, but he figured that he would quickly throw a go-bag together and then high tail it out of there.

When he rounded the corner, he saw that two police cruisers were blocking off the street, manned by none other than Officers Beef and Cake, clad in their bright reflective traffic patrol jackets.

Glorified crossing guards, Pierre thought to himself. Now he just had to hope for a helpless little old lady that needed help crossing the street to distract them so he could sneak past.

He quickly ducked beside a brick building and peeked out around the corner of it towards them.

Officer Beef was offering Officer Cake a bite of his pastry, a doughnut, perhaps, possibly even an eclair. Pierre shook his head to try to set himself straight. It didn't matter which it was, but Pierre still hadn't eaten all day, except for the granola bar, and the hunger was setting in. Officer Cake politely declined his partner's offer. The two men were leaned up nonchalantly against the hood of their cruisers.

Maybe if you just act like you belong there, Pierre thought. *You can just waltz right by them.*

It had worked in the file room hallway of the police station, until it hadn't. Besides, every officer in France probably knew his face by now. It was just a matter of time before that beautiful face was spread over the front page of every newspaper in the country, and soon, the world.

So much for the greatest art thief in all of France, Pierre scoffed. The *greatest* thieves were the ones that nobody has ever heard of. Pierre, on the contrary, was about to be headline news. There's a distinct difference between the *greatest* thief of all time and the most well-known. He decided that at some point, he was probably going to have to figure out how to have facial reconstruction surgery, but right now, he had a more pressing issue— how was he going to get around the police blockade?

Something caught Pierre's attention out of the corner of his eye. He must have done something good in a past life, because karma was seemingly on his side. There, just down a little way in the street in front of him, was a manhole cover.

Pierre felt a ray of optimism and then grief wash over him all at once. *A sewer?* He thought and groaned. *I'd rather have another air duct.*

"*Come on, Pierre,*" the necklace pleaded from his pocket. "*Do it for me!*"

"Now you're just being needy," Pierre mumbled and then groaned again when he looked down at his feet. He was wearing his new shoes today, his brand new, white trainers. Now, he was about to go gallivanting through the Toulouse sewer system.

"*I'll buy you a new pair,*" the necklace assured him.

The necklace could probably buy him a *million* new pairs, but it didn't really matter, since he hadn't paid for this pair anyway, he'd stolen them.

"Yeah, yeah," Pierre mumbled. He peeked out again at the officers just down the street. Unfortunately, he realized, the manhole cover was directly in their line of sight. There was no way they wouldn't see him if Pierre were to run over and try to slip under the cover.

As if in answer to his prayers, an enormous produce delivery truck signaled in front of him and then turned onto the street. It wasn't a helpless old lady, but this would do just fine. Karma was *very* much on his side.

The enormous truck turned onto the street, nearly blocking the entire width. Officers Beef and Cake ran towards it, waving their hands in the air frantically to flag it down and stop it.

Pierre darted out from his hiding place along the side of the building and slid on the pavement towards the manhole cover under the cover of the truck. He lifted the cover up, but it was much heavier than he had initially anticipated, and it slipped from his fingertips, slamming back on the metal grating that it rested on. Pierre quickly lifted it again with all his might and then slid under it and into the sewer just as the cover rattled closed on top of him and nearly took his fingers along with it.

The rattling manhole cover caught the attention of Officer Cake out of the corner of his eye, and he watched it curiously.

29

Sunday, the 1st of January, 11:11 p.m.

In the minutes following the discovery of Pierre's escape, the police units scrambled into position. The Chief had the fire alarm system finally shut off, restoring the station to its original pale saffron hue.

Matthieu had disappeared but returned with a rolled-up map of the city of Toulouse and stretched it across the long table on the station floor. He drew a wide circle around the station, spanning the five-block radius of the perimeter.

When the Chief finally emerged from his office with a loud sigh, he walked over to the chalkboard that hung from one of the station walls that read, "It's been 398 days without an incident." He erased the number and replaced it with a big, fat 0.

"Guess this counts," he said with another sigh. "Where are we so far?"

"No sign of him yet," Matthieu answered. His eyes were still fixated on the map, scanning every corner.

"How in God's name did he get out of there?" The Chief asked.

"This is the same guy that scaled a three-story building in under twenty seconds," Genevieve mentioned.

"Allegedly," Matthieu corrected.

"What happened to being *with* us?" Genevieve asked.

"This isn't the time for that," Matthieu answered.

Genevieve shot a wicked glance at her ex-husband who failed to notice.

"We've got Simone combing through the footage from the interrogation room," she said.

"The poor woman," the Chief remarked. "I don't think she's going to be the same ever again after today."

"Yeah, yeah," Matthieu said, distractedly. "She's doing great. Where are we on that address?"

"We just now got a hold of his employer," Thomas said, the phone still to his ear. "She's checking her records now."

"Let us know when you have something," Matthieu replied.

"Do you really think he's stupid enough to go back to his apartment?" The Chief asked.

"I think he's arrogant enough," Matthieu said. "I mean, he walked into the police station the day after his alleged involvement with the whole Boutrel incident."

"Oh, brother," the Chief grumbled. "I've got some calls to make. Let me know what you get."

With that, the Chief retired to his office.

Genevieve came over to Matthieu and sat down on the desk beside him.

"Why can't you just say it?" She asked, quiet enough that only Matthieu could hear.

"Say what?" Matthieu asked, distractedly. He was still scanning the map.

"Say that I was right, and that Pierre is our murderer."

"Because I don't think it's true."

"You're still hung up on the wife and the mistress?" Genevieve asked. "After everything that just happened?"

"Because I know that one or both of them are involved," Matthieu said.

"Are you sure it's not because you're too stubborn to let me be right?" Genevieve asked. "They had nothing to do with this and you know it. It was Pierre."

"You would take their side," Matthieu said. "Don't think that I didn't notice how buddy-buddy you were being with them when you escorted them in earlier."

"I was apologizing to them on behalf of the entire department," Genevieve said. "For bringing them in like that under the circumstances."

"Of course, you would start your apology tour with them," Matthieu said. "Gotta keep the money coming in."

"You're ridiculous," Genevieve continued. "You know, this is all your fault."

"All my fault?" Matthieu asked, looking up from the map at her. "How is any of this my fault?"

"He escaped under *your* custody."

"While you were conniving behind my back to take my position as lead interrogator!"

"I wasn't conniving," Genevieve assured him. "It wasn't even my idea."

"I don't have time for this," Matthieu decided, turning back to the map. "Where are we, Thomas?"

"Well, you're going to have plenty of time after this is over," Genevieve said, coldly. "In fact, you're going to have nothing *but* time."

"Shoo," Matthieu said and waved her away.

"I hope that you enjoyed your vacation, Martin," she continued. "Because you're going to be taking an extended one pretty soon."

Matthieu turned to her with a burning intensity in his eyes that Genevieve hadn't seen in years. His eyes screamed passion, but his words spewed hatred.

"Why are you so intent on bringing me down, you evil, vile woman?!" He demanded. The station floor became deathly silent. "Wasn't it enough that you ripped my heart out of my chest? Now, you have to come for my career as well?!"

The Chief came out of his office when he heard shouting. Everyone was standing motionless, Genevieve and Matthieu looked like they were either going to kill each other or rip each other's clothes off.

"I have that address," Thomas interrupted awkwardly.

Genevieve stared at her ex-husband. She had never been more attracted to him in her entire life, not even in the conference room some 24 years ago over their shared doughnut.

"What are you waiting for?!" Matthieu demanded.

"Right," Thomas said and read from the Post-it note in his hand. "56 Rue Bedelieres, apartment 2B."

Matthieu scanned the map until he located the Rue Bedelieres. It was just outside of the perimeter, just off the Rue Saint-Rome. He circled the position on the map.

"Do we have any officers stationed near there?" Matthieu asked.

The Chief looked at his sheet of assignments for the perimeter.

"Two officers," he answered. "Stationed along the Rue Saint-Rome."

"Tell them to hold their position, we're coming their way," Genevieve said, trying to take the reins back from Matthieu. "If they see him, tell them, 'do not approach.' We don't know who we're actually dealing with here and who knows what Pierre is actually capable of when his back is against the wall."

"You honestly believe that Pelletier is capable of murder?" Matthieu asked.

"That's why we're sending you over there, Matthieu," the Chief declared.

"Me?" Matthieu asked. "Why not Genevieve? She wants him so bad; she can go get him herself."

"I don't have a gun," Genevieve answered.

"Neither do I," Matthieu replied.

"You do now," the Chief said. "Catch."

He tossed the pistol over to Matthieu who caught it and held it for a moment in his palms.

"I thought that you said not until I passed the psychological evaluation."

"Exigent circumstances," the Chief replied.

"Well, I can guarantee that I'm not going to need it," Matthieu said as he grabbed his cell phone off his desk along with the keys to his blue Renault. He grabbed the peacoat off of his chair and threw it over his tweed jacket. "I don't think murder is Pelletier's style."

"You also didn't think that he was going to escape," Genevieve scoffed.

"Well, Thomas, are you coming?" Matthieu asked, turning to his partner. "Or are you just going to stand there with your mouth open, daydreaming about the Black Locust for the rest of the night?"

Thomas flailed his legs out wildly in pursuit of his partner.

"Oh, and Matthieu," the Chief called. Matthieu turned back one last time. "Pierre Pelletier is a dangerous fugitive. We underestimated him once before, we won't make that mistake again. I'm authorizing you to use deadly force at your own discretion."

30

Sunday, the 1st of January, 11:25 p.m.

Matthieu was right about three things. The first, was that Pierre was certainly one of, if not *the*, most arrogant people in all of France, rivalled maybe only by François Fouquet. The second, was that Pierre was completely incapable of murder. The third, was that Pierre was, indeed, headed straight for his apartment.

When Pierre slid through the gutter, it was a longer way down to the bottom than he had anticipated. He landed awkwardly on his feet and slipped, landing his entire bottom half into the sewage below.

"Yuck," he exclaimed as he stood up and tried to shake himself dry.

The first thing that struck him about his new surroundings was the smell. It was a strangely familiar smell, he thought. Not unlike the perfume that Genevieve had been wearing.

Pierre was ankle deep in standing water, flooded in the darkness of the sewer. He looked one way and he looked the other. Every direction looked the same, just a flowing stream of human excrement.

"Brilliant," he mumbled as he lifted his shoes to inspect them. In what light existed down here, he noticed that the white had turned a disturbing shade of brown. He immediately regretted not stealing the black pair. To make matters worse, the stream had already soaked through his socks as well.

He dunked his foot back into the sewage and then instinctively reached his hand against his pocket to make sure that the necklace was still there. Fortunately, it was. If it hadn't been, he may have given serious consideration to leaving it for good. If it came down to leaving it or bobbing for the necklace in this toilet water, the choice was obvious for Pierre. He was holding on for dear life to that one last shred of dignity that he had left.

"How could you even think that?" The necklace demanded, like a jilted lover, one of the *many* in Pierre's past. This one reminded him of Lucinda.

"You know that I would have come back for you," Pierre said as he rolled his eyes, the same thing that he had told Lucinda. He didn't come back for her.

"I know that you would have, mon cher," the necklace whispered sweetly to him. At least he still had his charm.

"This better be worth it," he mumbled to himself and then began trudging forward through the sewage.

A couple meters ahead of him, he could hear rushing water overhead and then a spray of fresh sewage burst in a waterfall that emerged from a pipe along the wall. The gushing waterfall strangely took him back to a robbery that he had committed in a convenience store when he was a teenager.

He was in the midst of stealing a silver wristwatch when his attention shifted to a rack of postcards beside the checkout counter. One in particular caught his eye, the picture on the front was of a secret beach with a glistening waterfall. He stole the wristwatch and the postcard and when he got home, he pinned the postcard on the wall across from his bed at his mother's house. Someday, he promised himself that he was going to find that tropical paradise. That was his happy ending. This, he realized, was probably as close to that as he was ever going to get.

When the waterfall had dried up, Pierre continued along. He knew that if he continued straight down the tunnel in the direction that he was already heading, it was basically like walking straight down the Rue Saint-Rome. It was a route home that he had taken hundreds of times before. Eventually, he figured, the sewer should split off at a junction, which would be the Rue Bedelieres, where his apartment building was located. Then, it would just be a matter of climbing back to the surface and then going inside. He was already planning out the things that he needed to take with him from there to save him some time.

He kept cash under his mattress, not much, but enough to maybe eat a decent meal for the next few days. A change of footwear was a must.

He lifted his shirt up to his nose and took a whiff.

Maybe a change of clothes while he was at it.

A little way up ahead, Pierre found the junction in the sewer that he had been looking for that split off, presumably at the Rue Bedelieres. It was much narrower, but he squeezed in and then continued down this junction a little further until he stopped and glanced up. Just a bit ahead of him was a manhole cover with a ladder underneath it sitting about a meter and half off the ground.

Pierre ran up to it, kicking up sewage as he went. He jumped at the base of the ladder and grasped it in his hands and hoisted himself up. He climbed the ladder to the top and then pressed his back up against the manhole cover. With as much force as he could muster, he pushed upwards and the manhole cover flipped over, landing on the pavement off to the side of the manhole. Pierre pulled his head up first and looked around.

The street was completely deserted. So, he pulled himself out of the sewer and then kissed the ground.

Pierre proceeded down the street to building number 56 and pulled the key from his pocket. Miraculously, he hadn't dropped it in the shuffle of things. Although, he could have picked the lock easily anyways.

Pierre jiggled the key into the lock and then pushed open the front door. He ran upstairs, across the perpetually dirty, beige carpet, to his own apartment, 2B, and reached out his key for the lock, but when he did so, he noticed that the lock was broken off and the door was slightly ajar. Pierre was sure that it hadn't looked like this when he had left this morning and he didn't expect to see what he saw next when he pushed the door open.

The entire apartment had been thrown apart, ransacked. Even more so than he had left it. Pillows on the sofa were ripped apart and stuffing was all over the floor. The sofa cushions themselves were scattered all around the apartment with their stuffing guts spewn everywhere. The dining room table had been turned over and all the drawers in the armoire in the living room had been emptied and their contents scattered around. Whoever did this had cleaned up all the Post-it notes on the kitchen floor, which Pierre was somewhat grateful for.

The first thought that occurred to Pierre was that this couldn't have been the police. It was too chaotic for a police search. Besides that, there would have been an officer stationed outside of the building and this whole complex would have been treated like an extension of a crime scene.

Whoever it was that had broken in was looking for something. His hand reached down instinctively again for the necklace.

"*I'm never going to leave you again*," she promised him.

Pierre's thoughts were interrupted by the distant wailing of sirens. He rushed for the bedroom. His mattress had already been turned over and with it, all of his cash that he had kept under it had been taken.

"Definitely not the police," he muttered, as he looked around at the chaos around him.

The sirens grew louder and louder until they seemed to stop right in front of his building and surround it.

"*That's* the police," Pierre groaned.

31

Sunday, the 1st of January, 11:52 p.m.

Matthieu skirted up onto the curb just outside of the old, brick apartment building at 56 Rue Bedelieres. Several other police cruisers followed and boxed him in, establishing a perimeter around the building.

Matthieu and Thomas slipped on their bulletproof vests over their jackets and emerged from the car. The first thing that Matthieu noticed in the street was the upturned manhole cover. He knew immediately that Pierre had managed to evade the police blockade, but he also knew that he couldn't run forever. This was his last stand.

Pierre could already hear the footsteps of the officers storming the building before he even had another moment to think. He quickly ran to his front door and closed it. The lock was broken off, so he toppled over the armoire in front of the door to block it.

There was only one entrance to the building, at the front entrance. There was, of course, the fire escape outside of his bedroom window that had been installed a few years back, but there was no way that rickety thing was up to code. The police were coming through the front door though, so that left Pierre with no other option.

Without a moment to lose, Pierre ran back into the bedroom. He threw open his bedroom window and was struck with a cold draft in the face as the curtains blew back behind him. He looked out. From his position on the second floor, he could see police cars already littering the street in front of him with more arriving every second. The fire escape in front of him was in plain view of the police barricade.

Matthieu led the way up the first flight of stairs inside the apartment with Thomas and Officers Beef and Cake.

They ran to the door of apartment 2B and Matthieu began pounding on it heavily.

"Police!" He cried. "Open up, Pelletier!"

Pierre gave one last look outside and groaned. There were several officers below with their guns drawn and pointed directly towards him. Before long, there was a spotlight cast from down below on Pierre's bedroom window.

"Come out with your hands up!" The Chief yelled into a megaphone.

"The jig is up, Pelletier," Matthieu called from the hallway. "We've got you completely surrounded. Either you come out or we're coming in to get you!"

There was no response from the other side of the door. So, Matthieu turned and instructed that the door be kicked in.

Officer Beef stepped up and swung his massive leg toward the door like a human battering ram. It only took a single kick for the armoire to slide across the floor and the door to collapse. The four of them entered the room with their pistols at the ready.

Pierre was startled by the slamming of the heavy front door to his apartment as it crumbled to the ground.

There goes my security deposit, he thought to himself.

In the next instant, Pierre leapt out onto the fire escape, which bowed a little under his weight, and began running along it. The spotlight followed his daring escape.

As soon as the door to the apartment had caved in, Matthieu got his first glimpse of the room.

"Good God!" He exclaimed at the state of the apartment before he noticed the curtains blowing from the open bedroom window. "This way!" He commanded.

The four men ran into the bedroom and Matthieu poked his head out through the window. From below, he could see Pierre's feet pattering on the fire escape on the third floor.

"Stop!" Matthieu ordered, as if Pierre had been completely ignoring him up until now but was suddenly going to reconsider his escape. Matthieu knew what he had to do.

He holstered his pistol and climbed onto the fire escape as well. The fire escape swayed a bit and began to wobble unsteadily. It felt as if the whole thing might soon collapse.

"Remind me to check the scaffolding permit for this building after this," he mentioned aside to Thomas as he tried to steady himself.

He began moving slowly along the fire escape and turned at the first level of stairs before finally gaining some momentum.

Thomas was down below, peering through the window at his partner when he turned to Officer Cake.

"Did you want to go next?" He asked.

Officer Cake shook his head.

"Nah," he answered. "I'm good."

Pierre rounded the corner of the fourth floor and was now onto the fifth and final level. Matthieu was not far behind him, just climbing now onto the fourth.

"Stop, Pelletier!" Matthieu called again. "I just want to talk!"

"Tell it to your diary!" Pierre called back.

He ran to the end of the fifth level of the fire escape and then hoisted himself onto the roof and out of sight of the officers on the ground below. Matthieu climbed the staircase to the fifth floor and then followed him onto the roof.

Pierre ran along the roof until he reached the very edge of it. He skidded to a stop just in time before he plummeted into the alleyway that was five stories below. He looked out across the alleyway at the roof of the adjacent building which was roughly three meters away. Matthieu pulled his pistol from the holster strap of his belt and pointed it at Pierre's back. The church bells of la Basilique Saint-Sernin in the Toulouse town square chimed in the distance.

"Nowhere left to run," Matthieu said in between gasps for breath. He hadn't sweat this much since he and Genevieve had signed up for that hot yoga class a few years back. The bells chimed a second time.

Pierre turned around slowly with his hands up.

"Are you going to shoot me?" He asked. The bells chimed for a third time.

"I don't want to," Matthieu replied. "But I will if I have to. So, don't try anything." The bells chimed for a fourth time.

"I didn't do it," Pierre still insisted. "I'm completely innocent."

"You sound just like every other low life in prison," Matthieu replied. The bells chimed a fifth time. "Why don't you come over here and we can talk about it?"

The bells chimed a sixth time.

"I think you're in over your head, Pelletier," Matthieu continued. "Let me help you."

The bells chimed for a seventh time.

Pierre turned his head to the side and looked down at the alleyway below.

"End of the line," Matthieu said. The bells chimed an eighth time.

"Maybe for you," Pierre replied and then turned and leapt with all his might across the gap between the buildings.

Matthieu's eyes grew wide. For a moment, it looked as if Pierre might take flight and just float over the gap between the buildings as the bells chimed for a ninth time. However, even the *Black Lotus* was not above gravity and Pierre came plummeting back down to Earth like a meteorite. Matthieu watched in bewilderment as Pierre disappeared between the two buildings just as the bells chimed a tenth time.

Pierre Pelletier was pronounced dead on Monday, the 2nd of January at 12:00 a.m.

Just kidding, at the very last second, Pierre reached his hand out and grasped the very edge of the adjacent building with only his fingertips. Matthieu had convinced himself that he had just seen the man fall to his death and felt a strange tinge of regret before he watched Pierre hoist himself back up and then smile back at the Detective.

"I'd love to stick around, Detective," Pierre called. The bells chimed an eleventh time. "But I've got a train to catch."

He ran across the rooftop of the building and then leapt from it, disappearing below.

Matthieu was certain that he had just watched the man leap to his death once more as the bells chimed for a twelfth and final time.

"Pelletier?" Matthieu called out in the silence of the night.

He was answered not by Pierre, but instead by a train whistle and then the train that the whistle belonged to flew out from in between the buildings. Pierre was standing on top of the second train car and waving to the Detective.

Matthieu burst out into a fit of laughter.

32

Monday, the 2nd of January, 12:03 a.m.

Pierre flipped down from the top of the midnight train to Paris and entered in through one of the passenger cars.

There was a middle-aged gentleman in the first seat. He was wearing a thick pair of spectacles and had his face buried in the newspaper in front of him that he held in one hand. His nose was nearly touching the words on the page. In his other hand, the man held a glass of merlot. Pierre noticed that the man's train ticket was sitting in the groove on the back of the seat, unpunched by the conductor.

He snatched the ticket as casually as he could and slipped it into his pocket before stopping in front of the gentleman.

"Is this seat taken?" Pierre asked, pointing to the seat across from the man whose ticket he had just stolen.

The man lowered the newspaper from his face. Pierre caught a glimpse of the front cover and immediately recognized Detective Matthieu's face splattered all over it.

"By all means," the man said. Pierre recognized the man's obvious American accent from the police shows on TV. "Help yourself."

"Don't mind if I do," Pierre said. After all, he had already helped himself to the man's train ticket.

Pierre wiggled past the man's legs and into the seat across from him. It was a long trip to Paris, so he thought he would appreciate the company. Besides that, he figured the best place to hide since he had just stolen something from the man was in plain sight.

The man stared at him for a moment. His piercing, bug eyes made Pierre rather uncomfortable. His glasses were so thick, that Pierre could barely see the man's eyes through them.

"The name's Neamon," the man finally said. He stuck out his hand to Pierre. "Norman Neamon."

"Norman Neamon?" Pierre repeated the name slowly and deliberately, as if he was skeptical that this was a real name at all.

"And you are?" Norman asked.

"Yes, of course," Pierre said. "I'm…" He hesitated for a moment. Pierre Pelletier was now a wanted fugitive. He stared at the newspaper that was folded in Norman's hand. "Martin Matthieu."

"Well, it's a pleasure to meet you, Martin," Norman answered. "What's bringing you to Paris?"

Truth be told, he hadn't exactly formulated a plan yet. But it was away from Toulouse and more importantly, the Toulouse Police.

"Travelling for business," Pierre answered.

He slipped his hand in his pocket and caressed the Han Sapphire necklace. He did intend to sell it, so he wasn't completely lying.

"Ah, I have the pleasure of travelling to Paris for business as well," Norman said. "My wife was jealous, let me tell you. She's always wanted to go to Paris, but the nature of my business prevented her from accompanying me."

"C'est la vie," Pierre replied.

"I don't think that I'm at liberty to discuss too much detail," Norman continued as he glanced around the train car suspiciously.

That's funny, Pierre thought. *I don't remember asking you to.*

He glanced down at the briefcase that rested between Norman's legs. It was seemingly the only possession other than the newspaper and the glass of merlot that his new companion was travelling with.

"But," Norman continued and then lowered his voice barely above a whisper once he was satisfied that nobody was eavesdropping. "I work for the FBI."

"The FBI?" Pierre repeated, suddenly intrigued. From his police shows, he knew that those letters stood for the Federal Bureau of Investigation.

"Yes, in the Art Crime and Thefts Division."

"Of course you do," Pierre said.

"Now, of course I'm *really* not at liberty to discuss the extent of my business here," Norman continued. "But, let's just say it involves a very high-profile forgery case."

He licked his lips excitedly and leaned forward in his seat.

"Forgery?" Pierre repeated, also leaning in.

"Forgery," Norman replied. "Now, I *really, really* can't say too much else. But, between you and me, the case involves a very famous Matisse painting."

"Did you say Matisse?" Pierre's eyes grew wide.

"That's right," Norman replied. "The painting was titled, *La Pastorale*."

"*La Pastorale*?!" Pierre suddenly shouted.

Norman's case involved the very painting that Pierre had stolen from the Museum of Modern Art in Paris six years ago. The coincidence was uncanny.

"Shh, shh," Norman insisted. "Please, lower your voice, Martin."

"Sorry," Pierre apologized.

"So, I take it from your reaction that you've heard of the painting?"

Pierre cleared his throat as another passenger of the train car walked past them. The two men sat back in their seats casually until the passenger was out of sight.

"Only from what I gleaned in the papers," Pierre said, leaning forward once more.

"Of course," Norman answered. "I much prefer the French newspapers to the publications in America," he said and flashed up the newspaper in his hands. "I can't read the words, but I can tell by the pictures that the information is much more interesting. Like, what do you think is going on here, Martin?"

He pointed to the image of the real Detective Martin Matthieu standing over the corpse of Bastien Boutrel.

"I haven't the slightest idea," Pierre replied.

"Either way," Norman continued as he studied the image. "All we have in America is celebrity gossip, fad diets and fake news."

"Can I ask you a question, Norman?" Pierre asked.

"I can't promise that I'll be able to answer it, but fire away."

"What does the Matisse painting have to do with the FBI? You mentioned forgery?"

"Did I?" Norman asked. "I wish I could say more, but I'm *really, really, really* not at liberty to discuss."

Pierre waited for the inevitable "but."

"But," Norman continued. "There was an FBI sting operation at a black market art auction in Tulsa, Oklahoma. The Matisse was recovered there along with a handful of other famous paintings that had been reported as stolen."

Pierre sat back in his seat.

So, that's what happened to her, he thought. *La Pastorale* was one of Pierre's first true loves, his most infamous heist. Until a few nights ago, that is.

"*Who is she?*" The voice of the Han Sapphire necklace suddenly demanded from his pocket. Pierre slapped the side of his pants and she quieted.

"But," Norman continued, trying to hook Pierre back in after noticing that his companion had become distracted.

"But?" Pierre repeated and leaned forward in his seat again. Norman had hooked a big one, but he didn't even know it.

"The painting was a forgery," Norman continued. "Trying to be moved on the black market as an authentic Matisse. We were able to trace it back to an infamous counterfeiter known to the FBI only as, Videl."

"Videl," Pierre mumbled the name under his breath. "I've never heard of him."

"That's because he's the best of the worst," Norman said. "The best criminals are the ones that you've never heard of."

Pierre felt personally victimized by this comment.

"So, why are you travelling to Paris?" He asked. "If the painting was recovered in Oklahoma?"

"I'm going back to the scene of the initial crime, where the painting was originally stolen from," Norman said. "The Museum of Modern Art. Or, should I say, Musée d'Art Moderne de la Ville de Paris."

Norman was investigating the man sitting right across from him and he didn't even know it.

"I have a hunch," Norman continued and leaned closer. Pierre leaned in as well so that the two were nearly nose to nose. Pierre could smell the merlot on his breath. "I think the painting may have been a forgery all along."

Pierre sat back in deep contemplation while Norman grinned. Did he really go through all that trouble just to steal a forgery all those years ago? Not that it really mattered anyways, because he had still been paid, nonetheless.

"Tickets!" A voice called harshly that broke Pierre from his trance.

Pierre looked around frantically until his eyes settled on the train conductor who was beginning to collect and punch tickets.

"Now, there's all of this business I've been hearing about all day about the murder of a Bastien Boutrel," Norman said. "And an expensive theft at his château."

"Are you thinking that Videl had something to do with it?" Pierre asked, turning his attention back to Norman.

"They're saying it's this *Black Lotus* character," Norman said. "The same one they believed was responsible for the heist at the Museum of Modern Art. Maybe he and Videl are one in the same." He shrugged. "All I know is that if some grown man is parading around with a nickname, pretending to be some kind of people's hero, masquerading around in his underwear and leaving behind flowers everywhere he goes, he's got issues."

"The *Black Lotus* doesn't masquerade around in his underwear," Pierre insisted, defensively.

"Tickets, gentlemen," the train conductor interrupted.

"Oh, yes," Pierre said and reached into his pocket for his ticket.

"Behind me," Norman motioned without looking.

Pierre handed the conductor his ticket and the conductor punched it. He handed it back to Pierre and then glanced behind Norman.

"There's nothing there, Monsieur," the conductor stated flatly.

"I beg your pardon?" Norman asked.

"There's no ticket behind you," the conductor informed him.

Norman whirled around in his seat and, to his dismay, there was no ticket. He dropped to his hands and knees onto the floor, spilling his glass of merlot in the process as he began searching under his seat for the ticket and stuttering.

"I swear I purchased one," he said. "I don't know where it could have gotten to!"

The conductor frowned.

"We don't tolerate fare evasion, Monsieur," he said.

Pierre tried to suppress a smile.

"Fare evasion?!" Norman repeated in disgust from the ground. It was as if the man had just accused Norman of murder. "*This* is how you treat your patrons?!"

146

"Our *patrons* have all purchased tickets, Monsieur," the conductor said.

"Well, *Monsieur*," Norman began mockingly. He rose to his feet and stared through his thick glasses at the conductor. "I purchased a ticket, and somebody has obviously stolen it!"

"Monsieur!" The conductor interrupted, trying to speak over Norman. "You can pay for a ticket, or you can get off here!"

Norman glanced out of the window as the rolling hills blazed by in the darkness.

"Right here?" he asked.

"Right here, Monsieur."

"Unbelievable," Norman grumbled to himself. "How much is it for a ticket?"

"€200, Monsieur."

"€200?!" Norman repeated in disbelief. "This is robbery!"

Pierre snickered and tried to suppress it by pretending he had been coughing.

"It would have been half of that price if you had planned in advance," the conductor said.

"I refuse to pay that much for a ticket!" Norman insisted.

"Then, this can be your stop if you'd like," the conductor said.

Norman glanced outside once again. He grumbled something incomprehensible and then reached into his back pocket to retrieve his wallet. He pulled out the leather wallet and his passport along with it as he continued to grumble.

The conductor pulled a ticket out from the fanny pack around his waist and punched it with his hole punch. Then, he exchanged it with Norman for the €200 they had settled on.

Norman sat back down in his seat as the conductor proceeded to the next passenger car.

"I have never been so mistreated in all of my years," he grumbled before turning his attention back to Pierre. "Did you see anyone take my ticket, Martin?"

"No, Monsieur," Pierre assured him. "I'm usually very observant when it comes to things like that too."

Norman calmed down and then slipped his passport and wallet back into his back pocket. He grabbed his glass of merlot off of the floor and tapped the glass.

"I'm going to need a refill of this after that," he said. "Can I get you anything?"

"No," Pierre said. "I can't."

"You don't drink?" Norman asked. "It's going to be a long four hours otherwise."

"It's not that I don't," Pierre said. "I can't."

"Ah," Norman began. "I understand, I know a lot of good men in programs."

"It's not a program," Pierre said. Norman was staring at him curiously. "You know what, never mind."

Norman shrugged and then disappeared into the lounge car. When he returned, he resumed chatting Pierre's ear off for the rest of the, roughly, four-hour trip about classified information that he *really* wasn't at liberty to discuss.

Pierre, meanwhile, was strongly considering turning himself in and spending the remainder of his days in solitary confinement when he glanced out of the window and could finally see the Saint Lazare Train Station terminal off in the distance. The train began to slow until the fields beyond the window were replaced by the scaffolding of the station.

Pierre was looking out of the window at the platform as the train pulled in and felt his heart sink.

The platform was *swarming* with police officers.

33

Monday, the 2nd of January, 4:49 a.m.

When the train came to a complete stop, Norman reached out and grabbed the briefcase from in between his legs and then stuck his hand out to Pierre.

"Well, Martin," he began with a sincere smile. "It's been a pleasure. I don't care what anybody says about the French."

Pierre took his hand and shook.

"My, are you alright, Martin?" Norman asked. "Your hand is quite clammy."

Pierre laughed nervously. He took his hand back and wiped it on his pants.

"And I don't care what anybody says about Americans," he said, trying to maintain the facade that he had been portraying. Pierre could feel the walls closing in around him.

Norman chuckled.

"Perhaps we can meet up sometime for coffee while we're both in town," he said. He reached into his pocket and pulled out a business card.

Pierre took the card and turned it over in his hands. It was a plain white card with simple black writing. The only thing written on it was Norman's name and a phone number. If you didn't spend five minutes talking to the man, you might assume that Norman was a very secretive gentleman.

"Only if you promise to give me the exciting conclusion of the case that you've been working on," Pierre said as he tucked away the card in his pocket, right next to the Han Sapphire necklace.

Pierre glanced nervously out of the window at the police officers that were stationed by all the doors. He could tell that they were scanning IDs, something that he didn't have. Even if he did, they were undoubtedly looking for him. He was nearly out of time.

"You know I can't divulge too much," Norman continued as he stood up. Pierre mimicked him as he stared at the man's thick glasses when all the sudden, a brilliant idea struck him. It wasn't foolproof, but it might just have been stupid enough to work.

"Of course," Pierre said. "Well, it would be a pleasure all the same."

Norman smiled at him and then Pierre moved out of the way to let Norman pass. When Norman was just in front of him, Pierre slapped the back of his head with enough force to knock the glasses off his face and onto the floor.

"Hey!" Pierre yelled out.

Norman doubled over and grabbed the back of his head in pain.

"What the heck?!" He proclaimed and went down on his knees. With his other hand, he began to scour the ground for his glasses.

Pierre quickly reached down and grabbed them off the floor before Norman could find them.

"Some guy just took off with your glasses, Norman!" Pierre cried. "I'll go after him!"

Pierre stealthily slipped his hand into Norman's back pocket with the delicate hands of an experienced pickpocket and retrieved Norman's passport, as well as his wallet, and then proceeded to the door. Along the way, he glanced at the ID photo of the passport. In it was a much younger Norman, but he still had on thick spectacles that pretty much engulfed his whole face. Pierre thought he might be able to pull off the look.

"Wait!" Norman cried out. "Martin! I can't see a darn thing without my glasses!"

Pierre ignored him and squirmed past a family that was struggling to unload their bags from the overhead compartment. He snatched a cap that was resting on the armrest, then slipped the cap onto his head and tucked in the curls of his hair.

When he got to the door, he stood in line behind another passenger ahead of the security checkpoint and slipped the glasses onto his face. Norman's prescription was so strong that Pierre couldn't see anything.

"Next!" The officer at the security checkpoint called.

Pierre assumed that was him and walked forward blindly before bumping into the side of the train door.

"Monsieur?" The officer asked, alarmed. He reached out to help Pierre through the door. "Are you okay?"

Pierre grumbled.

"Identification?" The officer said.

"Yes, of course," Pierre said in his best American accent.

He handed Norman's passport over to the officer. The officer looked down at the passport and then back up at Pierre. Pierre was looking slightly to the right of him unintentionally.

"Monsieur Neamon," the officer began, reading from the passport. "You're from the United States?" He asked, looking at Pierre suspiciously, not that Pierre could tell anyways.

"Yes, *sir*," Pierre answered, careful not to call the officer "Monsieur" and doing his best to act like a tourist.

"What's the nature of your visit to Paris?" The officer pressed.

"Business," Pierre answered without hesitation.

"Monsieur," the officer called. "I'm over here."

Pierre followed the sound of his voice and turned his head towards it.

"Business," he repeated.

The officer glanced down at the passport in his hands and the image of the man in the thick, wide-rimmed glasses, and then back up at Pierre. Pierre stood there in silence, smiling. Finally, the officer handed the passport back to Pierre.

"Enjoy your stay," he said. "Next!"

Pierre reached out for the passport and just grazed it at first, then grabbed at it with both hands. The officer eyed him curiously and then turned his attention to the next person in line as Pierre cautiously walked forward a few steps. He walked a little bit further until he was sure that he was out of the way and then took the glasses off. His eyes were crossed and struggled to correct themselves.

He slapped himself on the cheeks a couple of times and then began walking away. If he hadn't been so dizzy, he would have been more in awe of himself that his plan had worked. He removed the cash from the wallet and then dumped all the stolen items in the nearest trash bin as he moved toward the stairs of the platform.

He could faintly hear the same officer that he had just made it past shouting behind him, "Where's your identification?!" Followed by the familiar voice of Norman, pleading, "I don't know, sir! A thief made off with my glasses and I can't see anything!"

"Cuff him!" The officer ordered another officer. A whistle sounded and within seconds, Norman was thrown to the ground by half a dozen officers and handcuffed.

Pierre did feel bad for Norman, but not bad enough to turn around and help. Besides, Norman hadn't done anything wrong, and Pierre convinced himself that he had the utmost confidence that the police would be gentle with him. When it came to himself, on the other hand, he wasn't so sure that he could trust them. Right now, as much as Matthieu tried to convince him, Pierre's only friend was himself.

He climbed the staircase and emerged into the train station, which was also swarming with officers.

Pierre lowered his head and then proceeded out of the front door of the train station, into the familiar early morning Paris streets.

Pierre hadn't been back to Paris since the weeks following the heist of the Museum of Modern Art. He had decided at the time that a permanent relocation was what was best for him. Now, somehow, he found himself here once again. Pierre didn't know what his next move was, but he only knew one person still in Paris, so he knew what his next move had to be.

He walked for a couple of hours until he reached the familiar apartment complex of the 9th Arrondissement. He looked up at the white facade of the building with the newly painted green door with a pattern of square windows. Pierre took a deep breath, followed by an exaggerated exhale.

Here goes nothing, he thought and proceeded up the stone staircase. *I hope they still live here.*

He squinted as he read the names of the residents of the complex. The sun was just beginning to rise on the city, but it was still dark and hard to make out the writing. But Pierre finally settled on the name that he was looking for. He wasn't sure whether he was terrified or relieved. He clicked the button and heard the doorbell ring from the inside of the apartment.

Within the next moment, a figure emerged beyond the square windows of the green door and then slowly pulled the door open.

34

Monday, the 2nd of January, 5:59 a.m.

Matthieu came back to the station several hours after combing Pierre's entire apartment without a trace of any Han Sapphire necklace. The place had obviously been ransacked before the police had arrived, either by Pierre himself, or somebody else. Matthieu began to wonder if whoever it was had been looking for the same thing that he was looking for.

The one piece of damning evidence that they did find, was a couple of spots of blood on the carpet in Pierre's living room. Although Matthieu refused to believe it, he feared that they would belong to Boutrel. Nevertheless, he wasn't denying that Pierre was in the study with Boutrel, just that he believed that Pierre truly hadn't killed him. Unbeknownst to Matthieu, the blood that Pierre had tracked into his apartment was a consequence of Boutrel having toppled on top of him, displacing the dagger and allowing blood to trickle from the wound. During his escape, Pierre accidentally stepped in the puddle of it. Although, since Matthieu couldn't have known this, his theory was beginning to become more and more convoluted with each new piece of evidence that presented itself. Occam's Razor be damned.

Either way, he arrived back at the station deep in thought. Yes, Pierre was certainly the bane of his existence for the last, roughly, 24 hours, and he was now beginning to understand why they called him the Black Locust, because he was becoming a real pest. Still, he couldn't help but admire his persistence. He was a little like a cockroach in that way.

He had eluded the police at his apartment, but there was almost no way that he would be able to avoid the police that the Chief had ordered to be stationed at the Saint Lazare Train Station in Paris. Unless, of course, he had jumped from the moving train. Matthieu decided this possibility was highly unlikely. Pierre would be back in police custody soon enough, and then Matthieu would have a few more questions with him, granted that he was given the opportunity. The other scenario in which he could have escaped, which never occurred to Matthieu, was that he could have impersonated an American FBI agent while exiting the train and then passed right through the security checkpoint undetected.

As Matthieu slumped through the doors of the station, he had another thought. Besides his identification of Pierre, there was something that Baron William Worthington had said that struck the Detective as quite strange. So, he decided to pay the good Dr. Aveline a visit.

"Ah, Detective," she began without looking up from the microscope she was seated in front of. "I was wondering when you would return to hound me. I sent that report up there hours ago."

"How did you know it was me?" Matthieu asked in disbelief.

"Come now, Detective," Aveline said. "Who else would it be?"

"What have you got there?" Matthieu asked as he approached her.

"I've isolated the strain of the toxin from your victim," she said.

"Perfect, that's actually why I came down here in the first place."

"You didn't just come down to say hello?"

"Well," Matthieu stammered. "Of course, that too."

"Relax, Detective, I'm messing with you. See, I can have a sense of humor too sometimes."

"Right," Matthieu continued, uncomfortably.

"Do you want to have a look?" Aveline asked him.

She moved to the side and Matthieu peered in through the lenses of the microscope. In the center of the frame was a black, tar-like substance, floating in solution.

"That's it?" He asked. "The *Gu?*"

"A sample of it," she said and turned back towards the microscope.

"I actually wanted to come down here to discuss your other findings on the toxicology report," Matthieu said. Aveline didn't respond, so Matthieu continued. "Do you happen to remember Boutrel's blood alcohol content?"

"It's all in the report that I sent up," Aveline answered, bluntly. "Didn't you read it?"

"Yes, I could go up and read it again," he stuttered. "But I was hoping to ask you a few follow up questions as well. Something that might not be in the report."

"It was negligible," Aveline answered. "Practically non-existent."

Just as Worthington had suspected. Boutrel wasn't drinking heavily that evening. So, why was he acting so intoxicated?

"I called a colleague of mine with a little more knowledge on the poison," Aveline continued. "The toxin acts through the liver first and then the brain. It's quite fascinating really."

"In what way?" Matthieu asked.

"Let me show you, Detective," Aveline said and stood up. She walked over to a cabinet and pulled out a glass vial containing a pink liquid. "Have a seat," she instructed him. Matthieu took a seat at the microscope and peered in at the black substance on the slide.

"What are you doing?" He asked.

"Just watch," she said. She placed the tip of a pipette into the vial of pink liquid and drew some of it up. Then, she placed a droplet of the liquid onto the slide in front of Matthieu.

Before his very eyes, the black substance on the slide seemed to convulse and spread itself out, oozing slowly towards the edges of the slide.

"What's happening?" Matthieu asked. "Is it alive?!"

"It's not alive, but what I gave it was. This vial contains living hepatocytes," Aveline said. "The detoxifying cells of the liver."

"So, it's detoxifying the poison?"

"On the contrary," Aveline said. "It's *activating* the poison."

"I'm a bit confused."

"Of course you are," Aveline said, disappointedly. "I ran a few extra tests on your victim."

"What kind of tests?"

"Well, the most significant finding was from the test for liver function. Monsieur Boutrel's liver was shutting down. I presume that he would have been dead within the week anyways. Whoever killed him probably did him a favor."

"The irony," Matthieu mumbled.

"Do you know the significance of his failing liver?"

Matthieu couldn't even hazard a guess.

"It means that his body couldn't *activate* the poison," Aveline said.

"I thought I read that the report said he was given a lethal dose?"

"He was given a lethal dose, if he had a functioning liver. For Boutrel, it only had a few mild, secondary effects."

"Secondary effects," Matthieu repeated and then his eyes widened with realization. "Could intoxication be one of them?"

"When the toxin first crosses over the blood-brain barrier, it can cause the appearance of intoxication before it actually works. If activated, the toxin causes inflammation in the brain's capillaries. The victim will begin to seize shortly before their capillaries burst, leading to an extremely painful death."

"That's gruesome," Matthieu remarked.

"If the toxin was not activated," she continued. "It would simply cause the appearance of intoxication until the victim was able to flush it out."

"Fascinating," Matthieu remarked and stared in again at the black substance, which had nearly oozed to the microscope slide's edges.

"If somebody intended to kill Boutrel with the poison," Aveline stated. "They must not have known the poor state of Boutrel's liver."

"They could have realized that the poison wouldn't work and then stabbed him to finish the job," Matthieu muttered. The puzzle that he thought he had nearly pieced together was ripped apart.

Aveline shrugged.

"While his BAC was practically nonexistent," she continued. "He did have some wine in his stomach, mixed with some of the toxin and nothing else."

"Meaning…"

"Meaning that your perpetrator introduced the toxin into his digestive system via his drink."

This revelation didn't help the Detective as much as Aveline thought it should. Then again, she was just giving him the facts. With this information, Matthieu realized, it was possible that anyone at that soirée could have poisoned Boutrel. Hell, they could have spiked the punch bowl, for all Matthieu knew. But, no, because if that had happened, everybody else at the soirée would have been affected. Someone had undoubtedly served Monsieur Boutrel that tainted glass of wine, the only one that Worthington remembered him having. Somewhere in that château, Matthieu presumed, there was a wine glass with *two* sets of fingerprints on it, Boutrel's and the attempted murderer, who was also maybe the actual murderer too.

Matthieu's head reeled, but it was a start.

He thanked the doctor and then proceeded back upstairs to his desk with this new information. When he reached his desk, he sat down at the chair before he noticed the Post-it note there in front of him. Written out in pencil on the note was the number that he had requested several hours earlier. It was still early, but not too early to give the number a call.

Matthieu stared at the Post-it for a moment, debating on what to say in his head. He reached over for the phone on his desk and picked it up. Matthieu mumbled the numbers to himself as he carefully punched them in.

The phone rang once, and then twice, and then a third time before a small voice picked up on the other line.

35

Monday, the 2nd of January, 6:46 a.m.

"Hello?" The small, and tired, voice called. Matthieu could tell immediately that this was the voice of a young child.

"Hello?" Matthieu repeated back.

"Who is this?" The child demanded, rather abruptly.

"Who is *this*?" Matthieu repeated.

"You're the one that called us!"

Matthieu snickered. He was always humored by the antics of children. Although he and Genevieve had never had any, it was not for lack of trying.

"Is your father home?" He asked.

"Listen, Monsieur," the child began, sternly. "Whatever you're selling, we're not interested!"

Matthieu almost burst out laughing. In the background of the phone call, he heard another voice call out from a distance. It was obviously the voice of an adult, fortunately.

"Pepin!" The other voice called. "Poitier! What are you two doing?!"

Matthieu heard giggling come from two children and then a loud clanging on the other line. He heard footsteps scurrying away and then the phone being fumbled around.

"Hello? Hello?" The man called into the phone.

"Yes, hello," Matthieu began. "This is Detective Matthieu from the Toulouse Police Department. May I ask who it is that I'm speaking to?"

"Shoo, shoo," the man said, presumably to the two children and not to Matthieu. "It's the police."

Matthieu smirked.

"This is Phillipe Pelletier," the man answered.

"Just the man I was looking for," Matthieu replied.

"You said that you're from the Toulouse Police Department?" Phillipe repeated for clarification.

"That's correct, Monsieur Pelletier," Matthieu said. He winced a little at the name. "I'm calling about your brother, Pierre."

Phillipe let out an exasperated sigh.

"I was wondering when I was going to get this call," he began. "He's dead, isn't he? I must admit, the only thing surprising about this call is that it took a lot longer than I anticipated to receive it. In any event, I thank you for your call, Detective. I'll spare you the trouble of stumbling through your condolences and we can both just continue on with our days."

"Wait, wait, wait," Matthieu insisted just as Phillipe was about to end the call. "Your brother isn't dead!"

"I beg your pardon, Monsieur?"

"Your brother isn't dead," Matthieu repeated. "In fact, he's very much alive."

"That's almost more unbelievable," Phillipe said.

"I take it from your response that you haven't seen or spoken to your brother in a while?"

"Not since our mother passed thirteen years ago," Phillipe said.

"I'm sorry to hear that," Matthieu said.

"Sorry to hear what?" Phillipe asked. "That my mother passed? Or that I haven't had any communication with my brother in thirteen years?"

Matthieu didn't know how to answer the question.

"Both, I suppose," he decided after an awkward silence.

"If you're calling to express condolences for my mother's death, you're a bit late."

"No," Matthieu said and cleared his throat. "Like I said before, I'm calling with some questions about your brother, Pierre."

"Pierre is basically a stranger to me," Phillipe said. "But I'll try the best that I can."

"Right," Matthieu began. "Well, I guess we can start with your estranged relationship. If you wouldn't mind, could you tell me a little bit about that?"

"Sure, Monsieur," Phillipe answered. "But we have to make this quick. I've got to finish getting these two little devils ready for school."

Matthieu heard shrieking in the background.

"Of course," he said. "Any time that you can offer is valuable. You can even come by the station if you have the time to answer a few questions."

"No," Phillipe replied. "This will be brief. Anyways, let's see, where to begin…Pierre and I used to be very close. We were a few years apart in age, but it was always just the two of us. Thick as thieves, as my mother used to say."

Matthieu could appreciate the irony.

"What happened?" He asked.

"You know, now that you ask," Phillipe said, distractedly. "Boys!" He shouted. "I'm not entirely sure why we grew apart." He thought back and then began chuckling to himself. "Pierre always used to cook up all kinds of schemes when we were younger."

"Schemes?" Matthieu asked.

"For example," Phillipe began. "When I was five years old, Pierre would have been eight, I remember he concocted this elaborate heist to steal our mother's pearl necklace!"

Phillipe laughed to himself for a moment before he was able to continue.

"He got quite the spanking, let me tell you," he said in between laughs. "I wouldn't be surprised if he still had the bruises!" He burst out into a fit of laughter. "And you know the best part about it, Detective?"

"What's that?"

"I turned him in!" Phillipe pronounced. He was laughing so hard that tears were streaming down his face.

"I see," Matthieu said, concerned that the man clearly had some issues that he had tried to bury long ago.

"Oh, man," Phillipe tried to calm himself. "Anyways, after that, Pierre would spend hours in the top bunk of the room that we shared going over it with me, trying to figure out what had gone wrong with the 'mission,' as he called it. Little did he know, the reason he got caught was right under him the whole time, literally! I was in the bottom bunk!"

Phillipe burst out laughing again uncontrollably.

"So, you were the one that turned him into your mother?" Matthieu asked, trying to rein Phillipe back in.

His laughter finally began to subside and he cleared his throat.

"When he found out," Phillipe continued. "I guess maybe that's when we grew apart. Pierre never included me in another one of his schemes again after that. We just kind of…drifted apart."

"I see," Matthieu replied.

"Probably for the better," Phillipe decided. "I know all about his run-ins with the law, it used to break our mother's heart. She was always very protective of him, especially after his illness. I think all of that worrying is what killed her. The two of us would have ended up right in that cell together if things had continued along as they were. Now, a Detective from the Toulouse Police Department is calling. I can only imagine what kind of trouble he's gotten himself into this time!"

"Have you been following the news at all?" Matthieu asked.

"As much as I can in all of my free time juggling a full-time job as an attorney and these two little monsters."

"Are you familiar with the name Bastien Boutrel?"

"Isn't that the man who was killed the other night," Phillipe suddenly stopped. "Wait a minute!" He exclaimed. "I knew your name sounded familiar! That's where I know you from, you were in that picture in the paper!"

Matthieu was glad this conversation was taking place over the phone because he was blushing with embarrassment.

He cleared his throat.

"Your brother, Pierre, escaped police custody several hours ago," Matthieu said. "He was an important witness in our investigation."

"Witness," Phillipe scoffed. "You can forget about the political correctness with me, Detective. As I said before, I'm an attorney, myself. I know 'witness' in the sense you just used it is just another word for suspect."

"Okay," Matthieu began. "Then I won't mince words with you. Yes, your brother was a suspect. You don't sound surprised by his involvement, Monsieur?"

"That's because I'm not," Phillipe answered. "Nothing that Pierre does surprises me anymore. I haven't heard from him in thirteen years, it was just a matter of time before he got himself killed or he killed someone else."

"Between you and me," Matthieu said, lowering his voice. He glanced over his shoulder. "I don't think that your brother killed anyone. But I think he might have answers for who did. I just want to talk to him."

"You can cut the act, Detective," Phillipe replied. "I know why you're calling. To answer the question that you're dancing around, no. I haven't seen my brother, not since our mother's funeral, thirteen years ago."

"Yes," Matthieu stuttered. "Of course, I'm sorry to hear that again."

Phillipe thought about toying with the Detective again for a moment but decided instead to wrap this up.

"Is there anything else, Det—" he began before he interrupted himself and began shouting on the other end of the phone. "Boys, boys, boys!" He shouted, followed by a loud crash.

"Is everything alright?" Matthieu asked.

"The boys knocked over a vase," Phillipe groaned. "I've got to go, Detective. Was there anything else?"

"Just that if you hear from your brother, please give me a call," Matthieu said before adding, "ask for me specifically."

"Right, will do," Phillipe said and then nearly clicked the button to end the call but realized he had one more thing to say. "I can assure you though, Detective," he began. "I've already got two children to deal with. I don't need a third. If you're looking for my brother, this is the *last* place you'll find him.

"Of course," Matthieu replied. "I'll let you go now. You have a good—"

Before he could finish what he was saying, the line on the other end went dead.

"Rude," Matthieu mumbled.

Phillipe clicked the phone off and put it down on the table as he rushed over to the shards of vase that were laying on the ground. All the flowers and soil in the vase had spilled out onto the floor. The boys were dancing around in the soil, dumping it in their hair and Pepin was putting some in his mouth when the doorbell rang.

Phillipe groaned.

"Ugh, what now?" He mumbled and ran over to the door.

There in front of him, of course, was the *last* person that he would have expected to see in the *last* place that you would have expected to find him.

36

Monday, the 2nd of January, 7:02 a.m.

Phillipe's look of bewilderment quickly faded to a frown as the boys screamed with delight behind him. Phillipe was the spitting image of Pierre. He even had the same soft, azure eyes. However, even though he was Pierre's younger brother, he looked older and more distinguished.

"Hello, Phillipe," Pierre began, trying to muster the best puppy dog eyes that he could.

"What do you want, Pierre?" Phillipe asked.

"I was just in the neighborhood and—"

"You're going to have to do better than that, Pierre," his brother interrupted.

"You shaved off your curls!" Pierre cried.

"Yes, Pierre," Phillipe said, running his hand through his nearly shaved head. "I'm not five years old anymore. Did you come here to compliment my haircut? Or is there another reason why you show up on my doorstep at seven in the morning on a school day?"

Of course, there was another reason, but Pierre was too proud to admit that he needed help.

"This wouldn't happen to have anything to do with the murder of Bastien Boutrel, would it?" Phillipe struck.

Pierre was stunned by how fast the news cycle must have worked.

"The police called," Phillipe continued when his brother didn't answer. "If you're wondering how I know about that."

"What did they say?" Pierre asked, slightly taken aback.

"They said that you had something to do with the murder of Bastien Boutrel!" Phillipe declared.

"Come on, Phillipe," Pierre began. "You know that I could never do anything like that."

"Do I?" Phillipe asked. "I mean, look at you."

He gestured his hand out to Pierre and motioned to his choice of ensemble.

"You're wearing all black," he continued. "You look like you literally just came from the murder! And what in the name of all that is holy is that God awful smell?!"

Pierre looked down at his white trainers which were stained with sewer sludge and he knew the smell that his brother was referring to. He was surprised that Norman hadn't mentioned it.

"Listen, Pierre," Phillipe continued. "I'm glad that we could have this little reunion. We'll have to do it again sometime, maybe in the next thirteen years. But, as you can tell, I've got two children trying to tear down the house, and I'm running late for work. So, I really must be going."

Phillipe began to close the door, but Pierre stuck his hand out to stop it with genuine tears welling in his eyes. Phillipe had never seen his brother cry before. Not after the savage spanking delivered at the hands of their mother, not even at her funeral. He thought for a moment that this must be some new trick that Pierre had taught himself. However, the next words out of Pierre's mouth surprised Phillipe with their sincerity.

"Please, Phillipe," Pierre began. "I'm in over my head."

Phillipe studied his brother carefully and then sighed.

"What do you want, Pierre?" He asked. "I can't give you any money."

Pierre shook his head.

"I don't want your money," he said, hoping that he wouldn't have to ask Phillipe for the thing that he really wanted and that instead, Phillipe would just offer it to him.

"What do you want, Pierre?" Phillipe repeated.

"I need a place to stay," Pierre finally admitted.

"A place to stay."

"Just for one night," Pierre said. "Then I'm out of your hair for good."

Phillipe kept his eyes on his brother, looking for any signs of deceit. Either Pierre had become frighteningly good at lying, or he was being entirely genuine. For a moment, Pierre appeared to be eight years old in front of him and Phillipe felt like he was only five again. This was his big brother, who at one point had been his hero, standing in front of him. His cold heart began to melt.

"I would have to ask Penelope," Phillipe began, softening up a bit.

"Oh, thank you!" Pierre said and ran forward, embracing his younger brother in his arms. "Just one night, I promise! Two at the max!"

"Now, wait a minute," Phillipe tried. "I didn't say yes, I said that I had to ask Penelope!"

"Ask Penelope what?" Came a woman's voice from the stairs behind Phillipe. "Who was that at the door at such an early hour?"

"Penelope," Phillipe began, turning to face her nervously. She was wrapping her long, blonde hair into a tight bun. "I'd like you to meet my brother, Pierre."

Pierre was admiring the foyer inside of the apartment.

"I love what you've done with the place," Pierre said as he looked around.

Penelope shot her husband a disapproving glance. She only knew Pierre from the few stories that Phillipe told, but she could tell that he was a bad egg. Phillipe hoped that she hadn't heard yet that he was the suspect of a murder investigation that had escaped from police custody only a few hours ago. He decided it was probably best to keep that information to himself for the time being.

"So," Pierre continued. "Do I get your bed and you and Penelope will take the couch? Or—"

"Absolutely not," Phillipe declared. "You can sleep on the couch, but if you're going to wear those clothes then you can sleep on the floor, or even outside for that matter."

Penelope stared daggers at her husband who gave her a pleading glance that cried, "what else was I supposed to do?"

Pierre looked down at his ratty clothes and smiled sheepishly.

"Can I also borrow a change of clothes?" He asked.

Pierre scanned the rest of the room until his eyes found the two boys. They looked strikingly like Phillipe and Pierre when they were children. They're golden brown, curly mops of hair nearly covered their eyes. Plant soil was dripping from their mouths as they stared motionless at their long, lost uncle.

"And who might you be?" Pierre asked, dropping down to one knee and speaking down to them.

"These are your nephews," Phillipe answered, trying to pull himself out from the white-hot light that was his wife's stare. "Pepin and Poitier, say hello to your uncle." He turned to his wife and mouthed the word, "sorry."

The boys just stood there in the hallway over the broken shards of vase that Phillipe had neglected to finish picking up. They were staring at Pierre warily.

"They look identical," Pierre said to his brother and then turned his attention back to his nephews.

"They're twins, Pierre," Phillipe said. "You would know that if you bothered to keep in touch."

"I wrote you that Christmas card once," Pierre said.

Phillipe rolled his eyes.

"Hello, boys, it's a pleasure to meet you," Pierre began. "Which of you is Pepin and which of you is Poi—"

Before he had time to finish his sentence, the boys began sobbing hysterically, screaming as if someone had just been murdered. Pierre wondered briefly if they were old enough to have read the paper. Maybe they were crying because someone *had* been murdered.

"Oh, God," Pierre said. "What did I do?"

"They're not good around strangers," Phillipe said over their screams, rushing over to their side to try to comfort them.

"But, I'm their uncle!" Pierre insisted.

"And a complete stranger," Phillipe replied.

"Phillipe," Penelope said in between her clenched teeth. "We're going to be late!"

Pierre stood there in the foyer as Penelope eyed him bitterly, the boys screamed, and his brother tried to comfort them. He wondered what he had gotten himself into. Little did he know, Phillipe was wondering the same thing.

37

Monday, the 2nd of January, 7:02 a.m.

Matthieu hung up the phone with Phillipe and sat back in his chair in deep contemplation.

Pierre was the key to the investigation, or so he believed. The problem, of course, was that Pierre couldn't provide him with any useful information about Boutrel's murder without copping to some crime that he had been in the act of committing in the first place. Besides that, Pierre was in the wind.

He stared down at the clock on his desktop computer. There was no way that it would have taken the train that long to arrive in Paris. By now, they should have heard something about the police taking Pierre into custody at the train station, but there hadn't been a call and Matthieu was beginning to grow worried. Had Pierre jumped from the moving train? If so, he could be anywhere in France by now.

Matthieu decided that he had better start trying to piece things together without Pierre. So, he put in a request for all the glassware at the château to be dusted for fingerprints. He knew that this would take some time and it was a long shot considering it was now two days after the whole affair had taken place. On top of that, the more he thought about it, and considering Boutrel's alcoholism, the more he realized that Boutrel's fingerprints were already probably on every single glass in that residence. Finding the exact glass that he had used that night would be nearly impossible.

Most of the evidence had already been gathered in the case, he decided. The answer was in there somewhere, he just had to use some big brain power to figure it out. So, he started revisiting some of the trails that he had gone down in his mind many times since yesterday morning.

Lucile Lebas and François Fouquet had motive. François had mentioned that he had been serving drinks that night, so that meant he had access to Boutrel's glass. However, that was circumstantial because anybody could have had access to his glass if Boutrel had placed it down for even a second.

Besides all of that, Beatrice Boutrel also had plenty of motive.

Pierre Pelletier may have had motive to steal the necklace, but was his motive justifiable enough to kill Boutrel? Matthieu still didn't believe so.

Then of course, there were the Chinese and Russian Ambassadors.

Baron William Worthington couldn't be ruled out himself since he was last seen in a heated argument with Boutrel. Maybe even an animal right's activist or two could have been responsible. Really, it could have been anyone at that soirée. Boutrel seemed to have enemies everywhere that the Detective turned, all with more incentive to kill him than Pierre. The whole crime seemed more personal than a robbery gone wrong.

Remembering Worthington sparked another lead that Matthieu wanted to follow.

Worthington had mentioned the mystery woman in the sparkling, scarlet evening gown, who Matthieu assumed may have been Pierre's accomplice, maybe even the woman that he had an affiliation with, Colette Couvrir. If he couldn't find Pierre, maybe she was the next best thing. Maybe she had seen something too.

So, Matthieu put in a request to see all of the photographs taken that evening, to try to identify her from them. However, it wasn't long before he received a response back, informing him that there hadn't been any photos taken at the soirée. He dug a little deeper and discovered that all of the guest's cell phones and cameras had been collected at the door. This struck Matthieu as odd. Boutrel was a public figure, why did he want to keep the soirée so private? Unless, of course, he was hiding something. Either way, the scarlet dress was a dead end for now.

But, if Boutrel was hiding something, maybe there was something to Beatrice mentioning her husband's offshore accounts after all. This train of thought got Matthieu thinking about Beatrice Boutrel. Maybe even the mystery woman in the scarlet dress hadn't been Pierre's accomplice, but the murderer. She could have followed Boutrel up to the study and then killed him before Pierre came in. After which, Pierre's accomplice helped him into the window, where he stumbled across the body and fled from the scene. Maybe even Beatrice had been the woman in the scarlet dress. After all, in her interrogation, Matthieu had noticed her lips stained with dark red lipstick from the night before. That would probably go perfectly with a sparkling, scarlet evening gown, or so he thought. Truth be told, after Pierre had put him in his place, Matthieu realized that he knew nothing about fashion.

Nevertheless, in her interrogation, Matthieu believed that Beatrice was trying to pin the murder on Lucile. In which case, Lucile would have gained nothing from Boutrel's death except for a lengthy prison sentence. Beatrice would have acquired her entire fortune back, including the offshore accounts. Matthieu's train of thought switched tracks. So, if this were the case, why would she mention the accounts at all? Even if Lucile took the fall, and the accounts were discovered, Beatrice would never see any of that money if it had been obtained through "illicit means," as she had put it. If she *hadn't* mentioned the accounts to him, the police would have probably never known about them and Beatrice would have been able to collect all of that at her behest.

Lucile Lebas, on the other hand, had conveniently not mentioned anything about the offshore accounts. In fact, she acted as if she didn't even know what an offshore account was. However, from her crying episodes, Matthieu pegged her as quite the actress. Maybe it was because she was trying to keep them a secret, or maybe she was telling the truth and it was because she honestly didn't know about them. Either way, Beatrice was beginning to look less and less guilty in the eyes of the Detective. Besides, Lucile could probably pull off a sparkling, scarlet evening gown. A dress like that would be the center of attention.

The one thing that seemed to maybe tie things together was the offshore accounts. So, Matthieu decided that was the best place to start. He put in a request for the financial records of Bastien Boutrel through the attorney who was responsible for the handling of Boutrel's will. The Chief was able to get authorization from a judge to halt the dispersal of any funds from the will until the entire mess was sorted out. Matthieu believed that if Lucile was involved, and she and François had been in on it together, this might convince them to stick around a little longer. He thought about the subtle flinch on François' face at the mention of the poison.

"Working hard in here?" Genevieve interrupted her ex-husband's brain moving hundreds of kilometers a minute and completely derailing his train of thought.

Matthieu grunted.

"We found something that we thought you'd want to see," she said. "Maybe it would convince you to come around to our way of thinking."

"Oh, yeah?" Matthieu asked. "What's that?"

"Why don't you see for yourself," Genevieve said. She tossed down a photograph in front of the Detective.

"What's this?" Matthieu asked, staring down at the photo. It was a photo of Pierre. "Is this a joke? I'm not keeping this on my desk."

"*That* is an enhanced image of the security footage that we recovered from the château."

Matthieu glanced up at her.

"I thought the idiot in the lab misplaced the security tape," he said.

Genevieve shrugged.

"Apparently, he found it," she said. "Recognize anyone in the picture?"

"This is Pierre," Matthieu said, bluntly.

"That's right it's Pierre," Genevieve said. "With that and the blood spots that we recovered from his apartment that we matched to Boutrel, we have enough for a conviction."

Matthieu whirled around in his chair. His ex-wife was so giddy that she couldn't contain her excited smile.

"You matched the blood spots to Boutrel?!" He stammered.

"That's right," Genevieve declared proudly. "We just got the word back from the lab."

"And nobody told me?" Matthieu demanded.

"I'm telling you right now," Genevieve said.

Matthieu stammered for a moment to the delight of his ex-wife before he was able to compose himself.

"It doesn't mean anything," he said and turned around to the papers that cluttered his desk.

"If you're keeping score at home," Genevieve continued. "That's, Genevieve—3, Martin—0."

"It was just tied!" Matthieu declared and whirled around again.

"What?" Genevieve asked.

"Yeah," Matthieu insisted. "You embarrassed me in the conference room, but then I was right about the intruder being at the soirée—"

"Wait a minute," Genevieve interrupted. "You won that round initially with the footage of Pierre escaping, but what about the security footage of the shifting gutter? That proved that the intruder wasn't at the soirée."

"Dammit," Matthieu mumbled, he conveniently had tried to forget about that.

Genevieve smirked.

"So, are you going to sit here all day like a deranged lunatic, or do you want to come back with me and join the rest of civilized society in the conference room? We have doughnuts—"

"Keep your doughnuts," Matthieu spat and turned back around aggressively.

Genevieve shook her head.

"Martin, Martin, Martin," she mumbled and then walked away.

Matthieu stared at the scattered pages on his desk and he realized that she was right. He really was beginning to look like a deranged lunatic.

38

Monday, the 2nd of January, 7:15 a.m.

"You expect me to be okay with us leaving him here alone after everything you've told me about him?!" Penelope demanded harshly to her husband, but just barely above a whisper. Phillipe was scraping up what was left of the busted vase and throwing it all into a garbage bag.

"I think we can trust him," Phillipe assured her.

"*Think*?!" Penelope repeated. "You *think* we can trust him?!"

"We can trust him," Phillipe said. "Besides, it's only for a few hours. I'll try to see if I can get out a little bit early from work."

"Oh my God," Penelope said. "You've gone crazy, that's it. You've absolutely lost your mind."

"Penelope, where else am I supposed to tell him to go? Where can you turn to if not for family?"

She scowled.

Phillipe still didn't know whether she had heard about the Boutrel incident, or Pierre's involvement in it, but if she hadn't yet, she almost certainly would by the end of the day. Then, he wouldn't put it past her to race home and decapitate Pierre herself, him too for that matter.

"Hey, is everything alright over there?" Pierre called out. He was wearing a pair of his brother's silk pajamas as his own clothes rested in a dirty pile in the laundry room. Pepin was showing his uncle one of his miniature racing cars and was bragging incessantly about it.

"Everything's fine," Phillipe assured him and then looked back at his wife with the same puppy dog eyes that Pierre had conjured up before.

"I don't know if this is some kind of mid-life crisis that you're having here," Penelope said. "But if he's going to be sleeping on our couch tonight, then you're going to be sleeping with him."

Phillipe felt a wave of relief. He didn't like the idea of sleeping on the couch, but he could handle it for a night, or two if it came to that. For some strange reason, he felt an obligation to help his brother. After all, at one point in time, they had been as thick as thieves.

Penelope stormed off and sat angrily in the passenger seat of their minivan with her arms crossed defiantly.

"Run to the car, boys, I've just got something I need to talk to your uncle about in private," Phillipe said.

Pepin and Poitier scampered off through the door and down the staircase. Their backpacks bounced behind them. Once they were out of sight, Phillipe turned to his brother.

"I love those kids," Pierre said and then slapped his brother across the chest. "Look at you! All grown up!"

"At least that makes one of us," Phillipe said. "Listen, Penelope isn't a huge fan of this idea, so you've got to keep a low profile."

"Low profile was my nickname in high school," Pierre said.

"Whatever," Phillipe replied. "Help yourself to anything in the fridge, but don't touch the casserole that's in there. That's for dinner tonight. Other than that, the upstairs is off limits, the downstairs is off limits. As a matter of fact, everything except for the kitchen and the living room is off limits. Got it?"

"Got it," Pierre replied.

"Pierre, I'm serious," his brother warned. "If anything happens, the police are going to be the least of your worries."

"Alright, I got it," Pierre grumbled.

Phillipe turned to leave but then turned back to his brother once more.

"Oh, and Pierre," he began. "Don't steal anything while we're gone."

"Understood," Pierre declared.

Phillipe shook his head and mumbled the phrase, "I can't believe I'm actually doing this," a couple of times to himself before he joined the rest of his family in the minivan and drove off.

Pierre watched them from the window and then waved as the minivan disappeared down the street. He plopped himself on the couch and turned on the TV to try to forget about everything that had happened over the course of the last couple of days. However, every news channel was running with an image of his old mugshot and that he was wanted for questioning for his role in the Boutrel incident as the top story every hour. They kept referring to Pierre as a "dangerous fugitive."

The same media that had at one point made him out to be a hero had now turned against him. Pierre saw no other way out. If he couldn't escape it, then he was going to solve it and clear his name.

He thought hard about everything that he had learned over the course of the past two days from the police and some of the things that Norman said trickled in as well. Within fifteen minutes, Pierre was fast asleep.

39

Monday, the 2nd of January, 6:02 p.m.

On the dining room table that evening was the casserole that Penelope had prepared. The boys had finally been calmed and had their mouths full. Pierre sat in the chair across from the boys. He slowly nibbled at a bit of casserole that he had stuck to his fork. Penelope was scowling at him and then at her husband. Pierre could feel her piercing eyes burning a hole in the side of his head.

The dining room was completely silent except for the boy's occasionally chewing their food loudly. Penelope finally settled her eyes on her husband. It was as if the whole time she had been deciding who she wanted to take her wrath out on, and she had finally settled on Phillipe— poor, poor Phillipe.

"Can I talk to you in the kitchen, Phillipe?" She asked in between clenched teeth.

Phillipe stood up from the table and followed his wife into the kitchen. Pierre watched him march passed like an inmate on death row.

"No, no, no, a thousand times no!" Penelope said from behind the kitchen door. The door wasn't as thick as she thought it was and Pierre could hear every word that the couple was saying to each other.

"Do you boys like Star Wars?" Pierre asked.

"Mommy says that you're a bastard," Pepin informed him.

"Okay, then," Pierre decided.

"It's just one night!" Phillipe insisted. "Come on, Penelope, he's got nowhere else to go!"

"We're not a cheap motel, Phillipe!" Penelope replied. "And did you think I wouldn't see the news at all today?!"

"You saw that?" Phillipe asked sheepishly.

"Were you just not going to tell me that your brother was a…" she paused for a moment and then lowered her voice to a whisper and spelled out the next word carefully. "M-u-r-d-e-r-e-r?!"

"It wasn't him," he assured her. "I believe him. He's family, Penelope. What if this was your brother?"

"My brother would never be the suspect in a…" she lowered her voice to a whisper again for the next word she said. "*Murder* investigation and then escape from police custody!"

"You can't know that for sure," Phillipe replied.

"Really?" Penelope asked in disbelief. "Is that your answer?"

169

"I've got something that you boys might like," Pierre said and reached into his pocket. He held up the Han Sapphire necklace and dangled it in front of them as the light from the dining room beamed off it.

Pepin and Poitier's eyes grew wide. It was like they were in a trance, hypnotized by the necklace. The necklace seemed to have the same effect on a lot of people. Even Pierre wasn't immune to its pull. It was almost like it had some dark power to it.

"The only reason that I didn't call the police was because I knew that you would be held responsible as an accessory!" Penelope cried. "Do you want the boys to grow up without a father?!"

"Now that's not fair," Phillipe pleaded. "Besides, I grew up without a father and I turned out just fine!"

"That's not the point," Penelope insisted.

"Penelope," Phillipe tried. "Just the couch, please. Just for one night."

Penelope let out a wild grunt in anger and frustration.

"Fine!" She finally said. "But I was serious before. You can sleep with him on that couch. Don't say that I didn't warn you. That brother of yours is bad news for this family!"

She stormed out of the kitchen and returned angrily to her seat at the table. Pierre quickly shoved the necklace back into his pocket, breaking the boys from their trance, and he smiled at her. Penelope did not return his smile.

Phillipe emerged from the kitchen with the slumped shoulders of a man who was in the doghouse. He gave his brother an angry look. He didn't have to say anything, his accusatory glance screamed to Pierre that this was all *his* fault.

"The casserole is good," Pierre said, trying to break the awkward tension in the room. Penelope was staring daggers at her husband. "Like, *really* good," Pierre insisted.

"I've suddenly lost my appetite," Penelope said and then stood up and walked away from the dining room table. They listened to her stomp away until her footsteps disappeared upstairs.

"My mommy doesn't like you," Poitier said, matter-of-factly.

"No kidding," Pierre mumbled and stuffed a large bite of casserole into his mouth.

Phillipe shook his head.

———————

After dinner was put away, Phillipe and Pierre sat on the twin couches in the living room while the boys played with their miniature race cars on the carpet.

Pepin came up to Pierre with the best puppy dog eyes that he could. Pierre couldn't help but to appreciate that they reminded him of his own.

"Can we play with your pretty necklace, Monsieur?" He asked.

Pierre laughed nervously as Phillipe passed over a suspicious glance.

"Oh, you little rascal," Pierre said and rubbed Pepin's golden brown, curly hair until it was a complete, frizzled mess. "These kids have such a vivid imagination."

"I'm not a rascal," Pepin insisted. "I'm a human being."

"Go on and join your brother," Phillipe said to his son.

Pepin ran over to his younger brother and then the two scampered off together, disappearing behind a corner of the staircase.

Pierre and Phillipe were left alone in silence. Phillipe seemed perfectly content at keeping it that way. Pierre was fidgety.

Poitier reappeared from behind the staircase in a full sprint. His foot caught a corner of the carpet in the living room and he tumbled to the ground. He began screaming at the top of his lungs. Phillipe ran over to comfort him when Pierre felt something strange, like tiny little hands trying to reach into the pocket of his silk pajamas.

He reached his own hand down and caught the intruder by the wrist. Pepin smiled nervously as Pierre held him there. Pepin gave his brother a frantic look, like an animal in a trap. His eyes screamed, "Abort! Abort!"

Poitier, noticing that the jig was up, stopped wailing almost immediately and then got up and ran off. Pierre released Pepin's arm and Pepin trailed after his brother. Both disappeared behind the staircase once more.

"What a miraculous recovery," Phillipe said.

Pierre laughed.

"They remind me of us," he said, reminiscing. "Remember?"

Phillipe did for a moment and then stopped himself.

"Alright," Phillipe said and stood up. "Time for bed, boys."

Pierre watched his brother walk away without looking at him and then guide his sons to their bedroom upstairs. Pierre's heart swelled with regret once more.

Phillipe returned sometime later in his own pair of silk pajamas with a couple of pillows and two blankets under his arms.

"Here you go," he said and tossed Pierre a pillow and a blanket.

"Thanks," Pierre said and set up a makeshift bed on one of the living room couches. Penelope's threat apparently wasn't empty, and Phillipe set up his own bed on the couch across from him. He laid down on the other couch and turned away from his brother.

"You can leave the light on," Phillipe said over his shoulder. "Just turn it off when you're ready to sleep."

"I might as well turn it off now," Pierre said. He reached up and pulled at the lamp chain and the light turned off, casting the two brothers into a dark silence. Pierre could feel the words forming at the back of his throat and almost word vomited them all up at once.

Instead, he cleared his throat and arranged his thoughts carefully.

"So," he began awkwardly. "How have you been?"

"How have I been?" Phillipe repeated in a muffled voice. His face was buried into the back of the couch. "It's been thirteen years and *that's* what you have to say to me?"

"Sounds like not well," Pierre mumbled.

Phillipe flipped himself over violently and, in the dim light of the streetlight pouring into the living room through the window behind the couch, Pierre could see the faint outline of his brother's face and the whites of his eyes glowing. He was staring straight at him.

"Actually," Phillipe began. "I've been great. I have a loving wife, two beautiful children, and a roof over my head. Thanks for asking."

"I'm sensing some bitterness."

Phillipe scoffed.

"I'm not bitter," he insisted and turned over again.

Long silences made Pierre physically uncomfortable. It was like an itch that he couldn't scratch. He could feel the word vomit forming at the back of his throat again, but fortunately, Phillipe spoke instead.

"I needed you, Pierre," he said. "And you weren't there."

Pierre was speechless for maybe the first time in his life. Unfortunately, it came at a time where he probably should have had something to say. So, Phillipe continued.

"Our father died when I was just a boy, and mom died when I was 15. Do you know what it's like to be alone in the world at 15, with nobody to turn to?"

"No," Pierre answered, faintly.

"That's all you can say?" Phillipe asked.

"What do you want me to say? I'm sorry?!"

"It's a start!" Phillipe said, whipping himself around again. "You walked into my house and have yet to apologize to me."

"Well, I'm sorry," Pierre said. "I wish that I could take it all back, but I can't. Besides, it's not like you're completely innocent in all of this."

"Are you talking about when I ratted you out to mom?" Phillipe asked in disbelief. "I was five years old, Pierre! And you turned your back on me when you found out."

"I was hurt."

"I *needed* you!"

"I know. I just—"

"And what were you off doing while I was left completely alone?" Phillipe interrupted. "Pickpocketing, breaking and entering, *murdering people*?!"

"You know that I had nothing to do with that," Pierre insisted. He was answered with silence from his brother. "Don't you?"

"I don't know what to believe anymore," Phillipe said. He stared for a moment at Pierre with judgmental eyes that chilled Pierre to his core. Phillipe finally turned over and Pierre stared up at the ceiling. He hoped that the answer to everything would just flash right in front of him, but it never did.

"You were better off without me," he finally said.

"Is that what you convinced yourself to help you sleep at night?"

There was silence again as the steady metronome of a clock ticked somewhere in the room.

"Goodnight, Pierre," Phillipe finally said.

"Goodnight, Phillipe," Pierre replied. In the midst of the awfulness that he was feeling, and the twist that he felt in his stomach, it felt good to be reunited with his brother.

The morning didn't come quickly for Pierre. He tossed and turned sleeplessly for most of the night. If you had asked him, Pierre would have said it was because he was so uncomfortable on the couch, but really, it was because he was so uncomfortable with himself. He thought a lot about the direction that his life had taken that night, and he wished that he could do it all over.

He was finally able to fall asleep at the first break of sunlight through the window. It wouldn't last long though, as he was soon awakened by a loud knocking on the front door. His eyes shot open.

Pierre sat up on the couch and quickly rolled off it. He crawled over to the couch where his brother was still sleeping soundly and peered behind the curtain that draped the window behind the couch. When he looked out, he expected to see an entire SWAT team of officers waiting there with semi-automatic weapons at the ready to gun down the "dangerous fugitive." However, it wasn't an entire SWAT team, it was just a single person. For a moment, he believed that his eyes were playing tricks on him. But there, on the front stoop of his brother's apartment complex, was Colette Couvrir.

40

Monday, the 2nd of January, 6:02 p.m.

The rest of Matthieu's Monday continued in much the same way that it had begun. Unfortunately, every wine glass at the château had been recently hand washed and polished. The only fingerprints that Simone St. Clair could find on any of them belonged to the person who had cleaned them, François Fouquet himself, ironically enough. Matthieu knew that this would have been a long shot, and probably wouldn't have proven anything anyways, but he still felt disappointed, nonetheless.

When Matthieu finally got a hold of Boutrel's financial records later that evening, he began combing through them.

The first thing that he came across was the hefty life insurance policy that Beatrice had taken out on her husband just a week prior to his death. The premium that she would have been paying for a leech like Monsieur Boutrel hardly seemed worth it. Then again, maybe the premium was worth it if she only had to make one payment for such a staggering payout of nearly €100 million. Was the Boutrel name alone worth that much? Although he had become less suspicious of the "grieving" widow, she climbed his suspect list once again.

Matthieu began to delve deeper into Boutrel's finances and found that Boutrel had an account in nearly every French bank.

So, Matthieu decided to start by reviewing all of Boutrel's most recent transactions to see if he could make any sense of the numbers.

The numbers in his French accounts were confusing, to say the least. The balances remained relatively stable and Matthieu could see that it was mostly as Beatrice had said.

Every Friday, Boutrel received a combined transfer of €200,000 spread out amongst his numerous French accounts, Beatrice's allowance. There were also a number of other deposits into these French accounts, none with any details associated with them other than the amounts. The money that was deposited into these accounts was always a discreet cash transaction. There were never any names or identities linking any of them to anything. Matthieu now understood why Boutrel always preferred working in cash. If the police had ever come across these accounts, there was virtually no paper trail. The cash deposits could have been, theoretically, collected from anywhere. They were all seemingly innocuous, but Matthieu could tell that something unsavory was afoot.

However, strangely enough, all of the French accounts had been drained and closed on the 3rd of December. On the 17th of December, the accounts were opened again. From that day forward, his allowance was doubled. The pattern continued like this until his death.

When the funds had been drained, they had all been funneled into a mysterious account that didn't have any name associated with it, just an account number. The details of this mystery account were unavailable to Matthieu. He tried to look into the bank that the account was listed under, Financial Union, apparently located in a small Caribbean island called St. Kitts. This was, undoubtedly, part of the offshore accounts that Beatrice had spoken of. However, the further Matthieu dug, the less he came up with. After tracing the routing number into a dead end and several phone calls, Matthieu came to the conclusion that no such institution existed. The Caribbean account appeared to be at the epicenter of the tangled web of Boutrel's accounts, but from there the trail seemed to disappear.

On the 3rd of December, there were a number of large wire transfers to this mystery Caribbean account from his French accounts, the sum of which was €60 million, the exact price that he had paid for the necklace.

Shortly after that transaction, Boutrel's French accounts had been drained and closed. The trail went cold until they were reopened on the 17th of December and then business continued as usual.

Conveniently missing, Matthieu discovered, there were no recent transactions involving deposits totaling €100 million, the price that the Chinese Ambassador, Zhao Zhu, had negotiated with Boutrel for the Han Sapphire necklace.

While this, of course, could have been explained in the same way that Worthington had explained it, Boutrel had been murdered before the transaction had gone through, or before Boutrel had a chance to deposit the cash into his account, it circled Matthieu back around to an idea, nonetheless.

The Chinese Ambassador had connections to Hong Kong. The *Viper Triad* had connections throughout Europe but many of their operations were centered around Hong Kong. The *Gu* was a Chinese poison. It all seemed to wrap together in a box with a neat little bow, right in front of Matthieu. If you followed the trail, you could logically conclude that *maybe* the Chinese Ambassador decided that €100 million for the necklace was a bit steep. *Maybe* he intended to get himself a discount on the jewel the old-fashioned way, by stealing it. Through his connection with the *Viper Triad, maybe* he arranged for Boutrel to be poisoned and when the poison didn't work, they stabbed him. Then, they broke into the safe, stole the necklace and then fled back to Hong Kong.

However, this still didn't explain why Pierre was there in the first place. But maybe it was as simple as Pierre being in the wrong place at the wrong time, caught in the crossfire between Boutrel and the Chinese

Ambassador. Or maybe, just maybe, it was as Matthieu had suspected once before and that Pierre had been set up. Maybe whoever had killed Boutrel had hired Pierre for the job of stealing the necklace, knowing that he would leave behind his signature flower and would thus, in a sense, frame himself for the murder.

Matthieu fingers began to tingle as they tapped on the desk in front of him—*he was onto something.*

However, the bow on top of the box began to unravel when Matthieu remembered that they hadn't yet found the necklace. The Han Sapphire necklace was the key to it all, and Pierre may have been the key to the necklace. If he didn't have it, he might know who did. If he did have it, then he might have information about the killer. Matthieu needed to know what Pierre saw that night.

"I wonder what the big, bad, lone wolf is up to now?" A familiar voice called to Matthieu from behind, breaking him from his stupor—Genevieve's voice. Matthieu nearly fell out of his chair.

"I was looking through Boutrel's accounts," Matthieu grunted.

"Are you going to be here all night?" She asked.

"It's only six."

"Guess again, genius."

Matthieu glanced over at the clock on his computer which read that it was past eleven. He had been engrossed in the accounts for nearly five hours and hadn't even realized it.

"I probably won't be much longer," he grumbled, unsure of why she would even care anyways.

Genevieve shook her head and looked down on her ex-husband with pity.

"I have to say," she began. "I admire your stubbornness."

"Thank you," Matthieu replied. He resumed his focus on the numbers in front of him and tuned out his ex-wife.

"It wasn't a compliment," she said to which he grunted an indistinguishable response. "Anyways, a couple of us were going to go out for a few drinks, maybe discussing the case a little. We wanted to see if you wanted to come with us?"

"Why would I want to do that?"

"For old times," Genevieve replied.

Matthieu thought about it for just a moment before coming to a decision.

"Pass," he said.

Genevieve sighed.

"Fine then," she said. "Have it your way."

She started towards the front door before turning back once more, debating whether to offer some words of encouragement for the sorry state of the man she once loved or to rub everything in his face again. She opted for some sort of strange middle ground.

"Just one more thing," she began. "I know that you have this constant need to be right. But nobody will care if you decide to jump ship and join the rest of us."

Matthieu grunted.

"You're letting your own need to be right cloud your judgment," she continued. Matthieu didn't respond. "I mean, you had the culprit right here and you let him slip through your fingers!"

"You were the one with your fingers all over him," Matthieu said, coldly. "Don't think that I didn't see the two of you in there, canoodling."

Genevieve rolled her eyes.

"Did you ever stop to think that maybe I was doing that *intentionally* in front of you?"

Matthieu stopped for a moment and looked up at the wall blankly.

"Whatever," Genevieve said. "You can chase your ghosts. I'm going after the real 'ghost.' The *Black Lotus*, the killer *and* the thief. They're conveniently packaged into one Pierre-sized person, after all."

Matthieu grumbled again and turned around.

"Goodnight, Martin," Genevieve said and then walked away, leaving Matthieu completely alone in the station.

There were always rumors of the Toulouse police station being haunted by ghosts. Lights flickered on when nobody was around, water ran from the sinks in the restrooms when nobody had used them, and there were even footsteps on the linoleum floors down the long, dark hallways. But Matthieu never believed any of them. The only ghosts that were haunting Matthieu tonight were the ghosts of his failed marriage, and the ghost of Pierre that seemed to be mocking him at every turn.

Matthieu scanned the numbers in front of him, trying to make sense of them all, until he fell asleep on top of them.

While he slept, he dreamed up a solution to the problem that solved everything all at once. Like any dream, it made complete sense while he was asleep, but when he woke up with a violent start to the phone ringing, his face was pressed against a puddle of his own drool and his solution faded away.

Matthieu scrambled for the phone and picked it up on the second ring.

"Hello?" He called. "...What?! Are you sure it's him?!"

Matthieu slammed the phone back down. He grabbed his peacoat from the back of his chair and rushed towards the door of the station. He brushed past Genevieve on the way by. It seemed as if he didn't even notice her there.

"Where are you going?" She cried out to him, but Matthieu didn't respond.

He stormed right past her and disappeared beyond the station doors.

41

Tuesday, the 3rd of January, 6:33 a.m.

"Colette," Pierre stammered as he opened the door.

"Well, well, well," Colette began with a sly smile on her face. "If it isn't the infamous Pierre Pelletier."

"What are you doing here?" Pierre stuttered.

"What do you think I'm doing here?" she asked. "I'm here for you, you idiot."

Pierre loved the way that the final syllable of the word "idiot" just seemed to slide through her perfectly straight teeth and under those full lips. He could have listened to her call him an idiot for hours, and he might have, if it hadn't been for Phillipe sneaking up behind him. Phillipe elbowed Pierre in the side before yawning widely.

"Are you going to invite her in?" Phillipe asked, mid-yawn.

Pierre turned back to Colette who was looking at him expectantly and shivering a bit in the cold.

"Of course," he said and gestured inside. "Come in."

Colette came inside and looked around for a bit as Pierre escorted her into the living room. He took a seat on the couch that he had been sleeping on and Colette took a seat on the couch that Phillipe had spent the night on.

Phillipe shuffled his feet over to them with the Tuesday morning newspaper unfolded in his hands. On the front page was the image again of Detective Matthieu standing wide eyed over the body of Bastien Boutrel.

"Gets me every time," he mumbled under his breath and chuckled. When he flipped the paper over, there was Pierre's face, just below it. Phillipe pretended not to notice.

When he lifted his head up, he saw Pierre and Colette staring at him. Pierre cleared his throat loudly.

"Right," Phillipe said, taking the hint. "I guess I'll leave you to it."

He grabbed his pillow off the couch and then disappeared into the kitchen.

Pierre turned to Colette.

"What are you doing here?" Pierre repeated frantically, not caring to waste any more time.

"Wow, Pierre," Colette began, calmly. "Not even going to ask how I've been?"

"Fine," Pierre decided. "How have you been?"

"Pretty good, considering the circumstances."

"Glad to hear it," Pierre said. "Now, what are you doing here?"

Colette laughed.

"I guess we'll get straight to the point," she said.

"Do they have you wearing a wire?" Pierre demanded. He stood up and glanced out through the window, then closed the curtains.

"Don't be ridiculous, Pierre," Colette said. "I'm not wearing a wire."

"That's *exactly* what someone who's wearing a wire would say!"

"What, do you want to strip search me?" Colette asked.

"Could I?" Pierre replied.

Colette rolled her eyes.

"You're just going to have to trust me, Pierre," she said.

"Kind of like I trusted you to be my lookout the other night?"

"I gave you ample warning," Colette insisted. "The rest was all you."

"You think I killed him too, don't you? When you called me before, you said so."

"I know you didn't," Colette sighed. "Otherwise I wouldn't be here."

"How do you know I didn't? You seemed so sure of my guilt before."

Colette scoffed.

"I've seen you in a fight before, Pierre," she said. "Don't you remember? High school? Valerie Vivian? You tried to steal something out of her purse, and she beat the pulp out of you!"

"She was big for her age."

Colette chuckled.

"Whatever you say, Pierre," she said.

"How did you know you would find me here?" Pierre asked.

"It didn't take a genius to figure out that if you escaped from police custody, you would go to your only living relative," she answered.

"So, you found me, what do you want?"

"A glass of water would be nice."

"You travelled all this way for a glass of water?"

"Get me some water and then we can talk about why I came," Colette said with another roll of her eyes.

Pierre admittedly loved the way that she did that, he always had. With him, she usually had plenty of reason to.

Pierre got up and disappeared into the kitchen. There, he almost tripped over Phillipe who was laying on the tile floor.

"How's it going out there?" Phillipe asked, groggily.

"Swimmingly," Pierre answered and then finally found the cabinet with the glasses. He filled a glass with tap water and brought it back out to Colette.

"For the last time, what do you want?" He pressed again. "Couldn't we have done this over the phone?"

Colette took a long, drawn out sip from her water and then set it down on the table.

"I needed to see you, Pierre. This was too delicate to talk about over the phone," she finally began. "Seeing as you managed to escape police custody, and knowing you, I'm guessing that you didn't leave Toulouse without the Han Sapphire necklace?"

"I don't know what you're talking about," Pierre replied and plopped down on the couch across from her.

"Pierre," she insisted. "I'm *not* wearing a wire."

"Did they offer you some sort of immunity if you got me to confess?" Pierre asked. "Is that it? I bet there's a whole SWAT team in position outside of the house right now, isn't there?"

"Do you want to check?" Colette asked, trying to help quell his paranoia.

Pierre studied her eyes. He knew Colette well, maybe better than anyone else. Colette grew up in the house just next door to the Pelletier's. However, she had always been a third wheel when it came to the two Pelletier brothers. That is, until Phillipe ratted his brother out. Then, it was easy for Pierre to replace his brother for Colette and she often found herself involved in Pierre's little schemes, all the way through high school. They had grown apart after Pierre's mother had passed and had pretty much lost touch until Pierre realized that he would need a man on the inside of the château for the "mission" roughly two weeks prior. It had to be someone that he could trust. So, that was when he had decided to give his old friend a call.

Since he was so familiar with her, Pierre could usually tell when she was lying. She seemed genuine now.

"Let's say, *hypothetically*, that I do have the necklace," Pierre began. "What difference is it to you?"

"Well," she began. "*Hypothetically*, that would be good news for both of us."

"Why would that be good news for both of us?" Pierre asked. "*Hypothetically*."

"Because, Pierre, I have an interested buyer."

"Hypothetically?"

"No, Pierre," Colette answered. "I have a *literal* buyer."

Pierre remembered everything that his brother had said the night before. If there was a buyer, that meant that he was going to turn his back on him once again. Everything that Colette was offering was just another scheme for him to get himself sucked into.

There was a sudden voice that spoke up from Pierre's pocket.

"Don't be a fool," the necklace said. *"Take the opportunity. When will you ever have another chance at €60 million?"*

That was a lot of money, but was that worth the price of his soul?

"Do you know how many souls you can buy for €60 million?" the necklace continued. *"Hell, the Pierre that I know would have sold his soul for a pair of night vision binoculars."*

"Pierre?" Colette asked, calling him back to reality. "Are you having your daydreams again? What's it going to be?"

"I don't have it," Pierre stammered.

"What?" Colette asked.

"I don't have the necklace," Pierre said. "The police, they impounded it."

Colette stared at him skeptically for a moment and then frowned.

"Well," she began and sunk herself into the couch cushions. She seemed incredibly defeated by the revelation. "That's a real shame."

"Yeah," Pierre answered, indifferently.

"Then, I guess that's it for us," Colette decided and stood up.

"You're leaving?" Pierre asked.

"What else am I going to do here?"

For a moment, Pierre thought about his brother and the life that he had made for himself. He was married and he had two children, he had a family. More importantly though, he was happy. It was all that Pierre ever really wanted. He wanted to tell Colette to stay and suggest that they should run away together. Instead, he didn't say anything.

"Alright," Colette said while Pierre stared off into space.

She began moving toward the door. Pierre followed her and held the front door open for her. She looked back up at him for a moment and Pierre found himself flooded with emotion as he stared into her hazel eyes.

"Goodbye, Pierre," she said. "Take care of yourself."

Her goodbye stung like a thousand daggers. His tongue was dry and swollen. Colette kept her eyes on his for a moment before she finally turned away. She walked out and the morning sun glowed on her face.

"Oh, Pierre," she said before turning back around to him. Pierre looked at her optimistically, as if she might say everything that he wanted to. "Call me if the necklace ever turns up."

"Are you going to answer this time?"

Colette rolled her eyes.

"You'll be the first person that I call," Pierre assured her.

Colette's gaze lingered again from the sidewalk. She couldn't help but notice the shell of a man that he had become in less than 72 hours. This wasn't the same arrogant Pierre that she had known. This one almost seemed human.

She tried not to give it another thought and she turned to walk away. Before long, she had disappeared down the Paris streets.

42

Tuesday, the 3rd of January, 7:15 a.m.

"Alright, Pierre," Phillipe began, frantically trying to stuff things into his briefcase. "Same deal as yesterday. The kitchen and the living room *only*. Got it?"

"Got it," Pierre grumbled.

Penelope was coming down the stairs and was just finishing putting on her earrings.

"Good morning, Penelope," Pierre tried.

She grunted at him and then left through the front door. It was progress, at least, but Pierre wasn't satisfied.

I will win you over, he thought with determination.

"Alright," Phillipe continued. "There's leftover casserole in the fridge, you can have that for lunch if you want. Just please, please, *please* try to stay out of trouble while we're gone. And don't steal anything!"

"You have my word," Pierre said.

That was exactly what Phillipe was afraid of. He groaned and then yelled upstairs.

"Boys! Come on, we're going to be late!"

Pepin and Poitier began down the staircase, rubbing their sleepy eyes. Once they had reached the ground level, Phillipe put his hand behind their backs and began to push them outside.

"Goodbye, Uncle Pierre," Pepin said and waved back behind him.

Has a nice ring to it, Pierre thought.

He waved back and then, just like that, the door closed behind them and Pierre was alone in the apartment.

He looked around at the boy's miniature racing cars among the clutter of other toys that were scattered all around the floor.

"Right," he said aloud. "Well, what do I do now?"

Pierre glanced over at the clock which ticked slowly. The house was an absolute mess. Just then, the idea came to him to clean it. What better way to win over Penelope than by doing something selflessly for the family?

"*I can already see where this is going,*" the necklace burst in. "*This is the part where you have a change of heart and decide to do things for others. Yawn!*"

"What's so bad about helping others?" Pierre mumbled to the empty room.

"*It doesn't help us,*" the necklace replied.

"Helping others *would* help us," Pierre insisted. "A little manipulation can go a long way."

The necklace considered this for a moment.

"*There's the Pierre that I know,*" it said.

"Besides," Pierre continued. "That woman scares me."

"*Me too,*" the necklace agreed.

So, Pierre set out to clean the entire house.

He picked up all of the toys on the floor, cleaned all of the dishes in the sink from the night before, rearranged the contents of the fridge alphabetically, started the laundry, vacuumed and dusted the two rooms that he was allowed in until they sparkled and prepared dinner for the family for that evening. He even pulled all the shards of broken vase from yesterday morning out of the garbage and glued them all back together.

Once finished, he sat down on the couch, exhausted. Pierre found the remote to the TV and turned it on. The news cycle was continuing with footage about him. Pierre flipped through the channels until he found cartoons. Almost immediately, he fell asleep.

He slept for hours before he was finally rudely awakened by another booming knock at the front door.

Pierre got up groggily and began walking straight for the door, not even bothering to look first out through the window.

He rounded the corner until he was face to face with the door window and he could see through it. There, on the other side of the door, was Detective Matthieu.

Matthieu was looking around outside and didn't notice Pierre, which gave him enough time to scramble out of sight and duck down behind the couch under the living room window.

Matthieu stood there for a few moments and then frowned and knocked again. When nobody answered for a second time, he began to walk around the apartment building, studying the exterior.

There was a garden with some light shrubbery at the front of the building, behind which there was a large front window, the window that Pierre was beneath. Matthieu trudged through the garden to try to get a glimpse inside.

"Very clean," he mumbled to himself, looking right over the couch that Pierre was hiding behind before he noticed that the TV was suspiciously on inside.

At the same moment, Pierre could hear a car slow down and then turn into the driveway. He glanced up at the clock, it was just past four. He had slept for nearly the entire day.

Thank God, Pierre thought. *That must be Phillipe.*

Phillipe noticed the blue Renault parked in the driveway. He parked beside it when he noticed the strange man peeping in through his living room window.

"Excuse me, Monsieur," he called out. "Can I help you with something?"

"Yeah," Pepin shouted from his car seat. "Whatever you're selling, we're not interested!"

Phillipe shushed his son.

Matthieu stumbled back through the garden and approached Phillipe.

"I didn't mean to startle you," he assured him. "I'm Detective Martin Matthieu with the Toulouse Police Department."

He walked across the lawn and stuck his hand out to Phillipe.

"I was wondering when you were going to show up," Phillipe said and shook the Detective's hand with a sly smile that only a defense attorney could muster. "I take it that you didn't believe me? You probably get that spiel all of the time."

Matthieu laughed.

"More than you would think," he said.

"Well, what can I do to convince you?" Phillipe asked, cordially.

"How about a look inside?" Matthieu replied. "It would help ease my mind."

"Seems like you already got a good look inside," Phillipe said, less cordially.

Matthieu blushed sheepishly.

"Sorry about that," he said. "My curiosity got the better of me, I suppose."

Phillipe studied him intently for a moment.

"If it'll get you off my back," he decided. "I'll let you look around. You can follow me."

He released the two devils from the back seat of the car and the two began wrestling on the front lawn. Phillipe led Matthieu up the stairs. He unlocked the front door and pushed it open.

Matthieu stepped inside the foyer as the old, wooden floors creaked beneath him. He glanced around. Everything was immaculately clean and eerily still. He could hear the faint sound of the TV from the other room.

"Your wife keeps a very neat house," he said. "Speaking of, where is your wife?"

"She takes the train back from her office," Phillipe said. He was also surprised by the state of the house. It hadn't even looked this clean when they had moved in.

"I see," Matthieu said.

"Come on in, boys!" Phillipe turned and called to his sons.

Pepin and Poitier ran up the stairs and into the house, pushing their way past the Detective. He collected the boys winter coats and walked them over toward the coat closet in the front hall.

"Can I get you anything, Detective?" Phillipe asked.

Matthieu walked in a little bit further until he saw a shadow spilling out on the floor in the faint shape of a man from behind the front door. He quickly turned and saw what had produced the shadow, an umbrella holder. He frowned and turned the other way to face the living room.

Phillipe pulled open the coat closet door and found himself face-to-face with Pierre. He quickly closed it.

Matthieu slowly walked towards the living room as Phillipe watched him nervously. Matthieu stared at the area in front of the couch by the window where Pierre had been hiding. The spot was empty but what remained of Pierre's presence was a corner of the carpet which had been flipped over. Matthieu studied it curiously.

"Just some water would be nice," he finally said and smiled over at Phillipe.

"Water it is," Phillipe replied nervously and proceeded into the kitchen, carrying the coats with him.

"You have a lot of closets," Matthieu remarked.

He pulled open a closet door in the living room.

"Pierre!" He cried for a moment before realizing that he had mistaken an upturned mop head for his fugitive. To be fair, they had the same hair.

Pierre swallowed hard from the coat closet.

"Everything alright out there?" Phillipe called from the kitchen.

"Yes," Matthieu called back, slightly embarrassed.

He looked around at the picture frames on the mantle and the TV that was still running.

"The reason I stopped by," Matthieu called to Phillipe who was still in the kitchen. "Is because I received a disturbing phone call this morning."

"Oh, really?" Phillipe called back. The first thought that came into his mind was Penelope. She said the night before that she had thought about calling the police but the only reason that she didn't was that she didn't want her children to grow up without a father. Had she changed her mind on that front? Did she decide that the risks far outweighed the benefits?

"The caller informed me that Pierre is in Paris."

"Really?" Phillipe asked, emerging from the kitchen. Matthieu noticed that his hand was a bit shaky when he handed him his water.

Matthieu took it from him and took a sip.

"Do you always leave the TV on when you leave for work?" Matthieu asked, pointing to it. Phillipe looked over at the TV which displayed a colorful collection of some cartoon show that he didn't recognize.

"The boys usually watch cartoons in the morning," Phillipe lied. "We were running late today and must have just neglected to turn it off."

He reached for the remote and turned the TV off.

"Hmm," Matthieu grunted and then continued to look around. The ground creaked beneath him as he scanned the corners of the apartment. He walked back into the foyer and stopped right in front of the coat closet by the front door. The coat closet that Pierre was in.

"You said that Pierre was in Paris?" Phillipe asked.

"It would seem so," Matthieu said as he stared at the coat closet doorknob. "Pierre was last seen fleeing from Toulouse on board the midnight train to Paris. We had officers stationed at the Saint Lazare Train Station early yesterday morning to intercept him. However, when the train arrived, there was no sign of him. We were ready to assume that he had jumped from the moving train until earlier *this* morning when I received the disturbing call that an FBI agent had been detained at the train station claiming to have met *me*."

Phillipe was relieved that the call hadn't come from his wife, and he felt guilty for ever thinking that it could have. Matthieu reached down and wiped a smudge off the coat closet doorknob with a handkerchief.

Pierre could almost feel the Detective, just beyond the closet door. He felt a bead of sweat drip down his forehead and down his nose before it splashed on the floor. He held his breath.

"Of course," Matthieu continued, walking away from the door. Pierre breathed a heavy, but quiet, sigh of relief. "I wasn't on that train. When we looked at the passenger logs, the only person that was unaccounted for was the individual the FBI agent claimed to have met. Security footage from the train station verified that it was your brother who exited that train, impersonating the FBI agent. He stole his glasses, his passport and the man's wallet."

"That's quite the tale," Phillipe said. "I'm sorry that you wasted your time by coming all the way out here."

Matthieu chuckled.

"I wouldn't call a trip to Paris a waste of time," he said. "How long have you and your wife lived here?"

"We were both born and raised here," Phillipe answered, loosening a little. "I always wanted to get out of the city, but Penelope wanted to stay. I'm sure you know how that old argument goes. Are you married, Detective?"

Matthieu's mind wandered to the thought of the succubus that he used to call his wife back in Toulouse.

"No," he said, finally.

"Hmm," Phillipe grunted.

"Anyways," Matthieu continued. "You still haven't heard from or seen your brother at all?"

"Not since the funeral," Phillipe reminded him.

"Of course," Matthieu stuttered once more. Phillipe found it quite odd how uncomfortable the Detective seemed to be around death. "He seems to have a knack for evading the police. Slipped away from us in Toulouse and now apparently has slipped away from the police in Paris. He's developing quite the reputation. Even earned himself another nickname it seems. They've been calling him "the Eel" down at the station."

"Another nickname?" Phillipe repeated.

"Ah, that's right," Matthieu said. "The papers have a lot of details, but they don't have the whole story. You see, one key component has been left out of them. Perhaps you've heard of the Black Locust?"

"*Black Lotus*," Pierre mumbled under his breath between his gritted teeth.

"You mean the *Black Lotus*?" Phillipe asked, slightly taken aback. "Are you suggesting that my brother had something to do with the heist at the Museum of Modern Art right here in Paris? The last I heard, he used to work there for Christ—" he stopped himself short of finishing the sentence when he pieced the revelation together.

"I'm not suggesting that your brother *had* something to do with that crime, Monsieur. I'm saying he *was* that crime."

Phillipe was stunned.

"I probably shouldn't be telling you this, but we found a key piece of evidence at the Château de Boutrel that links the two crimes together," Matthieu said.

"What was that?" Phillipe asked.

"The flower. The black lotus origami flower," Matthieu said before continuing. "We also have evidence that your brother was an unwanted guest at the château the other evening. Therefore, the evidence would seem to link your brother to both crimes."

Phillipe was floored. A million thoughts raced through his mind.

"Why are you telling me this?" He asked.

"You know what I find odd," Matthieu began again. "You said that you and your wife have lived in Paris this whole time and you knew that your brother was living in Paris and working at the Museum of Modern Art. Yet, you never thought to pay him a visit and he never came to visit you, his only family?"

"I think he sent us a Christmas card once," Phillipe said. "But, it's the sad truth."

"The reason that I'm telling you all of this, Monsieur Pelletier, is because I wanted you to see the facts for yourself."

"I see them."

"Therefore, the only logical conclusion, and the conclusion that the police have come up with, is that your brother is the person responsible for the death of Bastien Boutrel."

Phillipe could hardly believe it, but all the evidence was right in front of him. His eyes shifted to the coat closet door. Matthieu noticed the subconscious flinch and followed his glance.

"But," Matthieu continued. "Personally, I believe that your brother is innocent."

"Innocent?" Phillipe repeated in disbelief. "How could he be innocent after everything that you've just told me?"

"Innocent in the sense that I don't believe that your brother had a hand in killing Monsieur Boutrel."

"But you said it yourself, all of the evidence—"

"There's other evidence in the case, other factors at play that have led me to believe that your brother was simply caught in the wrong place at the wrong time."

"But you said it yourself that the police have concluded—"

"Yes, yes," Matthieu interrupted. "The rest of the police have settled on your brother as the only suspect. That's why I want to talk to him."

"So, you're not working with the police?" Phillipe asked.

"I am, of course, but on my own accord."

"Do they know that you're here?"

"That's not important," Matthieu said. "What is important is that I get to Pierre before they do. If they make the connection and find out that you've been harboring Pierre here—" he paused for a moment. "Well, you have two young children in the house, Monsieur Pelletier. It would be a shame if they were to get caught up in the middle of this."

Phillipe had been just about ready to trust Matthieu and turn his brother in, but the trust quickly faded. He didn't appreciate Matthieu using his children as a weapon against him. He had decided instead that the Detective had worn out his welcome.

"I agree with you, Detective," Phillipe said.

Matthieu glanced around the room again, waiting for some admission on the part of Phillipe. There was none. The metronome of the clock filled the silence, rhythmically ticking on in the living room.

"I'm sorry, Detective," Phillipe continued. "I wish I could help you; I truly do. But I believe that there's nothing else that I can do."

Matthieu frowned.

"Of course," he said. He glanced around again before finally deciding. "Alright, Monsieur. I guess that I'll get out of your hair."

He began to walk towards the front door when the coat closet caught his attention again. He remembered when Phillipe had subconsciously glanced over at it. Matthieu walked over to it and thrust the door open.

"Aha!" He exclaimed.

The closet was completely empty except for the Pelletier family's winter coats and jackets.

"I think it's time for you to leave," Phillipe reminded him.

"Right," Matthieu said. "Of course."

He closed the closet door and proceeded back to the front.

"It's been a pleasure meeting you, Detective," Phillipe said, trying his best to will Matthieu out of the house. He pulled the door and held it open for him.

"Likewise," Matthieu said. He had the bitter taste of dissatisfaction on his tongue. He walked through the door before turning back once more. "One more thing," he began again. "If your brother does try to contact you, please call me. I would really hate to see you get wrapped up as an accomplice in all of this."

He reached into his pocket and pulled out a business card. He handed the card to Phillipe who took it and stuffed it carelessly into his own pocket. Phillipe couldn't tell briefly if this was genuine concern, or a vague threat. Either way, he wasn't prepared to give in.

"Like I said over the phone already," Phillipe began. Matthieu could sense the agitation in his voice, no matter how much Phillipe tried to mask it. "You'll be the first person I call."

Matthieu conjured the best smile that he could and then disappeared into his car.

Pierre burst out from another closet in the front foyer when Matthieu had driven away.

"That was *too* close," he exclaimed. His hair was a damp mess of nervous sweat.

"For all of us," Phillipe said and began to walk away.

"Thank you for covering for me," Pierre said, trailing after him. "But why'd you do it?"

"Because you stayed at my house last night and I didn't call him," Phillipe answered. "I already *am* an accomplice."

"You could have just told him that I threatened you or something if you didn't let me stay. But you covered for me instead."

It was just like the pearl necklace heist all over again, only this time, and with a lot more at stake, Phillipe hadn't turned his brother in.

"Thank you, Phillipe," Pierre said genuinely.

"I've got to start dinner," Phillipe said. "Penelope should be home soon."

"There's no need," Pierre informed him. "I've already prepared something."

Phillipe turned to his brother with a concerned look on his face. He wondered if there was something wrong with Pierre, because it wasn't like him to do something for anybody else.

43

Tuesday, the 3rd of January, 6:11 p.m.

Penelope sat at one end of the table, adjacent to Pierre. Her scowl was a little less visible tonight and her stare didn't feel nearly as hot in the back of Pierre's head. He thought that she must be warming up a little.

At the center of the table was the casserole that Pierre had prepared for the family. He had never made a casserole before. As a matter of fact, he had never made anything that didn't come from a box. However, the recipe that he found online for the ham and swiss casserole seemed easy enough to make. Even if it was virtually the same dish that they had had the night before, Phillipe did appreciate not having to cook.

Dinner was mostly silent. The boys chewed their food loudly and stared at their uncle as if it was the first time that they had been introduced to him all over again. At one point, Penelope did compliment the casserole and told Pierre that he would need to share the recipe. That was about as deep as the conversation got, but at least it was an improvement from the night before.

After dinner was over, Phillipe offered to clean the dishes and Penelope volunteered to help. The two of them disappeared behind the door to the kitchen, leaving Pierre alone with Pepin and Poitier. Pepin had been staring at him throughout the course of the meal, but now that they were alone with him, he was trying to avoid eye contact following last night's failed robbery attempt.

"You know why I caught you," Pierre began.

Pepin lifted his head shyly and shook it.

"It's because you lack the subtle nuances of expert thievery."

"What's a subtle nuance?" Poitier asked, butchering the words.

"It's just a fancy way of saying that you boys were too obvious," Pierre said. "Someone once told me that a great thief is like a magician. Do you boys like magic?"

They both nodded their heads.

"The difference between a good thief and a great thief is how well they can steal their audience's attention," Pierre said.

He grabbed one of the miniature race cars that the boys had set on the table in front of them. Their eyes followed his every move.

"And then deceive them using nothing more than sleight of hand or misdirection," he continued, concealing the car in one hand. "A good thief can steal something from you, but a great thief can make it disappear…"

He knocked his hands together and then opened the hand that previously concealed the car. His palm was empty.

"It's in your other hand," Pepin said in an unamused tone. Pierre thought that he was very snarky for a five-year-old. However, he still admired him because Pepin reminded Pierre a lot of himself. After all, Pierre was still basically a snarky five-year-old.

Pierre shrugged and opened his other hand. To the boy's dismay, his other hand was also empty.

The two boys looked at Pierre's empty hand in amazement and then at each other.

"Where'd it go?" Pepin demanded.

"Don't you see?" Pierre said and closed his hand again. "It was here all along."

He opened the original hand and there, resting in his palm was the miniature racing car. Pepin snatched it from Pierre's hand and studied it carefully with wonder and amazement.

Pierre sat back and laughed.

"How did you—" Pepin began, shocked.

"Now, you two have got the misdirection down," he said and motioned over to Poitier who had taken the dive on the carpet the evening before. "You just need to add a little subtlety."

Pierre could hear the faint rushing of water from the sink faucet in the kitchen. Before long, Penelope and Phillipe began talking again to each other in hushed whispers, but still loud enough for Pierre to hear.

"I have to admit," Penelope began. "It was very nice of your brother to make us dinner *and* clean the house. I really didn't think that he had a decent bone in his body."

Pierre grinned and gave the boys a thumbs up.

"I'm just as surprised as you are," Phillipe answered.

They returned to silence again for a moment as Pierre could hear the dishes clanging beyond the door.

"Can we also agree that the casserole was atrocious?" Penelope asked.

Pierre looked over at the kitchen door both shocked and offended.

Phillipe snickered.

"When you asked for the recipe, I almost lost it!"

"I don't think he realized that you're supposed to break the eggs *before* you put them in," Penelope said.

"I think my gums might still be bleeding!" Phillipe cried and the two giggled like school children.

"Shush," Penelope insisted, unsure if Pierre could hear them in the dining room. He could. Pierre's face was red with embarrassment.

"Anyways, it's the thought that counts," Penelope said. "Call it an act of good faith, if you will."

Pierre's face began to regain its normal color. He was still offended, but he could tell that her jest did seem to come from a good place. She really did seem to be warming up, until she continued talking.

"But you know that he can't stay here," she said.

"He's family," Phillipe tried.

"And what am I? What are our children? You would risk their safety to protect this brother of yours that you barely even know?"

Phillipe sighed.

"You're right," he decided.

Pierre's heart sank as he looked over at his two nephews across from him. They were listening in too and apparently, they could comprehend what this all meant, because they frowned towards him.

"Tonight's the last night," Penelope insisted. "After that, I don't care where he goes, but he can't stay here."

Pierre was crushed. He hoped for a minute that his brother would speak up and defend him. But he knew that Penelope was right. He was no good for any of them.

After the dishes were done, Pierre played miniature cars with his nephews for a while and taught them everything he knew about thievery before Phillipe put them both to bed. He came back downstairs and sat down on the couch across from Pierre, unsure of quite how to break the bad news to him.

Pierre decided to take the pressure off his brother, and he spoke first.

"I'm leaving tomorrow morning," he said. "First thing."

"You are?" Phillipe asked. He was surprised and slightly relieved. Although, there was also another feeling that was somewhere clouded in between those two, disappointment.

"I told you yesterday," Pierre said. "Two nights max."

"I've never taken you as a man of your word," Phillipe said. "But that's your decision."

Pierre nodded, leaving the two men alone in silence once again. Phillipe laid down on the couch and flipped over so that his back was facing Pierre. Pierre reached up for the lamp chain and turned off the light. He laid down and faced the ceiling. The space between them was filled with words that they wanted to say but didn't know how to.

"When this whole thing blows over," Phillipe finally said. "I hope that you'll come back."

Pierre brightened up immediately.

"You want me to come back?" He asked.

"I saw the way that you played with the boys tonight and I think they've really warmed up to you," he said. Pierre had mistakenly thought the same thing about Penelope. "I think that they need you in their lives."

He knew that he was saying it was for the boys, but it was really about what he, himself, needed, his older brother. He tried to suppress the feeling.

"Should we make this an annual thing?" Pierre joked, half-heartedly. "How about every time I'm running from the police, I'll use your apartment as a safe house. You know, you make a great accomplice."

"Don't say it like that," Phillipe chuckled.

Pierre smiled.

"What are you going to do now?" Phillipe asked.

"Right now," Pierre began. "I'm going to go to sleep, then I'm going to say goodbye to you all tomorrow and start my new life."

"New life, huh?" Phillipe asked. "Pierre Pelletier is a changed man after two days?"

"I mean it," Pierre said in all seriousness. "I'm out."

"Out of what?"

"Out of the game," Pierre decided, and he felt like he meant it.

Phillipe shook his head.

"So, you're telling me that Pierre Pelletier, the *Black Lotus*, is going to settle down and work a normal, nine to five job? Maybe start a family of his own?"

"Well, when you put it that way," Pierre said. "Does sound pretty unlikely, doesn't it?"

They both chuckled. For a moment, it felt like they were kids again, scheming in the bunk beds of their once-shared bedroom.

"You know," Phillipe began. "I guess there was a part of me that always knew that it was you."

"You're just saying that because the Detective told you all about it today," Pierre scoffed.

"I'm serious!" Phillipe insisted. "But you know what, truth be told, I knew that it was you and I was weirdly proud of that fact."

"You were proud of it?"

"In a deluded sort of way, yes," Phillipe said and laughed before becoming serious again. He didn't know quite how to phrase the next question that he wanted to ask. So, he stumbled through it. "Were you really there that night, Pierre?"

Pierre sighed.

"I was there," he admitted. "But I swear to you, I never killed Boutrel."

Phillipe turned over and stared at his brother.

"I believe you," he finally said.

"You do?" Pierre asked, in disbelief.

"I do, and you know what else?"

"What?"

"I honestly think that the Detective does too."

"No way," Pierre insisted.

"I'm serious," Phillipe said. "I think that guy honestly believes you."

"So, what are you suggesting, that I go and turn myself into him?"

"I mean, you can do whatever you want, Pierre. But I think that he might honestly be the only friend that you've got. The news is out here painting you as a murdering, criminal mastermind."

Well, they're two-thirds of the way right, Pierre thought.

"I can't do it," he decided. "I just can't. I've got to figure this thing out for myself."

"Is that why Colette was here today?"

"What?" Pierre stuttered.

"Colette," Phillipe continued. "Are you two starting your own amateur detective agency? Whatever happened to the two of you anyways?"

"What do you mean?" Pierre answered.

"I just got to thinking when she was here yesterday," Phillipe continued. "You two used to be as thick as thieves—pardon the expression, but you know what I mean. I always thought that after you had worked through whatever it was that you were working through that you two would end up together."

Pierre considered this for a moment.

"I guess we were always just on two different trajectories," he decided. Yet, somehow, fate had brought them back together again. Or, maybe it wasn't fate, maybe it was something that Pierre had wanted all along, and *that* was why he had called her specifically for the Boutrel mission.

"That's a load of bull and you know it," Phillipe said.

Pierre knew that he was probably right.

"Pierre?" Phillipe called after a brief period of silence.

"Yeah?" Pierre called back.

"Maybe I can convince Penelope to let you stay a little longer," he said. "Just until you're back on your feet and we can sort this thing out together."

Pierre didn't know what to say, but he felt an actual tear forming in his eye.

"You don't have to do that for me, Phillipe," Pierre said, choking back his emotions.

"I want to," Phillipe insisted. "Anyways, go to bed. I can tell that you're crying over there. We'll sort everything out tomorrow."

"I'm not crying," Pierre said. "I've got allergies."

Phillipe rolled his eyes and turned over on the couch.

Pierre stared up at the ceiling before finally speaking again.

"Phillipe?" He called.

"Hmm?"

"I'm sorry," Pierre said. "For everything. You were right, I should have been there for you."

Phillipe grabbed a throw pillow off the couch and threw it over at Pierre.

"Go to sleep," he said.

Pierre laid there awake with the possibilities swarming around in his head. For the first time in as long as he could remember, he felt like he belonged somewhere. However, the doubt started to creep into Pierre's mind.

Pierre, of course, had his demons. He had done bad things in his life that he knew he could never undo. He knew that even though it seemed like he was being presented with a choice, it really wasn't a choice at all. He had outrun his demons so far, but they would always be there, and they were just now starting to catch up to him.

"*So, I guess you were just going to forget about me, Pierre?!*" The voice of a woman demanded from Pierre's pocket.

It was the Han Sapphire necklace, just one of his many demons. Only, this time, it wasn't the voice of Lucinda, the ex-girlfriend that had pined after Pierre. It was the voice of Valerie Vivian, the girl in high school that used to abuse Pierre both physically and emotionally. He had decided one day to get her back by stealing from her, but she had found out and beat him to a pulp. Now, she was back again for her revenge.

"Never," Pierre insisted.

This was true for both the necklace and for Valerie. Pierre would never forget either of them. No matter how much he wanted to.

"*That's so sweet that you and your brother are going to spend the holidays together,*" the necklace mocked. "*Maybe swap Christmas cards.*"

"What do you want, Valerie?" Pierre spoke, barely above a whisper.

"*You know, as well as I do, that you're only going to drag this family down with you.*"

"That's not true," Pierre insisted.

"*Of course, it's true. You're nothing, Pierre. Worse than nothing, in fact. All you ever were was a parasite. You suck the life out of whatever you cling to and then you're gone. You were going to do the same to them!*"

"No," Pierre tried.

"*Yes, Pierre,*" the necklace insisted. "*They're better off without you. Everyone is better off without you!*"

"No!" Pierre shouted.

"Hmm?" Phillipe called back from a dead sleep.

"Nothing," Pierre whispered. "Go back to sleep."

"Okay, honey," Phillipe replied from his dream state.

The necklace was silent for the rest of the night, but its words remained. Pierre tried to convince himself that everything that he had heard was a lie, but it was no use. Of course, they weren't actual words, because

196

the necklace's words were his own thoughts. Everyone *was* better off without him. Maybe everyone's lives would have been better if the illness that he had suffered from as a child would have just taken him long ago. There was no way that Pierre could hope to stay here long term, no matter how much he wanted to. It was just a matter of time before Matthieu, or equally as bad, Genevieve, returned with a warrant. If they found that Pierre was hiding out there, Phillipe would have been arrested and Pepin and Poitier would grow up without a father.

As much as Pierre tried to fall asleep and escape the thoughts, he could not. Sleep was the only thing that would escape Pierre again tonight.

44

Wednesday, the 4th of January, 6:15 a.m.

Phillipe was awakened violently the next morning by a heavy pounding on the front door that rattled the whole building.

"Jesus!" He exclaimed before calming himself back down. "What's with all of these visitors lately?"

He shuffled over to the door, still grumbling to himself, and opened it in a haze. His eyes were still a bit crusted shut but when he looked outside, they opened as wide as golf balls. The day that Pierre had anticipated had come much sooner than he had anticipated it so. There, on Phillipe's front lawn, was an entire SWAT team of police officers wearing bulletproof vests and heavily armed with semi-automatic weapons strapped across their chests. They were surrounding the entire apartment building and had barricaded off the street. Phillipe turned his attention to the woman at the front whom he did not recognize.

"Can I help you?" He stammered.

"My name is Detective Genevieve Gereaux," she said. "I'm with the Toulouse Police Department, Art Crime and Thefts Division."

"Art Crime and Thefts Division?" Phillipe stuttered.

"Monsieur Pelletier," Genevieve continued. "We have a warrant to search your home."

She slapped the piece of paper into Phillipe's open hand and then pushed her way inside. She was followed by nearly a dozen officers.

"You can't just come in here," Phillipe stammered.

"Yes, we can," Genevieve assured him. "It says so in the warrant."

She directed a handful of officers upstairs and told another few to search around back. Phillipe scanned the contents of the warrant. In his disorientated, sleepy haze, the words seemed like a jumbled mess of letters and he couldn't make out anything on the page.

"I have rights!" He insisted.

"Not today," Genevieve replied.

Phillipe could hear a scream come from upstairs followed by the sound of his children crying. When he looked back at Genevieve, she was grinning smugly. He thought for a minute about punching her square in the nose but decided instead to be with his family. He ran upstairs to comfort them.

The officers were tearing through the upstairs of the apartment. They were ripping doors open and throwing things carelessly onto the floor. Penelope had run in her nightgown into the boy's room and that was where Phillipe found them all huddled together. She was shaking.

Phillipe put his arms around all of them.

"What's going to happen to Uncle Pierre?" Pepin asked, sweetly.

Penelope scowled.

She thought for a minute about throwing it back into her husband's face that "Uncle Pierre" was the cause of this nightmare that they were currently living. But she could tell by the look on his face that her husband was fully aware, and he was terrified of the repercussions. She wondered briefly if he was more terrified about the trauma that this would have on their children, or if he was more concerned that they would find his brother.

"I don't know," was all that Phillipe could say.

After nearly a half hour of searching, the officers stormed back down the stairs and into the foyer. Phillipe could hear Genevieve's voice coming from downstairs.

"What do you mean you didn't find him?!" She demanded. "Look again!"

She stomped up the stairs and into the boy's bedroom before locking eyes with Phillipe.

"Where is he, Monsieur Pelletier?" She demanded.

"I don't know what you're talking about," Phillipe answered.

"Don't play coy with me," Genevieve replied. "Your brother, Pierre! Where is he?!"

"He's not here. He never *was* here. I haven't seen my brother in thirteen years!"

"Well, if he's not here, then where is he?!"

"Isn't that your job to figure out, *Detective*?" Phillipe mocked. "It's just as I told the other Detective yesterday."

"The other Detective?" Genevieve repeated.

"The one from all the newspapers, Matthieu, I believe his name was."

"Detective Matthieu was here?"

"Just yesterday. He didn't come in nearly as brazenly as you all did, but he pushed his way in, nonetheless. I gave him a look around the apartment but he didn't find anything, just like you won't."

Genevieve shook some sense back into her head.

"We just want to ask your brother a few questions," she said.

"Is that why you brought the guns and bulletproof vests with you?" Phillipe replied. "Storming into my house, trying to scare my family. You should be ashamed of yourself!"

"Monsieur Pelletier, your brother is a dangerous fugitive! If it means that I have to storm into a dozen more homes along this block, scaring every mother and child along the way, I would do it one thousand times over!"

Phillipe stared into her eyes.

"And, if I find out that he was here, you're going to be in a world of trouble, Monsieur Pelletier."

With that, Genevieve stormed out of the room and back downstairs. She barked orders at the officers that were present down below.

To be honest, Phillipe was just as confused by all of this as she was. Pierre had been there just last night, and Phillipe had told him that he was going to speak on his behalf with Penelope to let Pierre stay a little longer. Either, Pierre was just good at hiding, or he really was a ghost after all.

Eventually, when the initial fuss had died down, Penelope was able to get ready for work and then took the minivan and dropped the kids off at school. Phillipe took a personal day from work so that he could monitor the police activity in the apartment. If they found anything, he wanted to be there. However, he was glad that the rest of his family had left, just in case they did find something. If it came down to it, he didn't want them to see him led out in handcuffs.

Fortunately, no handcuffs would be necessary. Hours passed before Genevieve was finally convinced that Pierre wasn't here. She still wasn't convinced that he had never been here, but she found nothing to even support that theory.

Slowly, but surely, the officers began filing out of the apartment. Genevieve was the last of them to leave.

"You'll be hearing from my lawyers," Phillipe said to her as she left, trying to sound intimidating before he remembered that he *was* his lawyer. "Me, I mean."

"I'm sorry to have taken up your time," Genevieve grunted, slightly embarrassed as she brushed past Phillipe towards the door.

Phillipe slammed the green door shut, nearly hitting her with it on the way out. He found himself finally alone in the apartment and he looked around both relieved and confused. He remained by the door and listened intently as the last officer drove off.

"Pierre?" He finally called out.

There was no response.

"Pierre?" He tried again. "I know that you're here."

There was still no answer.

Phillipe shrugged. He wondered if maybe Pierre had found some tight little crawl space and was just struggling to get out of it before he presented himself in typical grand fashion. Only, he never did.

While he was waiting, Phillipe decided to clean up the house. The search party left his apartment looking like the aftermath of a war zone. He picked up the living room first, then the kitchen before heading upstairs. All in all, it probably took him another couple of hours until the place was finally clean enough.

That afternoon, he finally changed out of his silk pajamas and tossed them into the overflowing hamper. He decided that it would probably be best to start a load of laundry.

So, he carried the hamper downstairs and set it by the washing machine in a closet off the kitchen. He reached up for the bottle of liquid detergent on the shelf and poured some into the machine as he opened the door. When he opened the door, he accidentally dropped the open bottle of liquid detergent on the floor and it began to ooze out. He reached into the door of the washing machine in awe.

The search party had, of course, searched behind the washing machine, but they had neglected to look inside of it, thankfully.

Within it, he found the silk pajamas that he had loaned to Pierre in the days before, folded up neatly at the bottom of the washing machine. What had surprised Phillipe wasn't the fact that Pierre had folded his own clothes. What did was the black lotus origami flower that had been placed neatly on top of them.

45

Wednesday, the 4th of January, 6:08 a.m.

It was a good thing that Pierre left when he did. There was no deceit or elaborate escape plans this time. He simply slipped out through the front door before Phillipe woke up, and just moments before the SWAT team had arrived that morning.

If this were a story with a sappy ending, Pierre would have chosen to move past his life of crime and live out the remainder of his days with his estranged brother and his family, atoning for his sins and trying to make up for all of the lost time. Unfortunately, there was one key factor that wouldn't allow Pierre to have a sappy ending, he was still a wanted murderer.

Nevertheless, if he was going to get his, he needed to solve this mystery without the help of the police and clear his own name.

He held out his cellphone in one hand and stared down at the contact that he had opened it up to. He was contemplating what to say when his finger slipped, and the phone began ringing.

"Well, well, well," came the familiar voice of Colette from the other end of the phone before she was interrupted. If he was going to clear his own name, he would probably need the funds to do so. He needed to get rid of the necklace anyways, why not try to sell it?

"Yeah, yeah, yeah," Pierre said. "We get it, if it isn't the infamous Pierre Pelletier. Why is that always the first thing that you say?"

"Did you call me to criticize me?" She asked. Her voice was direct.

"I called you because I have the necklace. I'm in."

"Took you long enough to come around," she said. "I'll pick you up. Where are you?"

Pierre looked around and noticed a small cafe behind him. He hadn't walked very far from his brother's apartment. As a matter of fact, it was still within sight, just across the street and down the ways a little.

"I'm in front of the Cafe de la Paix," Pierre said, reading off the sign of the cafe behind him.

"So am I," Colette said.

Pierre looked around wildly until he saw Colette waving at him from behind the cafe window.

"I figured that you would change your mind," she said. "So, I stuck around."

She paid her bill in cash and then left the cafe. Pierre was glancing over his shoulder nervously when she emerged and began leading him to her car parked just down the street.

It was not more than a minute before they reached Colette's car, a small, peach Peugeot, that the SWAT team arrived at Phillipe's apartment and stormed out onto the lawn. If Pierre had left the house five minutes later, he would have been caught in the firestorm.

Colette peeled off slowly in the opposite direction of the SWAT team.

"So, can I see it?" She began.

Pierre reached into his pocket and pulled out the Han Sapphire necklace. She followed the swaying motion of the necklace almost as if it had her hypnotized. There was that strange power that the necklace seemed to have again.

Pierre was watching the expression on her face with an uneasy feeling. When he turned back to face the road, they had veered a little into the other lane.

"Colette!" Pierre cried.

Colette looked forward again and swerved just as a car in the other lane blazed past them in the opposite direction, blaring its horn. Pierre slipped the necklace back into his pocket and breathed a heavy sigh of relief.

"Where are we going?" he asked.

"Marseilles," Colette answered without looking at him.

Pierre turned to look out of the passenger side window.

"I see that you're growing out your beard," Colette began.

Pierre stroked the rough stubble that had grown in patches across his face.

"It's my depression beard," he said.

"Depression beard?" Colette repeated.

"You know, like in the movies."

"I'm not following."

"In movies, during times of hardship, the protagonist always grows out a beard to signify their depression visually. Then, they shave it off right before the climax to signify the start of a new beginning."

Colette rolled her eyes.

"You're so dramatic," she said. "I'll give you a few minutes to sulk, but that's all you get."

Pierre sighed heavily and continued to stare out through the window at the buildings as they passed by.

––––––––––

"Who is it?" Pierre finally asked.

"Who?"

"The buyer," Pierre said.

Colette was silent.

"I don't have a name," she said.

Pierre turned to face her.

"You don't have a name?!" he repeated in disbelief.

"It's not that strange," Colette said. "We work with people all the time and we don't know their last names. Anonymity is important in this business."

"I think the circumstances have changed," Pierre said. "We have to be even more careful now. How do we know this isn't a sting operation?"

"It's not a sting operation," Colette assured him. "And before you ask, no, I'm not wearing a wire. And no, you may not strip search me."

"Well, do they know who we are?"

"If you're asking if they know who *you* are, all of France knows who you are by now, Pierre."

"So, they know me, but I don't know them. That seems to put us at a disadvantage. How do you even know that you can trust them?"

Colette was silent for a moment again.

"I don't," she finally said. "But that's the nature of our business."

"The nature of our business is based on nothing *but* trust!"

"So, you're a philosopher now?" Colette mocked. "Either way, Descartes, I don't have a name, so I don't know what you want me to tell you."

"How did you get into contact with them?" Pierre asked.

"What is this, twenty questions? It was through a mutual acquaintance. They called me. Especially now that it's been so highly publicized, everyone wants a piece of it."

"Wouldn't that make it less valuable?" Pierre asked.

"How should I know? High risk, high reward. All that I know is that the buyer wants it and they're willing to pay us a hefty price for it."

"How much?"

"€50 million."

Pierre stammered.

"Where are we meeting them?" he asked.

"They haven't given me the rendezvous point, yet," she said. "Just told me to meet them somewhere in Marseilles. But sometime today they're supposed to call me with details."

Pierre shook his head.

"I've got a bad feeling about this, Colette," he said.

"Do you trust me, Pierre?" She asked.

Now, there was a loaded question. Pierre didn't know if he could trust anyone. He thought about it for a moment and then nodded his head.

"Then, trust me, Pierre," she continued. "Besides, how can things possibly get much worse than they are now?"

Pierre could think of a few ways off the top of his head, but he decided to keep them to himself.

He spent the rest of the, roughly, eight-hour car ride gazing silently out of the window. Pierre was lost in thought, thinking about everything that he had just walked away from, and tried to rationalize his decision with everything that he was walking toward. He had closed the door on a life with his family for the time being, but he had still left it slightly ajar to return. It was, of course, a long shot that he would be able to clear his name and come away with his fortune, but the fantasy seemed to work out in his head.

A few hours into the trip, Colette's phone rang. She answered it, holding it against the ear opposite Pierre. He tried to listen in, but he couldn't hear the person on the other end of the call.

"We're on our way," Colette said.

She was silent and Pierre could hear faint, indistinguishable rumbling from the phone's speaker.

"Yes," Colette said. "We have the necklace…we'll be there."

Short and sweet. She hung up the phone and Pierre stared at her. Colette didn't look back at him. She was focused on the road in front of her. Pierre eventually looked away and continued his silence.

A few times throughout the course of the trip, Colette did look over to make sure that he was still awake. It wasn't like Pierre at all to be in a confined space with her and not be constantly trying to hit on her. For a moment, he seemed so human again.

———

They arrived in Marseilles that afternoon where they rented a motel room with cash. Colette had a small travel bag with her, Pierre had nothing more than the clothes on his back and the priceless Han Sapphire necklace in his pocket.

Their motel room wasn't a large room by any means. There was a separate bedroom off the living room with only a single bed and a small living room with a couch that sat across from the TV. Pierre would be spending another evening on the couch.

"What do we do now?" He asked, once they were settled.

"I have the location," Colette said. "Let's go get our money."

They left the stuffy motel room and the Peugeot behind in the parking lot. They walked a little way along the Quai de Rive, the paved pathway that ran right alongside the water line, admiring the Mediterranean Sea shining brilliantly in the afternoon sun. Along the way, Pierre managed to pickpocket a cap and a pair of sunglasses from some unsuspecting tourists to help himself blend in. After all, his face was everywhere these days. Apparently, the detail of the lotus flower had been leaked to the press and the same media that made the Black Lotus into a hero was now painting him as a villain.

Colette led him along the path until they arrived at the ferry port. She walked over to the booth and stood in the small line that had formed in front of the window. Pierre couldn't help but notice that she looked nervous.

"What's this?" Pierre asked.

He read the sign above the booth window, it had prices listed for guided tours of the Château d'If.

"This is where our buyer wants to meet," Colette said. "The Château d'If."

"I think that I've had enough châteaus for one lifetime," he answered.

Colette rolled her eyes in the way that only she could.

"Maybe you can pick up a little culture while we're here," she said.

When they reached the front of the line, she purchased two tickets for the ferry. They boarded it and shortly after, it began its voyage across the Mediterranean Sea.

Pierre was slumped down in his seat, keeping a paranoid eye on all the tourists around him. Every one of them seemed to be looking at him strangely, especially the man sitting a few rows behind with a cap pulled down over his face and big sunglasses. Pierre couldn't get a good look at his face without looking overly suspicious. What made matters even worse was, on the ferry, there was nowhere for Pierre to run except for jumping overboard, and Pierre was never a good swimmer.

Finally, off in the distance, an island with a massive stone fortress sprung up along the horizon. Pierre forgot everything for a moment and gawked at the impressiveness of it.

"Pretty neat, huh?" Colette asked, noticing his increased interest.

Pierre remained silent.

"Have you ever heard of the Count of Monte Cristo?" She asked.

"I can't say that I have," he answered.

"You've lived in France your whole life and you've *never* heard of the Count of Monte Cristo?"

"Alright," Pierre said. "I don't go around pointing out all of the things that you don't know about."

"Yes, you do," she reminded him. "All of the time."

Pierre rolled his eyes.

"It's a book, written by Alexander Dumas," she continued. "A man is falsely imprisoned in the Château d'If for about twenty years but manages to escape and exact an elaborate revenge scheme on the people who put him there."

Pierre could appreciate the parallels between this Count of Monte Cristo and his own situation. He didn't think that he could make it twenty years in prison.

"Is that supposed to be a metaphor for me?" Pierre asked.

"No," Colette answered. "It's just a good book."

"How does he escape?" Pierre asked.

"I guess that you'll just have to read the book and find out, won't you, Pierre?"

"I'll wait to see the movie," Pierre replied, gazing upon the massive stone architecture. He couldn't imagine a real-life scenario where a real person could break out of here. He seriously doubted that there were any air ducts.

When the ferry made port, they got off and walked around for a bit inside of the fortress while Colette kept glancing nervously at her cell phone. Pierre studied the prison cells that had been transformed into tourist attractions, but it was almost as if he could still feel the helplessness that anyone imprisoned here must have felt.

At the base, the Château opened to a lawn with a magnificent scene of the Mediterranean Sea. It was like something out of a painting. The sea looked like glass that continued forever into the horizon of the setting sun.

Pierre glanced over at Colette whose hazel eyes reflected the glimmer of sun off the water. He was about to speak when he was interrupted by her cell phone ringing. She answered it.

"Hello?" she called into it.

Pierre heard rumbling coming from the speaker.

"On our way," Colette said and clicked off the phone.

She turned to Pierre.

"They're downstairs," she said.

Pierre could feel his heart thumping in his chest as they proceeded down the large stone steps to an underground area of the Château d'If. Colette slipped under a chain that was there to prevent visitors from going deeper, but, since they had already committed one felony this week, trespassing didn't bother them.

At the base of the staircase, they found themselves in a long, dark hallway. At the other end of the hallway, a flickering light was pouring through. Suddenly, a hooded figure emerged from the shadows. Pierre felt Colette grasp his hand with her own.

The figure stared at them for a tense moment. Outside, the horn from the ferry blared loudly, signaling that it would soon be making its last return to port.

Colette and Pierre were frozen in place, staring back at the hooded figure down the hallway, until they heard the sound of a footstep on the stone floor behind them. They immediately turned and saw a man standing there in the shadows. It was the same man that Pierre had been suspicious of before on the ferry, wearing a hat and large sunglasses.

The man began stuttering like a fool.

"Oh my," he said. "This isn't the restroom."

Pierre and Colette turned back and saw the hooded figure disappear frantically back into the shadows. Colette took Pierre's arm and led him off in the other direction, brushing past the man that had accidentally followed them down there and back up the stairs.

"What happened?" Pierre asked.

"Something's not right," Colette said.

They boarded the last ferry back to the port of Marseilles, just before it departed. The strange man that had gotten turned around on his way to the restroom and had accidentally followed them underground, further down into the Château d'If, boarded just after them. He took a seat behind them, in the shadows. Pierre still couldn't get a good look at his face, but the man didn't concern him. He seemed like a blubbering halfwit. The ferry departed soon afterwards and then arrived back at the port of Marseilles. They headed straight back to the motel and Colette closed the blinds on the windows.

"What happened back there?" Pierre asked.

Colette was cautiously peering through the blinds.

"I'm not sure," she said.

"Why did that hooded figure run?" Pierre asked.

"I'm not sure!" Colette snapped.

"Do you think that bumbling idiot that was looking for the restroom spooked them?"

"Maybe," Colette said.

"Well what do we do now?" Pierre asked. "Can you call them?"

Colette shook her head.

"I don't have a number," she replied.

"So, we're at their mercy," Pierre remarked. "That's just great."

He sat on the couch and flipped on the TV.

"How can you be so calm?" Colette asked.

"Well, what else are we supposed to do?" Pierre asked. "If they're really that interested in the necklace then they'll call back. Until then, we can't really do anything else. Why are you so nervous?"

Colette was silent, so Pierre searched through the on-demand movies on the motel room TV.

"Maybe we can see if they have your Count of Monte Cristo," he suggested.

He was able to find a version of the film that was produced in 1961, in all its technicolor glory.

Colette kept watch through the window blinds, but eventually, she joined him on the couch.

She was stiff when she sat down and he could notice how heavy the bags looked under her eyes. She let out an exasperated sigh as the back of her head hit the couch cushion. It wasn't more than fifteen minutes later that Pierre heard Colette snoring like an old man. She snored heavily and for a moment after each snore, it sounded like she had stopped breathing. The lack of breathing was frightening, but Pierre thought that her snoring was cute. A couple of times, Pierre thought that she may have stopped breathing entirely and had to elbow her awake.

The third time he did so, she came to and glanced around the room in a daze before putting her head back down. Only, this time instead of resting her head back on the couch, she rested it on Pierre's shoulder and nestled herself into him.

Pierre looked down at her and smiled as he brushed the loose hairs from her face.

I could get used to this, he thought.

"*Who is she?*" The necklace called back, jealously.

"Oh, pipe down," Pierre whispered, and the necklace was quiet.

He decided right at that moment, with the drool dripping out of her mouth and pooling on his shirt sleeve, that once they sold the necklace, he was going to forget about everything else. He was going to take Colette and run away together, something that he should have done years ago. Pierre decided that he was going to find that secret beach with the glistening waterfall in the tropical paradise from the postcard he had pinned up in his room. He could send his brother a Christmas card from there every year and live out the rest of his days in peace.

That sounded good to him.

46

Wednesday, the 4th of January, 4:37 p.m.

"I'm going to kill him," the Chief mumbled into the phone. "Are you absolutely sure that it was him?"

"Pierre's brother said that it was Matthieu," Genevieve informed him. "He recognized him from the papers. He said that he came by yesterday and had a look around the apartment."

She had parked her black SUV a little bit down the street from the Pelletier residence, but still within eyesight. She watched the front door intently for any signs of movement.

"Well, he better have a good explanation for all of this," the Chief declared.

"If he does, he doesn't seem to want to share it with us," Genevieve informed him.

"What do you mean?"

"He's not answering his phone. He sends it straight to voicemail every time."

"I'll try to call him after we hang up here," the Chief said. "What does he think he's doing over there?"

"From the sound of it, he's gone rogue."

"I would have to agree," the Chief said and began rubbing his temples. "I knew that it was probably a bad idea to give him his gun back. Reinstating him at all was probably a bad idea."

Genevieve mumbled a grunt of agreement.

"So, there was no sign that Pierre was there?" The Chief asked.

"None whatsoever," Genevieve replied. "If he was here, he must have left some time yesterday after Matthieu tipped him off."

"What are you going to do now?"

"I'm going to stay here just a little longer and stake out the house," she said. "Maybe now that everything seems to have died down, he'll show himself again."

"Matthieu or Pierre?"

"Either would suffice," Genevieve answered.

The Chief sighed.

"Alright, but afterwards I want you to come straight back here," he said. "We need to start thinking about other contingencies. If Pierre is no longer in Paris, then he could be anywhere in France right now. Matthieu, on the other hand, is a loose cannon as well, maybe even more dangerous than Pierre. Oh, what a mess, what a mess…"

"I'll wrap things up here and then head back to Toulouse, Chief," Genevieve informed him. "I should be back late tonight. Don't wait up."

The Chief grunted and then hung up the phone. Without hanging up the receiver, he dialed Matthieu's cell phone number. It rang twice and then went to his voicemail. He had screened the call and purposely ignored it. The Chief tried again. It rang twice and then went to his voicemail once more. He waited until the beep and then left a scathing message.

"Matthieu," he began, his face was becoming red with rage. "I know that you're there. If you don't call me back immediately with a good explanation of what you're doing, then whatever you *are* doing will be the last thing you ever do…as a police officer. Call me back when you get this."

He hung up the phone and then turned around and stared at the bust of himself on the shelf behind him.

"What are we going to do?" He mumbled.

47

Wednesday, the 4th of January, 4:43 p.m.

Matthieu's phone rang again as he carelessly pressed the button on the side to send the call straight to his voicemail. He wasn't currently accepting any calls, not until he had something concrete. But, boy, was he close.

The phone rang again shortly after. Matthieu sent the call to voicemail again without averting his eyes from what was in front of him.

He was parked in his blue Renault just across the street from a cheap Marseilles' motel and was staring straight ahead at room 217. Parked just underneath the room was the peach Peugeot that he had tailed here.

He had put in a call to Simone St. Clair back at the station and she confirmed that the Peugeot was registered to Colette Couvrir, just as Matthieu had suspected. He now had an identity for the mystery woman that he had seen Pierre leaving Paris with.

When Matthieu had been unsuccessful in finding Pierre at his brother's apartment the day before, he wasn't ready to give up easily. He staked out the building for the next twelve hours. With no signs of movement, he was just about to give up when who else showed his pretty, little face early this morning, but Pierre. He watched nearly the entire Paris police force pull up on the lawn just moments later.

He could have taken him down there, but he decided, instead, to follow him and try to catch him in the act of something. So, he tailed the peach Peugeot all the way from Toulouse to Marseilles, where it stopped at the cheap motel that he was now sitting across from. He watched Pierre and Colette head into the rental office and then upstairs to room 217, where they currently were.

Before long, they emerged from the room. Matthieu thought that this was strange. If he were Pierre, he would have stayed there until he had to leave. Matthieu wondered if this was it, if this was the moment that he had been waiting for. Pierre was on the move.

Matthieu put the blue Renault in drive and pulled off slowly. He hung a little bit back to not arouse suspicion and followed the pair along the Quai de Rive. Matthieu watched Pierre swipe a cap and sunglasses from a couple of unsuspecting tourists and continued to trail them until they stopped at the ferry port. There, he pulled into the parking lot and decided to trail them on foot.

Matthieu grabbed his own cap and sunglasses from the backseat of his car. He fitted the cap onto his head and slid the sunglasses over his eyes.

He examined himself in the rearview mirror. It was a weak disguise, but it would probably do as long as he lurked in the shadows. He got out of the car and then waited in line a few people behind Pierre and Colette at the booth. When he got to the front, he purchased a ticket for one.

On the ferry, he sat a couple of rows behind them and while everyone else was looking out of the windows at the beautiful, sprawling sea, his eyes were locked on Pierre, slumped over in his seat. He wasn't going to let him escape this time. Matthieu wondered what he could possibly be up to now.

When the ferry docked, he followed Pierre and Colette through the Château d'If and watched from an upper level window as the pair gazed out at the sea. He watched as Colette answered her cell phone and then began leading Pierre down into the depths of the Château. Matthieu stayed close behind.

He followed them down into the hallway, where he saw them standing across from a mysterious, hooded figure. He tried to get a closer look, but when he landed on the last step, he accidentally stumbled on a chip on the staircase and landed clumsily on the floor. Pierre and Colette turned around to face him and Matthieu grumbled the best excuse he could think of.

"Oh my, this isn't the restroom."

The hooded figure quickly disappeared, and Colette and Pierre brushed past Matthieu and back upstairs towards the ferry.

Matthieu followed them again. His cover had been exposed, but Pierre hadn't seemed to recognize him, thankfully.

When they caught the last ferry back to the port of Marseilles, Matthieu was just behind them. He and Pierre locked eyes for just a moment before he walked by him and returned to the shadows of the ferry. Matthieu followed them slowly back to the motel, creeping along in his blue Renault, and then parked across the street again. He watched Pierre and Colette head up to their room, where they retired for the night. He watched the door to room 217 for the rest of the evening.

48

Thursday, the 5th of January, 7:19 a.m.

Pierre woke up the next morning alone on the couch. The only thing that remained of Colette was the drool stain that she had left on his shoulder. He got up to peek into the bedroom to try to catch a glimpse of her sleeping peacefully. It was creepy, he knew, but he was in love. He never thought that he would say *that* word.

He crept over to the bedroom door and cautiously pushed it open. The door creaked lightly on its hinges. Pierre poked his head through to peek inside. When he did so, the room was completely empty. The bed was still made up as if it had never been slept in.

Pierre backed away slowly in disbelief. He reached his hand down instinctively for his pocket, feeling for the impression of the Han Sapphire necklace. There wasn't one.

He frantically reached for his other pocket which he found was also empty.

Before he had another moment to think, the handle of the door to the motel room began to jiggle.

It was a setup! He thought wildly.

Pierre stood there, frozen in horror as the handle clicked all the way and then pushed open. There in the doorway was Colette.

"Colette?!" Pierre stammered. This was the last person that he had expected to see.

"Get your stuff, Pierre," she said. Her voice was direct. "We need to leave. Now!"

"But you—" Pierre began, unsure of the words that his mouth was forming. Finally, he spat out, "where's the necklace?!"

"The necklace?" Colette repeated. "You have the necklace, Pierre! Tell me that you didn't lose the necklace."

Pierre reached for his pocket again which was still just as empty as it had been a moment ago.

"Pierre!" Colette cried.

"You have it," Pierre stuttered. "I saw the way that you were looking at it yesterday!"

"We don't have time for this, Pierre, we have to go, now!"

"What's the big hurry all of the sudden?" Pierre asked.

"I can tell you in the car. But, right now, we have to leave!"

"What about the necklace?" Pierre asked. "If you don't have it, then it's got to be around here somewhere…" Pierre began, searching frantically through the drawers of the motel room.

"You really lost it?" Colette asked. She frantically ran over to the couch where they had both slept the night before. "Did you check the couch cushions?"

Pierre joined her and together they dug their hands in between them. Pierre finally felt something smooth but with a few distinct corners, like the beautiful curves of a woman. He recognized these corners immediately and as he pulled the object out from in between the cushions, there she was in all of her glory, the Han Sapphire necklace.

"I thought I'd lost you again!" He declared and kissed the center of the sapphire.

"Thank God," Colette said with a sigh of relief. "Now, we have to go!"

They exited the motel room and down the flight of stairs where they met back up in Colette's peach Peugeot. Colette didn't waste any time in turning the car on and then peeling out of the motel parking lot.

Pierre couldn't help but notice that she kept glancing back at the rearview mirror.

"What's going on, Colette?" He asked.

"We're being followed," she said.

"Followed?" Pierre repeated and whipped around in his seat. "By whom?"

"Turn around, Pierre!" She ordered. Pierre did as he was instructed and faced forward again.

"Who is it?" Pierre asked once more.

"I'm not sure, I didn't recognize the person in the vehicle. But I noticed the blue Renault trailing us along the Quai de Rive yesterday afternoon and then again following us from the port of Marseilles back to the motel. I noticed it parked right across the street and I stepped out to see who was inside. It was the bumbling fool who was looking for the restroom yesterday. He followed us intentionally. Is there anybody that you know of that drives a blue Renault?"

Pierre considered this for a moment. It seemed familiar. He had seen a blue Renault a couple of times, but it always seemed like it was in the background of his memories. Then, it hit Pierre all at once.

He had first seen the blue Renault screaming down the street behind his apartment, trailing the ambulance that was coming from the direction of the Château de Boutrel the night of the soirée. Next, he saw the Renault parked just outside of the Toulouse Police Station. Finally, the blue Renault was parked in his brother's driveway when Matthieu had come to Phillipe's apartment looking for Pierre. The blue Renault belonged to Detective Matthieu.

"Oh, crap," Pierre exclaimed.

"What, what is it?" Colette asked.

"It's that Detective," he said. "The one that won't leave me alone."

Colette glanced over at the side view mirror and noticed the blue Renault just a few cars behind them.

"Does he look like the guy in the newspapers? The one standing over Boutrel's dead body?"

"He doesn't just look like that guy," Pierre said. "He *is* that guy."

"Crap," Colette agreed.

"Well, what do we do now?" Pierre asked.

"We lose him."

Colette made a sudden turn onto a side street. The blue Renault screeched on its wheels as it followed the turn.

"Dammit," Matthieu mumbled to himself. "I've been made!"

The peach Peugeot accelerated forward, leaving a cloud of dust behind it down the side street. The blue Renault sped up just to keep up with them.

Colette whipped the steering wheel and slammed down on the brake. She transferred her foot from the brake to the gas and jammed the pedal to the floor as she took off down a narrow, unpaved alleyway. Matthieu's reflexes weren't as fast and he missed the turn before slamming down on his own brakes. He backed up and then turned into the alleyway, but Colette had put a little bit of space between them.

Pierre and Colette bounced along the gravel alleyway which finally appeared to open to a busy, four-lane street up ahead. Pierre could see the early morning traffic whizzing by in front of them, but Colette didn't slow. In fact, she pressed down the gas pedal harder. Pierre went to let out a scream, but nothing came out.

A horn blared as they emerged from the alleyway and just narrowly avoided a collision with a large food delivery truck. Colette jerked the steering wheel in the opposite direction and the car skidded on two wheels before settling once again on all four. She never let up on the gas for a second and she took off down the street.

As Matthieu approached the end of the alleyway, he slammed on his brakes as the cars whizzed by in front of him. He cautiously looked both ways and only proceeded when the coast was completely clear on all sides. He followed the path that they had taken but found himself stuck at a red traffic light behind several other vehicles. He threw open his car door and stepped out, trying to survey the street ahead for any sign of them. When he looked out into the sea of cars, they were gone.

49

Thursday, the 5th of January, 7:36 a.m.

"Y ou've got a little drool on you," Colette said. She was still glancing neurotically through the rearview mirror.

Pierre looked down at his shoulder sleeve which still had the drool stain that had been left by Colette the night before.

"Where'd you learn to drive like that?" Pierre asked, carelessly trying to wipe the stain off.

"I didn't," Colette said. "That was just pure instinct."

"Well, whatever that was, it worked."

"I can't believe that guy followed us all the way here."

"He came by the apartment," Pierre began. "Phillipe's apartment, a few hours after you left."

Pierre looked over at Colette who still looked incredibly nervous.

"Don't worry," Pierre assured her. "He doesn't know about your involvement in any of this. I'm not even sure that he's working with the police anymore. I don't know what he's doing to be honest."

"Well, he knows about my involvement now," Colette said.

Truth be told, Pierre knew that Matthieu had suspected Colette's involvement before too. Especially when Pierre had accidentally let her name slip during his interrogation. However, leaving that part out seemed to be in his best interest.

"Anyways, what now?" Pierre asked.

Colette shook her head.

"For the time being, we have to stash the car until they call," she said.

They found an abandoned parking garage on the outskirts of the city where Colette dumped the car. They sat in the car in silence until the phone finally rang, startling both of them.

"Answer it!" Pierre said.

"I will, I will," Colette replied, and she took the call.

Pierre could still only make out the one side of the conversation.

"Hello?" Colette called into the phone.

There was rumbling on the other end.

"No, it wasn't like that at all—" Colette began before she was interrupted by more rumbling. "He tailed us there. He wasn't with us. Yes. Yes. Okay. Yes, I can do that."

With that, the line clicked dead.

"Well, that sounded like it went well," Pierre said.

"It's still on," Colette informed him. "But they've changed the location and they want us to meet tonight."

"What happens after that?" Pierre asked.

Colette was silent for a moment, almost like she was stumped by the simple question.

"Then we disappear with our money," she finally decided.

Together, Pierre wanted to add. She wasn't looking at him as he stared at her. Finally, she turned to face him and they stared into each other's eyes.

It was almost as if she was looking at him expectantly, like she was waiting for him to suggest they run away together, grab her by the shoulders and kiss her passionately on the lips.

Instead, Pierre said, "that sounds good to me."

Colette nodded her head.

"So, what do we do until tonight?" Pierre asked.

"No more day trips," she said. "We lay low for the rest of the day until the sun goes down."

Pierre agreed, but he still felt a pit in his stomach.

50

Thursday, the 5th of January, 2:06 p.m.

Matthieu patrolled the Marseilles' streets for hours with no sign of either Pierre, Colette, or the peach Peugeot. The police scanner on his dashboard was turned up to the maximum volume but nothing about any of them came over it. He thought for a moment that he was strangely more relieved that the police weren't looking for the Peugeot than he was disappointed that they had gotten away.

Matthieu also began to hope that Genevieve hadn't recognized his car at Phillipe Pelletier's apartment building. Undoubtedly, she was upset, and the Chief probably was none too thrilled either. In fact, Matthieu had received so many calls between the two of them since yesterday, that he had turned his phone on silent and tucked it away in the glove box. The Chief would, of course, forgive Matthieu when it would ultimately turn out that he was right. Genevieve he wasn't as concerned with. She could stay mad at him forever for all that he cared. In fact, he would prefer it, because that would mean that he had been right. She may have won the first few rounds, but Matthieu was going to win the game. For now, Matthieu was just relieved that the description of his own car wasn't being broadcasted over the police scanner.

A smug grin spread across his face, but quickly disappeared when he remembered that the one thing standing between him and his victory was locating Pierre. He had no idea where to go next.

So, he tried to place himself in Pierre's shoes. If he were Pierre, and he knew that Matthieu was hot on his tail, he would get out of Marseilles as fast as he could. What this meant for Matthieu was that Pierre could be anywhere in France within a roughly six-hour radius. You could nearly span the entire country in that amount of time, or even cross the border to Italy or Switzerland. He could even be halfway to Spain by now. Searching for Pierre would ultimately be a fruitless effort and a complete waste of time.

For the time being, Matthieu decided, he needed to take a different approach to this whole thing. That was when he was struck with an idea.

He reached into the glove box and pulled out his cellphone. He flipped the phone open and ignored the 48 missed calls and 12 voicemails. Matthieu reached back into the glove box where he retrieved the Post-it note with the phone number that he had requested before he had left, just in case it would come in handy.

He dialed the number into his phone. It rang three times before it was answered.

"Yes, hello, this is Detective Martin Matthieu with the Toulouse Police Department. I was wondering if you would be available to meet with me…Yes, today, if possible…I can be in Paris in about seven hours…I know a place, the Cafe de la Paix…around 9? Excellent, then I'll see you then."

He ended the call and then tapped the phone repeatedly to the side of his head. The familiar tingling in his fingers began again. It wasn't Pierre, but maybe the person he had just set up a meeting with could help find him or at least find out what Pierre was doing.

51

Thursday, the 5th of January, 8:48 p.m.

Nightfall didn't come quickly for either Pierre or Colette, but Pierre was somewhat glad that the transaction would be taking place at night instead of broad daylight, like yesterday. The *Black Lotus* was more of a nocturnal creature anyways.

Colette made the turn onto the dusty, dirt road and flipped off her headlights.

"Is this the place?" Pierre asked. In the dark, he could see the outline of tremendous concrete buildings. In the dim lighting from a few streetlamps, he could tell that the buildings were decaying. This place looked more like a place where you would have your organs harvested than a place for high end jewelry transactions.

"This is the address that they gave me," Colette said. Her voice was barely above a whisper and it was unsteady. Pierre looked at her curiously. She should have been excited. This was the beginning of the rest of their lives, but for some reason, she seemed incredibly nervous. She was acting as if this were the end.

She crept along the road until she finally saw the building that she was looking for. She turned the wheel and parked in front of it. Then, turned the key in the ignition and the soft purring of the engine quieted to nothing.

Pierre stared out through the passenger side window. There were no other cars around and not another soul in sight.

"Are you sure?" Pierre asked.

"Positive," Colette said.

Just before she pushed open the car door and got out, she glanced over at Pierre. She looked worried, but Pierre thought that she also looked distraught, like something was weighing on her. She turned away from him finally and got out of the car. Pierre followed.

Colette walked right up to the front door and pulled at the handle. Locked. Pierre glanced around until his eyes settled on a camera that was hanging from a crumbling corner of the building. The camera was pointed toward the front door, more specifically, right at them.

Suddenly, there was a jarring buzzing noise that came from a small intercom that rested on the side of the door. A man's voice followed the buzzing.

"You must be Colette," the man said. "Hold on, I'll buzz you in."

There was another jarring buzzing noise and Colette reached for the door handle. It was unlocked and the door opened effortlessly.

"Ladies first," Pierre insisted.

Colette graciously proceeded into the building. Pierre followed closely behind. The door closed behind them.

It was dark and damp within the stone walls of the building. Somewhere, Pierre could hear water dripping. The place reminded him of a cave. There was a faint glow from a desk lamp on the opposite end of the room. Pierre could make out the broad figure of a man who was seated at the desk in front of it.

"Not much security," Pierre mumbled.

"You should be more worried when it seems like there is no security," Colette whispered and then continued forward, towards the man.

She was right, Pierre would have been less worried if there had been armed guards out in front of the building. This encounter felt far more personal, and far more threatening. Pierre swallowed hard and followed. It seemed like there were threatening figures in every shadowy corner of the room.

When they got a little closer, Pierre could see that the man's attention was engaged elsewhere. He was tinkering away at something small that he held in his hands. The man placed the small object down on the desk carefully and then turned to them and rose from his seat. He had some sort of contraption around his head which Pierre recognized as a sort of magnifying head loop. It made the man's eyes look huge when viewing them through the other side.

218

The man stuck his hand out excitedly and smiled at them, revealing a set of brilliantly white teeth.

"Devereaux Dupin," the man said, exchanging his name freely.

Colette and Pierre were silent. They felt small in front of this intimidatingly large man.

"You must be Colette Couvrir and Pierre Pelletier," Devereaux said. "It's a pleasure to finally meet you both. It'll just be the two of you joining me this time, I hope?"

Pierre recoiled at the mention of his own name. Colette stuttered an affirmative that it was just the two of them, but Devereaux turned his attention to Pierre.

"Since she's Colette," Devereaux continued. "You must be the man that killed Bastien Boutrel."

Pierre stammered.

"I had nothing to do with that," he insisted.

Devereaux studied him cautiously for a moment and then let out a hearty burst of laughter.

"Ah, the old bastard had it coming," he said. "Besides, if you didn't get to him, his liver surely would have done him in."

Pierre was unsettled by the way Devereaux spoke so casually about another man's death. For all intents and purposes, Devereaux seemed like a nice guy, but there was a cold-blooded ruthlessness that seemed to reside just below the surface.

"Anyways," Devereaux continued. "Since we're through with the formalities, let's get down to business. You have the necklace, I presume? Of course, you do, no fool would walk into this meeting without it."

Pierre felt that that sounded vaguely like a threat. He reached into his pocket and caressed the necklace for a moment in his own hand. He turned it over a few times. His eyes remained locked on Devereaux's. Devereaux licked his lips and met Pierre's stare, greedily.

Finally, Pierre pulled the necklace out of his pocket and shined it up to the dull glow of the desk lamp. The Han Sapphire necklace sparkled magnificently, even in the dull lighting. Devereaux's eyes lit up on the necklace and he licked his lips once more. Pierre would have sworn that the man was salivating.

"The Han Sapphire necklace," Devereaux said, gluttonously. "May I?"

Pierre held the necklace out to the man but for an instant, hesitated to release it. Finally, though, he let go and Devereaux held it in his hands. It felt as if Pierre had just transferred a great power to someone else and for a moment, he felt empty inside.

"What now?" Colette demanded. She sounded direct, but Pierre could sense the trembling in her voice.

Devereaux let out another sharp burst of laughter that was almost frightening. Pierre tried to exchange a glance with Colette, but Colette was focused on Devereaux. Devereaux waddled the necklace over to his desk and studied it in the direct light under his magnifying lenses.

Although Pierre still had an uneasy feeling about the entire situation, a slight glimmer of hope found its way to him. If this worked out, they were going to be rich beyond their wildest dreams and then they were going to live happily ever after. It was the sappy ending that Pierre had always despised but had secretly always wanted. It was right at that moment that reality came crashing back down on Pierre's beautiful, little, curly-haired head.

"This is a fake," Devereaux said, curtly.

52

Thursday, the 5th of January, 9:02 p.m.

Matthieu arrived at the Cafe de la Paix exhausted after the long car ride. The lighting in the cafe was dimmed and quaint. Matthieu noticed the man with the thick, wide-rimmed glasses sitting alone at a table in the corner and sipping from a tiny espresso cup, the man that he was meeting. He walked over to him.

"Norman Neamon?" Matthieu asked.

The man nodded as he struggled to swallow the scalding hot sip he had just taken.

"Thank you for agreeing to meet with me," Matthieu continued and took a seat at the table across from him.

"Of course," Norman said, straightening the glasses that rested on his nose. "You must be Detective Martin Matthieu. The pleasure's all mine. I'm delighted to be able to work with a brother of the shield from overseas."

He tested the temperature of his espresso again with his tongue and his glasses slid down his face.

"Right," Matthieu said. "Anyways, I wanted to talk to you about Pierre Pelletier."

Norman chuckled to himself.

"You know," he said. "He used *your* name when he introduced himself to me. I guess that I'm really meeting Martin Matthieu for the second time this week."

Matthieu wasn't nearly as amused by this as Norman was. It was astounding, however, that Pierre could seemingly still mock Matthieu, even when he was nowhere to be found.

"Anyways," Matthieu continued, adjusting himself into a more comfortable position in his chair. "What did the two of you discuss?"

Norman shrugged.

"Not very much," he answered. "He did ask a lot of questions. You know, now that I think about it, the whole situation is comical. The man didn't even bring any luggage with him!"

"In police work, we call that type of behavior suspicious," Matthieu replied in a mocking tone. He was dumbfounded by Norman's sheer lack of common sense.

"Of course, Detective," Norman replied. "As you know, I'm a member of the FBI."

Matthieu's insult had sailed right over his head.

"You said that he asked a lot of questions," Matthieu said, trying to get back on track. "What kind of questions was he asking?"

Norman thought for a moment.

"He definitely seemed interested in the case that I'm working on," he said. "Yes, actually, most of his questions were related to that."

"Can you tell me a little bit about the case that you're working?"

"I'm not really at liberty to discuss an ongoing investigation," Norman answered. "But all I'll say is that it involves a high-profile forgery case. Mr. Pelletier seemed very interested in the details of it."

"Forgery?" Matthieu repeated, deep in contemplation. "From one brother of the shield to another, can you fill me in on any more details of this case?"

Norman's face contorted as if to suggest that he couldn't say much else on the subject. However, his mouth said otherwise, and he continued talking.

"It involved a specific Matisse painting, Detective. One that had been identified as a forgery, found during a sting operation in Tulsa, Oklahoma. *La Pastorale*, was the name of the painting. He seemed very interested in that."

The name of the painting rang a bell for Matthieu, but he couldn't quite place where he had heard of it. He shrugged it off as insignificant.

"If it was discovered in Tulsa, Oklahoma, as you say, then why are you here, in France?" Matthieu asked.

"The FBI had reason to believe that the painting was forged in France and then smuggled over to the US."

Matthieu was beginning to have reason to believe that the FBI had done the opposite with this Norman character, shipping him from the US to France just to get him out of the country for a bit.

"But why France?" Matthieu asked.

"Well, you see, Detective, the painting in question was the very same painting that was stolen six years ago from the Museum of Modern Art in Paris, by your infamous, *Black Lotus*."

Of course, that was why Pierre had been so interested in the painting, Matthieu realized. It was the same one that he had stolen already. But, if that were the case, wouldn't he have already known what had happened to it?

"I had an appointment to meet with the head curator of the museum before I became...indisposed," Norman continued. "I, unfortunately, have had to reschedule my appointment with her until early tomorrow morning, before business hours."

"You said that you believe that the painting was forged in France?" Matthieu interrupted.

"There's an infamous art forger, named Videl," Norman continued. "I believe that the work can be traced back to him."

"I've never heard of anyone by that name," Matthieu said.

"The working theory is that the name is just an alias."

"Hmm," Matthieu grunted. "Where can you find this character, this, Videl?"

"That's just it, Detective," Norman began again. "All that we have to go off of is the name."

"How did you manage to trace the forgery back to him?"

Norman grinned from ear to ear.

"Videl is good," he said. "*Very* good. You almost couldn't tell his forgeries from the real thing because they're so conscientiously constructed."

"So, how did you do it?"

"The brush strokes," Norman said. He pretended to be holding a paintbrush in one of his hands and running it along a canvas.

"I'm not following," Matthieu said. He was beginning to grow more and more sure by the minute that the man in front of him was completely delusional.

"The brush strokes on the painting are different from the brush strokes of the actual Matisse painting."

"Meaning?"

"Meaning that it wasn't Matisse that had painted it, Detective."

Norman picked up his espresso, which was almost certainly still too hot. He pretended that it wasn't as he swallowed hard.

"Okay, so if that explains that it wasn't the real thing, how does it explain that it was Videl that painted it?" Matthieu asked.

"There were a number of other factors that went into the identification of the forger," Norman began. "The amount of pressure applied on the canvas or the swirl patterns of the paint, for example. You see, each artist's brush strokes are unique to them. Sort of like their own individual fingerprint. No two are identical. If you study them long enough, as I have, you can tell one from the other. This Videl, whoever he may be, his work is incredibly detailed and precise. He could have probably had a successful art career of his own if he weren't so singularly focused on forging the work of others."

Matthieu sat back in his chair. He thought that this man was simply an idiot. As it turns out, he might have been some sort of idiot savant.

"Of course," Norman continued. "Maybe it's simply because Videl lacks the creativity necessary to be a real artist."

"So," Matthieu began again. "You're telling me that this man can't be found? Nobody knows who he is?"

"I suspected that your *Black Lotus*, Pierre, and my Videl were one in the same. Where's Pierre now?"

That's where their opinions differed. While it didn't seem too far off from the realm of possibility that Pierre would assume another nickname, Matthieu didn't suspect Pierre of being an expert forger. Videl and Pierre were two different individuals. Unfortunately, they did share a couple of things in common. One, their connection to *La Pastorale* and the heist at the Museum of Modern Art. Two, Matthieu had no idea where either of them was.

But he thought to himself. *I bet that Genevieve could find Videl.*

The thought had seemingly come from nowhere, against his will. He groaned at the prospect of having to recruit his devil of an ex-wife for help. If there was one thing that she was good at, it was these kinds of crimes. She had some of the best connections all throughout the art world. Somebody that she knew must know *something* about this Videl character. Maybe looking more into Pierre's previous crimes could help Matthieu find him. He was starting to regret going rogue.

"Pierre's gone," Matthieu informed him.

"Hmm," Norman grunted. "What a shame."

"Wait a minute," Matthieu interrupted. "So, if you're telling me that *La Pastorale* was a forgery, then where's the original?"

"That's what I'm in Paris to find out, Detective," Norman replied. "I suspect that the painting may have been a forgery all along. If he and Videl are two different individuals, then I believe that your *Black Lotus* may have unwittingly stolen a forgery from the museum six years ago."

Matthieu chuckled. The idea of Pierre having been duped was a moderately amusing one.

"Anyways," Norman began again. "Seeing as your Pierre is in the wind, what will you do, Detective?"

Matthieu considered this for a moment.

"I suppose that I'll have to return back to Toulouse and atone for my sins," he replied with a sarcastic grin. "Unless, of course, there was anything else that you can think of that was odd from your encounter with Monsieur Pelletier?"

Norman tried to recollect the entire encounter.

"Only that he hits like a girl," he said.

53

Thursday, the 5th of January, 9:07 p.m.

"A fake?!" Pierre stammered.

"Hold on," Colette interrupted. "What do you mean?"

"It's a forgery," Devereaux said, blankly. His face was devoid of any emotion. "A rather impressive one at that, nearly undetectable. However, the stones embedded in the necklace are common stones, completely worthless."

Pierre and Colette exchanged a nervous glance.

"I'm judging by your reactions," Devereaux continued, turning to face them. He stared intently at Colette. "You genuinely had no idea that you were carrying around a fake this whole time?"

He stood up from his chair. His large body towered over the two of them. Devereaux slapped the necklace down in Pierre's hands. Pierre stared down at it in disbelief.

"Or, maybe, you were trying to deceive me?" Devereaux suggested, coldly. "Do you know what happens to people that try to deceive me?"

"No, of course not," Colette stammered. "We're just as surprised as you are!"

Devereaux studied them through his magnifying lenses. If he could spot a forgery that looked as real as the real deal Han Sapphire necklace, he should be able to see the genuine shock in Pierre and Colette's eyes.

The necklace felt heavy in Pierre's palms and he couldn't look away from it.

"*I promise, Pierre,*" the necklace whispered sweetly to him. "*I had no idea—*"

Pierre shook himself free from its trance and then stuffed it back into his pocket.

Devereaux turned his back on them and went back to his seat at the desk. He began fiddling around with the same small object that he had been when they had first entered.

"Well," he said without looking up. "Feel free to show yourselves to the door."

"That's it?" Colette asked.

Devereaux silently tinkered away.

Colette grabbed Pierre by the arm and pulled him toward the door. This mission had gone completely south, and she wasn't going to stick around to see how it all played out. Every object in the shadowed corners of the room looked like it intended to kill them. Colette kept her eyes locked on the door to the building which seemed to get more and more distant with each step.

"If you find the real thing," Devereaux called out to them. "You know where to find me."

Colette struggled with the door handle in her shaky hands before finally getting it open.

"Colette," Pierre began. "I—"

"We'll talk about this in the car," Colette interrupted. "Don't stop moving."

She pushed the dazed Pierre into the car and then climbed into the driver's side. She started the engine and skidded out of there as fast as she could, glancing back in her rearview mirror neurotically to make sure that they weren't being followed.

"I swear that I had no idea!" Pierre assured her.

"I know, I know," Colette answered when she was sure that they were alone on the road.

She sighed to try to compose herself.

"What the hell happened at the château that night?" She asked. Her voice was still shaking.

Pierre was at a loss for words, which didn't happen very often.

"I don't know!" He cried. "I got the necklace from the safe and then— I don't know!"

"Think, Pierre, what about Boutrel?"

"He was already dead when I came into the room," Pierre answered. "Like I told you! You let me in through the window, I cracked the safe and then I found him in the closet!"

Pierre froze.

"Wait a minute," he began again. He slowly craned his head to face Colette. "You were in the room before me."

Colette silently watched the road in front of her.

"Brilliant, Pierre," she finally replied. "Are you suggesting that I killed Boutrel? Maybe stick to the other side of the law. You're not the ace detective that you think you are. Besides, if I *had* killed him, why would I come back for you?"

That was a valid point, except when he considered that he had the necklace. There was also something else that he couldn't explain and that he needed an answer to.

"How did Matthieu know about your sparkling, scarlet evening gown?" he asked.

"My what?" Colette asked.

"When Matthieu interrogated me, he knew what dress you had been wearing that night."

"That doesn't make any sense, Pierre."

"It *doesn't* make any sense," Pierre replied. "That's why I'm asking you to explain it."

"I can't explain it," Colette said. She was silent for a moment before continuing. "Nothing makes any sense. Why would Boutrel keep a nearly identical fake of the Han Sapphire necklace in his safe?"

"Maybe he never *had* the real one," Pierre suggested.

"No," Colette replied. "He was smart. He would have made sure that it was the real deal before he forked over all of that money."

"So, then where did the fake come from?"

"The hell if I know," Colette answered. "And what happened to the real thing?"

Pierre's stare remained fixed on her.

"You were there before me," he said again. "And Matthieu knew your dress which makes me think that it was significant. If anything, you know more than I do."

"Wait a minute," Colette said. "The dress!"

"What about it?"

"There *was* someone else," Colette remembered.

"Someone else where? In Boutrel's study?"

"I didn't notice anyone else in the study, but I noticed them coming down the stairs just as I was going up them."

"What did they look like?"

"It was a woman," she said, hesitantly.

"Was it Boutrel's mistress, Lucile? Or his wife, Beatrice?"

"I'm not sure," Colette answered. "I was a little distracted. The only reason that I'm remembering it now, is because I remember that she was wearing the same dress as me."

"The sparkling, scarlet evening gown?" Pierre asked.

226

"Yes," Colette replied, deep in thought before her concentration finally broke. It was as if it was on the tip of her tongue, but then it had slipped away. "I don't remember, but maybe the Detective thought that he saw me, but he really saw the woman who looked like me?"

Pierre was skeptical, but he had known Colette for a long time, and he decided that he didn't think that she was capable of murder, or setting him up. Especially after the tender moment they'd shared together the night before.

"But what does it mean?" Pierre asked.

Colette thought for a moment, but ultimately came up with nothing again and shrugged. Pierre groaned.

"Well, where do we go from here?" He asked.

"I was hoping that you had an idea," Colette said.

Pierre shook his head.

"Either way," Colette continued. "We've got to split up."

"Split up?" Pierre repeated in disbelief. "I thought that we were in this thing together—"

"The trail's too hot, Pierre!"

Pierre wondered for a moment if Colette was trying to turn her back on him to save herself, but to make it seem like it was in both of their best interests. His mother's words echoed again, "there's no honor among thieves."

"Maybe you're right," Pierre said.

The reason that she had to do that, of course, was because Pierre was a wanted fugitive. Just as Boutrel's corpse had done that fateful night, reality came crashing down on Pierre.

She's better off without you, everyone is better off without you!

He tried to shake the negative thoughts.

All you ever were is a parasite!

There was no use. They were all true. Pierre was toxic, poisoning everything that he touched.

"Where do you want me to take you?" Colette asked, breaking Pierre from his own self-deprecating thoughts.

Although Pierre was sure that she was doing this for selfish reasons, he could sense the empathy in her eyes.

"Just drop me off at the train station," he decided.

"Where will you go?"

Pierre shrugged.

———

When Colette pulled up to the Gare de Marseilles Saint-Charles, she looked over at Pierre.

"I guess this is your stop," she said.

End of the road, Pierre thought as he stared at the bright lights above the train station's front entrance.

He suddenly turned back to Colette.

"Come with me," he said.

Colette started laughing, hysterically laughing. This was not exactly the reaction that Pierre had been expecting or hoping for.

"Oh," she said after a moment when Pierre's facial expression hadn't changed. "You're serious."

"Yes, I'm serious," Pierre said, defensively.

Colette cleared her throat.

"There's nothing for us," she said.

"But last night, you fell asleep on top of me and I thought—"

"You thought what, Pierre?" Colette interrupted. "That we would be together forever and ever? This isn't a fairy tale, this is real life and everything that happened yesterday was strictly business!"

"So, you're telling me this whole time that there has never been anything between us? Don't tell me that my radar was *that* off."

Colette was silent.

"Maybe at some point there was," she finally admitted. "But we could never be together, Pierre, and you know that."

"And why's that?"

"Because you love yourself far more than you could ever love someone else."

Her words crushed him. They were hurtful, but more importantly, they were true.

Without another word, Pierre turned and got out of the car. He closed the door behind him, physically and metaphorically, and began walking towards the front entrance of the train station.

"Pierre," Colette called once she had rolled down her car window. Pierre turned to face her optimistically. She didn't really know what it was that she wanted to say. "Call me if you ever find the real necklace."

Pierre smiled at her as well as he could. His smile wasn't fooling her, and she could tell that his eyes were tired. He was tired of running, but he had so much more to do. Once more, Colette couldn't shake the feeling that there was something so human about the way that he looked. She watched as Pierre disappeared beyond the front doors of the train station.

―――――――

Pierre slumped his way over to the ticket counter.

"Where to, Monsieur?" The attendant behind the window asked.

"Nowhere," Pierre said and sighed heavily.

228

"That's nice," the attendant replied. "But this is a train station and you need an *actual* destination to purchase a ticket."

"When's the next train?" Pierre asked. "I don't care where it's going."

The attendant stared at him suspiciously for a moment and then back at the computer screen in front of her.

"The next train leaves in five minutes," she said. "They're finishing boarding now."

"I'll take it," Pierre said.

The attendant tapped away at the keyboard in front of her.

"That'll be €50, Monsieur," she said.

Pierre reached into his back pocket and pulled out the last €150 that he had liberated from Norman's wallet before dumping the wallet into the trash. He handed over €50 of it to the attendant.

She pressed a button and then the computer whirred to life and spit out a ticket.

"Enjoy your trip," she said and handed him the ticket through the gap in the window. Pierre had never purchased a train ticket before this moment, but he didn't have it in him to scheme again.

He sighed exaggeratedly and walked away from the window, toward the platform and then onto the train. There, he found an open seat by the window.

Nothing makes sense anymore, he thought to himself as he stared out through the window. He tried to close his eyes and get some rest. At this point, he almost didn't even care if he was caught.

His mind began to wander as he could feel the train beginning to shift beneath him and then pull away from the station without a happy ending in sight.

What the hell *had* happened that night? It all seemed like a bad dream. He had taken the necklace from the safe, the fake necklace, he now knew and then had been rudely interrupted by the intruder. He tried to find a place to hide in the coat closet when Boutrel's body just plopped out, right on top of him.

Plopped.

A strange thought suddenly occurred to Pierre. It was like the first break of a spring flower through the frozen ground. It didn't burst through, but a faint idea took root. The seed of which was something seemingly innocuous that he had heard a few days prior and for some reason, it struck him now.

The wife found the body, Genevieve had said.

But the thought continued beyond that. *She must have opened the coat closet door and he just plopped right out.*

Pierre's eyes suddenly shot open.

Plopped.

How did Genevieve know that Boutrel's body had been in the closet? Maybe the killer *had* said something that only the killer could know. Sometimes, maybe it was that simple.

Act III
The Hero

54

Friday, the 6th of January, 3:11 a.m.

Remy Rochefort woke up to a heavy knock on the front door of his small, one-bedroom apartment. It was the same apartment in which he lived alone, not with his wife and two children. That was just one of the many lies that he had told Pierre only a few nights prior.

He shuffled over to the door and peered into the peephole. He grumbled a bit to himself before undoing the deadbolt.

"What do you want?" He mumbled.

"Well, are you just going to make me stand out here all morning or are you going to invite me in?" The unwanted visitor asked.

Remy sighed and opened the door.

"I was wondering when you were going to show up, Genevieve," he said.

Genevieve had made the trip back to Toulouse late last night and had been briefing with the Chief until the early hours of the morning before she decided to pay her friend a visit.

She entered the small apartment and looked around. The blinds were drawn and Remy was wearing his favorite robe, the extravagantly shiraz-colored one with the gold lace around it that made him feel more important than he was. Under it, he was wearing a white tank top and boxer shorts.

"Nice place you've got here," Genevieve remarked.

Remy grunted and then shuffled his way into the kitchen. Once there, he fired up the coffee maker.

"I would offer you some," Remy called. "But I only offer coffee to my guests."

"Am I not a guest?" Genevieve asked. She found a light switch that lit up the bulb hanging above the dining room table. She closed the door behind her and locked the deadbolt in place.

In the light, the apartment didn't look too dissimilar from Pierre's. There were things scattered everywhere and Remy's beige couch had a long tear down the back of it.

Remy emerged from the kitchen with a steaming hot mug of coffee and sat down at the dining room table.

"So, what do you want?" He asked flatly.

"I came to talk to you about that night," Genevieve answered.

"Well, you'd better start talking. Killing Boutrel was never a part of the plan."

"Well, plans change," she said coldly.

The casual way that she said this really rubbed Remy the wrong way. It was as if she was talking about cancelling lunch plans, not murdering a man.

"Don't give me that look," Genevieve said. "We knew what was going to happen to him after the fact anyways, when he couldn't produce the real necklace."

"You said that we were just supposed to frame Pierre. Nobody said anything about murdering Boutrel!"

Genevieve shook her head and scoffed.

"This whole mission was sloppy," she said.

"How did you know that Pierre Pelletier was the same Pierre?" Remy asked, taking a slow sip of his coffee. "The papers said that he was in your police custody before he escaped, but he and I never exchanged last names, just like the arrangement you and I had."

"I had my suspicions about him," Genevieve said. "It's no coincidence that the man parading around as the *Black Lotus* is named Pierre and the expert on Chinese art that used to be the head curator at the Museum of Modern Art is also named Pierre. I've told you before that my connections in the art world go way back. I suspected from the beginning that the two were one in the same."

Remy scoffed.

"Well, aren't you just a regular Nancy Drew," he said.

Genevieve winced. Her ex-husband always used the same, demeaning phrase.

"What I didn't account for," she continued. "Was how much of a fool he really was."

"What do you mean?"

"I mean that I didn't think that he would get himself caught so soon. I thought he was supposed to be the expert, the ghost!"

"I guess that he didn't plan on finding a dead body in that room either," Remy said.

"*You* were supposed to keep Pierre from finding the body. Pierre was never supposed to know that there was a dead body in that room. Your job was to make sure that he got the necklace, left behind his stupid flower, and then got out."

"Why does it matter anyways?" Remy asked. "I thought that was the plan from the beginning. Pierre would take the fall for the heist. Now, the only thing that changes is that he's going to take the fall for the murder as well."

Genevieve shook her head.

"We needed him to take the fall, yes," she said. "But we needed him to stay hidden much longer. The only reason that I called him into the police station was so that I could keep an eye on him for the next week until our buyer was ready."

"So, Pierre came willingly to the police station?"

"Yes," Genevieve replied. "I figured we could pretend that we needed his expertise on the case. Keep him busy for a little while and out of trouble. I never planned on him being identified so easily."

"Who was it that identified him?"

"Some old, British diplomat," she said bitterly. "The same one who *you* also failed to keep Pierre away from that night. He walked in on Pierre because of your ineptitude."

"Did the police ever find the fake necklace?" Remy asked.

Genevieve shook her head.

"That's the one thing that he did right," she said. "I don't know where Pierre managed to hide it, but I'm grateful that he did before he was captured. Otherwise, the forensics lab might have spotted it for a forgery and known that there was something more going on here before I had a chance to disappear. Our whole cover could have been exposed."

Unbeknownst to Genevieve, Pierre had dropped the necklace in the file room completely by accident.

"Well, at least his little escape will help buy us some more time," Remy said.

"Yes, but will it buy us enough?"

"When are you supposed to meet with this buyer of yours?"

"Not until his private jet is scheduled to make a return trip back into the country on Saturday."

"I'm sure that Pierre can go one more day without showing his stupid face," Remy said.

"I'm not so sure," Genevieve replied. "Pierre loves to show that stupid face. The next day after the crime, he walked right into the police station." She shook her head again and mumbled to herself, "there are far too many loose ends."

"Well, that's what happens when you *murder* people, Genevieve."

She sighed but began to casually nod her head in agreement.

"Fortunately," she said. "I've thought of a way to tie them all up into a nice little bow, my dear, Remy Rochefort."

Remy was taking another sip of his coffee when he froze. Some of the coffee slid down his windpipe and he began to choke.

"How do you know my last name?!" He cried in between gasps of breath.

"The same way that I knew where you lived, Remy, didn't that strike you as odd?" In his haze, it hadn't, but it certainly did now. "And the same way that I'm sure that you know mine. The same way that you seemed to know just now how I was a member of the police force when you said that Pierre had escaped from *my* police custody. I never shared any of that information with you. You see, just like you, Remy Rochefort, I did my research. I had to make sure that I was protected."

Remy continued to choke uncontrollably.

"But I'm sure as you can understand," Genevieve continued. "I can't keep you around knowing that you know who I am."

The choking fit began to subside but when Remy tried to speak, his voice was hoarse.

"How do you propose we tie up the loose ends?" He asked desperately.

"I'm not really proposing that *we* do anything," Genevieve said and slipped something out from her back pocket.

Remy's eyes grew wide. He dropped the coffee mug, spilling hot coffee all over the dank carpet. At first, he didn't know what she had been reaching for, but the sharp glimmer of the stainless-steel blade in her gloved hand was unmistakable.

"What are you doing with that?" Remy stammered, resuming his coughing fit. His eyes were fixated on the knife that Genevieve held in her hand.

"Tying up loose ends," Genevieve said. A wicked grin spread across her face nearly from ear to ear as Remy recoiled in his chair.

"He doesn't know my name!" Remy pleaded between gasps, squirming in his seat. "I swear it! I won't say a word! I'll leave France and never come back! Please, what are you doing with that thing?!"

Genevieve placed a gentle hand on his shoulder and, without another word, plunged the knife directly into his heart. The knife almost penetrated out through the other side. Genevieve twisted it for good measure. The grin never left her face.

Remy tried to speak, but nothing came out. His hacking gasps for breath were replaced by a wet, gurgling sound. He looked up at her eyes with a desperate plea, but they looked cold and empty as the light began to fade from his own. He glanced down at his chest. Dark, red blood began to leak out from the fresh wound. The last thing that he saw before everything went black was Genevieve reaching back into her pocket and pulling something from it. She placed the object on the table beside Remy.

"You know," she began. "You're a difficult man to find, Remy Rochefort. I've been trying to hunt you down for days. But I'm glad that we could finally have this little visit. We'll have to do it again sometime."

She left Remy alone, dying and staring at the black lotus origami flower on the table beside him that she had left behind.

55

Friday, the 6th of January, 3:54 a.m.

Matthieu was struggling to stay awake on the long drive home to Toulouse, but he had nearly arrived back already. The time spent on the road the last couple of days had afforded him ample time to think. He tried to imagine every scenario of his return and all of them seemed to end the same way, with his termination. When his mind shifted gears back to the case, he was beginning to feel like he was spinning his wheels. It was like he had collected 100 different pieces to 100 different puzzles and had been trying to jam them all together.

If he put all the pieces together the way that it looked like they should fit, they formed an image of Pierre with that familiar, arrogant grin on his face. However, Matthieu was still not ready to accept this as a possible solution, no matter how much it seemed to be the case. The more he thought about it though, the more unsure he became that he really believed what he was chasing after. He began to wonder if he was just desperately trying to convince himself that Genevieve was wrong.

That was when his phone rang.

He reached for the phone which rested on the passenger seat and looked at the caller ID. It was a blocked number.

He immediately assumed that it was probably either the Chief or Genevieve that were trying to disguise the call to try to trick him into answering. He decided that since he was coming home anyways, maybe it was best to finally answer their call. He could feel them out a bit to see where they stood and then maybe give them a little time to cool off. However, when he answered the phone, he was immediately greeted by a loud, raspy, hacking cough.

"Hello?" The mysterious caller spoke. Matthieu was almost positive it was a man, but he couldn't be too sure.

"Hello…Monsieur?" Matthieu began.

"I'm a lady," the woman said in an offended manner and then hacked again, directly into the phone.

"Of course," Matthieu mumbled. "But, in any event, I believe that you have the wrong number."

"Is this Detective Matthieu with the Toulouse Police Department?"

"It is," Matthieu answered, surprised.

"Oh, good, Detective," the woman said. "I'm glad that I caught you."

"Do I know you?" Matthieu asked.

"No, but I saw your name in the papers, your picture too. You know, the one where you're standing over that dead body with that stupid look on your face?"

The woman began cackling to herself. Although, Matthieu wasn't entirely convinced that she wasn't just hacking again.

"Of course," Matthieu replied. "I don't think I'll ever forget it."

The hacking began to subside.

"Anyways," Matthieu continued. "Is there something that I can help you with Madame—"

"I'm calling about my neighbor," the woman interjected.

"Your neighbor?" Matthieu repeated.

"His name is Remy Rochefort."

"I'm afraid that I don't know the name."

"Right, well, anyways, he's dead and I think that you'd better come quickly."

"I'm sorry?" Matthieu asked as he fumbled for words. "Did you say that he's dead?"

"Yes," the woman answered. "And you'd better come quickly!"

It's not like he's going to get any more dead, Matthieu thought to himself.

"Do you have an address Madame—"

"Yes, it's 31 Bis Rue du Puits Vert," the woman spat. "You have to hurry!"

Matthieu plugged the address into his car's GPS. It was off the Rue Saint-Rome, just down the street from the Rue Bedelieres, the street which housed Pierre's apartment building. Matthieu didn't believe in coincidences.

"Can I get your name?" Matthieu asked.

In the next second, the voice on the other end of the phone was gone and Matthieu was left alone with the dial tone.

On the other end of the phone line, Genevieve rubbed her throat and hacked once more before slipping the phone back into her pocket. She headed down the carpeted hallway and out of Remy's apartment building.

Matthieu made a quick turn off the next exit. He called in the report on the police radio along the way and sped the entire length of the way there.

He blazed past the Rue Bedelieres and then turned quickly through a red light onto Bis Rue du Puits Vert. He was the first officer on sight. Without removing the keys from the ignition, he ran upstairs, across the hideous beige carpet, until he found Apartment B.

The door to the apartment was wide open and there at the dining room table was Remy Rochefort, the next victim in the series. A dagger had been plunged into his heart and a black lotus origami flower rested on the table beside him. His face was frozen in surprise and his eyes were wide open. Matthieu's face reflected this same expression.

It wasn't long before the crime scene unit arrived on scene and the entirety of the Toulouse Police Department had swarmed the apartment building. This time, at least, Matthieu had beaten Genevieve to the punch, or so he thought.

Genevieve arrived a short while later and came upstairs.

"Well," she said as soon as she walked in the door and saw her ex-husband, canvassing the crime scene. "If it isn't the lone wolf himself."

Matthieu scowled. Genevieve turned her attention to the black lotus flower on the table.

"I think it's pretty obvious what we have here," she declared.

"What are you doing here?" Matthieu interrupted. "This isn't an art crime."

"This is *my* case, Martin, and *my* suspect."

"What happened to working the case together?" Matthieu asked.

"Oh, so now you want to work the case together?" Genevieve challenged.

Matthieu grunted and kneeled in front of the body. The handle of the dagger in his chest was made from polished wood and had some sort of Chinese writing on it. The blood was still somewhat fresh.

"Besides," Genevieve continued. "I don't think we'll be working together much longer."

"What's that supposed to mean?" Matthieu demanded.

Genevieve grinned but ignored his question.

"The working theory," she continued. "Was that Pierre had an accomplice on the inside, one that helped him in through the third-story window. The same window that he escaped from which would have been otherwise impossible to open from the outside. Maybe this—" she paused for a moment and glanced at the ID that the officers had already found that belonged to the dead man and began reading from it like she didn't already know his name. "'Remy Rochefort' *was* the accomplice that we've been looking for. Pierre must have killed him to keep him quiet."

"Makes sense to me," Thomas replied.

Matthieu hadn't even noticed his partner enter the room and he shot him an angry glance. This battle royale was strictly between him and his ex-wife.

"I'm not buying it," he said. "Besides, I don't think this man could pull off a sparkling, scarlet evening gown."

Genevieve seemed to tense up.

"What do you mean by that?" She asked.

Matthieu shook his head and grumbled to himself.

"This seems pretty cut and dry to me, Detective," Genevieve insisted.

"If you're referring to the wound, then it doesn't seem very cut and dry at all, *Detective*," Matthieu challenged. "In fact, the cut seems pretty fresh and the blood still seems fairly wet."

"What are you babbling on about, Martin?" Genevieve asked, unenthused.

"Alright," Matthieu said. "I'll play along, because that seems to be what you've wanted from the beginning. Let's say that Pierre did kill Boutrel, for whatever reason. Maybe he did walk in on him stealing his priceless necklace, maybe Pierre just didn't like him, maybe Pierre decided that Boutrel would look much more handsome with a dagger in his chest, whatever. Now, Pierre's on the run from police, meanwhile he decides to come back to Toulouse, kill an old accomplice of his that may incriminate him and then leaves behind a signature at the crime scene that points us directly to him? Does that make any sense to you?"

"Maybe he did it before he left?" Thomas suggested.

"I don't think so, Thomas," Matthieu replied, shaking his head. He was catching a full head of steam now. Any doubt that he had about Pierre killing Boutrel now was dismissed. "The blood suggests that this was done recently. Probably within the last hour or so."

"It's like a compulsion," Genevieve insisted. "Pierre *needs* to leave behind that signature. He's a serial thief. Just like a serial killer likes to leave their own personal touch on the crime scene. Only, they don't just *like* to leave behind that personal touch. They *need* to do it. It's like a ritual to them. They get off on that stuff. As for Pierre returning to Toulouse, who knows why he did it? But you know what they say, the perpetrator always returns to the scene of the crime, or the city, in this case. *Especially* if he's got loose ends to tie up."

Matthieu just shook his head again.

"Very convincing argument," he said. "Pierre is arrogant, I'll give you that. But I don't think that he's even *that* arrogant. Without the flower, we might have never even suspected him for this murder. The whole thing just seems very...staged."

Genevieve scoffed.

"I guess it doesn't matter what it seems like to you," she said.

"What's that supposed to mean?" Matthieu repeated.

"Oh, you'll find out soon enough," she said with a smirk.

Matthieu didn't like how cryptic she was being.

The Chief interrupted them by appearing in the doorway and casting a long shadow from the hallway lighting over Matthieu. Matthieu turned to face him and saw that he was staring straight at him.

"Matthieu," he began.

He was calm but, in a way, like the calm before a storm. The Chief was about to explode. He wiggled his magic finger and a detective appeared in the hallway of the apartment building.

"If this were the old days, Matthieu, I'd probably be strangling you right now," the Chief began. "Fortunately for you, I've been feeling a lot more relaxed ever since seeing the office psychologist."

"Why did you call me out of there?" Matthieu interrupted. "And why is *she* even here anyways?"

"Because she's the lead on the case," the Chief informed him.

"What?!" Matthieu exclaimed. "We were working the case together!"

"Is that what you call running off to Paris without telling anybody and then tipping our dangerous fugitive off that we were onto his whereabouts? You were *supposed* to be working the case together. Now, you're not."

"What does that mean?"

"It means that you're off the case, Matthieu," the Chief replied. "As a matter of fact, you've been suspended."

"Suspended?!" Matthieu repeated.

"Without pay."

"Without pay?!"

"Indefinitely," the Chief finished.

"Indefinitely?!"

"You make a lousy detective, Matthieu, but an even lousier parrot."

"On what grounds?!" Matthieu demanded.

"It may have something to do with our prime suspect escaping and making a mockery of the entire Toulouse Police Department!"

"Okay, well, the first time was not my fault and you know that—"

"It doesn't matter whose fault it is, Matthieu! You're always trying to pass blame on everybody else, but you can't admit when it's *you* who's at fault! It's just like everything else this week, you're too stubborn for your own good!"

"Chief," Matthieu tried. "I'm so close, I can feel it. You can't pull me off this."

"It's not my call," the Chief said. "I just got the order from Internal Affairs about an hour ago. But just so you know, even if it was my call, you'd still be gone in a heartbeat. I made a mistake, Matthieu. I never should have had you reinstated."

"But, Chief, I—"

"The only *butt* that I want to see is yours walking out of this crime scene," the Chief interrupted. "Now, turn in your badge and your gun."

Matthieu glanced back through the open door of Apartment B and saw Genevieve staring back at him with a devious grin.

He turned back towards the Chief and slowly began to unholster his pistol. He stared at it for a moment before finally clicking the safety on and slapping it into the Chief's hands. Next, he unclipped the badge from his belt. He stared at the shiny gold plate in his hands for another moment, unable to let it go.

"You want this?" He asked, holding up the badge to the Chief. "Then go and get it."

He leaned back and then hurled his badge down the hallway. It skidded across the carpet before coming to a stop in front of one of the other apartments.

"Real mature, Matthieu," the Chief said.

Matthieu didn't care. He stormed past the Chief and out of the building. Once outside, he lit up a cigarette and then he climbed into his blue Renault and disappeared down the street.

56

Friday, the 6th of January, 4:11 a.m.

Fortunately for Pierre, or unfortunately, depending on how you looked at it, the train ticket that he had purchased at random was for the train that was travelling straight back to Toulouse and right back into the firestorm. Unbeknownst to Pierre, there was another body on his hands.

He didn't know why Genevieve had done it. Although, he assumed that greed was one of the primary reasons. A €60 million necklace with dark powers of persuasion at the center of the puzzle was certainly enough to justify his reasoning. However, it wasn't the necklace that caused people to act the way that they did around it, it was their own greed. He also didn't know how she did it, but he was sure that she did.

She mentioned that the wife, Beatrice, had found the body, but she didn't say that Beatrice had mentioned the body plopping out on top of her. No, that was what Genevieve had been pretending that she had "surmised." Only, she didn't really need to surmise what had happened because she already *knew* that Boutrel was in that closet to begin with. The only two people that would know Boutrel had been in that closet were the person who found him there, Pierre, and the person that had put him there, the killer.

Sure, she could have just assumed by the positioning of the body that Boutrel had plopped out of the coat closet, but that was too much of a coincidence for Pierre to believe. Besides, he remembered reading in the autopsy report something about dependent lividity suggesting Boutrel was face down shortly after his death. He had no idea what it meant, but obviously, it was caused by Boutrel falling out of the closet on top of Pierre, and Pierre leaving him face down on the ground. If the wife had found him in the closet the next morning, as Genevieve pretended to presume, the dependent lividity, whatever it was, would not have suggested Boutrel was face down shortly after his death. Genevieve would have known that and she never would have mentioned Beatrice finding the body in the coat closet this morning, unless she accidentally let it slip, like she had.

Besides that, there was something else that Pierre had remembered from that evening. It seemed like nothing at the time, but the more that he thought about it, the more the pieces of the puzzle began to fall into place.

In between the intermittent radio static that came through his earpiece that night, he had heard a voice that he assumed was a radio broadcaster speak the words, "…Eve…MURDER."

He had thought before that the person who had spoken those words had been referring to New Year's Eve and that the second word was completely incidental, if it had even been real at all. Now, he was certain that the "Eve" had been referring to Genevieve and that the "MURDER" had been referring to Boutrel's fate. Put the two together and you have that Genevieve had something to do with Boutrel's murder. The more that he thought about it, the more that he began to wonder if it had even been a radio broadcaster at all, or had it been Remy's voice, disguised through the static? Was Remy involved in the setup? The voice that had spoken the words seemed frantic and when Remy returned to Pierre's earpiece, Pierre remembered thinking that he sounded short of breath. Maybe Remy and Genevieve had been working together, Genevieve killed Boutrel unexpectedly and Remy had exclaimed something to the effect of "Genevieve, murdering him was never part of the plan!" Of which, Pierre only caught bits and pieces through the static.

If it was a setup, that could also explain why when Pierre had accidentally mentioned the anonymous *Black Lotus'* letters to the police, denouncing an affiliation with the *Viper Triad*, to Genevieve, she hadn't even batted an eye. The only people that should have known about those letters were the police, and the *Black Lotus* himself. Pierre obviously wasn't a member of the police, so that should have easily exposed him, but Genevieve didn't seem to notice. It wasn't because she didn't make the connection, it was because she had already made the connection. Genevieve had known that Pierre and the *Black Lotus* were one in the same from the beginning. A setup would also explain why she had been so obsessed with pinning the murder on the *Black Lotus* to begin with, because she needed him to take the fall for her crimes.

All of that hit Pierre at once with the force of four separate trains running into him, one after the other and his eyes shot open in sudden realization. If thievery didn't work out, Pierre certainly had a future as a detective. He immediately reached into his pocket and pulled out the two cell phones that he carried with him, both were dead. At this hour, there was nobody else in the passenger car. Pierre was on a four-hour train ride back to Toulouse, bursting at the seams with his discovery, but with nobody to share it with.

———

When the train finally arrived at the Gare de Toulouse Matabiau, Pierre ran off it as fast as he could, nearly barreling over the conductor who was standing by the door. Fortunately, this time, there was no swarm of police officers checking IDs. Nobody, of course, knew that he was here. He had managed to disappear completely off the grid. After his brother's apartment, Toulouse was probably the last place that anyone would have expected to look for him.

He emerged from the train station and out onto the streets of Toulouse. The cold air struck him first, a taxi that rushed by nearly struck him second. Pierre didn't know what time it was, but it was dark, so he assumed it was sometime after midnight, maybe even closing in on morning by now.

He ran across the bridge which spanned Le Canal à Vélo, the canal which ran straight through the front of the train station and divided traffic into two distinct directions. He ran down the street until he spotted the Hotel ibis Styles Toulouse Centre Gare across the way. Assuming they would have a phone that he could use, Pierre ran to the hotel and then burst through the door, surprising the young, blonde concierge who was sitting behind the front desk.

"Can I help you, Monsieur—" she began before Pierre interrupted her.

"I need to use your phone!" He shouted and ran up to the desk. He placed his elbows on the granite countertop to catch his breath.

The concierge looked down at his elbows disapprovingly and cleared her throat. Pierre promptly removed them.

"I need to use your phone," he repeated. He was breathing heavily.

"The phone is for guests of the hotel only, Monsieur," she said.

"You've got to be kidding me," Pierre mumbled. "Can't I just borrow it for a moment? This is an urgent police matter!"

"You're with the police?"

"Well, no," Pierre admitted. "But it involves the police and I need to use your phone immediately!"

"You don't look like you're in any immediate danger," she said, scanning Pierre up and down. "I can call them for you, if you'd like."

"No," Pierre said, shaking his head. "This is a private matter that is top secret, privileged information."

This seemed to intrigue the concierge. She raised a quizzical eyebrow at Pierre, but her interest quickly faded.

"The phone is for hotel guests only," she repeated. "You can rent a room, or you can leave back through the door that you came."

Pierre groaned in frustration.

"Then, I guess you leave me no choice," he said, almost threateningly. "How much for a room?"

"€100," she answered.

"€100?!" Pierre repeated. "That's the cheapest room that you have?"

Here he was, thinking that *he* was the greatest thief in all of France.

She nodded her head indifferently.

Pierre grumbled and reached into his back pocket, pulling the last two €50 notes that he had stolen from Norman. He handed them over to the concierge.

She took them and held them up to the light to make sure that they were authentic.

"The phone?" Pierre asked impatiently.

She lifted the phone from the counter below, next to the computer monitor and placed it on the counter in front of him before turning it to face him.

"Dial 8 to call out," she said. "And make it quick."

Pierre picked up the receiver and held it against his ear before he froze.

"Do you have the number for the Toulouse Police Department?" He asked sheepishly. He remembered that he had dialed the number accidentally when he had been trying to contact Remy. The two numbers were identical except for one number. However, he couldn't remember the full number then, and in his frantic state, he certainly couldn't remember it now.

The concierge sighed and searched for the number on her computer before reciting it back to him. The other end of the line began to ring.

Pierre began tapping his fingers on the countertop anxiously and then looked over at the concierge who was still standing there and staring at him.

"Do you mind?" He asked.

She rolled her eyes and then disappeared into the back office to give him some privacy.

On the third ring, a woman's voice answered.

"Toulouse Police Department," she said. "How can I direct your call?"

Pierre suddenly remembered that he hadn't completely thought this plan through and that he didn't know *who* he was calling for. After all, he didn't know who there was left to trust. He had no idea how high up this thing went. The entire police department could be compromised. Pierre thought of Genevieve placing her hand on his thigh. It was the same hand that she had probably used to *murder* Boutrel. He felt unabated hatred for her swell in his chest. This *vile* woman had set him up. He hated her probably more than anyone else on the face of the planet.

"Hello?" The woman called into the phone.

That was when Pierre had another realization. He remembered the only other person that could have possibly hated Genevieve more than he did. It was the one person who might just believe a tale as insane as his. The person who, at one point, claimed that he was Pierre's "only friend." Maybe it was time to put that claim to the test.

"I'm hanging up now," the woman threatened.

"Detective Martin Matthieu, please," Pierre spat out all at once.

The woman on the other end of the phone sighed.

"One moment, please."

Matthieu was the only person left in the station, other than the Chief, and he was cleaning out his office desk when the phone rang. He placed the mug that read, "World's Best Detective" into a cardboard box next to the framed portrait of himself in his police uniform on the first day out of the academy before he looked up at the ringing phone. He reached for it slowly and then picked it up from the receiver.

"Yes?" He called into it.

But nobody answered him.

"Hello?" He called out again. "Hello?!"

Still no answer. He became angry.

"Listen, if this is another one of those kids who thinks it's funny to keep prank calling here and asking for me, then I've got a couple of things to say. I want you to know that there are *four* walls that are holding up my roof and that my refrigerator is running on electricity, *not* physically running away from me!"

With that, he slammed the phone back down.

"Matthieu!" The Chief roared. "This isn't time for you to make social calls. Clean out your desk and get out!"

Matthieu grumbled to himself. This is what years of hard work and dedication had gotten him.

On the other end of the phone, as soon as Matthieu had picked up the call and then began speaking into it, there was a reason that nobody had answered. It was because nobody was there.

The last thing that Pierre could remember was a prick in the side of his neck, like a bee sting, and then everything faded to black.

57

Friday, the 6th of January, 5:17 a.m.

When Pierre finally regained consciousness, there was a ringing in his ears, and he had a pulsing headache. His vision was beginning to clear, but his thoughts were jumbled. It was almost like he could see the words that formed in his brain bouncing off the walls of it. In his unconscious state, Pierre had felt euphoric.

"That was some party," he said and tried to reach his hand up to rub his temples. The only problem was that his hand didn't comply. He glanced down at his arms and noticed that they were zip tied to the armrests of the wooden chair that he was seated at. A few moments later, he realized that his legs were bound to the chair's legs as well. Normally, a situation like this would have sent Pierre into a panic, but he felt strangely Zen.

"I didn't know that it was *that* kind of party," he said and chuckled to himself.

There was a swaying lamp overhead, but the rest of the room was shrouded in darkness.

"That's just the drugs speaking," said a mysterious deep, almost demonic, voice. Pierre couldn't tell if he had imagined the deep pitch of the voice or if someone was trying to alter it using some sort of voice changer. The other option was that Pierre had hallucinated the voice altogether.

"God?" Pierre asked and looked back at the swaying lamp overhead. "I swear, I'm not on any drugs."

The deep voice laughed demonically.

"I didn't give you *that* much," the voice said. "You're a lightweight, Pierre."

"Am I dead?" Pierre asked in amazement.

The deep voice laughed again.

"Not yet," the voice said. "Now, let's make this quick, Pelletier. I've got other places to be."

Slowly, Pierre's memory began to come back to him in small fragments. He remembered the concierge at the hotel, he remembered dialing the phone and asking for Matthieu and then he remembered feeling the prick in the side of his neck. After that, there was nothing.

"Did you drug me?" Pierre asked lazily. It was like his mouth was struggling to keep up with the words that his brain was sending down to it.

"Just a little something to take the edge off," the voice said.

"My head is killing me," Pierre said and slumped it over, slipping out of consciousness again.

"Wake up, Pierre," the voice instructed.

Pierre felt a slap on his neck right in the spot where this figure had injected him with something. The site was sore. Pierre regained some semblance of consciousness and stared out beyond the dim light overhead until he could just barely make out a shadowy figure beyond the darkness.

"Genevieve!" Pierre cried out in his drug-induced haze.

"Try again."

"Dad?"

"What?" The voice repeated in disbelief. "No! It doesn't matter anyways. Now, start talking Pierre, or you're a dead man."

"I don't want to be a dead man," Pierre replied.

He knew that those were bad words, but it was strange because he still didn't have a care in the world. Whatever drugs he had been given; they were good.

"Then, you'd better start telling me what I want to hear," the voice instructed.

"What do you want to hear about?"

"The necklace," the voice demanded. "Where's the necklace?"

"The necklace," Pierre mumbled. Those fragments of memories hadn't made their way back to him yet. When it finally clicked and Pierre remembered the necklace, his lover that had betrayed him, he shifted in the chair so that he could feel his pocket pressed up against his arm. It was the pocket that he had last placed the necklace, only now, it was empty once again. Pierre threw his head back in a fit of laughter.

"Stop that!" The voice demanded. "Where's the necklace?!"

"Oh, man," Pierre began, his laughter was slightly subsiding. "I've got to get pants with deeper pockets."

He burst out laughing again.

"Where is the necklace?!" The voice roared, carefully annunciating each syllable.

"I don't have it!" Pierre declared.

"Obviously," the voice said. "All that you had in your pockets was two dead cell phones, a mysterious business card for someone named, Norman Neamon, a paperclip and an excessive amount of pocket lint! More than any person should have! Where did you hide the necklace?!"

Pierre shrugged his shoulders casually.

"I never had it," he insisted, slurring his words. His head slumped over once more.

"What do you mean that you never had it?" The voice demanded.

Pierre didn't respond so the figure slapped him awake once more.

"Where am I?" Pierre asked.

"What do you mean that you never had the necklace?!" The voice asked. "You broke into the château, killed Boutrel and stole the necklace!"

Pierre made an exaggerated flail of his head.

"Well, you got one of those things right," he said. "I didn't kill anybody, and I don't have the necklace! The real one at least."

"The real one?" The voice repeated. "Where's the necklace, Pelletier?! I'm tired of your games!"

"Keep your pants on," Pierre slurred again. "I don't know where your precious necklace is."

"Well, you better start remembering, Pelletier," the voice said coldly. "Because pretty soon, you're not going to remember anything."

"What's that supposed to mean?"

"It means that just before you woke up, I injected you with something else," the voice replied. "And you have about fifteen minutes before it takes effect."

"What did you give me?" Pierre asked.

The voice began chuckling maniacally.

"Tell me, are you familiar with *Gu*?"

"I've been poisoned?!" Pierre exclaimed. His eyes widened and his mouth dropped open like an excited child who isn't in full control of his own movements yet. "That doesn't sound good!"

"That's right, Pelletier," the voice said. "It *doesn't* sound good. You've been poisoned, just like Boutrel was. It's too bad that the *Gu* didn't have a chance to work on him. I'll be honest with you, I'm not sure what exactly went wrong, but I won't make the same mistake again with you. It can be a particularly nasty substance, as I'm sure that you know, and the Supreme Dragon wanted to make sure that Boutrel suffered."

"You're the one who poisoned Boutrel?!" Pierre declared.

"That's right, Pelletier," the voice said. From the shadows emerged a hand and in that hand was a glass vial which contained a black, tar-like substance. "Right now, that same poison is coursing through your veins. It's only a matter of minutes before the *Gu* reaches your brain and makes each individual blood vessel pop one at a time."

Pierre was still strangely apathetic.

"Just tell me where the necklace is, Pelletier," the voice tried once more.

"I've already told you, Monsieur, I don't know where it is."

"Then you leave me no choice."

The man who the voice belonged to walked forward into the light and Pierre recognized him immediately. Although, in his haze, Pierre couldn't remember his name which would have made the reveal so much more dramatic.

"You!" Pierre shouted.

"That's right, me," the man said with a sinister smile, turning off the voice changer.

"You're that handsome guy!"

"You flatter me, Monsieur Pelletier," he said.

Pierre fumbled for the name.

"Lucile Lebas!" He shouted. "You're her lover!"

"François Fouquet," the man said. "It might serve you well to remember it because it's going to be the last name that you call out right before you die."

58

Friday, the 6th of January, 5:20 a.m.

Norman Neamon arrived at the Museum of Modern Art in Paris exactly ten minutes before the time that he and the curator had previously agreed upon. He always liked to be early and would frequently repeat the phrase, "if you aren't ten minutes early, you're late." Much to the chagrin of his coworkers.

He walked up the tall, stone steps and could see a silhouette of a woman standing in the doorway. The woman pushed open the large glass door and Norman entered the building.

"You're late, Monsieur," the woman said.

Norman glanced down at his watch.

"I'm ten minutes early, actually," he said.

"My father always used to say that if you aren't fifteen minutes early, you're late."

"Your father sounds like a smart man," Norman remarked. "You must be the museum curator?"

He stuck his hand out for her to shake.

"Evian," the woman replied and stared down disgustedly at his hand without taking it. "You must be Norman?"

"Norman Neamon," he replied and awkwardly placed his hand back by his side. "I'm sorry, did you say Evian?"

The woman nodded her head and then adjusted her wide, red-rimmed glasses that had no lenses in them.

"Like the bottled water?"

"I'm not familiar, Monsieur," she said. "Please, come this way."

Norman shrugged and then followed the woman upstairs.

"I'm afraid that I never caught your last name," he said.

"It's just Evian," the woman replied.

The stairs opened into a large room that was lined with a strange assortment of sculptures. There was one sculpture that was simply a tin can with a stick protruding from the top and another that had been made from melded and twisted iron that was particularly phallic.

"Is this the room where all of the paintings were stolen from?" Norman asked.

"It is," she replied.

"Then where are all of the paintings?"

"We don't really *do* paintings anymore," she said. "We've embraced the cultural impact of contemporary sculpture."

Norman walked over to one of the exhibits.

"Is this a banana, duct taped to the wall?" He asked.

"Don't be ridiculous, Monsieur," Evian said. "That's a plantain."

"Of course it is," Norman mumbled. "Anyways, so, the thief came in from that skylight up there?"

He pointed to a large window that was above them. The moon shone brilliantly through it and spilled onto the floor.

"That's correct," Evian said.

"Interesting," he said.

251

Norman walked over to a large window on the opposite side of the room and looked down. It was a three-story drop, straight down to the bottom of the pavement.

"How did the thief manage to evade the cameras?" Norman asked. In each corner of the room there was a camera that was sweeping the area.

"Six years ago, there was only one camera," Evian said. "It was on a rotating loop. Every twenty seconds it would complete a full revolution."

"I see," Norman muttered. "Why wasn't there more security here at the time? The paintings here were priceless."

"There was plenty of security," Evian informed him. "There were cameras downstairs and by every exit and entrance. They never thought that we would need to take such drastic security measures by the third-floor windows, especially the skylight."

"You said, 'they,' Miss. Does that mean—"

"I wasn't working here at the time, no. I believe the man who previously held my position was named Pelletier. Or something like that."

"What about the alarms?" Norman asked, pointing to the infrared, laser, trip wire alarm that lined each of the windows.

"Same story, Monsieur. They never thought they would need an alarm on the windows up here."

"Security guards?"

"There were guards patrolling the museum throughout the night, from what I heard. None of them heard or saw anything out of the ordinary."

Norman nodded his head.

"Anyways," he continued. "I'm not really here to discuss the initial heist. I'm more curious about the *origins* of the stolen paintings themselves."

"Even though we don't work with paintings anymore, it's a shame that they have never been recovered," Evian said. "But we do have a backlog of all of the paintings that we've acquired over the years."

"So, these would include a backlog of all of the stolen paintings as well?"

Evian nodded.

"Yes," she said. "We have acquisition dates, photos of the condition that they were in when they arrived—"

"Photos?" Norman interrupted.

"Yes, Monsieur," Evian said. "They would take photos of every painting when it came in, so that they could catalog its condition."

"Can I see the photos?" Norman asked. "The one of the stolen Matisse, *La Pastorale*, in particular."

"I don't see why not," Evian answered. "Come with me, the records are kept in the storage room."

She led Norman down a long corridor and into a back room with tall filing cabinets from the floor to the ceiling. Each was lined with binders filled with documents.

"You'll have to excuse the mess," she said. "Paper is such a dated means of record keeping. We're in the process of trying to go paperless."

She finally found the binder that she had been looking for and pulled it off the shelf. She opened it and then began scanning through the documents that it contained.

"Ah," she exclaimed. "Here it is."

She turned the binder around so that it was facing Norman.

Norman straightened the thick spectacles that rested on his nose and then grasped the edges of the binder in both hands. There was an image of *La Pastorale* on the page in front of him, but Norman never saw the forest through the trees, as it were. He was more focused on the trees themselves, or the brush strokes in this instance. He studied it for a moment and then lifted his head. His eyes were even wider in the magnification of his lenses than they had been before.

"This was the painting that was stolen?" He asked.

"It was, Monsieur."

"You're absolutely sure about that?"

"As sure as I am breathing. You don't see it anywhere along the walls of the museum, do you? And you certainly won't find it in storage."

"This *exact* painting was stolen?" Norman repeated, pointing emphatically at the photo of the painting on the paper.

"Is there something wrong with you?" Evian asked. "As I've been saying, *that* painting was stolen!"

"This isn't the painting that was in Tulsa," Norman mumbled. He glanced back down at the photo.

"I beg your pardon, Monsieur?"

"Sorry," Norman replied. "I'm afraid that sometimes my mouth skips a few steps between when my brain sends it signals. That's what my wife always tells me anyways."

Evian had a frightened look on her face. Who was this lunatic that she was alone with in the storage room?

"What I was saying," Norman continued. "Is that this painting in the photo is *not* a forgery."

"Obviously," Evian said. There was a hint of annoyance in her voice. "This is the Museum of Modern Art, Monsieur, we verify the authenticity of every work of art that passes through here."

"So, the forgery in Tulsa was *not* the same painting that was stolen from the museum," Norman mumbled.

253

"I'm afraid that I don't understand," Evian tried, but Norman was engaged deeply in his own thoughts.

"No, no, no," Norman continued mumbling to himself. "So, what does it all mean? It means that the real painting was stolen from the museum and then switched out with a fake after. If the fake was brought to Tulsa, then where's the real painting?"

"Monsieur!" Evian tried again.

This time, she startled Norman back into reality, and he dropped the binder in his hands. The binder smacked on the floor and flipped to a random page.

"Oh, I'm terribly sorry," Norman said. "Here let me get that—"

He bent over to pick up the binder but then he froze in his tracks, staring at the page in front of him.

"Where is this painting?" He asked, entranced.

"Monsieur?"

"Where is this?!" He demanded.

"Monsieur, I think that you'd better leave."

"Please," Norman begged. "I *need* to see this painting."

Evian glanced at the number that was associated with the painting in the binder and then turned back to a larger filing cabinet behind her.

"It's probably stored in here," she said, nearly cowering.

Norman greedily reached for the filing cabinet handle and pulled it open.

There had to have been a hundred or so paintings that were lined up in there. The filing cabinet was like a casket for all of them because they would probably never see the light of day again. At least, not until vintage art came back in style. Norman fingered through the paintings until he found the one that was wrapped up in paper and marked with the same number as the painting he was so fascinated by in the binder.

"This is it," he cried and then tore the paper off like a child on Christmas morning.

"Monsieur!" Evian cried.

"I think there's a lot more going on here than we think, Evian," Norman said delightedly.

"I don't know what's going on here to begin with," she tried, but it was almost no use. Norman was lost in his own head.

When he had finally unveiled the painting, he gazed upon it in all its glory.

"Where's this painting from?" Norman asked.

"That was from a collection of local artists that were spotlighted six years ago," Evian said, reading from the binder.

"Who painted it?!"

"Henri Harquin," she read.

"Henri Harquin," Norman repeated.

Evian tried to run her hand in front of his face, but it was no use, Norman was hypnotized. The painting was of a canoe that was docked along a shoreline, but Norman wasn't interested in that. His eyes danced from brush stroke to brush stroke. The amount of pressure applied, and the swirl patterns of the paint produced a sort of artistic fingerprint on the canvas. No two were identical. Norman should know whose fingerprint this painting belonged to. God knows, he had spent countless hours studying the same print.

"Videl," he whispered to himself.

This Henri Harquin and Videl were one in the same. He remembered thinking that Videl could have had a successful art career of his own if he wasn't so singularly focused on forging the work of others. As it turned out, he did.

59

Friday, the 6th of January, 5:37 a.m.

Former Detective Martin Matthieu was sitting on his living room couch in the dark, wrapped up in a blanket from head to toe. A bottle of red wine was caressed lovingly in one arm and a photo of Genevieve was in the other. There was a roaring fire in the fireplace in front of him. Matthieu didn't know what time it was, but he was drunk, so it didn't matter. He was staring at the bare living room walls and mumbling to himself.

"They're chartreuse, Martin," he mumbled mockingly in a high-pitched whine that was supposed to mimic Genevieve's voice.

He grabbed the photo of Genevieve tightly in his hand before throwing it against the wall.

"They're yellow!" He cried as the photo smashed against the wall. The frame snapped and the glass shattered to pieces on the carpet. Everything was silent again.

The fire crackled as it was beginning to die down.

"Needs another log," Matthieu grumbled and stood up from the couch.

He grabbed the fire poker and pushed over the charred remains of the fire to make room for more fuel. Then, he took another framed picture of Genevieve from the wooden bin in front of the fireplace and tossed it into the flames. However, even though the picture seemed to burn easily, the memories that the two of them shared together didn't. What made it even more difficult was that he was still living in the house that they had shared together. He contemplated dragging the hot coals into the living room and setting the whole house ablaze.

Instead, he stumbled over to the photo of Genevieve that he had thrown against the wall and picked it up. He stared at her for a moment as his eyes welled with tears. Then, he silently walked it over to the fire and tossed it in. This one landed face up, and he watched as the flames reached over the photo like fiery hands and engulfed her. Her piercing eyes were the last thing to burn and Matthieu felt for a moment that they were penetrating right to his soul. However, they quickly disappeared under the red-hot flames.

"I'll drink to that," he said and held up the bottle of wine for a toast.

He put the rim of the wine bottle to his lips and slugged it back with a long guzzle and then a satisfied, "ahh."

His cell phone started ringing on the end table beside the couch.

"Stupid kids," Matthieu grumbled to himself.

He was far too busy to answer it. Matthieu let the call go to voicemail and took another slug out of the wine bottle. If it was important, they would leave a message. If it wasn't important, they could screw off. Hell, they could screw off if it was important too. Another minute later, the phone dinged.

Matthieu sat there for another moment as the fire crackled in front of him. However, his curiosity got the best of him and he reached over to pick up the phone. The light from the phone was blinding but he could read as clear as day that he had one missed call from an unsaved number and a voicemail. The number wasn't a French number, he could tell that for sure. He played the voicemail and put the phone up to his ear.

"Hello, Detective Matthieu?" A man's voice began frantically, almost as if the man were being chased. "It's Norman, Neamon Norman—I mean, Norman Neamon. I need you to call me back as soon as you get this message. It's regarding an urgent matter and I need to speak to you right away. We shouldn't even waste time exchanging greetings when you call because there's something very important that I need to share with you, and I think you'll want to hear it. Either way, I'm going to call you back in just another sec—"

The cell phone began ringing again, right in Matthieu's ear. In his surprise, he dropped the bottle of red wine onto the floor. The blood red liquid oozed onto his white carpet. Matthieu thought that it resembled a crime scene.

"Hello?" Matthieu grumbled as he fumbled to answer the phone in his hands. "You've reached the number of the unemployed and the clinically depressed."

"Detective Matthieu?" Norman called into the phone.

"Formerly," Matthieu replied.

"Matthieu, I'm glad that I caught you," Norman said. "I hope that I'm not interrupting anything."

Matthieu glanced over at the spilled wine bottle on the carpet and the incinerated picture frames in the fireplace.

"I thought you said this was urgent, Norman," he said bluntly.

"Right, of course," Norman stammered. "I thought that you would want to hear this because I found Videl."

"You found Videl?" Matthieu repeated, unsure of what this meant. All at once, it clicked and Matthieu declared excitedly, "you found Videl!" Then, he remembered his present circumstances. "I'm not working the case anymore, Norman. I'm—"

"He's dead," Norman interrupted.

60

Friday, the 6th of January, 5:41 a.m.

"Can we get back on track, Pelletier?" François began again. "You tell me where the necklace is, and I'll give you the antidote to the poison."

"Poison?!" Pierre declared. "I've been poisoned!"

"We've been over this already, Pierre," François said frustratedly.

"That doesn't sound good."

François slapped his palm to his forehead. Then, he walked over to Pierre and put the heel of his shoe on Pierre's hand. He pressed down with his heel against Pierre's fingers and they crunched under his weight. Pierre grimaced in pain. Even the drugs couldn't take it away.

"Tell me what I want to hear," François demanded between teeth that were clenched in fury.

"I didn't kill Boutrel," Pierre said between teeth that were clenched in pain.

François pressed down harder on Pierre's fingers.

"You stabbed him and then left your stupid, little flower right in the safe when you robbed it," he said. "You saved me the trouble of having to kill the old bastard, but you also took the thing that I was after! Just tell me where the necklace is, Pelletier!"

"I didn't stab him," Pierre insisted. "He was already dead when I came in the room and the necklace was already gone. I was set up!"

In the pain, his memory was becoming lucid again.

"Who would want to set you up?" François asked and removed his foot from Pierre's hand for a moment. Pierre tried to stretch his hand out and could notice the tread marks all along the back of it in the pattern of the underside of François' shoe.

"Genevieve," Pierre grunted.

"Genevieve?" François repeated. "The lady cop? Why would she set you up?"

"I can think of about 60 million different reasons," Pierre replied. The feeling was just beginning to return to his hand.

"What if I don't believe you?" François asked.

"Believe what you want, but it's the truth!"

"So, you're saying that you don't have the necklace and that you've never had the necklace?"

"That's what I've been saying," Pierre said and then began chuckling to himself uncontrollably.

François considered for a moment and then stomped his foot back onto Pierre's hand.

"Wait!" Pierre cried in between fits of laughter. "Please!"

"I don't believe you," he crunched down on Pierre's fingers once more. "You're going to tell me where the necklace is, or there's no antidote for Pierre."

"But I need it!" Pierre exclaimed. "Don't you know that I've been poisoned?!"

The pain, which had previously produced a lucid effect on Pierre, was now having the opposite effect. In conjunction with the drugs that he had been given, Pierre's head was spinning. He continued laughing but it was a horrified laughter that he couldn't escape from.

"Come on, Pierre, you're a smart guy," François began with a devious smile. "Tell me where the necklace is, and I'll let you live. It's as simple as that."

"It was in my pocket," Pierre tried, his thoughts jumbled around once again, rattling like ping pong balls in his head. "The fake one!"

François pressed his heel down nearly as hard as he could.

Pierre erupted into a fit of laughter.

"Not exactly the effect that I was hoping to have," François said. "It's usually more fun when they show fear. But I guess that this will do."

A moment later, he finally released his foot from Pierre's hand again. Obviously, torture wasn't working. He glanced down at his wristwatch.

"Oh, dear," he said as Pierre struggled for breath. "It looks like you've only got about a minute left before the poison takes full effect, Pierre. Better start talking."

"I told you everything already!" Pierre pleaded.

François stared into his frantic eyes.

"You really don't know where it is, do you?" he asked with a frown.

"That's what I've been saying the whole time," Pierre said. "Just give me the antidote and let me go."

François laughed.

"There is no antidote, Pierre," he said. "You were never going to make it out of here alive."

Pierre's eyes widened in horror, but yet, inside he felt numb.

"The way I see it," François began. "You've got ten seconds to say any last words before the poison takes effect."

There were so many things that Pierre had always wanted to say as last words in case an opportunity like this presented itself. They had been carefully designed to leave a lasting impression. However, in his haze, he couldn't think of any. He was going to die in silence.

François glanced down at his wristwatch and began the countdown.

"4..."

"Wait!" Pierre cried.

"3..."

"Please!"

"2..."

"There's so many things I haven't done yet!"

"1..."

Pierre was silent. An image of Colette's smiling face flashed in front of him. If he ever wanted to see her again, he needed a way out of this, but Pierre was out of schemes.

"Zero," François finished.

He looked up at Pierre. Pierre looked back at him, expecting the most gruesome death imaginable to take hold, but nothing happened.

"Oh, what the hell?" François exclaimed. "It didn't work again?!"

He pulled out the vial of the black, tar-like substance from his pocket.

"Absolutely worthless," he sighed. "Nevertheless, there are still other ways to kill you."

He reached into his back pocket and pulled out a sharp dagger. He held out the pointy end to Pierre.

Pierre knew that he should be panicked, but he started laughing uncontrollably again.

"What are you doing with that?" Pierre gasped for breath between laughs.

"What do you think I'm going to do with it?" François asked, taking a step closer. "I'm going to stab you with it."

Pierre's eyes followed the blade of the dagger as it poked against his chest and François rested it there for a moment.

"Au revoir, Pelletier," François said, he pressed the blade in so that it penetrated Pierre's skin. "Send my regards to Boutrel…"

Pierre glanced down at the fresh blood that was trickling out around the blade and he passed out.

61

Friday, the 6th of January, 5:50 a.m.

The taxi dropped former Detective Matthieu at 221 Rue Malaret, the address that Norman had given him over the phone. It was an old stone apartment building nestled in between two larger buildings just about a block and a half away from the Toulouse Police Department. The apartment building looked almost uninhabitable, the perfect place for squatters or drug addicts to call home. Vines twisted up the crumbling exterior. The first thought that Matthieu had was that if you were looking for a dead body, this was certainly the first place that you should look. He had no thoughts beyond that, he was absolutely wasted.

The front door of the building was missing, so Matthieu stumbled his way inside.

"Hello?" He called into the open hallway.

"Detective!" Norman called and poked his head out from a doorway on the second floor. "I'm up here!"

Matthieu began to climb the creaky staircase. He had to brace himself a couple of times to prevent himself from tumbling backwards. Finally, he reached the top and proceeded into the room.

"Ugh," Matthieu exclaimed, plugging his nose with his thumb and index finger. "What's that smell?"

"I can assure you that it isn't me," Norman said. "Must be our friend here."

He pointed to a corner of the room which was nearly an identical scene to the Remy Rochefort crime scene. The only difference was that it was a little less fresh.

There was a man seated in front of a round, wooden dining room table. Matthieu's mind was absorbing every detail but found none of them to be particularly relevant. What he did find relevant was the dagger that was protruding from the victim's chest.

"Probably been dead a few days at least, maybe even a week or so," Norman said, noticing the look of disgust on Matthieu's face. "Looks like it was your guy."

Norman pointed to the table where there rested a black lotus origami flower surrounded by a scattered pile of loose pills.

"First of all, he's not my guy," Matthieu slurred. He plugged his nose and then leaned in to study the body more closely.

The victim had a series of dark track marks up his arm, suggestive of chronic intravenous drug use. The dagger in his chest was nearly identical to the one that they had recovered from the Remy Rochefort crime scene. The handle was made from polished wood and had Chinese writing along the side of it. The two must have been part of the same set. What disturbed Matthieu about this revelation was that whoever killed Boutrel had appeared to have done so with his own dagger in the heat of passion. Whoever had killed the last two victims had done so completely intentionally. These were planned killings.

"Secondly," Matthieu continued. "Did you call the police yet?"

"I thought that you *were* the police."

"I tried explaining that to you over the phone, but you kept insisting that I come over immediately…how do you know this is Videl?"

"Look around," Norman replied and motioned with his hand around the room.

Matthieu glanced around at the canvases and half-finished paintings that were sprawled out throughout the apartment. In one corner of the room, there was a large object that was concealed under a dingy sheet.

"I thought that nobody had ever heard of him and yet, you managed to track him down in a couple of days," Matthieu said. "How'd you do it?"

"There was a painting at the museum," Norman replied as he walked into the kitchen.

"I'm not following."

"Oh, yes, forgive me. I always miss a few steps in my explanation when I get excited," Norman said. He pulled the refrigerator open. It was completely empty. Videl took the role of the "starving artist" quite literally. "I had my meeting with the curator earlier. The curator at the Museum of Modern Art. I was following up on the heist six years ago when I spotted an original."

"An original what?"

"An original Videl! Or, I suppose an original Harquin."

"Who's Harquin?"

"He is, Detective," Norman replied when he returned to the room and pointed down to the decaying corpse. "I knew that it was Videl's work from the moment that I first laid eyes on it. Only this time, it wasn't a forgery. It was an authentic, produced by a local painter named Henri Harquin."

Matthieu glanced over at the corpse and frowned.

"Anyways," Norman continued. "The museum curator had the contact information and address for Mr. Harquin on file. He was a frequent contributor to the museum in the past, especially when they presented the exhibit to shine the spotlight on local artists. The curator gave me the address, I got here, found him dead, called you, and here we are. Less than two blocks from the police station too. I guess you know what they say, keep your friends close and your enemies closer!"

"It wasn't Pelletier that did this," Matthieu said.

"What about the flower?" Norman asked. "It's the same flower that was found at the original heist of the Museum of Modern Art and the same one that was found at the Boutrel crime scene from what the papers are saying."

"And the same flower that was found at the Rochefort scene," Matthieu replied.

"Rochefort, Detective?"

"Another piece to the puzzle."

Matthieu wandered around the room but stopped in front of the object that was blanketed by the sheet.

He yanked the sheet off of the object, revealing a large contraption with a magnifying lens attached to it.

"What's this?" Matthieu asked.

Norman walked over and examined the contraption.

"It's an industrial laser diamond cutting machine," he said. "How does someone with no food in his fridge and with a nasty drug addiction afford something like this?"

"Easy," Matthieu began. He had heard about a contraption like this once before. "He steals it."

This was the exact kind of machine that would have been in the back of a jewelry store, he realized. In the Chief's office, earlier in the week, Matthieu had learned that three weeks ago, almost four now, Genevieve had been working a case in which a jewelry store had been robbed. The Chief had mentioned that no jewels had been stolen, just one of the store's machines. Here it was. If this was the man who had stolen it, why was he dead and why was there a black lotus flower beside him?

"Hmm," Norman grunted. "I wonder what the significance of it is. The plot thickens."

Matthieu considered everything that he had learned over the last week but then blanked his mind and shrugged.

"Not for me," he said. "I've been suspended."

"Suspended?" Norman repeated. "Then you shouldn't be here, this is an active crime scene!"

"That's what I've been trying to tell you from the beginning—"

"Well, I guess it's a little late now," Norman interrupted. "So, if it wasn't Pelletier, then who was it?"

"If I had the answer to that question, then I probably wouldn't have been suspended in the first place," Matthieu answered.

"Do you have a hunch?"

Matthieu shrugged.

"My money was on Lucile Lebas and her lover, François Fouquet," he said. "Although, I don't understand why the murders have continued if it was them. They would have already gotten what they wanted. But I did always suspect that there was something else that they were sticking around for…"

"Seems like quite the conundrum," Norman remarked. "It sounds like you just don't have enough answers yet.

"And he doesn't really give us any either," Matthieu said and pointed over to the body of Henri Harquin, also known as Videl, decomposing more and more with each passing second. "He just adds more questions."

62

Thursday, the 5th of January, 11:53 p.m.

After Colette had dropped Pierre off at the train station the night before, she sat there with the engine idling for a bit. She couldn't seem to get the image of Pierre's pathetically sad face out of her head. She knew that it was obviously in her best interest to drive away and never look back, but it was like some unseen force was preventing her from doing so.

There was suddenly a knock at her window that interrupted her thoughts. She turned her head and stared in disbelief at the police officer standing there before rolling the window down.

"Is there a problem, officer?" She asked, innocently.

"You can't park here, Mademoiselle," the officer said.

"I'm sorry, I was just dropping someone off," she replied, absentmindedly.

"You've been idling here for twenty minutes," the officer informed her. "You need to either park in the lot or follow the road to the exit."

Colette stared at the two options that the officer had presented in front of her. The decision seemed to split her right down the seams, but when she really thought about it, the choice wasn't really a choice at all.

"I hate you, Pierre," she mumbled and then turned the wheel. She guided the peach Peugeot into the parking lot and left it there while she ran inside.

———————

Inside the train station, there weren't many people around. She scanned the scene for a moment but no matter where she looked, she didn't find Pierre.

"Excuse me, Mademoiselle," she began as she approached the ticket window. "I'm looking for someone, I don't know if you've seen him."

The woman behind the counter frowned.

"Aren't we all," she answered bitterly. "We sell tickets here, Mademoiselle."

"This'll be quick," Colette assured her. "He was here probably no more than twenty minutes ago. He may have purchased a ticket from you, he may not have. He's got a mop of curly, golden brown hair and a sad, puppy dog look in his eyes."

"Yes, I actually do remember the man that you're talking about. He purchased a ticket to Toulouse about twenty minutes ago."

"Toulouse?!" Colette repeated. "Why would he want to go back to Toulouse?"

"He didn't ask to go there specifically, he just said that he wanted a ticket for the next train that would be leaving the station and he didn't care where it was going."

"Then, I'd like a ticket please, for the same train."

"I'm afraid that the train has been closed for boarding," the woman said. "They should be leaving any second, if they haven't already."

"Which platform is it?"

"Platform G," the woman replied.

Colette took off running toward the platform and yelled a "thank you" back to the woman. She grunted.

When Colette finally reached the platform, the train to Toulouse was just beginning down the tracks. She ran alongside it and peered into the windows of the empty train cars until she finally saw the curly-haired mop of a head that she had been searching for.

"Pierre!" She cried out. "Pierre! Down here!"

Pierre turned his head out through the window and sighed, but he never saw her. He closed his eyes and leaned back in his seat.

Colette yelled and waved her arms spastically as she chased after the train until the very end of the platform, but it was all in vain. The train continued along, and Colette could do nothing else except watch, helplessly.

264

However, she decided that she wasn't ready to give up that easily, so she ran back to the parking lot and started up the peach Peugeot. She sped the entire length of the trip back to Toulouse as fast as she could and made it there in record timing. She still arrived there after Pierre's train and when she ran through the station and over to it, he was already gone.

She knew that he couldn't have gotten too far by now, so when she emerged from the train station, she glanced out across the Toulouse streets, just in time to catch a glimpse of Pierre disappearing through the front door of the Hotel ibis Styles Toulouse Centre Gare across the way. As fast as she could, she ran to the hotel. She was nearly there and could see him talking on the phone through the glass doors when she watched a masked figure approach him from behind and jab a syringe into the side of his neck. Pierre went limp and collapsed to the floor.

Colette froze in her tracks and then dove out of sight as she watched the masked figure load Pierre into the back of the trunk of a black SUV and then drive away. Colette immediately ran to her own car and pursued them.

The SUV stopped at an abandoned warehouse not far from the train station. She watched the figure emerge from the vehicle without the mask, it was a man that she didn't recognize. Then, the man grabbed Pierre from the trunk and dragged his lifeless body into the warehouse. She crept in behind them and then watched from the shadows as the man zip tied Pierre to a wooden chair and shined a dim overhead, swaying lamp above him.

Next, she watched the entire interrogation of Pierre. From a distance, she could only make out some of what they were saying as she sat there in silence, contemplating what she should do, if anything. When François began piercing the blade into Pierre's chest, Colette felt around frantically in the dark for something, anything, that she could use to help. Her fingers finally settled on something in the shadows that was sturdy and heavy, but not too heavy that she couldn't lift it. She grabbed the object in her hands, ran up behind François, and smacked him across the back of the head with it.

François collapsed to the ground. The dagger that he had been holding slipped from his hands and pattered across the floor.

63

Friday, the 6th of January, 5:55 a.m.

"Pierre!" Colette cried frantically.

She dropped the object that she had used to incapacitate François, a solid, wooden two by four, and she straddled Pierre. She ripped the small hole in his shirt from François' dagger wider so that she could assess the damage. She hoped that it hadn't been fatal and when she looked down at the mark left behind by the dagger, she saw the superficial mark that François had formed into the shape of an "F." A little something that Pierre would always remember him by, but nowhere deep enough to kill him. Another few seconds though and François may have finished the job.

Pierre's eyes began to flutter open.

"Colette?" He cried. His voice was weak. "Where are we?"

"We've got to get you out of here, Pierre," she said. She reached down for the dagger and cut loose all the zip ties that were binding Pierre to the chair.

Pierre began to chuckle.

"That tickles," he said.

"Are you drunk?" Colette asked as she undid the last of the zip ties. "What the hell's gotten into you?"

"Drugs," Pierre replied and then burst out into another laughing fit.

"Come on," Colette instructed. "We need to get out of here before he wakes up."

"Shouldn't we just kill him?" Pierre asked as he rubbed at his wrists. The laughter subsided just enough for Pierre to be able to think somewhat clearly. However, his head swirled when he stood up. He reached back for the chair to balance himself.

"Have you ever killed anyone before?" Colette asked. She slapped the dagger down into Pierre's hands.

The dagger felt warm and inviting there. Pierre stared down at the unconscious, albeit still handsome, man on the floor.

"Let's just go with your idea," he decided.

They ran out of the building just as the sun was beginning to rise over the horizon. Pierre began to wander off and Colette had to grab him by the arm and shove him into the passenger side door of her car. She slid across the hood of the car and around to the driver's side.

"That was cool," Pierre grumbled.

She jumped into the seat next to him and quickly started up the engine. Colette reached over and strapped the seatbelt across him. She shifted the car into reverse and then pressed the gas pedal to the floor. The tires squealed to life beneath them. She shifted into drive and then they squealed off in the opposite direction, kicking up a cloud of smoke behind them.

Pierre was digging around in between the seats until he finally found what he was looking for. He pulled his hand out from the crack and held up the fake Han Sapphire necklace.

"I've got to get deeper pockets," he repeated and then burst out laughing once again. He passed out a few seconds later.

64

Friday, the 6th of January, 7:59 a.m.

When Pierre finally came to once more, he only had a faint recollection of what had happened along with a raging headache to go with the amnesia. The fragments of distorted memories seemed like they had happened years ago, not hours, and not to him.

He found himself on an unfamiliar couch and he sat up to have a look around.

It was a small living room that he found himself in. The decor of the apartment left much to be desired. There were at least three different pieces of wall art with the phrase, "Live. Laugh. Love." Or at least some form of it.

"What year is it?" He asked.

He rubbed his eyes which were heavy and sore from the light of the morning sun that was peeking through the window. Colette was facing him with a steaming hot mug of coffee in her hand and her back against the living room wall.

"Were you watching me sleep?" Pierre asked.

"I was making sure that you didn't asphyxiate yourself last night," she answered.

"I'm not really into that kind of stuff," he said. She rolled her eyes. "Hey, is this your place?"

"It is," Colette answered.

"Who would have thought that I just needed to be kidnapped and tortured to get to come back to your place? If I knew that in high school, I would have done it a long time ago."

"Alright, Pierre."

Pierre chuckled and then rubbed his head.

"Why do I feel like there's something very important that I need to do?" He asked. "Wait a minute…the poison! I've been poisoned, Colette! I need the antidote!"

"Relax, genius, I think if you were going to die from the poison it would have happened by now."

"But how could you be sure that I wouldn't?!"

"You're alive, aren't you?"

"But François said that he—" Pierre began.

"I heard him. But, whatever happened, it didn't work."

"But you couldn't have *known* that it wouldn't," Pierre said.

"I took a chance," Colette admitted. Pierre stared at her in disbelief. "Did you want me to take you to the hospital? You'd have been taken into police custody immediately!"

"You'd rather that I die on your couch?"

"You'd rather be in prison?"

"Good point," Pierre said and rubbed his temples. "I feel like there was something else though. What was it?"

"How should I know?" Colette asked. "You passed out in the car and just kept mumbling the same thing over and over again."

Pierre looked up at her. He couldn't help but notice that she seemed slightly annoyed.

"Wait a minute, you came back for me!" He suddenly remembered.

"Yeah, yeah, yeah," Colette said. "Don't get too excited. It was strictly business."

"Strictly business, eh?" Pierre repeated with smug satisfaction.

"I thought about what you were saying," Colette said. "And we *are* still in this together. So, we deserve to see it through to the end. Besides, I'm still entitled to half of whatever we make from selling that necklace. You should be thanking me for coming back to save your sorry self. If I didn't, you'd be deader than Boutrel right now!"

"Boutrel," Pierre mumbled. "François was saying that something also went wrong with Boutrel's poison…"

Unbeknownst to Pierre, the reason that the *Gu* had no effect on him was the same reason that he had been hospitalized as a child and the reason that he had to refuse the drink from Norman on the train. It was also the same reason why the *Gu* had no effect on Boutrel: Pierre's liver cells had been ravaged by a severe case of childhood hepatitis. They couldn't activate the poison and instead only produced mild, secondary effects, like the appearance of intoxication. The disease that had nearly ended his life before it had even begun was the reason that he was still alive now, sitting on Colette's couch.

"I thought that Boutrel was stabbed," Colette replied. "His picture was all over the papers."

"He was, he was," Pierre remembered. "But in the autopsy file, it also said that he was poisoned, *prior* to him being stabbed."

"Why would somebody poison him and then stab him?" Colette asked. "That doesn't make any sense, Pierre. I think that you need to sleep off the drugs a little bit more."

Pierre shook his head and shushed her.

"Did you just shush me?" Colette asked, annoyed again.

"Sorry," Pierre said. "I'm just trying to think. If François poisoned Boutrel with the *Gu*, then he must have some sort of connection to the *Viper Triad*. He mentioned something about the Supreme Dragon wanting to make sure that Boutrel suffered…"

"Pierre, what are you talking about?"

"Maybe François was using Lucile Lebas to get close to Boutrel so that he could steal the necklace for the Triad. The fake necklace, that is."

"Maybe it wasn't always a fake," Colette suggested.

Pierre closed his eyes and concentrated.

"Maybe it *was* the real thing at some point. So, François poisons Boutrel, but the poison doesn't work. Besides that, François doesn't have the necklace. Otherwise, what would he need to kidnap and interrogate me for? So, the real necklace was stolen before François had a chance to get to the safe. Boutrel was stabbed sometime in between being poisoned by François and then us stealing the fake necklace. Somewhere in between those two events, Genevieve must have stabbed Boutrel, stolen the real necklace and then swapped it out with the fake! It's exactly like the pearl necklace heist…Genevieve has the real necklace!"

His eyes shot open.

"I need to use a phone!" He shouted.

"There's that name again," Colette said.

"What name?"

"The same name that you kept mumbling to yourself over and over again last night when you were passed out in my car," Colette said. "*Genevieve*."

Pierre thought that he could detect a slight hint of jealousy in her tone.

"No, no, no," he assured her. "It's not like that…at all!"

Colette rolled her eyes.

Pierre got up from the couch and nearly fell back over before his vision corrected itself and he stumbled over to the phone on the wall in the kitchen.

"Genevieve is the murderer," he said.

He picked up the phone and dialed the number for the Toulouse Police Department. Somehow, through it all, he had managed to retain the number by heart this time.

"It's ringing," he said and glanced over excitedly at Colette.

"That's what phones do, Pierre," she mumbled.

"Toulouse Police Department, how may I direct your call?" The woman on the other line asked.

"Yes, hello," Pierre began. "I called a couple of times last night. Something came up and we got disconnected."

The woman on the other end sighed.

"How may I direct your call?" She repeated, uninterested.

"Right," Pierre said. "Detective Matthieu, please. I'd like to speak with Detective Matthieu."

The woman punched in a few buttons and the line began to ring again.

"It's ringing," Pierre said again to Colette.

"You're calling the police?" Colette whispered harshly. "Are you out of your mind?!"

"On the contrary," Pierre answered. "I can see things clearer now than I've ever seen them before. Maybe I should do drugs more often."

"Those *things* you're referring to are hallucinations, Pierre. Give me the phone!"

She lunged for it, but Pierre turned his back to her and fought off her advances while trying to hold the phone against his ear.

On the third ring, the phone finally picked up.

"Matthieu, don't say anything," Pierre began. Colette was on his back and was trying to get her arms around his head. "It was Genevieve! I don't know how or why, but it was *definitely* her. I'm sure of it!"

There was silence on the other end, but Pierre could hear someone breathing into the phone.

"Pierre, is that you?" Said the voice of a woman on the other end. It was an easily recognizable voice. After all, it belonged to Genevieve herself.

65

Friday, the 6th of January, 8:12 a.m.

The line on the other end went dead and Genevieve was left with nothing but the dial tone. She could feel her heart thumping heavily in her chest and it was filling her ears with every pulse.

"Good morning, Genevieve," Thomas said. She looked up to meet his eyes.

At first, it had almost seemed as if he had been calling to her through a tunnel.

"Are you okay?" He continued. "You look kind of pale."

"I'm fine, I'm fine," she assured him. She was more so trying to convince herself than him. The thumping in her ears began to slowly subside.

"The crime scene unit should be wrapping up that Harquin crime scene shortly," Thomas said. "I don't know about you, but I couldn't sleep a wink after seeing that body. That's up to three now for Pierre, who knows how many more he's going to kill before this is all said and done?"

Genevieve didn't have an answer to this question because she didn't know how many more she was going to have to kill on behalf of Pierre before this was all said and done. However, she was sure that, by the end of it, she would have a considerable body count on her hands. She could now add Pierre Pelletier to her ever-growing hitlist, although it would be difficult to frame him for his own murder.

How could that idiot have figured it out?

It felt like the walls were closing in on her. If Pierre knew, it was just a matter of time before everyone else found out.

"I need to use the restroom," she suddenly declared.

"Oh, okay," Thomas said. "I'll talk to you when you get back. Maybe we can discuss the evidence in the Henri Harquin case. Sound good, partner?"

Genevieve didn't respond. Instead, she rushed right by Thomas and into the ladies' room where she immediately pulled out her cell phone. She punched in the number from memory, but her fingers were shaking so badly that she misdialed twice and had to re-enter it. When she finally got it right, the phone began ringing.

"Come on," she mumbled to herself as she paced the tiled bathroom floor. "Pick up."

Finally, after what seemed like ages, but was only a couple of rings, the line on the other end did as she had instructed and picked up.

"This had better be good," the man on the other line began with a deep voice in a thick, Russian accent.

"Monsieur Yachnitch," Genevieve began. "Ambassador Yachnitch," she corrected herself. "There's been an incident and you need to come back…*now.*"

"What kind of incident?" Yachnitch asked. "This had better not be a, *you lost my necklace*, kind of incident."

"It's more like a, *my cover is blown*, kind of incident."

Yachnitch began chuckling on the other end of the line. This was not exactly the response that Genevieve had been hoping for when she had made the call.

"I fail to see how this is *my* problem," he said.

"If I get caught, that means you can say goodbye to your necklace, too," Genevieve said.

"Eh, I will buy another," he said coldly. "Or, once you are captured, I will pay someone to take it out of the police evidence room. Of course, that would make you a loose end. You know I do not like loose ends, Ms. Gereaux."

Genevieve shook her head.

"You need to come back, now," she insisted once more.

"I am afraid that is impossible, Ms. Gereaux. Like we previously agreed upon, I will be back no sooner than tomorrow morning and we can continue with the deal as planned."

"You're just as involved in this as I am," Genevieve said.

There was silence on the other end of the phone.

"You may as well have killed those three people, same as I did," she continued.

Genevieve could hear him breathing calm and rhythmically into the phone, but he was otherwise silent for a tense moment.

"You would not be trying to blackmail me, Ms. Gereaux, would you?" He asked directly.

"Of course not, of course not," Genevieve assured him, when this, in fact, was what she had, indeed, been trying to do.

"That is good, Ms. Gereaux, because if you were, then I would have to remind you that you are simply the dealer. In Mother Russia, we have a saying—sometimes, you are the dealer and sometimes, you are the one who is being dealt with. Do you understand what I am telling you?"

"Yes, I understand," she answered. Goosebumps crept up her spine.

"Good," Yachnitch replied. "Do not be more trouble than you are worth, Ms. Gereaux. I will be back early tomorrow morning, like we agreed upon. If you can manage to keep your head above water until then, we will go through with the plan as scheduled."

"I may need to disappear for a while," Genevieve tried.

"I would not do that if I were you," Yachnitch said. "If you make me come find you, I will be the last person who ever does. Am I making myself clear?"

"Crystal," Genevieve replied. She swallowed a hard lump in her throat. "I'll take care of it."

"Good," Yachnitch said and then hung up the phone, putting an abrupt end to the conversation.

Genevieve didn't feel any better than she had before she had called the Ambassador. In fact, she felt worse.

66

Friday, the 6th of January, 12:00 p.m.

Former Detective Matthieu woke up on his couch at the crack of noon with his arm draped lovingly around an empty bottle of wine. He wasn't exactly sure how he had gotten home after he had been excused from the Harquin crime scene. He simply couldn't remember. He did, however, have a faint recollection of stumbling into the nearest bar and promptly being thrown out and landing face down on the street. He figured that from there, he must have stumbled right back to this familiar spot. The fire from the night before was now just a dwindling pile of ash in the fireplace. The first thought on his mind when he woke up was that it had been almost five weeks now since Genevieve had left him, but the wound was still so painfully fresh.

He didn't know why his body had decided to wake him up now. Matthieu was fully content to sleep through the whole day. However, for some reason, he thought that he had heard a heavy knocking on his front door. He was just beginning to think that he must have imagined it when, sure enough, to confirm his suspicion, there it was again—three obnoxious pounds that shook the whole house.

"I'm coming, I'm coming," he grumbled to himself.

As he approached the door, he could hear voices coming from the other side of it, a man and a woman. They sounded to Matthieu like an old, bickering, married couple.

"This is a bad idea," the woman was saying.

"Just trust me on this," the man insisted.

"Trust you like I trusted you with the mission?" The woman asked.

"Oh, you want to get into that again?" The man challenged. "You were the one who bailed on me, remember?"

Matthieu pulled open the door and found himself face to face with Pierre Pelletier and Colette Couvrir.

"Detective!" Pierre exclaimed delightedly.

Matthieu was speechless. He rubbed his eyes.

"I've got to lay off the sauce," he mumbled.

When he opened his eyes again, Pierre and Colette were still standing in front of him. Pierre was smiling up at him like a buffoon.

"What the hell are you doing here?" Matthieu stammered.

"I'm here to turn myself in," Pierre said. "Just kidding, but I do have something to tell you. Is it alright if I come in and use your restroom first?"

"I told you to go before we left," Colette interrupted.

"I didn't have to go before we left," Pierre replied.

Matthieu was almost positive that he was hallucinating.

"I must have died last night," he said. "That's it. I died and I'm in hell. This is my reward for all my good deeds. I'm stuck here, for an eternity, with Pierre Pelletier!"

"I feel the same way, pal," Pierre said and slapped Matthieu on the shoulder. "So, can I come in now?"

"This is a dream," Matthieu tried again. "It's just a bad dream and if I close my eyes, I'll be at home and you'll be gone."

He did just that but when he opened them once more, Pierre was still in front of him.

"Maybe try clicking your heels together, Dorothy," Colette said. "But trust me, he doesn't go away that easily. He's like a parasite that way."

Matthieu's face suddenly became blistering red and Pierre thought that he could see the beginning of smoke billowing out from his ears.

"What, in the hell, are you doing here?" Matthieu asked, annunciating every syllable carefully between his tightly clenched teeth.

"What you said back at the station," Pierre replied. "And at Phillipe's house. You said that you knew that I didn't do it, which was true. But I know who did."

"Well, you'd better start talking, Pelletier, or I'm calling the police."

Pierre shook his head and chuckled to himself.

"I don't think that *either* of us want you to do that," he said. "May we come in?"

"Why shouldn't I call them?"

"First of all," Pierre began. "I thought you *were* the police."

"Not anymore, thanks to you."

"You're welcome then," Pierre said.

"That does it," Matthieu began again. "I'm calling the police."

He marched over to the cellphone on the end table, but Pierre shouted after him.

"The police have been compromised!"

Matthieu turned back to face him.

"What are you talking about?" He asked.

"It was an inside job," Pierre said. "I think that your wife had something to do with it."

"Genevieve?" Matthieu asked. He put the phone down on the end table in disbelief and returned to the front door.

Pierre nodded his head.

"That's right," he said.

"Let's clear up one thing first," Matthieu began. "Genevieve is my *ex-wife*," he spat bitterly. "And what makes you believe that she's involved in any of this?"

"Can we come in and I'll explain everything that I know to you?" Pierre asked, shifting his weight on his feet from left to right like a child that can't hold it in for much longer.

Matthieu contemplated it for a moment, but eventually, he reluctantly decided to let them in. Pierre immediately made a break for the little boy's room and Matthieu offered Colette a seat on the couch adjacent to him. By "offered," he pointed and grunted at it.

"I love what you've done with the place," Colette said, looking around and observing the bare walls that had collected dust where photos used to be hung. She looked over and saw a large, wooden bin of framed photos by the fireplace. "Are you moving?"

"Why don't we skip the small talk," Matthieu replied.

The sound of the toilet flushing from the restroom interrupted their pleasant exchange.

"Oh, thank God," Colette mumbled to herself.

Pierre came out of the restroom and plopped down next to Colette.

"I see you're growing out a disgusting beard, Pelletier," Matthieu said.

"It's my depression beard," Pierre replied.

"Your depression beard?"

"Don't get him started," Colette warned.

"Alright, so, why don't you start with something else, Pelletier," Matthieu said. "You've got five minutes to convince me not to call the police."

"Fine," Pierre agreed. "Genevieve did it."

"You said that already," Matthieu replied. "You're going to have to do better than that. What proof do you have?"

"I know that it was her because of something that she said when we were working on the case together," Pierre said.

Matthieu's face became red again when he remembered how cozy the two were getting in the conference room.

"What did she say?" He asked.

"She knew that Boutrel was in the closet."

"What does that mean?" Matthieu asked.

Pierre sighed.

"I guess I should tell you the whole thing," he said.

"Pierre," Colette whispered sharply. "Are you sure that's a good idea?"

"I'm right here," Matthieu said. "I can hear you."

"I've got to tell him," Pierre said. "So, I'm going to start from the beginning, Detective. Unless you'd like me to start from the end and then sprinkle in little flashbacks to the beginning with the occasional reveal in the middle."

"Just tell me what the hell you're talking about."

"Right," Pierre said. "So, you were right all along. I *was* there that night."

"I knew it!" Matthieu declared.

Pierre continued to recount every detail of every event that had happened to him the previous week, sparing none of them, except doing his best to keep Colette's name out of it. He told him about the château break-in, stealing the necklace, finding Boutrel in the closet, running away, going to the police station, climbing through the vents, escaping from police custody, his brother, being in the coat closet while Matthieu was just outside, trying to sell the necklace to Devereaux and finding out that it had been a fake all along, being kidnapped and tortured by François, and then finally looking up the Detective's address online and showing up on his front steps. By the end of it all, Matthieu had never been so fascinated and so exhausted at the same time.

"Do you still have the fake necklace on you?" Matthieu asked.

Pierre slipped the fake Han Sapphire necklace out of his pocket and held it up to the Detective. It was strange that Matthieu didn't seem to react in the same, lustful way that everyone else did. Maybe since he knew that it was fake, it had lost some of its power. Pierre slid it back into his pocket.

"So, what I think happened," Pierre said. "Is that François poisoned Boutrel, waiting for the right moment for him to drop dead so that *he* could rob the safe. Instead, somebody else swooped in and stabbed Boutrel, took the real necklace from the safe and swapped it out with this fake. That's when I came in through the window, stole the fake necklace, found Boutrel, already dead, and then fled the scene."

Pierre stopped to catch his breath.

"And you left the black lotus flower there because—"

"Come on, Detective, it's my signature! Where's your sense of style?"

"And, let me get this straight," Matthieu continued. "You think that this *somebody else* that swooped in was Genevieve?"

Pierre nodded his head.

"Genevieve?" Matthieu repeated and turned to Colette to see if she could talk some sense into her partner. However, her gaze was elsewhere. She was peering into the wooden bin of framed photographs that rested in front of the fireplace.

"There were only two people that would have known Boutrel was in that closet," Pierre said. "The person who found him, me, and the person who put him there."

"And you think that was Genevieve?" Matthieu asked. He shook his head. "That's circumstantial at best, Pelletier. At worst, it's downright slander."

"Wait a minute," Colette interrupted. "Is *that* Genevieve?"

Matthieu followed her gaze.

276

She stood up from the couch and reached into the bin of photos by the fireplace. She pulled out one. It was the one that Matthieu used to keep on the table by the door. The one of their engagement dinner where Genevieve was wearing her favorite, red dress with her arms draped lovingly around Matthieu's neck.

"Yes, that's her," he answered. "It's an old photo, obviously, but it—"

"This is her," Colette said and looked over at Pierre.

"Yes, that's what I was just saying—" Matthieu tried to continue.

"This is the woman that I passed on the stairs that night," Colette finished.

"The one that you said was wearing the same dress as you?" Pierre asked.

Colette nodded her head.

"She's wearing the *same* one in this photograph!" She cried. "The sparkling, scarlet evening gown!"

"It's not scarlet!" Matthieu suddenly erupted. "It's red, just say red—"

He trailed off when it all finally clicked. He had had a similar outburst when Worthington had suggested that he had seen a woman following Boutrel upstairs in a sparkling, scarlet evening gown. Earlier, he had thought when he had seen this photo of their engagement dinner that Genevieve could still fit into that dress, maybe she had, for that night at the château. Maybe Worthington had seen *Genevieve* going up the stairs in the sparkling, scarlet evening gown after Boutrel. The only reason that Matthieu hadn't made the connection sooner was because of his lack of creativity when it came to colors. There were the chartreuse walls that he insisted were yellow, Pierre's azure eyes that he insisted were blue, and now, there was Genevieve's scarlet dress that he had overlooked from the very beginning because he would have insisted that it was red. However, the fact alone that it was the same dress was all circumstantial.

"So, you were there too that evening?" Matthieu asked Colette suspiciously.

"She wasn't involved," Pierre lied. "She was invited there by one of the guests. It was a coincidence."

"Right," Matthieu said. "Anyways, alright, hold on. If what you're suggesting is true, then that would mean that Genevieve would have forged a nearly undetectable replica of the Han Sapphire necklace. Genevieve wouldn't know how to craft something like that, she would have needed someone like—"

He trailed off again.

"Someone like Videl," he finished.

He remembered thinking that with her connections, Genevieve could have found him. He never stopped to think that maybe she already had. After all, a laser diamond cutting machine was found in Videl's apartment, probably the same one from the case that Genevieve had been working about four weeks ago. The puzzle was coming together.

"I've heard the name before," Pierre said as he tried to remember back. He snapped his fingers when he came to the realization. "Norman…oh, what was his last name, it almost rhymed, didn't it?"

"Neamon," Matthieu finished for him. "Norman Neamon, FBI agent. The one that you impersonated in Paris."

Pierre blushed with embarrassment.

"So, you met Norman?" He asked. "How's my old friend doing?"

"Well, he's not in prison anymore, no thanks to you," Matthieu replied. "Anyways, he was the one that told you that he was looking for Videl."

"So, then we've got to go find this Videl character!" Pierre shouted. "He would be able to confirm her involvement."

"He's not going to talk to you, Pelletier," Matthieu said frankly.

"Well, then we'll make him talk! You know, just like those police shows. The rogue cop with nothing to lose, on the hunt for information that he probably can't handle, and he doesn't care how many kneecaps he has to break along the way."

"I admire your enthusiasm," Matthieu said. "But he's not going to talk because he's dead."

"Well, that's a shame," Colette replied.

Matthieu nodded.

"Whoever killed Boutrel now has three bodies on their hands," he said and held up three of his fingers. "And you're looking pretty good for it in the eyes of the police, Pelletier. Your stupid, little flower was left behind at every scene."

"Three bodies?" Pierre asked. "Who was the third?"

"Something Rochefort," Matthieu answered. "Remy?"

"Remy?!" Pierre repeated.

"You know him?" Matthieu asked.

"Oh, he was there that night at the château as well," Pierre said. "That bastard. I knew that he was involved with setting me up. Now, it's all coming together. They *knew* that I would leave behind the flower, setting myself up for the theft *and* the murder. Genevieve probably hired him to get into contact with me and then killed him to keep him quiet. What I don't understand though is how she found Remy in the first place. They said that I was a ghost, but that guy's the real ghost."

"I have no idea," Matthieu said. "But you really think that Genevieve has the necklace?"

"Oh, I'd stake my life on it," Pierre answered.

Matthieu sighed.

"I must be really losing it, because I believe you," he said.

"You do?!" Colette asked in disbelief.

"But recent events might also be clouding my judgement," Matthieu admitted. "Still, if what you're saying is true, then we're going to need a lot of evidence to support this. Otherwise, I'm taking the word of a confessed criminal and another assumed criminal. If Genevieve really was in on this, there's got to be a trail of some kind that ties her to it. For all that we know, the entire Toulouse Police Department could be in on it too. We need to find out how deep this thing goes, and we're probably going to have to do it alone until we know who we can trust."

"You keep saying we," Pierre said. "*We're* going to go after them. *We're* going to have to do it alone. I assume by that you mean *you*?"

"I mean all of us, including you two goons," Matthieu said. "I think it would also probably be best if I had my pistol for protection."

"Okay, where's your pistol?" Colette asked. "And where are we going to find the evidence that we need?"

"Fortunately, we can find both of those things at the station," Matthieu answered. "My pistol is probably tucked safely away in one of the drawers of the Chief's office and the case file should be in the file room."

"Okay," Pierre said. "So, we'll just swing over there and pick up your pistol and the case file. Piece of cake."

Matthieu shook his head.

"It won't be that easy," he said. "I'm suspended. That means that I'm not allowed in the building."

"So, what are you suggesting that we do?" Pierre asked warily.

Matthieu and Colette were both looking at him expectantly.

"Wait a minute," Pierre said. "Oh, no. I'm not breaking into the police station. Are you both crazy?"

"Do you expect one of us to do it?" Colette asked.

Pierre groaned.

"There was one more thing that I forgot to mention to you, Detective," he said.

"What's that?" Matthieu asked.

"Genevieve knows that I know."

67

Friday, the 6th of January, 2:23 p.m.

"**I** look ridiculous," Pierre said.

"You look fine," Colette assured him.

She was lying, of course, Pierre looked ridiculous. Then again, anybody would have looked equally ridiculous in the police uniform he was wearing that was about three sizes too large and the obviously fake mustache. The empty bag from the party planning store where they had purchased the ensemble was crunched up on the floor. The uniform itself was nearly identical to the normal Toulouse Police Department uniforms except for one key difference. The uniform that Pierre was wearing was tear away.

Matthieu, Colette and Pierre were sitting in the peach Peugeot just across the street from the Toulouse Police Department.

"Do you really think that this is going to work?" Pierre asked.

Matthieu shrugged.

"Only one way to find out," he said. "Now, remember, we need the case file from the file room and my pistol which is probably in one of the drawers in the Chief's office. You got it?"

"Yeah, yeah," Pierre said. "This isn't a grocery run, I'll get what I can."

"I can't help you if you don't bring me what I need, Pierre," Matthieu said.

Pierre groaned.

"Whenever you're ready, Pierre," Colette said.

"Remember," Matthieu began. "If you see Genevieve, steer as far clear as you can from her. If she gets spooked, she might try something desperate."

"Good thinking," Pierre began sarcastically. "And here I was, thinking that it might be a good idea to go right up to her and reminisce on how long it's been since we've seen each other."

Pierre adjusted the mustache that tickled his upper lip and then emerged from the car. He closed the car door behind him.

"Is he always this snarky?" Matthieu asked.

Colette nodded and rolled her eyes.

Pierre took a deep breath and then began walking slowly, but deliberately, toward the police station.

"This definitely isn't going to work," Colette said as she watched Pierre's pants slip down and he reached down to adjust them.

"No chance," Matthieu replied.

There were a couple of officers that were posted outside and as soon as he was within sight of them, he nodded casually.

If he acted like he belonged, he thought maybe he could slip past them.

The officers congregated by the door nodded to him, but they each had a puzzled look of unfamiliarity with him, like they didn't recognize Pierre. As casually as he could, Pierre continued past them and in through the glass doors of the station. Their eyes followed him the whole way, but eventually, they turned away, uninterested.

Pierre breathed a sigh of relief once inside.

When he climbed the familiar stairs in front of him, the station floor was swarming with officers. This fact alone probably shouldn't have surprised Pierre as much as it did, considering he was in a police station. He felt as if he had been thrown into the lion's den and slathered with barbecue sauce.

In front of Pierre, seated at a desk was Thomas. His head was buried in a stack of files and he didn't even look up when Pierre casually strolled by him.

He kept his eyes on Thomas as he walked right past and around him, toward the long corridor. Pierre remembered that the file room was to the right, a little down the hall from the Chief's office. He could get everything all in a row, it was almost too easy. However, he knew that he wouldn't be able to just walk in through the front doors of the two rooms. He was going to have to go through the all too familiar air duct system again, through the restroom. He was just going to have to hope that his pants didn't fall off along the way.

He was lost in thought and when he finally looked up again in the direction that he was walking, there in front of him, barreling down the hallway like an angry bull, was Genevieve.

Pierre quickly turned around and walked as casually as he could in the opposite direction, but Genevieve was storming down the hallway, and she was gaining on him. Her footsteps were right behind him when Pierre whipped around to turn himself in, just praying that she didn't kill him on the spot. However, much to his surprise, she continued past him, too distracted to really notice him. Then, she disappeared around the corner. Pierre followed and peered around the corner. He watched as she headed for the front door and wondered where she was going. Either way, it didn't matter to him and Pierre continued toward the restroom.

When he finally arrived, he checked under each of the stalls to make sure that he was alone. Then, he made his way to the last stall closest to the wall. He pushed it open and looked up at the air vent. To his dismay, the vent had been bolted to the wall.

Pierre wasn't entirely surprised by this discovery as, of course, the police would have reviewed the footage from his daring, interrogation room escape and then they would have taken the necessary precautions to ensure that kind of thing didn't happen again. Unfortunately for Pierre, if he wanted Matthieu's help, he was going to need it to happen one more time, but now, he was going to need to find an alternate way into the file room.

The Chief's office would be easy enough, if he wasn't in there. The file room, on the other hand, would be a problem. The door to the file room was locked and only accessible by key card. This would mean that he would either need to find a way to override the locking mechanism, or he would need to lift an ID badge off of an unsuspecting officer without them noticing. One scenario sounded impossible, the other sounded improbable, but far more likely. After all, Pierre had survived for a few, desperate years off pickpocketing alone.

He left the restroom with some semblance of a plan and emerged out into the hallway where he literally bumped into his old friends, Officers Beef and Cake. The force from the blow nearly knocked Pierre onto the ground, staggering him backwards a little, but he was able to maintain his footing. His fake mustache, on the other hand, hadn't been so fortunate. It tumbled from his lip and Pierre just barely caught it in his hand. He frantically tried to fit it back onto his face.

"Whoa didn't see you there," Officer Beef said. "Are you alright, pal?"

"Oh, yes," Pierre said, struggling to hold the mustache in place. The adhesive on the back of it was less sticky than it had been before.

"Did you bite your lip?" Officer Cake asked, trying to get a closer look.

Pierre laughed nervously and tried to turn away.

"You know how it is, with mustaches and all," Pierre said. Even he didn't know what this meant.

"Right," Officer Beef replied, staring at Pierre suspiciously.

Pierre glanced over and noticed the ID badge clipped loosely to the officer's belt.

"Yes, anyways," Pierre began. "I should really get going, I'm late for that meeting."

He began to walk and tried to squeeze past them in the hallway, but Officer Beef stuck his hand out.

"The meeting is that way," he said and pointed toward the conference rooms down the hall.

"Did I say meeting?" Pierre asked. "I meant restroom."

"You're late for the restroom?" Officer Cake asked.

"Yes, yes, you know how it goes. Crohn's Disease! That's it!" Pierre shouted emphatically. "Yes, Crohn's Disease. It's like clockwork. You can set your watch to it."

Officer Beef grimaced.

"Good luck with that," he said. "Make sure you wash your hands."

The two officers brushed past Pierre in the hallway, but not before Pierre first slyly unclipped the ID badge from Officer Beef's belt. The officer didn't even flinch.

He watched the two officers disappear into the conference room and then casually strolled by on his way to the file room. He looked up at the camera that was recording the entire hallway, but there was no way to avoid it. Besides, it wouldn't matter anyway. If the mission was successful, nobody would suspect a thing.

He approached the door and looked down at the ID card.

"Officer Timothy Twigs," he read aloud. "What a strange name for such a large man. He looks more like an Officer Beef."

He shrugged and then held out the ID card toward the little black key card reader on the side of the file room door. The light above the key card reader lit up green. Pierre reached his hand for the door handle which turned without issue. Just like that, Pierre was back inside.

He immediately ran over to the shelf that was lined with folders and scanned through them. He couldn't remember the number of the case file, but if he saw it, he was sure that he would recognize it.

His eyes finally landed on it.

"1593," he read aloud. "Come to papa!"

Pierre reached out and pulled the folder from the shelf. It was much heavier than he remembered and, when he flipped it open, there was his own stupid mugshot photo from his teenage years, grinning up at him like an idiot. There he was, in all his glory, prime suspect nombre un in the Boutrel case.

He flipped the folder shut and then placed it under his armpit before walking back over to the door.

"Don't forget to get milk, dear," he mumbled, mocking Matthieu. "Oh, and can you just get my pistol while you're at it? I'll just be waiting in the car."

He pushed the door open and proceeded back down the hallway. Fortunately for Pierre, the Chief was occupied by the meeting that was conveniently taking place in the conference room at the time. So, his office was empty.

Pierre stealthily slipped his way into the office and the door closed behind him. It was easy enough, and Pierre couldn't believe it had been so. The only problem was, and if he didn't see this one coming from the beginning, then he was only fooling himself, the tear away police uniform he was wearing had been hanging so loosely that a part of his shirt had gotten caught in the door as it closed behind him. When he took one step forward, instead of tugging against it, the entire uniform completely ripped apart at the seams and stripped Pierre down to his boxers with a loud ripping noise.

"That can't be good," he said as he glanced down at himself.

He tried to pick up the tattered remains of the clothes, but it would be no use trying to put them back together. So, he ran over to the Chief's desk and began rummaging through the drawers frantically. There was random junk in nearly every drawer but finally, Pierre found the pistol and held it in his hands. Pierre never liked guns. He acknowledged their usefulness on some occasions, but he thought that, overall, they lacked style and finesse, two things that Pierre was most concerned with over practicality.

That's when the doorknob to the office began to jiggle.

"Seriously?" Pierre mumbled. "Again?!"

Without another moment to lose, Pierre slammed the drawers shut and hid underneath the Chief's desk.

The door pushed open and the Chief came in, a doughnut in one hand and his cell phone in the other. He nearly tripped over the pile of tattered clothes on the floor.

"What the hell?" He exclaimed and looked down at the disassembled police uniform that lay in ruins. "People need to pick up after themselves."

He grumbled to himself and then stepped over the pile, walked over to his desk and then sat down. He looked around his desktop surface for a moment and he suddenly felt that something didn't seem quite right. It was as if a few of the objects had been slightly displaced from their original positions.

Before he had another moment to think about it, Pierre darted out from under the desk and toward the door. He had the pistol in one hand and the case file under the armpit of his other arm. The Chief's mouth dropped open in disbelief when he saw the barely clothed man running through his office in nothing more than his boxer shorts.

"Stop!" He finally stammered.

Pierre didn't listen. Instead, he ran out of the office and through the station floor. He continued past the bewildered onlookers, before arriving at the stairs.

"Stop him!" The Chief yelled.

Nobody knew what to do.

284

Pierre ran through the front door, across the street and jumped in through the open back window of Colette's car.

"Drive, drive, drive!" He instructed.

"Did you get everything that I asked for?" Matthieu asked.

"What happened to your clothes?" Colette tried.

"Just drive!" Pierre shouted.

Colette slammed down on the gas pedal and the tires of the Peugeot screeched beneath them. They disappeared down the street just as the officers in the building were making their way outside.

"Was that the streaker again?" Thomas turned to the Chief and asked.

The Chief nodded, out of breath from the chase.

"I don't know how the hell that guy keeps getting in here," he said.

Simone was standing beside them. Her eyes were twitching in the sunlight. When she caught the last glimpse of the peach Peugeot, she watched it curiously before it disappeared down the street.

68

Friday, the 6th of January, 5:12 p.m.

The two amateur detectives, Pierre and Colette, and the blossoming criminal, Matthieu, were gathered around the coffee table in Matthieu's living room. The case file was laying closed on top of the table in front of them.

"Now that we've got this," Matthieu began. "Before we go through it, we've got to be careful. In the words of the great Sherlock Holmes, we need to find theories to suit facts instead of twisting facts to suit theories. In other words, we need to go into this with a clean slate and the eyes of an unbiased observer."

"Is that a friend of yours?" A freshly clothed Pierre asked.

"Who?" Matthieu asked.

"Sherlock Holmes?"

"Just ignore him," Colette said.

Matthieu rolled his eyes. It was not nearly as cute as when Colette did it, Pierre noted. Then, Matthieu flipped open the folder.

Colette reached in and grabbed the top sheet of paper.

"Can I get a blown-up copy of this?" She asked, holding up Pierre's old mugshot.

Pierre snatched it from her hands.

"Can we focus?" Matthieu asked.

"*She* started it," Pierre said.

"How is it possible that you two bicker like an old, married couple, but at the same time sound as if you're five years old?"

Matthieu flipped through the file until he found the first item that he was most interested in, the guest list for the soirée.

"What do you have there?" Colette asked. She reached in and grabbed another sheet of paper.

"Genevieve was at the party," Matthieu said. Although he was trying to remain unbiased, he was probably the worst person to be so in this situation. "She told me that she was there. I just wanted to confirm that her name was on the guest list. Which, it is." He pointed to the name "Genevieve Gereaux."

"So, is that enough proof?" Pierre asked.

Matthieu shook his head.

"The whole city was at that soirée," he said.

"So, you were there too?" Pierre asked. "Then you must have seen something—"

Matthieu scowled.

"I wasn't invited," he mumbled.

"Well, at least that proves that she was there," Colette interrupted.

"What's this?" Pierre asked, pulling another sheet from the large pile.

"Those are numbers, Pierre," Colette said, peering over his shoulder.

"I know what numbers are, Colette," Pierre replied. "I'm wondering what their significance is."

"Hmm?" Matthieu asked. He was absorbed in the crime scene photos now. "Oh, those are just Boutrel's bank transactions."

"A lot of red," Pierre remarked.

"Those are transfers out of the accounts," Matthieu said absentmindedly. He had spent so much time studying them he could probably recite the numbers in order by heart.

"They're all going to a place called Financial Union," Pierre said.

"It's not a real institution," Matthieu informed him.

Pierre chuckled.

"No kidding," he said and flipped the page around, pointing to the first letter of each of the words, "F. U. Seems like Boutrel's last middle finger to us all."

Matthieu grunted.

"And then he closed all of his accounts dating back five weeks ago," Pierre remarked. "Looks like Boutrel was about to be on the run."

Matthieu looked up from the photographs.

"What did you just say?" He asked.

"Boutrel was about to be on the run?" Pierre repeated.

"No, before that."

"I know what numbers are, Colette?"

"*No*! After that!"

"Something about closing his accounts dating back five weeks ago?" Colette repeated for him.

"Five weeks ago," Matthieu mumbled.

He reached over and snagged the document from Pierre's hands. He had obviously seen the closure of all Boutrel's accounts in France, dating back to the 3rd of December. Something else significant happened on that day, but Matthieu had never made the connection until now because he had not been following the dates. However, he was certainly keeping track of the weeks.

Pierre and Colette looked at each other and both exchanged the same confused look and a shrug.

"Do you know what else happened five weeks ago?" Matthieu asked.

Pierre and Colette shrugged.

"Genevieve left me five weeks ago," Matthieu said. "Five weeks ago, tomorrow."

"Oh, I'm sorry to hear that," Pierre said with the fakest sincerity that he could muster.

"No, it's not about being sorry," Matthieu said. "But thank you. Why do you think she would leave me?"

Pierre looked the former Detective up and down and then cleared his throat.

"I can't think of anything," he said.

"She was trying to cut ties!" Colette declared.

Matthieu placed one finger on his nose and pointed another at Colette.

"That's why she gave up the house so easily too," Matthieu realized. "She didn't even try to fight me for it. In fact, she offered it to me. It's just as you said Pelletier. She did all of that because she was about to be on the run."

"But, if Boutrel and Genevieve were about to run away together, then why did Boutrel's accounts reopen on the 17th of December?" Colette asked.

Matthieu stared down at the transaction sheet.

"Three weeks ago," he mumbled.

"Wait a minute," Pierre realized. "Do you know what else happened three weeks ago?"

Matthieu and Colette looked at him expectantly.

"The 17th of December was the day that Remy called me," Pierre said. "That was the time that we began preparing for the heist!"

"Strange coincidence," Matthieu mumbled, lost in thought.

"Why would Boutrel reopen his accounts if he was planning on running?" Colette asked.

"Beats me," Pierre said.

"Let's start from the beginning, I guess," Matthieu began. "If Boutrel and Genevieve were both planning on running about five weeks ago, that would mean that they were in on the robbery together?"

"Well, that would mean that Boutrel set up his own murder," Colette said.

"Maybe they were initially in on a plan together," Pierre suggested. "Maybe it was something that involved the fake necklace. Then, Genevieve switched sides and turned on him."

Matthieu reached for the evidence list at the Boutrel crime scene.

"Boutrel was stabbed with his own dagger," he said. "The other two victims were stabbed with identical daggers to each other, but they didn't belong to the victims. I suspected from the beginning that Boutrel was stabbed in the heat of passion."

"But that still doesn't explain three weeks ago," Pierre said. "Say that Boutrel changed his mind around that time. Maybe that was why Genevieve decided to kill him."

"So, you're saying that Genevieve set it up to look like it was a crime in the heat of passion?" Matthieu asked. "Like a robbery gone wrong?"

"Maybe," Pierre said.

"That seems to strangely add up," Matthieu decided. "But it's still just speculation. I would venture to agree, however, that something went sour between them right around that time three weeks ago. I know that Boutrel was trying to move the necklace. In fact, he was trying to do it at the New Year's Eve soirée. He had a couple of interested buyers there as well, the Chinese Ambassador, Zhao Zhu and the Russian Ambassador, Yuri Yachnitch."

"Maybe Genevieve and Boutrel had the fake necklace crafted so that they could sell that to the buyer and then they were going to disappear with the real necklace," Colette suggested. "From there, they could cut the real necklace up into pieces and then sell it for the sum of its parts. I've seen it done before. It's like a chop shop but for expensive jewelry. Maybe Genevieve got greedy and changed the plan on him."

"That could make sense," Pierre began. "But where do I fit into all of this?"

"You always have to make it about *you*, don't you, Pierre?" Colette snarked.

"You were set up to take the fall for the heist *and* the murder," Matthieu reminded him.

"Right," Pierre said. "But let's say that Genevieve called Remy three weeks ago to stage the heist. This would have been right around the time that she decided to backstab Boutrel, or, front stab him, I guess. How would she have even gotten his number? Like I said, Remy's like a ghost. Besides that, how did she even know that he had a connection with me? We've only worked together once before that night and that was during the heist of the Museum of Modern Art."

"The simple answer is that Genevieve has unbelievable connections throughout the art world," Matthieu said. "But, nothing about any of this seems simple. So, I don't have the answer for you, but maybe we can find out."

"How do you propose that we do that?" Colette asked.

"By finding out exactly what went down three weeks ago," Matthieu said. "The three-week and five-week coincidences might not be enough for a conviction, but it's enough to convince me that something suspicious is going on here. Maybe Beatrice Boutrel or Lucile Lebas can shed some light on it. After all, Genevieve seemed pretty cozy with them the few times that I saw them together. We should start with them at the château. While we're there, maybe we can have a word with our mutual friend, Monsieur François Fouquet."

Matthieu tapped the pistol which he had holstered on the strap across his shoulder.

"Not *him* again," Pierre groaned.

69

Friday, the 6th of January, 6:43 p.m.

The pink terra-cotta bricks of the Château de Boutrel were ablaze and almost appeared red in the fading sunlight, but none of those present outside of the château that evening were there to admire its beauty.

Pierre and Colette were arguing on the staircase, under the watchful eyes of the looming lion statues, and Matthieu was threatening to, "turn this thing around and go home." He sounded more like a tired parent who has had enough of his two young children during a long road trip than a seasoned detective.

Finally, one of the large, front, double doors of the château swung graciously open and there, standing in her nightgown, was Beatrice Boutrel.

"Detective Matthieu," she said with a surprised look on her face which quickly changed to a delighted smile. "To what do I owe the pleasure?"

"Good evening, Madame Boutrel—"

289

"Call me, Beatrice," she interrupted.

"Yes, good evening, Beatrice," Matthieu said. "Is it alright if we come in? We just have a few more questions for you regarding your husband's death."

"Of course, Detective," she said and stepped aside to let them in.

Matthieu glanced around the familiar foyer and his eyes were drawn back, yet again, to the numerous paintings of naked people in various positions that lined the magnificent staircase. It was still the second most butt-cheeks that he had ever seen exposed in one place.

Pierre and Colette were too busy with Beatrice to notice their surroundings.

"I don't believe that we've had the pleasure of meeting," she said, intrigued. She extended a hand out to both, but to Pierre in particular.

Colette intercepted her hand.

"Detective Couvrir," she said and shook the widow's hand.

Matthieu turned around and scowled at her.

"Detective Pelletier," Pierre said next. He took the widow's hand and kissed it gently. "But my friends just call me Dr. Detective Pelletier."

"Charming," Beatrice replied. She studied Pierre with a flirtatious smile for a moment. "Please, come in."

Beatrice led them all into the parlour where Pierre admired the expensive furniture. There were magnificent vases scattered throughout and paintings that lined the walls. He had been in the château once before, of course, but this was the first time that he had been *invited* in. The last time that he had seen this room, he was staring in through the bushes in the garden outside and wishing that he could belong to this world. For the moment, at least, he could pretend that he did.

He sat down on the couch, which probably cost more than a year's rent at his current apartment. However, he soon realized that price didn't always equal comfort. When he sat, the cushion didn't give at all. It was like sitting on a wooden board. Pierre shifted around uncomfortably.

"Is Mademoiselle Lebas still staying with you?" Matthieu asked, looking around.

The smile that Beatrice was trying desperately to hold on to quickly faded to a frown.

"Oh, you're here for her?" She asked. Pierre could detect a hint of annoyance in her tone.

"Both of you, actually," Matthieu answered.

Beatrice stood up and disappeared beyond the doorway without another word.

"I take it that they're not as friendly with each other as they may appear to be from an outsider's perspective?" Colette whispered. She had seen the photos in the paper of Lucile crying into Beatrice's shoulders.

"You should have seen them in the interrogation room," Matthieu replied.

Beatrice returned a few moments later with Lucile Lebas in tow. Lucile was crying into Beatrice's shoulder as Beatrice was stroking her hair soothingly. The two ladies sat down on the couch across from their guests. Colette exchanged a skeptical glance with Matthieu.

"What's this about?" Lucile asked in between sobs.

"Can we cut the act for a minute?" Matthieu asked.

Colette suddenly whipped her head in shock over to the former Detective.

"Act?" Lucile repeated. "Her husband, *my* lover, is dead! And you dare have the audacity to come into *our* house and say this is an *act*?!"

"So, you two are sharing the house now?" Matthieu asked calmly.

He noticed Beatrice flinch.

"Fine," Matthieu said. "Since you want to bring lovers into this, then let's talk about lovers. I take it that Madame Boutrel knows about François Fouquet?"

Beatrice didn't just flinch this time. Her eyes widened and she glared down at the young girl in her arms with the crocodile tears still streaming down her face. Lucile wailed and buried her face in the widow's arm.

"I take it by your reaction, Beatrice, that you didn't know about the affair between Mademoiselle Lebas and Monsieur Fouquet?" Matthieu asked.

"You little witch!" Beatrice cried. She pushed Lucile off her disgustedly and rose to her feet.

"Oh, boy," Pierre mumbled.

"It wasn't enough that you could have my husband," Beatrice roared. "But you had to have *my* lover as well?!"

"Wait a minute," Colette interrupted. "So, you were both sleeping with the same château servant while also both engaged in a relationship with Monsieur Boutrel?"

"My head hurts," Pierre muttered.

"Please, Beatrice," Matthieu began. "Have a seat."

Beatrice sat down on the opposite end of the couch a meter away from Lucile. The look of pure disgust still hadn't left her face.

"So, you were having an affair with Monsieur Fouquet as well?" Matthieu asked.

Beatrice corrected herself and regained some of her composure.

"It was strictly sexual, Detective," she answered. She glanced over at Lucile who had her face buried in her hands and was sobbing uncontrollably.

"I believe that Lucile said that she and Fouquet spent most nights, if not every night together," Matthieu said.

"François and I never spent the night together, Detective," Beatrice replied. "He was usually gone by 9 o'clock. I much preferred sleeping alone. When you've been married for as long as I have, obviously you still have needs," she winked toward Pierre. Pierre recoiled a bit. "But you prefer the solitude."

"And Boutrel couldn't meet those needs?" Matthieu asked.

Beatrice shook her head and scoffed.

"Bastien was a wet noodle, if you know what I mean," she said.

"Ew," Pierre mumbled.

"So, it sounds to me like Fouquet was quite the servant," Matthieu noted. "Servicing you both on the same night. First, you, Madame Boutrel. Then, you would kick him out and once Monsieur Boutrel had passed out, Lucile would join him in his sleeping quarters for the rest of the evening. What a guy."

Beatrice was scowling at Lucile.

"Is Fouquet here today?" Matthieu asked, glancing around the room again. He casually reached his hand in through his jacket and tightened his grip around the handle of his pistol. "We'd like to have a few words with him as well."

Lucile burst out crying again.

"I'm afraid that we haven't seen him in a couple of days," Beatrice said. "He hasn't been around since Sunday."

"Hmm," Matthieu said. "*You* haven't seen him around recently either, or have you, Mademoiselle Lebas?"

Lucile lifted her head briefly from her hands and shook it.

"Shame," Matthieu said suspiciously.

"Do you think that François had something to do with my husband's death?" Beatrice asked.

"We believe that he may have played a part, yes," Matthieu replied.

"A *big* part," Pierre added.

"Yes, we believe that he may have poisoned your husband."

"Poisoned?!" Beatrice repeated. "But my husband was stabbed!"

"Very true, Madame," Matthieu said. "It does appear to be quite the enigma, doesn't it? You wouldn't happen to know anything about it, would you, Mademoiselle Lebas?"

Matthieu turned his attention towards Bastien Boutrel's mistress with the observant eyes of a seasoned detective.

Lucile's sobbing came to a screeching halt and she glared up at Matthieu.

"I didn't have anything to do with that," she said suddenly, dropping her previous routine and growing defensive at the accusation.

"What's going on here, Detective?" Beatrice asked.

"I believe that Fouquet poisoned your husband, Madame Boutrel. I think that Mademoiselle Lebas may have also played a hand in it."

"I did no such thing," Lucile insisted.

"You're quite the actress," Matthieu said. "It seems like you can even cry on command! Look at you, you have real tears streaming down your face! It's not a far leap for me to assume that you could easily lie about your involvement."

"You little witch," Beatrice spat venomously.

"If I really had something to do with it, don't you think that I would have run along with François?" Lucile asked.

Matthieu stared into her eyes intently.

"I had thought about that as well," he said finally, after a tense stare off. "I believe that you truly are quite the little manipulator. But I think that while you thought that you were playing Fouquet, he was playing you all along."

"What do you mean?" Lucile demanded.

"I think that he was using you to get closer to Monsieur Boutrel," Matthieu answered. He suspected that François was using both women to that effect for that matter.

Lucile was scowling.

"I do have another question for you both," Matthieu said.

Lucile looked like she was about to lunge at Matthieu and rip his head off. Beatrice looked as if she was ready to slap Lucile across the face.

Matthieu reached into his back pocket and pulled out the crumpled up photograph that he had brought with him. It was the photo of he and Genevieve at their engagement dinner. He unfolded it and held it up for them to see.

"How well did you know this woman?" He asked and pointed to his ex-wife.

"Genevieve?" Beatrice began. "She was a good friend of Bastien's."

"A good friend," Matthieu repeated suspiciously. "Can you elaborate?"

"She was here from time to time," Beatrice said. "My husband was a very 'generous donor' to the police. I assume it was because he wanted to make sure that they were in his back pocket."

Matthieu had had the same assumption.

"You say that she was here from time to time. Did you ever overhear what they discussed?"

"Art, mostly," Beatrice recalled.

Lucile nodded.

"It bored me half to death the way that they would sit there and babble," she said.

"Uncultured swine," Pierre mumbled under his breath.

"Nothing nefarious?" Matthieu asked.

"What do you mean, Detective?" Beatrice asked.

"Did you ever hear them discussing anything illegal?"

"Nothing like that," Beatrice replied.

"Me neither," Lucile agreed.

"Hmm," Matthieu grunted. "Did either of you notice a change in Monsieur Boutrel, dating back roughly five weeks ago?"

"What kind of change?" Beatrice asked, she stared back at Lucile.

"Were there any sudden plans that he made, any change in temperament?"

"There was one," Lucile piped up.

Beatrice focused her eyes sharply on the girl.

"One what?" Matthieu asked.

"Plan," she said. "Bastien was planning a trip about five weeks ago, but then about three weeks ago, he said that he had to cancel it. He said that something else came up."

"Did you know about this trip, Madame Boutrel?" Matthieu asked.

"I never heard anything of the sort," she replied.

"That's because you weren't invited," Lucile informed her. "He said that it was just for the two of us!"

"Where was he planning on taking you?" Matthieu asked.

"He wouldn't say," Lucile answered. "No matter how much I pressed him."

"When were you supposed to leave?"

"This coming Sunday," Lucile said.

Her face contorted into a hideously ugly crying face, but before she could begin the waterworks, Beatrice reached over and struck Lucile across the face with the open palm of her hand.

Lucile recoiled from the blow and then reached for her lip with her hand. When she pulled it back, she revealed a bright, red streak of fresh blood.

"You old witch," she cried and lunged for Beatrice, grabbing her by the hair.

Matthieu and Colette tried to intervene and pull the two women apart. Pierre sat there, in shock, taking in the ensuing catfight with his mouth agape.

When they were finally pulled apart, Matthieu sat them down on opposite couches.

"When did Monsieur Boutrel change his mind about the trip?" Matthieu asked.

"I don't remember," Lucile said in between whimpers.

"You said it was three weeks ago," Matthieu replied. "What was the date?"

"The 17th maybe?" Lucile said.

"Did you remember seeing Genevieve that night?" Matthieu asked.

"She was here all right," Beatrice interrupted coldly. She was still straightening her nightgown and patting her hair down from the brawl.

"She was?" Matthieu asked.

"I remember because the 17th is my birthday, not that Bastien bothered to remember. That was also the night where Bastien accidentally stumbled into *my* room, bumbling drunk. Maybe even more so than I had ever seen him, which is saying a lot. I remember that Genevieve and he were discussing the paintings in the foyer again. I could hear Bastien babbling like a drunken fool when I was upstairs."

"You said that they were discussing the paintings 'again,' Madame?"

"Oh, he always loved to brag about those things. It gave him a sense of superiority or something. If you ask me, I'd say all of those expensive art purchases were just his way of overcompensating."

"And later that evening, he stumbled into *your* room," Matthieu repeated for clarification. "What led you to believe that was an accident?"

"He knew better than to disturb me," she said. "Besides, he was whispering Lucile's name."

Lucile erupted into tears again. There was no way to tell if they were real or fake. Although everyone present assumed the latter. She stood up and ran off. She slammed the bedroom door shut behind her and then from the parlour, they could hear the lock to her door clicking in place.

Beatrice watched her leave with fiery hatred burning in her eyes. She turned this intense stare back to her guests. It was as if she intended to take her wrath out on them next.

"Well, then," she began. "Was that everything?"

Matthieu stammered.

"Just one more question," he began. "Do you remember seeing Genevieve the night of the soirée?"

"She was there," Beatrice grumbled.

"Do you remember what she was wearing?"

"She was wearing the same dress in the photo that you just showed me," Beatrice said. "The sparkling, scarlet evening gown. I remember because she looked like a trollop. Anything else?"

She looked like she was about to snap at any moment.

"No, um, no," Matthieu stammered and then turned back to his associates. "Are you guys good?"

"Yeah, yeah," Pierre said. "I'm good."

Colette nodded in agreement.

"Alright," Matthieu said. "Thank you for your hospitality, we'll see ourselves out."

The three rushed for the front door and Matthieu pulled it open as Colette and Pierre stood in the foyer waiting impatiently. Pierre hadn't gotten a good look around when he first walked in. His eyes curiously were drawn to the paintings of naked people in various positions that lined the staircase.

Matthieu pulled the door open and Colette followed him outside, but Pierre didn't. When Matthieu looked back, Pierre seemed to be entranced by the butt-cheeks.

"Pierre!" Matthieu exclaimed and reached back. He grabbed Pierre by the arm. "We're leaving!"

"I know how Genevieve found me," Pierre said. The words seemed to drool out of him. It was almost as if he had been hypnotized.

"What are you talking about?" Matthieu asked.

Pierre slowly lifted his arm and pointed to the paintings along the wall of the staircase. He was pointing at one painting in particular. It was of two naked people, stretched out on a grassy terrain with their butt-cheeks exposed.

"*La Pastorale*," Pierre said, the real one.

70

Friday, the 6th of January, 2:30 p.m.

Genevieve had also taken an interest in this painting as well. As the head detective of the Art Crime and Thefts Division, she was aware of the painting's status. Namely, she was aware that the painting had been stolen.

She had finished tying up whatever loose ends that she had at the police station, and she was on her way to the rundown motel where she was currently staying to pack up what remained of her belongings. When she had moved into the motel room five weeks ago, after her separation with Matthieu, she had packed lightly. She knew at the time that this wasn't going to be a permanent relocation.

While driving home from the police station that day, hopefully for the last time, she was thinking a lot about Bastien Boutrel.

She could remember meeting him for the first time at an art gala a few years ago. Truth be told, she had never liked him. He was a pompous and arrogant man, and those were two of his better qualities. However, back then, she never had any intention of killing him, or maybe she did, and she just wasn't ready to admit it.

On her first visit to the château, for one of Boutrel's famous soirées, she recognized *La Pastorale* on the wall almost immediately. This was a few years ago, and a few years after the heist of the Museum of Modern Art in Paris. She wondered if Boutrel knew of its status and the fact that the painting had been infamously stolen from the museum. She assumed that he had been cautious at first to expose the painting, but after enough time had passed, he displayed the painting in the foyer intentionally. She assumed that he was very aware of the painting's status. Its presence was the reason why Boutrel refused to allow cameras or cell phones at any of his soirées, including during his New Year's Eve soirée on the night that he had been murdered.

So, she thought about trying to bring a case against him, but ultimately decided, what was the point? Her husband always mocked how trivial her work was and maybe he had been right all along. Boutrel was just another cog in a greater machine. Genevieve could spend her whole life doing this, but for what? It was just a job at the end of the day, one that wasn't very financially rewarding but incredibly demanding. Everyday there was a new case just like this one. Most went unsolved. Everyone was getting a piece of the pie, everyone except for her. So, she thought of another idea, one to get her a seat at the dessert table. She was going to confront Boutrel privately about the painting, with the intent of blackmailing him.

Genevieve had never done anything like this before, but for such a tremendous potential payout, she didn't hesitate to take advantage. Besides, there was truthfully no harm that could come of it. It was only a victimless art crime, after all.

However, instead of blackmailing Boutrel, she came up with an even better idea. She proposed to Boutrel that they make a forgery of the painting. Since the real painting had been stolen, and only Boutrel knew of its whereabouts, it would be easy to pass off the forgery as an authentic. She said that they could make a fortune doing so.

It wasn't hard for her to find a young Henri Harquin and she commissioned him to produce the forgery. Genevieve already knew of his prowess and attention to detail when it came to his painting and sculpting. If he were born in a different era, Harquin could have been one of the world's great painters. However, when she met him, he was a struggling artist with a drug addiction and desperate for an opportunity to make some extra cash. So, he agreed without much convincing and began producing the high-quality forgery.

For a time after that, Genevieve and Boutrel enjoyed a prosperous relationship. Harquin had discovered a new passion and continued producing forgeries under the alias, Videl. Boutrel sold the forgery to some rich prick from Tulsa, Oklahoma for a hefty amount. It wasn't an incredible amount, but it was a modest fortune. After all, the value of the painting had skyrocketed with the amount of press that it had received. Genevieve hid the money from her husband. She returned to the trivialness of her job but, although she should have probably felt guilty about the whole ordeal, the thought of having pulled it off was exhilarating. Nevertheless, she told herself that she would never do something like that again.

When Boutrel was first introduced to the Han Sapphire necklace at a private auction, he was enamoured by it, struck by its beauty. This was when he hatched the plan and had decided that this would be a wonderful opportunity for an even bigger payout. One that could hopefully release him from the clutches of his miserable wife, Beatrice. Although the painting forgery had been quite successful, he still relied on her financially to fund his criminal ventures, unbeknownst to her. Still, her "allowances" felt like a spit right in Boutrel's face. But, with a score like this, he could disappear from her forever.

Boutrel was the one who had approached Genevieve with the idea. She tried to decline at first, but he threatened to expose her for her role in the forgery of *La Pastorale* and she quickly changed her tune. Obviously, she didn't appreciate being threatened, but since she had recently turned 50, she had been looking for a way out of her own banal existence with Matthieu. Besides that, she also needed to catch that exhilarating high that she had felt from her first crime once more. She decided that this could be her ticket.

It would be simple enough. They would find an interested buyer for the Han Sapphire necklace and commission Videl for a forgery. At the last moment, they would swap out the real necklace for the fake. Later, they would break the necklace into pieces and then sell it for the sum of its parts. That way, they could both enjoy a tremendous fortune from the sale of the necklace. Since Boutrel had fronted the money for the original purchase of the necklace, he would obtain the lion's share for its sale, of course. However, Genevieve's cut would be nothing to scoff at.

Genevieve's hands tightened on the steering wheel when her mind drifted back to the night that everything changed, three weeks ago.

On that night, she remembered that Boutrel was already three sheets to the wind by the time that she had arrived at the château and he was fumbling over his own words.

Lucile joined them in the parlour as they made small talk, casually discussing some of the movers and shakers in the art world. Beatrice passed by the parlour every so often, glaring in at them. Genevieve didn't know it, but Beatrice was upset about Bastien having forgotten her birthday that evening. It wasn't like there was any love left in their marriage anyways, but the least that he could have done was get her a cake.

When Lucile had grown bored and decided that she was going to sleep, she retired to her bedroom. That was when they turned to business. Boutrel led Genevieve into the foyer and began bragging about the paintings that lined the walls of his staircase. At some point during the discussion, he turned to Genevieve and informed her of his new plan, one that didn't involve her at all. He had decided that he was going to sell the necklace legitimately.

Genevieve suspected that he had finally grown a pair and asked for a raise in his allowance from Beatrice and that was why he decided that he no longer wanted to run. He could sell the necklace for more than he had purchased it and, along with an increased allowance, what more would he need? The only problem was that this meant Genevieve wasn't going to get a cut at all, and she wasn't particularly fond of that idea. The other problem came when she realized Boutrel had her wrapped around his finger, and she didn't like that either.

Initially, she had rejected the entire plan, but now, she was all in. She had already separated from Matthieu and had gone through all the trouble of procuring the fake necklace from Videl. Only a week after her separation from her husband, she had helped orchestrate the robbery of the jewelry store to steal the laser diamond cutting machine to produce it. That was, of course, the reason that the investigation into the robbery had reached a dead end, because Genevieve never actually investigated it since she was the one responsible. After all of that, what good would the forgery be to her now? Besides all of that, anytime Boutrel told her to jump, as long as he could lord this blackmail over her, all she could do was ask, how high? He had her in his back pocket, and that enraged Genevieve.

At the time, when Boutrel had broken the news to her that the deal was off, she was infuriated, but she tried her best to control her temper. She wanted to kill him right then and there for betraying her, but cooler heads would prevail. She decided that Boutrel could make his own plans, but then she was going to make hers.

Some semblance of a plan began to take root, but it didn't formulate completely until Boutrel stopped in front of *La Pastorale* itself that night and he began bragging about it, just as he always did. Genevieve wondered if he got off on the idea that he displayed the painting out in the open like that.

In the next moment, a plan to solve both of her problems at once sprouted to life; the first part was that the old, fat bastard had to die. She knew it, and she wasn't sorry about it. After all, he was the only one that could point to her involvement with the forgery of *La Pastorale*. Well, him and Videl. They were both loose ends. Genevieve hated loose ends, but she discovered that she really enjoyed tying them up. Stabbing them seemed to her the best way to do this. Forgery to murder was a far leap, but Genevieve was determined to make it.

However, her plan was still lacking one important component. She couldn't very well kill Boutrel outright in his home, as much as she wanted to reach over and strangle him as he continued to babble on about *La Pastorale*. No, that would be far too messy. She needed someone to take the fall for Boutrel's death. It had to be some blissfully unaware, yet completely arrogant simpleton.

Fortunately for her, the idea was staring her right in the face, *La Pastorale*. Throughout the remainder of the evening, Genevieve encouraged Boutrel to become more and more intoxicated and he became more and more loose with his words. Drinking made Boutrel feel invincible and by the time he had told her everything, he was more full of himself than she had ever seen him. That was, of course, why Boutrel had been so belligerently drunk that he had accidentally stumbled into Beatrice's room later that night.

It didn't take long for Genevieve to pry the entire story of *La Pastorale* out of Boutrel, which included the *Black Lotus'* involvement and the contact information for Remy Rochefort, who had been contracted to steal the painting initially from the Museum of Modern Art. The reason he had all of this information was quite simply because Bastien Boutrel had been the mysterious art dealer who Remy had been dealing with from the very beginning. Boutrel was behind the entire *Black Lotus'* heist of the museum.

The next part of Genevieve's plan was easy. Pierre had agreed to the deal, no doubt because of the hefty price tag it came with. Genevieve was going to steal the necklace, kill Boutrel and then set up this poor idiot for both crimes.

On that fateful evening, it happened exactly as she planned it. With Remy in her ear, switching frequencies between Pierre's earpiece and hers, which caused the static that Pierre had heard that night, the plan was put in motion. Remy, of course, was aware of the plan to frame Pierre for the heist, but he wasn't aware that Genevieve had intended to kill Boutrel from the very beginning.

During the soirée, Genevieve could tell that Boutrel was more intoxicated than he usually was, and he was a lot more cooperative, which played to her advantage. She followed him upstairs to the study where she thought that she was going to have to threaten him to give her the passcode to his safe, but he did so without any fuss. In fact, he was even laughing about the whole ordeal. Unbeknownst to her, he wasn't actually intoxicated, this was merely a secondary effect from the poison. Regardless, he wouldn't be laughing long.

Genevieve retrieved the Han Sapphire necklace from the safe and gazed upon its wonder as Boutrel stood there, swaying in place. Next, Genevieve grabbed the dagger from the display case on his desk. This was all a part of her plan as well because it would make it look as if Boutrel had been killed in a crime of passion, like a robbery gone bad, instead of one that had been meticulously orchestrated.

As she pictured herself plunging the dagger into Boutrel's heart on that evening, her hands relaxed a bit on the steering wheel. The blade passed through him effortlessly. It was a cathartic moment of release for her. In her mind, she settled for a moment on the satisfying look of helplessness on his face as he took his last breath.

With the real Han Sapphire necklace in her purse, and the decoy in the safe, Genevieve stuffed Boutrel's lifeless body into the closet. She struggled a bit under his weight, but finally got him in there. She left the room and headed down the stairs just as a woman wearing an identical dress as her own and that she didn't recognize, but knew was part of the heist, Colette, was heading up them.

Everything had seemed so easy from there. Genevieve could have simply staged the scene to make it look like Pierre had been there, but she needed Pierre to actually believe that he had played a part in this. Otherwise, he may have run and without Pierre in custody, the case would have remained open and the investigation may have inadvertently veered to her.

She had invited Pierre to the station to keep him close until the timing was right. After Remy had dropped contact from Pierre, and thus, removed any hope for Pierre to find a buyer, Genevieve knew that Pierre would be desperate. In that desperation, he would almost certainly agree to come down to the station because he *did* have a role in the crime that had occurred at the château. She knew that he would want to try to get ahead of them, to prevent his name from coming up in the investigation. So, she let him play detective for a little bit.

When Pierre had asked about the château's security tapes, she had lied and assured him that image enhancement technology was pretty poor in an attempt to prevent him from becoming desperate and trying to run. This wasn't the case at all, in fact, it was very effective, which could have potentially been bad for both of them if Pierre was identified on the tapes before Genevieve wanted him to be. Genevieve took care of that problem.

When Simone had come across the mysterious figure on the one security tape, Genevieve had offered to take it down to the lab to see if they could enhance the image. However, the tape never made it to the lab. The Chief was informed by the analyst on duty that he thought he must have misplaced the tape. After all, the paperwork for it was there, but not the tape itself. Problem solved.

The whole time that Pierre was trying desperately to stay one step ahead of the police, Genevieve was one step ahead of him. Her advances that Pierre thought he was playing into weren't even genuine. She just enjoyed playing with her food and watching him squirm like a fly caught in her web.

From there, she had steered the investigation towards Pierre and the *Black Lotus*, and everyone at the Toulouse Police Department bought into it, and why wouldn't they? Everyone that is, except for Matthieu. She tried to bring him over to her side, against Pierre, by resurrecting the missing security tape and enhancing the image of Pierre, fleeing from the château. In addition to that, she also told Matthieu that she was only acting flirtatiously towards Pierre to make Matthieu jealous, hopefully winning back his favor.

Nevertheless, Matthieu remained steadfast in his stubbornness, but he was at least three steps behind everyone. Genevieve soon realized that it was simple enough to make him look unhinged and remove him from the picture altogether. In fact, he pretty much did that to himself and she found his downfall rather amusing.

When the timing was right, she needed to have Pierre be discovered with the necklace and then take the fall. The case would be closed. Genevieve had already cut ties from her husband the same day Boutrel had purchased the necklace and closed his accounts. There was no turning back. All that would be left to do would be to put in her retirement and then disappear off the grid with her fortune. Nobody would ever look for her as the *Black Lotus* withered away in the darkness of a prison cell.

The one thing that Genevieve hadn't accounted for throughout this conscientiously constructed ruse was the discovery that Boutrel had been poisoned, but it didn't matter to her either way. She was certain that there were probably a lot of people that wanted Boutrel dead.

The day after the murder, she tracked down Videl and killed him, leaving behind Pierre's signature black lotus flower. Finding Remy was a bit trickier, especially once he was aware that she had killed Boutrel. But when she did, he met the same fate. That was everyone that knew of her involvement, all the loose ends, tied up into a neat little bow.

Genevieve couldn't help but smile at the neatness of it all. However, a dark cloud drifted in. That dark cloud's name was Pierre.

Unfortunately for her, Pierre was becoming a real thorn in her side. That imbecile just wouldn't go quietly and somehow, he managed to escape from police custody and, even more miraculously, figure it all out. After he'd escaped, Genevieve was panicked for a time, but developed an even better plan. If Pierre was killed in a shootout with police, that was an even cleaner solution to her problem. However, when they still couldn't find him, she was the one who had leaked the detail of the lotus flower to the press to turn the whole country against the *Black* Lotus, the mysterious figure they'd once revered as a hero. She was starting to realize that she was going to have to do the deed of killing him herself. The problem was, she had no idea where he was. But, at the very least, as long as he stayed hidden, she didn't have to find him. She just had to wait him out until tomorrow night when the deal went through. It wasn't as neat as she had wanted it, but she could make it work. After the deal, she would have enough money to disappear forever.

Genevieve tried to calm herself.

Her mind wandered back to the memory of the look on Boutrel's face as she sunk the blade of the dagger into him and she felt a calm serenity wash over her.

71

Friday, the 6th of January, 7:02 p.m.

The sunlight faded beyond the horizon as the rag tag group of investigators drove away from the Château de Boutrel that evening. When they arrived back at Matthieu's house, they decided to try to run through the puzzle again, but they were still missing some crucial pieces.

"Alright, I'm convinced," Matthieu said. "Everything seems to add up. The evidence is good, but unfortunately, I still don't think it's enough."

"What else do you need?" Pierre asked.

"It's all circumstantial," Matthieu replied. "Besides, we still don't know who else might be involved, so we have to be careful. The only thing left for us to do, to really nail her, is to catch her in the act and put an end to this once and for all."

"What about François?" Colette asked.

Matthieu grunted.

"I'm afraid he's in the wind," he said. "For now, we need to focus our attention on Genevieve."

"What makes you think that Genevieve isn't in the wind already too?" Colette asked. "Especially if she knows that Pierre knows."

"I did see her at the station, earlier today," Pierre remembered. "But she stormed right past me and out of the building."

"Maybe we don't need to even find her," Colette said. "Maybe she'll come straight to us. We could dangle Pierre out as bait to lure her out."

"I, for one, would like to suggest that we come up with an alternate plan," Pierre suggested.

"I don't think that Genevieve would come for him anyways," Matthieu decided. "She's too smart for that. She's going to stay hidden as long as she can until she can disappear forever."

"Well, why did she remain so involved in the investigation to begin with?" Colette asked. "Why didn't she just disappear after the night that she killed Boutrel?"

"Because she needed to make sure that Pierre took the fall," Matthieu said. "And because she's waiting."

"Waiting for what?"

"Waiting to move the necklace," Matthieu said distractedly.

"You think that she still has it?" Pierre asked.

"I'm sure of it," Matthieu said. "It's the only thing that makes sense."

"Well, when does she intend to move it?"

"I have a hunch," Matthieu began. "The Chinese Ambassador is flying back into France tomorrow. I think that he may be our buyer."

"What makes you so sure that it's him?" Colette asked.

"The Hong Kong connection," Matthieu replied. "The *Viper Triad*, the *Gu*, it all seems to point back to China."

"François mentioned something about the 'Supreme Dragon,'" Pierre remembered. "Do you think that's the Chinese Ambassador? Is he secretly running one of the most powerful crime syndicates in the world?"

"But that wouldn't make any sense," Colette interrupted. "By that logic, the Chinese Ambassador and François are working together."

"And if that were the case," Pierre interrupted. "François wouldn't have needed to kidnap and torture me because the Chinese Ambassador would have already known that I didn't have the necklace. And he would have already had a plan to secure it from Genevieve."

"Thank you, Pierre," Colette said. "For stealing my thunder."

"So, you think that it was the Russian Ambassador?" Matthieu asked.

"Maybe he made a contingency plan to get the necklace in his hands when he lost the bidding war," Colette suggested. "Maybe he partnered up with Genevieve to make sure that he would have it in the end."

"It doesn't really matter at this point though," Pierre reminded them. "If they're both coming in tomorrow, we still don't know where Genevieve is or where they're going to meet."

"But we don't have to if we can find out where the Ambassador is flying into," Matthieu realized. "It would be nearly impossible to hide that sort of arrival."

"How do you propose that we get that information?" Colette asked.

"I've got someone on the inside that I know I can trust."

"No police," Pierre insisted. "It's too risky.

"For once, I'm going to have to agree with Pierre," Colette said.

"Trust me," Matthieu assured them. "The only person that's invested more into this case than I have, is her."

"Who?" Pierre asked.

Matthieu didn't answer. Instead, he punched in the number for the Toulouse Police Department into his cell phone. The line rang a couple of times before the woman on the other end picked up.

"Toulouse Police Department," the woman said. "How may I direct your call?"

"I don't like this," Pierre mumbled.

Without thinking, Colette reached her hand over and placed it on Pierre's arm to reassure him. Their eyes met for a second and she quickly recoiled when she realized what she had just done. Things were getting a little too comfortable with Pierre for her.

"Yes," Matthieu said. "Put me through to forensics. I'd like to speak with Simone St. Clair."

A few moments later, the phone was ringing again and then it was answered. Matthieu could hear someone fumbling around on the other line and then the familiar squeaking voice of Simone.

"Hello?"

"Simone," Matthieu began. "Is that you?"

"Detective Matthieu?" Simone stammered when she recognized his voice.

"Yes, Simone," Matthieu said. "I need you to do me a favor. Do you think you can do that for me?"

Simone hesitated.

"I'm not sure if I can," she replied. "The Chief's got us all on a tight watch over here, and you've been suspended!"

"It's nothing significant, Simone," Matthieu assured her. "Nothing that could get you into any trouble. I just need you to do a little checking for me."

"About what?"

"I need you to find out when the Russian Ambassador's flight is scheduled to come in tomorrow."

"I don't know if I can do that," Simone hesitated again.

"Simone, please," Matthieu implored. "I really need you to find this out for me."

Simone was quiet on the other line.

"I'll see what I can do," she finally decided. "Is this a good number to call you back at?"

"Yes, Simone," Matthieu said. He gave a thumbs up to Pierre and Colette. "I can't thank you enough. I promise, you won't regret this."

"I hope not," Simone said.

With that, the line clicked off on the other end.

"So," Pierre began in the uncomfortable silence. "Now what?"

"Now, we wait," Matthieu said.

Pierre nodded his head and cleared his throat to fill the silence.

"So, anyways, Detective," he began. "How do you feel about cheese?"

Matthieu looked over at Pierre and rolled his eyes.

After a couple of painstaking hours dodging small talk, Simone finally called back with the information that Matthieu had requested. The Russian Ambassador's private charter was scheduled to land at the Toulouse-Blagnac Airport at 5:50 a.m. the following morning.

Matthieu thanked Simone again. When Simone asked why he had needed that information, Matthieu said that unfortunately, he couldn't tell her, but he promised that he would be sure to fill her in with the details tomorrow. He also warned her to be ready for anything. Simone didn't like the sound of that. She hung up with an uneasy feeling in her stomach.

"So, what's the plan?" Pierre asked.

"Obviously we're going to intercept him at the airport," Matthieu replied.

"Oh, brilliant," Pierre mocked. "Yes, hello, Monsieur Russian Ambassador. We know that you've just had three people killed off and are on your way to purchase a nearly priceless Chinese artifact. Would you care ever so much if we were to tag along?"

"Obviously we're not doing that," Matthieu assured him. "We're going to make a citizen's arrest at the airport."

"I actually think that Pierre's plan is more realistic," Colette replied.

"Thank you, Colette," Pierre said.

"Don't be ridiculous," Matthieu interrupted. "Unless you have any *real* ideas that you'd like to share?"

306

Pierre and Colette contemplated for a moment but shook their heads.

"Then, we're going with my plan," Matthieu said. "We're going to arrive at the airport before their scheduled arrival time and stake it out. Then, we can place the Ambassador under a hold and convince him to give up the details of his plan and who else was involved. We'll get him to tell us where Genevieve is expecting him, and then we can alert the police, whoever we find out that we can trust from them, anyways, and intercept her there."

"Brilliant," Pierre repeated. "So, we're going to take down the most influential Russian man in the country by ourselves. Then we can arrest him, arrest Genevieve and live happily ever after. Is that it?"

"There is one more thing, Pierre," Matthieu continued.

"What's that?"

"I just wanted to give you fair warning now that if we make it out of this thing alive, I'm still coming after you."

"Wait a minute," Pierre interrupted. "What do you mean, 'if we make it out of this thing alive?!' I didn't sign up for a suicide mission!"

"All I'm saying is that it's a possibility," Matthieu said. "These are dangerous people, and anything could happen. The question that you have to ask yourself now, is do you want to die a hero, or die a villain?"

"Why are you so sure that I'm going to die?!" Pierre asked. "I'd rather not die at all!"

"We're not going to die," Colette assured him. She turned back to Matthieu. "You're really going to come after him, Detective?"

"I can't, in good conscience, let you just run free, Pierre. I would say the same for you, Colette, but Pierre assures me that you weren't involved, and I can't pin anything to you...yet. But rest assured, when I can, I'll be coming after you as well. Especially now that I know about Pierre's role in the heist of the Museum of Modern Art in Paris, I can't let you go. If you cooperate now though, Pierre, I'm sure that they'll go easy on you at your sentencing."

"Well, that's reassuring," Pierre said. "What's there to stop me from running right now?"

"Nothing," Matthieu said.

"Well, then I guess that makes my decision easy," Pierre said and stood up. "Good luck, Detective. Colette, let's get out of here—"

"If you walk out of here now, then the mission's over," Matthieu said. Pierre froze halfway to the door. "I can't go after them alone. If you run, that's the end of my involvement."

"So, you're blackmailing me," Pierre said and plopped back down on the couch.

"I'm not blackmailing you, Pierre," Matthieu said.

"You're telling me that if I don't do what you want, you're going to let Genevieve get away with this. The police will still think that I killed Boutrel and I'll have to spend the rest of my life running or in prison."

Matthieu laughed.

"Well, when you put it like that," he began. "Then yes, I guess I am blackmailing you. But, let's not act like you're completely innocent here either. It's time for you to own up to what you've done, Pelletier."

"So, it's going to be like that, Detective," Pierre said.

"It's your decision, Pelletier."

Pierre sunk back into the couch and contemplated his options for a moment. He knew that he couldn't spend the rest of his life running, even if he wanted to. The simple reason was that he couldn't afford it. If he owned up to his crimes, he would do time in prison, probably at a reduced rate, if he cooperated, like Matthieu had said. Once he was out, there'd be a huge weight off his chest. He wouldn't have to constantly be looking over his shoulder anymore. He could finally be free. Free to enjoy a life with his brother and maybe even with Colette. He sat in silent contemplation for a moment but when it came down to it, the choice wasn't really a choice at all, and he realized what he had to do.

"I'm going to need a gun," Pierre said.

"You're not getting a gun," Matthieu replied.

"Then how am I going to protect myself?"

"I'm sure you can hold your own in a fight if you have to."

Colette scoffed.

"He's going to need a gun," she said.

72

Friday, the 6th of January, 8:03 p.m.

After Genevieve had returned to the rundown motel where she would be staying for the evening, hopefully for the last time, she packed up what remained of her belongings and then fell asleep on the couch with visions of Boutrel's lifeless body dancing in her head.

It wasn't a restful nap, by any means, and she hadn't intended to sleep at all. However, the stress from the last week had finally caught up to her, and she crashed. When she woke up and the calming visions faded, her paranoia began to creep up on her once again.

Right about now, the Chief would surely soon begin to wonder why she had left work so suddenly, especially with the recent breaks in the case. Besides that, Pierre knew of her involvement and Genevieve had no idea who he could have told. While she was sleeping, there could have been a manhunt in the Toulouse streets, searching for *her*, for all that she knew. At this point, everything could be in jeopardy. She hadn't exactly "taken care of it," like she'd promised, and she didn't want to upset the Russian Ambassador again by calling. If she let on that she was worried that they'd been compromised, he might never show up, and then the whole plan was foiled. Instead, all that she could do was simply hideout in this fleabag motel and hope that morning came early. The motel was overrun with addicts and ex-criminals. It was probably the last place that anybody would have expected to find her anyways. For God sakes, she had standards. Nevertheless, she crept over to the window and peered out through the curtains neurotically.

When she pulled them back, the parking lot outside was empty, just as it had been when she'd arrived. Other than her black SUV, there were no other cars there. Genevieve breathed a sigh of relief and returned to the couch. She was alone, and that was a reassuring feeling. Alone with the only two other companions that she had brought with her, the *real* Han Sapphire necklace, which was resting comfortably in a steel-lined briefcase at the foot of the couch, and the Glock 22 which rested on the coffee table beside her. She felt safer next to it than she had ever felt next to her ex-husband.

She was staring at the pistol when her cell phone began buzzing on the table next to it. The jarring vibrations made her jump. She scrambled over and reached out for it.

When she picked up the cell phone, the caller ID listed it as an unknown caller, which, in fact, confirmed the identity of the person on the other line. There was only one person that called her from a blocked line.

"Ambassador Yachnitch," Genevieve began as she answered the call as calmly as she could.

"How do you always know that it is me?" Yachnitch asked. "I call you from a private, blocked number and yet you always know! How do you do that?"

"Call it a hunch," Genevieve said.

"Anyways," he continued. "I hope that everything is in order for our meeting tomorrow. I am very much looking forward to it."

Genevieve noticed that the Ambassador sounded like he was in a much better mood than he'd been earlier. However, his mood was prone to changing at the drop of a hat.

"Yes, of course," she replied.

"What about our… *problem* that we were having?" Yachnitch asked.

"Taken care of," she lied.

"Good," he replied delightedly before continuing. "You will forgive me for my mood earlier, Ms. Gereaux, yes? I had been in such high spirits, but I have had a stressful visit back home. I am afraid that I may have taken it out on you unfairly."

"It's no trouble," Genevieve said, tip toeing on eggshells.

"Okay," he said. "My plane will be landing just before 6 a.m. tomorrow. So, we will still meet at the cemetery at 7, yes?"

"Yes," Genevieve answered, staring intently at the Glock 22. It was as if the pistol was trying to tell her something.

"You are sure that everything is fine?" Yachnitch asked. "You sound a bit distracted."

"Everything's fine," she insisted. "I'm eagerly awaiting your arrival tomorrow."

"I look forward to it as well," Yachnitch said. "Enjoy your last night as a poor woman."

He laughed heartily.

"You too," Genevieve replied distractedly and clicked the phone off. Her gaze was mesmerized by the pistol.

You know what you need to do, it seemed to be whispering to her. She couldn't tell if it was her own thoughts or if it was the pistol speaking to her. Either way, she picked up the phone again. She punched in the number and the phone began ringing. A woman answered on the other line.

"Toulouse Police Department," she said. "How may I direct your call?"

Genevieve knew exactly who she was calling for. It was the person who would least suspect anything from her. The same person who would be most willing to give up any information to her no matter the cost because they were so concerned with their job performance that they couldn't see the obvious signs right in front of their face. Besides, she needed to make sure that the police didn't know about her yet. Otherwise, that could put a damper on things tomorrow.

"Put me through to the forensics unit," Genevieve said. "Simone St. Clair."

In the next moment, Simone was on the line.

"Hello?" She called.

Genevieve was hesitant at first.

"Simone," she began. "It's me."

"Genevieve?" Simone asked. "Where are you, the Chief is *not* happy…"

She doesn't suspect a thing, Genevieve thought delightedly.

"I wasn't feeling well, so I decided to come home early and work from here," she said.

"Gotcha," Simone replied. "Well, what can I do for you?"

"I hadn't heard anything yet, so I wanted to know if anybody had found anything on Pierre Pelletier's whereabouts, or maybe heard anything from him? Like a list of demands or something of the sort?"

"Not to my knowledge," Simone replied. "There hasn't been anything like that."

"Hmm," Genevieve said. "Well, okay. Can you call me if anything changes?"

"Absolutely!" Simone said excitedly. It sounded like the conversation had reached a conclusion, but Simone continued. "Hey, Genevieve, thank you for calling. It's not everyday someone calls me down here. Sometimes, I can't help but feel like I'm some sort of deranged cave woman that everyone's afraid of. Now, *two* calls in one day, this is great!"

"Two calls?" Genevieve repeated.

Simone let out a squeak on the other end of the phone.

"Simone," Genevieve continued. "What did you mean *two* calls? Who else called you?"

"I think that I hear the Chief yelling for me," Simone tried nervously. "I should really get going. You know how he gets."

"Simone St. Clair," Genevieve cried like an angry parent.

"Okay!" Simone squeaked. "It was Matthieu, it wasn't a big deal or anything. I didn't tell him anything important. He just wanted to know when the Russian Ambassador's flight would be landing!"

Genevieve was silent for a tense moment, but suddenly erupted.

"And you told him?! You do know that he was suspended, Simone," Genevieve said. "Don't you?"

"I didn't tell him," Simone lied. Lying made Simone feel physically nauseous, but what other choice did she have?

"Good," Genevieve said with a quiet sigh.

"I'm sorry," Simone squeaked.

"Trust me, Simone," Genevieve began. "You didn't do anything wrong."

"Please don't tell Matthieu that I told you he called," Simone pleaded. "Or the Chief that I told Matthieu, or anybody!"

"My lips are sealed," Genevieve replied slyly.

She thanked Simone and then hung up the phone. Genevieve sank into the couch in deep contemplation.

Somehow, Matthieu had figured it out, or maybe he thought that he had, but he really hadn't. Either way, this warranted further investigation. Genevieve grabbed the Glock from the table and put it into her belt holster before leaving the motel. She might need to use it, and she was fully prepared to. After all, what was one more body, or three?

73

Friday, the 6th of January, 8:48 p.m.

Genevieve arrived at her destination that evening as if she had been drawn there by some, unseen force. She parked her black SUV directly across the street from the Matthieu residence, the same place where she had spent the golden years of her life.

The house was mostly dark except for a dim light which shined through the living room window. The curtains were drawn, but Genevieve could still get a glimpse of the inside through a small sliver in between them.

The first thing that she noticed was that there had to have been over two dozen bagged newspapers that were scattered across the lawn, some were in the bushes and there was even one on the roof. Matthieu hadn't bothered to retrieve any of them. Genevieve thought about how he would have made a lousy dog. He made an even lousier husband.

However, she wasn't sure that she even actually believed this, but she kept repeating it to herself, like a mantra, until she finally did. She'd been involved with Matthieu for nearly half of her life, Boutrel not nearly as long. It was only very recently, within the last several weeks, that Genevieve had had to decide between the two.

If only Boutrel had just stuck to the plan, Genevieve thought. He might still be alive to this day, well, maybe not, considering the sorry state of his liver. Maybe she'd done him a favor. In any event, they could have both disappeared and nobody would have ever been the wiser.

But, Boutrel hadn't stuck to the plan. Even after she had left her husband and gone all in on it herself. Sure, things weren't perfect between Matthieu and her, Matthieu would demean her work and say some hurtful things, but he was also a very loving and passionate man. No relationship is perfect. But, five weeks ago, Genevieve had been forced to choose between money and keeping her secrets buried over loyalty. She, of course, chose the former. Genevieve probably would have made a lousy dog too.

As she stared in through the sliver of space in between the curtains, there wasn't much that she could see. If she tilted her head, she could see that some of the picture frames that used to hang from the walls had been taken down, leaving a dust outline on the chartreuse paint. Genevieve remembered when she had finally convinced Matthieu to settle on that color for the living room when they had moved into the house. She quickly dismissed the thought. She couldn't look back now, only forward. Genevieve was there for one reason and one reason only, to find out what Matthieu was up to.

After a few moments, Genevieve saw a figure pass by behind the windows. The curtains swayed as they passed, and the sliver of space became slightly more open. Then, Matthieu appeared in between the space and stood there for a moment. Genevieve ducked down in her car but focused her gaze sharply on him. It was dark out and Matthieu wouldn't have been able to see through the tint in her car windows anyways, but Genevieve's paranoia was causing her to think more and more irrationally.

As she watched him, Matthieu appeared to be talking to himself.

"He's officially lost his mind," she mumbled to herself before realizing that the very same thing was happening to her.

Matthieu moved out of view, towards the kitchen, but re-entered her field of view only a few moments later. His mouth hadn't stopped moving since Genevieve had pulled up.

Suddenly, a woman appeared in the window. It was a woman with sweeping brunette hair that Genevieve recognized from somewhere although she couldn't quite place it. She felt a strange tinge of jealousy which quickly faded when another figure appeared in the window and her heart sank into the pit of her stomach.

"*Pierre.*"

She would have recognized that curly, golden brown mop of a head anywhere.

There, just beyond the window, was Pierre Pelletier, in the flesh. Genevieve's paranoia sprouted to life. If Pierre and Matthieu were on the same side, that meant that Matthieu knew of her involvement now too, but would he even believe it? She was sure that she had left no evidence behind. For God sakes, she was the lead investigator on the case. The only person that would have been able to come after her *was* her.

Still, here they all were, like a bad rendition of the *Three Musketeers*. Pierre, Matthieu and some other woman that Genevieve now realized must be Colette, the woman wearing the same sparkling, scarlet evening gown as her that she had encountered on the stairs that fateful evening in the château.

She was staring through the window at them when she realized that her hand was already resting on the Glock 22 which was still holstered to her hip. Maybe it wasn't such a bad thing that they were all together. After all, it made them all that much easier to kill. Three neat little bows for the price of one.

Slowly, Genevieve unclipped the pistol and pulled it from the holster. She held it in her hands which she noticed were completely steady. Although this *really* meant that there was no turning back, that didn't matter. She had already made her decision.

Her breathing rate remained steady as she rolled the window down. Once more, she felt a calm serenity wash over her.

Genevieve poked the barrel of the Glock out of the driver's side window of the car and pointed it towards the living room window of the Matthieu residence. More specifically, it was pointed towards the bouncing curls that rested on Pierre's head through the sliver in the curtains.

Without even a second thought, she pulled the trigger.

74

Friday, the 6th of January, 8:55 p.m.

On the other side of the living room window of the Matthieu residence, the merry band of *Three Musketeers* were finalizing their plans for tomorrow morning when they were rudely interrupted by the shattering of the glass window. A bullet whizzed into the room and right through Pierre as it buried itself into the back wall.

Pierre collapsed to the ground.

"Get down!" Matthieu yelled.

He instinctively reached over for Colette and pulled her down.

However, that wasn't the end of the assault. The first shot was followed by a second and then a third. In total, there were eight shots fired into the room. The bullets whizzed by and ricocheted all around them. Some buried themselves into the chartreuse-painted walls, some into the couch, and one broke through the back window on the other side of the house.

When finally, there was a ceasefire, Matthieu heard tires screeching off outside and crawled over shards of broken glass to the window just in time to see a black SUV fleeing the scene in the dull streetlights.

"Who is it?!" Colette called out in a panic.

"I don't know!" Matthieu yelled back as he peered through the shattered glass window cautiously. "But I think they're gone now."

Pierre was laying on the ground looking up at the ceiling. His eyes were glassy and hollow, and he was making horrible gurgling noises, the kind of death cries that would make even the toughest of men want to curl up into their mother's arms.

"Oh, God," Colette shouted. "He's been hit!"

She fell on top of Pierre and Matthieu crawled frantically over to him.

"I don't see an entry wound," Matthieu said.

He scanned Pierre's full body and felt his fingers along the seams of his clothes until he finally found the bullet's entry point in the sleeve of his shirt.

"Oh my God!" Pierre shouted in his haze. "I've been shot. I'm going to die! Colette is that you?! I see a light!"

"Pierre!" Matthieu called.

"Oh, Matthieu, is that you?" Pierre asked. "I can't see your sweet face, but I can hear your voice. Oh, it's so beautiful, Matthieu. The light is calling me home, I'm going towards it!"

"Pierre!" Matthieu repeated and ripped the hole in Pierre's sleeve slightly larger. "Stop staring up at the ceiling lights, that's not good for your eyes."

"Watch the shirt," Pierre said with his last, dying breaths. "This is a poly fiber blend."

Pierre Pelletier was pronounced dead at 9:02 p.m. on Friday, the 6th of January. Just kidding again.

Matthieu sighed and sat back onto the floor.

"There's your mortal wound," he said and revealed to Colette the tiniest little flesh wound on the side of Pierre's left arm that was just barely beginning to bleed.

"Pierre, you idiot," Colette said and slapped him down hard on the chest. "I thought that you were really hurt!"

"So, I'm not going to die?" Pierre asked.

"Not yet," Matthieu said. "But if you pull a stunt like that again, I'm going to kill you."

"It's a miracle!" Pierre cried.

Colette rolled her eyes.

"That shooter was a horrible shot," she said.

"Or just incredibly desperate," Matthieu added. "They must not have accounted for the change in trajectory from the bullet breaking through the window."

"Either way, are you sure that they're gone?" She asked, turning her attention back to the shattered living room window.

"I'm not sure," Matthieu said. "But, even if they are, it won't be for long. Whoever that was could come back."

"Or worse," Colette interrupted. "With all that gunfire, I'm sure one of your neighbors called the police. They could be here at any minute."

"We can't stay here," Matthieu decided.

"I've got a place that we can go," Colette said.

Matthieu crawled back over the window as the broken glass crunched under him. He peeked out through the window at the dark street. A couple of his neighbors had turned their front lights on and were standing on their front porches. Somewhere in the distance, there was the sound of dogs barking.

"It looks clear enough," he said.

Colette stayed crouched down and crept over to the other side of the window and looked out at her car which was parked in the driveway. One of the tires must have been hit by a stray bullet because it was sitting on only three wheels. The fourth had been flattened. Matthieu seemed to notice this as well.

"We can take my car," he said.

"Guys," Pierre interrupted. "I don't think I can walk."

Matthieu rolled his eyes. He crawled over to the table by the door and grabbed the car keys. He tossed them over to Colette.

"You're driving," he said.

"Me?" Colette asked in disbelief.

"I never let anyone drive her," Matthieu said. "But with the way that you handled that thing back in Marseilles, we might need that again."

He crawled back to Pierre and put his arm around Pierre's shoulder as he hoisted him up from the ground.

"You're a good person," Pierre whispered into his ear, seemingly delirious from the trauma.

Colette turned the doorknob and then ran out, staying as low to the ground as she could. Matthieu was not far behind, supporting all of Pierre's weight. Pierre may as well have been a dead body.

———————

Colette got in the driver's seat of the blue Renault. Matthieu tossed Pierre into the back seat and then climbed in up front. Colette turned the key in the ignition, threw the car in reverse and then slammed on the gas pedal. The tires turned and screeched in place and then the car flew off backwards.

"Careful!" Matthieu cried. "These are new tires!"

She slammed the brakes once they were out of the driveway and then threw the car into drive and screeched off again. Matthieu winced.

"Who do you think that was back there?" Colette asked, glancing back every few seconds into the rearview mirror.

"Guys," Pierre wailed. "I don't think that I'm going to make it!"

"I don't know," Matthieu said. "But we've got more enemies than friends at this point. It could have been the Chinese, it could have been the Russians, it could have been Genevieve."

"Whoever it was isn't interested in talking anymore," Colette said. Matthieu nodded.

"Are you sure that this place that you're taking us to is safe?"

"Safe is a subjective word, Detective," she said. "But nobody will find us there, that I can promise you."

316

After driving for a bit, Colette turned the blue Renault onto a narrow side road. Many of the houses on the road were decaying and had been tagged with graffiti. Finally, she pulled into a small parking garage.

"We used to get calls in this neighborhood all of the time," Matthieu said. "When people were still living here."

"It has its moments," Colette replied.

Matthieu turned around and looked out through the back window.

"Are you sure that you weren't followed?" He asked.

"Positive," Colette said.

"I need to go to a hospital!" Pierre wailed loudly. He had stretched himself out across the backseat.

"Pierre," Colette said and then shushed him. "Keep your voice down."

"And take your feet off the leather," Matthieu said.

"How about a little sympathy?" Pierre asked. "Did either of you just get shot?!"

Colette rolled her eyes.

"Let's get this idiot inside," she said.

Between her and Matthieu, they were able to carry Pierre up through the parking garage staircase to the fourth level which opened into an apartment complex.

Colette felt around in her pocket for her keys. When she found them, she placed the key into the door lock. Matthieu noticed that although she was acting like she was in control, her hand was shaking. She finally opened the door. Matthieu followed her in and then tossed Pierre's limp body onto the couch.

"Who would have thought that I just needed to be shot to get to come back to your place?" Pierre asked. "If I knew that in high school, I would have done it a long time ago."

"That bullet barely nicked you, Pierre," Colette said. She walked over to the window and pulled the curtain back. The street below was eerily quiet.

"Oh, I'm sorry," Pierre said. "Where did your bullet hit you?"

"You're ridiculous," Colette muttered.

Matthieu took a seat in the chair across from Pierre and rubbed his eyes.

"What a mess," he mumbled to himself.

After watching the street below for any signs of movement, Colette finally declared, "I think that we're in the clear."

"We should get some rest," Matthieu decided. "We can sleep in shifts and keep watch outside of the window."

"Agreed," Colette said, but when she turned to Pierre, he was already fast asleep.

It was a peaceful sleep, one of the first real ones that Pierre had had in a while. The trauma he had recently experienced produced some of the most vivid dreams that he had ever had.

He dreamed that he and Colette were together, holding hands as they walked off into the Toulouse sunrise.

"Pelletier!" Interrupted a jarring voice. "Wake up, or we're going to be late!"

Pierre could feel his whole body shake and the dream faded before him into the nightmare of Matthieu hovering over him.

"I'm up, I'm up," Pierre insisted groggily.

"Good," Matthieu said. "Because it's go time."

75

Saturday, the 7th of January, 5:02 a.m.

Pierre slipped on his shoes and double knotted them. Today would be a bad day for an untied shoe. His arm was still sore from the gunshot wound yesterday, but he decided that, although it had been touch-and-go there for a while, he was going to survive.

Matthieu stood in the bathroom of Colette's apartment and tucked his pistol into its holster. He slicked back his hair as he delivered a mantra to himself in the mirror. Colette was standing by the front door waiting impatiently for them both.

"Shall we?" Matthieu said as he emerged from the bathroom and marched proudly towards the door.

"Wait," Pierre said. "There's something that I have to do first."

"We're going to be late," Colette mumbled to Matthieu. She was tapping her foot and glanced down at her watch.

Pierre rushed into the bathroom. Matthieu gave Colette a quizzical look and she shrugged. The buzzing of an electric razor came from the bathroom and Pierre emerged shortly after with a freshly shaven face.

"Your depression beard?" Matthieu asked.

Pierre stood in front of them proudly.

"Did you just use my razor?" Colette asked. "That's gross, Pierre."

"Just before the climax to signify the start of a new beginning," Pierre said.

"You're so dramatic," Matthieu replied. "Can we go now?"

Pierre glanced over at Colette whose eyes met his gaze. Matthieu caught the two of them staring at one another.

Pierre cleared his throat.

"Unbelievable," Matthieu mumbled. "I'll give you a minute. I guess that I'll go and warm up the car."

With that, Pierre and Colette were alone in the apartment.

"So…" Pierre began, trying to break the uncomfortable tension.

"So…?" Colette pressed.

"I guess that I'll start," he said. "What happens to us from here?"

Colette scoffed.

"Haven't you figured it out yet, Pierre?" She asked. "There is no *us*. After this is all over with, you're probably going to jail. Don't you get it? He knows about your involvement in everything. Your role in heist of the Museum of Modern Art, your role in the Boutrel heist, lying to the police. Even with your cooperation, you'll probably still be doing five to ten, and that's if you get a judge that's lenient."

Pierre's heart sank.

"Five to ten, you think?" He asked. "I'll be almost forty."

Colette sighed. She couldn't help but notice that Pierre looked defeated and strikingly human again. She finally realized what it was. He looked vulnerable. The *Black Lotus* had been built up as this immortal figure, like a God amongst men. But Pierre wasn't any of those things. He was simply Pierre, the boy that she had grown up with and who loved to scheme if for no other reason than just to prove that he could.

"With good behavior, maybe not that long," she tried to reassure him. "But I'm afraid this is the end of line for us, Pierre. There is no happy ending."

"Why don't we just say screw it all and run away together?" Pierre asked. "Who cares if Matthieu tries to pin the murder on us. At least we'll have each other."

"Where would we get the money for that?" Colette asked. "I bet you don't even have a single euro to your name right now in those pockets."

"If I did, it's probably fallen out," Pierre joked. "Well, there's always petty theft to support ourselves!"

Colette laughed and shook her head.

"Oh, Pierre," she said. "I've already made my decision."

"What if we did have the money for it?" Pierre asked.

"I'm not going to get your hopes up and fill your head with fantasies."

"It's already filled with fantasies."

Colette laughed again.

"Maybe in five to ten years," she said. "When you're a free man. If you ever pull off the heist of your life, look me up."

Pierre sighed. He could feel a pit in his stomach. He wanted to lean in and press his lips up against her own, but it didn't feel right to soil potentially the last moment that they might share together with false promises that he wasn't sure that he could keep. Unbeknownst to him, Colette was feeling the same way.

Pierre was an insufferable, arrogant child. But recently, Colette had seen his humanity. She suspected that there were many levels to Pierre that she couldn't even fathom. When she witnessed him nearly die in front of her twice, she finally realized how much he meant to her. Truth be told, she'd always been drawn to him. However, she knew they couldn't be together because of what came next. As she stared into his eyes, she wished there was some way that they could disappear together into the Toulouse sunrise.

"I'll do that," Pierre interrupted her thoughts and put on the best smile that he could muster.

"Alright," Colette began again. "Matthieu's waiting and you know how he gets."

"Do I ever," Pierre mumbled.

Colette and Pierre walked out of the apartment and down to the car garage where Matthieu was waiting for them in the passenger seat with the engine idling. Colette climbed into the driver's seat and Pierre into the back.

"I thought for sure that you were going to run, Pelletier," he said.

"Not this time," Pierre replied.

"Are you ready to do this?" Matthieu asked.

"Ready as I'll ever be," Pierre answered.

———

They pulled out of the parking garage when it was still dark outside and drove to the Toulouse-Blagnac Airport. There was a dense fog that had blanketed the streets that morning. They arrived at the airport just as the sun was beginning to rise and parked on the grass beside the metal fence lined with barbed wire that barricaded the landing strip. Shortly after, a small private charter plane passed by low overhead. It touched down on the runway until it pulled up to a stop.

"That must be him," Matthieu said.

A black SUV drove up to greet the plane right on the tarmac.

"Who do you think that is?" Colette asked.

"Could be our friend from last night," Matthieu said. "There was a black SUV that I saw fleeing the scene. It screeched away after it laid waste to my windows."

Three large men emerged from the SUV to meet the plane's arrival. They were dressed in black suits, white collared shirts and black ties. They were also heavily armed, in the sense that their sweltering biceps were nearly bursting through their suit coats, but more so the fact that they were all strapped with semi-automatic assault rifles.

"Still want to make a citizen's arrest?" Pierre asked.

An armored truck pulled up shortly after and stopped right behind the black SUV. Another heavily armed man stepped out.

"Change of plans," Matthieu said. "We're just going to follow them to the rendezvous point where we can intercept all of them and Genevieve at the same time."

"Are you mad?" Colette asked. "You want to go right into the lion's den?"

"You're damn right I'm mad," Matthieu said. "I'm pissed! If they thought they could kill us that easily last night, they don't know who they're messing with. We're going to take them all down at once."

"For the record," Pierre began. "Everything that you just said right there, completely insane, but really cool."

The Russian Ambassador, Yuri Yachnitch, stepped off the plane. He was carrying a steel-lined briefcase as he disappeared immediately into the back of the black SUV. Matthieu and company waited until their targets proceeded out of the airfield and then began to drive off. The blue Renault followed closely, but not too closely, behind until the black SUV and the armored truck slowed and turned into the brick entrance of the Saint Martin du Touch Cemetery. The rest of the cemetery was surrounded by a tall, wrought iron fence.

"Fitting," Colette said. "Seeing as we're all going to die here."

She didn't follow the Russian Ambassador's caravan into the cemetery, that would have been far too obvious. Instead, she flipped her headlights off and then kept driving until the fence surrounding the cemetery ended. She turned down the side street that ran parallel to the fence and picked the caravan back up. Fortunately, there was a line of trees on the other side of the fence that obscured them from the caravan's view. Additionally, the darkness of the dawn kept them out of sight.

The caravan continued until it reached an old monastery deep inside of the cemetery. The monastery itself was decrepit. The stained-glass windows which had, at one point, probably filtered in brilliant colors that Matthieu probably couldn't even name, were nearly all shattered and the beautiful but crumbling terra-cotta brick walls suggested that it had been abandoned long ago. There was already another black SUV that was parked by the front entrance.

Colette pulled up alongside the grass and the *Three Musketeers* kept their eyes focused on the Russian Ambassador's caravan.

Another moment later, the Russian Ambassador emerged from the back seat of his SUV, followed by his heavily armed security detail. Two of them escorted him into the building, out of sight, while the other two remained outside and kept watch.

"What's the plan?" Pierre asked.

"I don't have one," Matthieu said without breaking focus from the monastery.

"You don't have one?" Colette repeated in disbelief. "I've got a plan. How about we give up this little charade and go home!"

"We're not giving up," Matthieu said. He turned back to Pierre. "Besides, don't you want to clear your name, Pierre?"

Pierre nodded solemnly. His gaze was fixated on the monastery as well.

"I think that I'd rather live," Colette said.

Their argument was suddenly interrupted by a sharp knocking at the back window. The color drained from their faces as they turned, ready to meet the fate that they all assumed would come.

76

Saturday, the 7th of January, 6:00 a.m.

On the inside of the monastery, Genevieve was already waiting to greet the Russian Ambassador and his men. At the opposite end of the monastery was an old, wooden altar. Genevieve was in front of it, pacing back and forth, checking the time on her watch every few seconds. Finally, when Yachnitch appeared in the doorway, Genevieve held steady. She felt like a groom waiting for his bride as Yachnitch strolled down the aisle towards her. Genevieve could almost hear the church bells sounding in her head. Although, those could have been the church bells of la Basilique Saint-Sernin, marking the hour at 6 o'clock. The bells reminded her of her own wedding day. She thought that she could even faintly hear the ghostly tune of the organ playing the wedding march. It was almost as if the memory of her wedding were haunting her. That had been a joyous day some twenty-plus years ago, without a doubt, but today was going to be much sweeter than her wedding day. Today was payday.

"Ambassador!" She called out once Yachnitch was in earshot. She bowed a little as a sign of respect to him.

"Ms. Gereaux," he began. He continued along the dingy, brown carpet of the monastery in step with the wedding march in Genevieve's head.

When he finally arrived at the altar at the back of the monastery, he placed the steel-lined briefcase that he had carried with him on top of it.

"I am glad to see that you made it here in one piece," he continued. "I trust that you were not followed?"

"Of course not," Genevieve assured him. "Everything's in order."

"And your problem?"

"Like I said, it's been taken care of."

She was almost sure of this fact, almost. She convinced herself that there was no way that any of her "problems" had survived that onslaught of bullets. If there was one thing that she had learned from this whole experience, it was that virtually any problem that you had could easily be solved by murdering someone.

"Good," Yachnitch said with a pleasant smile. Genevieve thought that it almost seemed sincere.

She reached down to her side and picked up a nearly identical, steel-lined briefcase and set it on the opposite end of the altar, across from his.

"Ah, you have great taste," he said, admiring her briefcase.

"It's really the only option when it comes to briefcases," Genevieve replied. "Fashionable *and* practical."

"You just don't see that anymore these days," Yachnitch said.

Genevieve nodded and then turned the briefcase to face her.

"Did you have a good trip home?" She asked.

Yachnitch sighed.

"I am glad that it is behind me," he said. "Now, I think that is sufficient small talk. Please, let us get down to business. I actually have a meeting with your boss shortly."

"My boss?" Genevieve repeated.

"Chief Jambalaya, or whatever," Yachnitch scoffed. "Just the ripple effect from your *problem*..." He seemed to grow irritated for a moment but quickly calmed himself. "It is no matter. If the problem has been taken care of, as you say, then there should be nothing to worry about."

"Of course," Genevieve said. She sounded confident, but inside, she was beginning to second guess everything. The reason that Yachnitch had a meeting with the Chief was at Matthieu's request. Considering that Matthieu was suspended, and hopefully dead, it was too bad that he wouldn't be there to greet the Ambassador. "I'm sure that you're a very busy man. I, for one, also have plans shortly. There's a plane ticket with my name on it, or, at least, the name of the identity that I'll be assuming. So, let's make this simple. If you show me yours, I'll show you mine."

The two of them turned their attention to their own individual briefcases. At the front of each, there was a digital passcode interface that required a six-digit numeric code for them to unlock.

They both entered their codes. What followed was a clicking sound and the top part of the briefcases unlatched and swung open. However, their contents were still obscured from the other party's view.

"Should we do it at the same time?" Genevieve asked.

"Ladies first," Yachnitch insisted. He was always the gentleman, especially when it came to back alley, black market dealings.

Genevieve swiveled her briefcase to face Yachnitch. His eyes lit up with lust as he gazed upon the briefcase's contents.

"The Han Sapphire necklace," he proclaimed in a trance-like state. The necklace even seemed to sparkle in the dim early morning sun that poured in through the broken shards of the stained-glass windows of the monastery. "May I?" He asked as he reached his hands greedily toward the treasure.

"Let's see yours first," Genevieve insisted. She slid her briefcase a little closer to herself, just out of the Ambassador's grasp.

Yachnitch chuckled.

"You do not trust me, Ms. Gereaux?"

"Don't take it personally," she answered. "I don't trust anyone."

"I like that about you, Ms. Gereaux," he said, wagging a finger at her. "In Mother Russia, we call someone like you *zhenshchina, kotoraya nikomu ne doveryayet.*"

"What does that mean?"

"It means, the woman who does not trust anyone."

"That's very descriptive," Genevieve said.

"The Russian language may not be beautiful, but it is descriptive," Yachnitch said. He reached down for his own briefcase and swiveled it around to face her.

Genevieve's eyes mimicked that of the Ambassador's from a moment ago, lustfully nearly protruding from her head like a cartoon character. There, in the Russian Ambassador's briefcase, she counted 25 neatly piled up stacks of €100 notes that each had to be nearly half a meter thick.

"It is all there," Yachnitch said, breaking Genevieve from her trance. "Just like we agreed upon, €50 million. Would you like to count it all?"

"That won't be necessary," Genevieve stammered.

With this amount of money, she truly could disappear forever. Up until this moment, there had been a nagging thought in the back of her mind that wouldn't go away, no matter how much she had tried to suppress it. While this was her endgame, she was almost certain that she would never make it to this point. Somewhere along the way, she had feared that something would have gone wrong. Now that she was face to face with her €50 million, her wildest dreams were about to come true. She almost couldn't believe it.

Yachnitch closed his briefcase.

"So," he began. "We will exchange cases now and then be on our way, yes?"

Genevieve closed her briefcase as well, concealing the Han Sapphire necklace within its confines.

She nodded silently. She could feel a warmth rise in her cheeks and she fought to suppress a delighted smile. Words were escaping her.

They each slid their briefcases across the wooden altar to one another.

"Perfect," the Ambassador said. "Now, we will transfer the passcode simultaneously through the smartphone app, yes?"

"Why are you describing everything that we agreed upon?" Genevieve asked.

"Just for clarification," Yachnitch replied. He reached into his pocket and pulled out his cell phone. "I cannot seem to figure out how to use this thing."

Genevieve snatched the phone from his hands. She didn't have time to explain how cell phones worked to this old man.

She pulled up the app which opened to a screen requiring an input for a six-digit numeric sequence to be entered.

"Once we've both entered the passcode to our own briefcase, it will send the passcode to the other person," Genevieve said. "That way, we'll both receive our respective passcodes at the same time. The app also won't let you send a fake passcode since it's linked to the real briefcase. Didn't you read the manual that came with the briefcase? This was all in there."

"I do not have time to read manuals," Yachnitch answered. "Why can we not just tell the passcode to one another? These kinds of things were so much easier before all of this technology."

Genevieve groaned.

"Do I have to spell this out for you again?" She asked. She noticed the blank expression on the Ambassador's face and realized the answer to her own question. "Because it lets us both leave here alive. This briefcase is a Doettling, they're the safest in the world, virtually uncrackable, tamper proof, bullet proof, flame proof."

"Explosive proof?"

"Yes."

"Waterproof?"

"Probably?" Genevieve answered, unsure of why that would be important.

"Ah, now I remember our previous conversations," Yachnitch said. "Those Germans certainly are crafty bastards."

"Agreed," Genevieve said. "Without the passcode, the briefcase will *never* open. Oh, and one more thing. If you enter in the wrong passcode, whether it's by mistake or if you're not the one who's supposed to be opening it, there's a failsafe in place. The passcode will reset randomly to one of a million different combinations. My app will alert me that the passcode has been changed and I'll be the only one who will know it. This ensures that the passcode can't be guessed easily. So, make sure you enter the right number, because I wouldn't want to hear from you again after this."

"Ah, yes," Yachnitch said. "I suppose that would make me a loose end. I share your hatred of loose ends, Ms. Gereaux. However, isn't it a bit ironic that we are both loose ends for one another?"

Genevieve glanced over at the Ambassador's security team as they tightened their grips on their assault rifles. However, as long as she was the only one with the passcode to the Han Sapphire necklace, she was safe. Thank God for technology. The only downside was that she also couldn't kill the Ambassador. He was one loose end that she would, unfortunately, have to leave dangling. However, the necklace should be more than enough to buy his silence.

"Well, I think that you've answered all of my questions," Yachnitch said and then turned to his companions. "Is there anything else that you can think of?"

Both men shook their heads.

"Alright then, Ms. Gereaux," Yachnitch began again. "It has been a pleasure working with you."

"Likewise," Genevieve replied. In one hand, she grabbed the briefcase that now belonged to her. €50 million was much lighter than she had initially anticipated. In the other hand, she caressed the Glock 22 on her belt. Even though the passcode system that she had in place secured her safety, there was always the possibility that Yachnitch and his men could still try to kidnap and torture it out of her. Genevieve's paranoia was preparing her for anything.

The Russian Ambassador began walking toward the door and Genevieve followed. What had just transpired, however, would ultimately turn out to simply be the opening act. The real show was just about to begin.

77

Saturday, the 7th of January, 6:02 a.m.

As Matthieu and company turned to face the potential threat that had just knocked at the back window, they each fully expected to see the barrel of a semi-automatic weapon pointed right at them. Instead, they came face to face with something far less threatening, maybe even the least threatening thing in the world, Norman Neamon, standing outside and smiling at them.

"How the hell…" Matthieu mumbled to himself as he rolled down the passenger side window.

"Hello, friends," Norman began. "Mind if I join you?"

"How did you find us?" Matthieu stammered.

"Oh, I figured it out too," Norman said. "Can I come in?"

"Yeah, uh, yes," Matthieu stuttered and unlocked the car doors.

Norman pulled the back door open and took a seat right next to Pierre who was trying to avoid eye contact.

"Hey," Pierre began. "Um, sorry about the whole train mistaken identity thing."

He laughed nervously.

"We'll talk about it later," Norman interrupted.

"How did *you* figure it out?" Matthieu asked, astonished that the idiot savant seemed to have struck again.

"It was quite simple, really," Norman began. "Back at Harquin's, when you said that it couldn't be Pierre, it all kind of came together and I realized that you were right. So, from there I decided that the murder must have been staged to look as if Pierre had done it. From there, I came to your house to ask you a few more questions, but as I drove by, I saw you all fleeing in Matthieu's car and that the house had been riddled with bullets. I have to admit, that I didn't really figure everything out, but I followed you to the parking garage and then here this morning. And, well, here we are."

Matthieu turned to Colette.

"I thought you said that you were sure that you hadn't been followed," he said.

"I was!" Colette declared.

"Ugh, never mind."

"Anyways, what have we got here?" Norman asked.

"The Russian Ambassador, Yuri Yachnitch, is in there having a private meeting with my ex-wife," Matthieu said.

"Seems personal," Norman remarked.

"So, what's the plan?" Colette asked. They all turned their attention back to the monastery and the two heavily armed guards that were keeping watch out front. The fog had settled on the tombstones and, from a distance, the guards appeared to be knee deep in it.

"Well, at least we've got two guns now," Matthieu said and motioned back to Norman.

"Who, me?" Norman asked. "Oh, no. I'm not allowed to carry a gun. They took that away from me at the bureau."

"Alright," Colette said. "So, back to one gun."

"I told you that you should have given me a gun," Pierre mumbled.

"You're not getting a gun, Pelletier," Matthieu said. "You were never going to get a gun!"

"Okay, Officer Rambo," Pierre began. "So, you're going to take on all four of the Russian Ambassador's men and your murdering sociopath of an ex-wife with that little pistol that you brought? Absolutely brilliant."

"It's not little," Matthieu assured him. "This is a perfectly average size for a pistol."

Pierre rolled his eyes and then pulled the handle of the back door open.

"Where are you going, Pelletier?" Matthieu demanded. "You can't run now!"

"Relax," Pierre answered. "I'm not running, I'm improvising. Somebody's got to do something. You guys can stay here and play with your thumbs if you want. I'm going in for a closer look."

He shut the car door behind him and walked a little bit down the dirt path that ran along the wrought iron fence of the cemetery. In one fluid motion, he leapt up and grabbed the top bars of the fence. He pulled himself up and over, landing safely on the other side but still concealed by the trees that lined the cemetery perimeter.

"What's he doing?" Matthieu asked. He was irate but also slightly a bit impressed by Pierre's acrobatics.

"He's doing what Pierre does best," Colette answered and rolled her eyes.

Pierre crept along the side of the fence a little way until he was facing the side of the monastery. The two armed guards were patrolling the front door and keeping watch, so they never even saw him.

Pierre hesitated for just another second and then took off across the lawn, weaving through the tombstones and staying as low as he could, until he finally reached the side wall of the monastery. He pressed his back up against the cool terra-cotta bricks.

"He's going to blow this whole thing," Matthieu cried. "And probably get himself killed in the process!"

Pierre then began to scale the protruding bricks of the building using nothing but the tips of his fingers at some points to hoist himself upwards. He climbed until he reached a brick ledge on the second story where he could stand and peer in through one of the busted out, stained glass windows. When he looked down, he was standing right above the heads of the armored truck and the armed guards. They were saying something to each other that Pierre couldn't understand, but neither of them seemed to have any clue that he was there.

Inside of the monastery, in the light of the early morning sun, Pierre could see Genevieve and the Russian Ambassador towards the back of the room. Pierre was still at the front of the building so he couldn't quite make out what they were saying. He shimmied his way along the narrow strip of the brick ledge until he was in a better, closer position and could hear them more clearly.

When he peered into this other window, he was right over Genevieve's shoulder. He would have to be extremely cautious because he was right in the Ambassador's line of sight. He looked in just as Genevieve was asking how the Ambassador's trip was. Next, she was opening her briefcase, revealing the Han Sapphire necklace, the *real* one. Pierre's foot suddenly slipped as a brick came loose from underneath him and cracked in half on a tombstone below. Pierre froze and held his breath. He slowly peeked at the two armed guards at the front of the building, but they were deep in conversation, neither of them heard a thing. Pierre breathed a sigh of relief; he was safe for the time being.

He grabbed the side of the window and steadied himself. He didn't want his skull to end up in two pieces like that brick. He peered in through the window again and saw Genevieve and the Ambassador swapping briefcases and discussing some sort of smartphone app.

The next thing that he knew, Genevieve and the Ambassador were heading for the door. The time for him to formulate a plan was leaving along with them.

Pierre followed them from his position along the ledge on the outside of the building until he was perched back in his original position, just over the heads of the two armed guards. Only, this time, when another loose brick slipped out from underneath his feet, it didn't crack on a tombstone. Instead, it projected into the air and landed on one of the heads of one of the armed guards who collapsed to the ground just as Genevieve and Yachnitch were exiting the monastery.

The other guard whirled around and looked up in the direction that the brick had come from. There, perched on the ledge like the world's stupidest gargoyle, was Pierre Pelletier.

"Um, hello," Pierre said, laughing nervously and waving toward the guard.

The Russian's face turned beat red and he roared as he turned the barrel of the semi-automatic rifle right at Pierre.

"This is for Ivan!" The man shouted and opened fire.

Genevieve and the Russian Ambassador had just exited through the front door and hit the deck as the sound of assault rifle fire echoed all around them. Pierre did the same and took cover behind a front pillar of the building. Bullets ricocheted off the bricks and whizzed past his head.

"Jesus, Pierre," Matthieu mumbled and emerged from the blue Renault. He had his pistol in hand and he aimed it in the direction of the mad Russian over the roof of his car.

Matthieu carefully steadied himself and pulled the trigger. A spray of blood spurted from the back of the Russian's leg. He grabbed at the fresh wound and his knee buckled to the ground. However, the Russian never took his finger off the trigger and as he went down, wincing in pain, he sprayed bullets wildly into the air in all directions.

Genevieve was facedown with her hands over her head but when she heard a pistol firing, she turned in the direction it had come from just in time to see her ex-husband ducking for cover behind his blue Renault. When he was safe, he peeked out from his cover and locked eyes with his ex-wife.

"Pierre!" Matthieu yelled, never breaking his stare from her. "Get out of there!"

Genevieve lost all control and stood up in the midst of the rifle fire and pulled out her own Glock. She let off a few shots towards Matthieu. One missed wide and struck the dirt just in front of him and another ricocheted off the hood of his car.

"Come on!" Matthieu cried out. "I just got this thing waxed!"

One of the Russian Ambassador's men helped Yachnitch off the ground and began escorting him into the back of one of the black SUVs. Another Russian, the one that had been hit by Matthieu's bullet, was still firing shots back and forth at Pierre and Matthieu. He limped over to his unconscious comrade, Ivan, picked him up and began dragging him into the back of the same vehicle. The fourth Russian was laying heavy rifle fire cover towards Matthieu. He took the briefcase from Yachnitch and proceeded toward the back of the armored truck. He thrust open the truck's steel lift gate and tossed the briefcase carelessly into it before closing the gate and climbing into the driver's seat of the truck.

Norman rolled out from the back of Matthieu's car and landed beside Matthieu.

"Where do you think you're going?" Matthieu roared over the gunfire.

"I'm going after the Russian Ambassador," Norman replied. "I've had a score to settle with him ever since the Cold War. This is personal!"

"You're unarmed," Matthieu reminded him.

"I can handle myself," Norman said and crawled to his own car which was parked just a little way down the dirt road behind the blue Renault. Before long, he was in full on, hot pursuit of Yuri Yachnitch.

78

Saturday, the 7th of January, 6:18 a.m.

Norman climbed into his rental car as bullets soared all around him. He was normally a mild-mannered man, he and his wife usually enjoyed simple pleasures such as reading before bed, gardening or stamp collecting. The most adrenaline that Norman had ever experienced at one time was when he was finishing a sudoku. However, today, he finally understood what it meant to be a hot-blooded American. He smashed his foot down on the gas pedal and peeled off from the scene in pursuit of the Russian Ambassador.

The black SUV was turning recklessly out of the Saint Martin du Touch Cemetery just as Norman was turning off the dirt road adjacent to it. Just after the black SUV passed the front, brick entrance of the cemetery, the armored truck turned recklessly in the opposite direction. Norman nearly collided with the truck in pursuit of the SUV and had to swerve to avoid it. As it passed, he saw Pierre dangling helplessly from the side of it, but there was nothing Norman could do to help him.

Once he finally caught the SUV on the two-lane road, he sped up to get alongside it. Then, he signaled with his hands for them to roll down the window.

"Pull over!" Norman shouted, trying to get their attention. He was turning his head back and forth between the black SUV and the road in front of him as they barreled down the street. "FBI!"

The Russian driver was happy to oblige in rolling the window down. Not so much when it came to pulling over. He smiled at Norman, then reached his arm down and out of sight. It reappeared as he pulled it out through the window, pointing the barrel of his semi-automatic assault rifle right at Norman's face.

Without even giving it a second thought, Norman swerved his rental car into the side of the black SUV just as the Russian pulled the trigger and sent a spray of bullets into the side of Norman's car. When Norman's car collided with the SUV, it crushed the Russian's arm in between the two vehicles. The Russian cried out in pain and released the assault rifle from his grip which pattered harmlessly along the asphalt behind them.

The Russian was wincing in pain as he tried to retrieve his pinned arm from in between the two cars. In his delirium, he quickly lost control of the SUV, swerving it likewise into Norman and taking out the passenger side view mirror. The SUV grinded against the rental with a horrible screech of metal against metal. It was right around this point that Norman remembered that he had declined the optional €25 rental insurance.

Norman tried to turn the steering wheel but could not, it was locked in place as the two intertwined cars continued to barrel through the street.

"Darn Commies," Norman mumbled to himself as he tugged and tugged at the locked steering wheel. He was glad that he had at least made the decision to leave his wife at home. She would have been shocked by his foul-mouthed antics.

Just up ahead, there was a traffic light with a single car, a small, silver Smart car, waiting beneath it for the red light to turn green. Norman was in the same lane and was heading straight for it. He instinctively slammed on the brakes, violently separating the two cars. Norman fell back as the Russians continued to plow ahead.

With his mangled arm finally free, the Russian driver turned his attention back to the road. He swerved the SUV at the last second, but it still pummeled into the back right tail light of the Smart car, sending shards of plastic from the bumper and tail light in a scatter throughout the street and thrusting the vehicle into the intersection.

Norman swerved over into the other lane and followed the path that the SUV had created. The other vehicles that were travelling through the intersection came to screeching halts as the SUV and Norman blazed past them.

"Sorry!" Norman shouted pleasantly with a sheepish smile as he waved at the irate drivers that he passed.

Within a moment, he was right back on the tail of the SUV when it's trunk suddenly shot open. The injured Russian man, who Matthieu had wounded with a shot to the back of his leg, leaned out and pointed his semi-automatic assault rifle at Norman. He wasted no time and began spraying rounds into the Toulouse streets, laughing like a madman.

Norman swerved from side to side to try to avoid the heavy rifle fire. However, some of the rounds ricocheted off his hood while others came through the windshield, burying bullets into the rental car's upholstery. Norman swerved into the other lane and floored the gas pedal again so that the hood of his car was nearly even with the back corner of the SUV. The relentless Russian continued firing into the side of Norman's car, busting out the passenger side window as Norman ducked for cover. Norman tried to peer out through the bullet hole riddled windshield through the crack in the steering wheel as he kept his head low.

When he peered out, he could see that the two cars were coming up on another intersection. Nobody was waiting beneath the traffic light, but the traffic that was whizzing passed the intersection was much heavier. He realized that if he didn't act quickly, both him and the Russians, along with everyone driving through the intersection, would be going down in a blaze of glory.

He jerked the steering wheel forcefully into the direction of the SUV and clipped the back end of it. The Russian that was spraying rounds from the trunk wobbled unsteadily and then fell forward from the impact and tumbled out onto the street.

The impact sent the rest of the SUV reeling to the side while its momentum was still carrying it forward. So, as it screeched on the asphalt and then became perpendicular to the direction that its momentum was carrying it, the car flipped and rolled over.

Norman slammed on the brakes so that he wouldn't collide with them as the Russians rolled over a second and then a third time, each time sending chunks of debris into the air, before finally settling upright, right in front of the white lines of the crosswalk.

Norman sat still for a moment in shock. His knuckles were white from gripping the steering wheel so tightly and his foot was pressed down as hard as he could on the brake pedal. This sure beat the hell out of sudoku.

When he came to his senses, he pulled the emergency brake of the rental car and emerged onto the street. His knees wobbled beneath him. He first saw the Russian that had been firing through the trunk, unconscious on the asphalt. He grabbed the assault rifle from him and held it in his hands, it felt right. Then, he went over to the black SUV as quickly as he could. Shards of safety glass and broken bits of unidentifiable car debris littered the asphalt. There was a plume of smoke billowing from the hood of the SUV and in the distance, Norman could hear emergency vehicle sirens. They were no doubt on their way to the scene to find out what the heck was going on.

He approached the SUV cautiously but when he got close enough, he noticed that the driver's side window was completely shattered. Through it, he could see the driver, passed out with his head pressed against the steering wheel. Blood was trickling from a small gash on the side of his head. Norman confirmed that he was still alive by reaching in and feeling for a pulse in his neck. Then, he looked behind the man and into the back seat where the Russian Ambassador was cowering behind Ivan, the man who was still unconscious from the brick that had collided with his head.

"Who are you?" Yachnitch asked in bewilderment.

"The name's Neamon," Norman said and pointed the barrel of the assault rifle towards him. "Norman Neamon, and you're under arrest."

79

Saturday, the 7th of January, 6:18 a.m.

J ust as Yachnitch's black SUV had begun to pull away, the gunfire from Genevieve ceased. Matthieu peered over his shoulder and could see her reloading her Glock behind one of the monastery's brick pillars. The armored truck began to pull away from the scene behind the SUV.

"Pierre!" Matthieu yelled again. "Get out of there!"

"I'm going after it!" Pierre shouted back.

"You're what?!" Matthieu called out and scanned the area for his companion.

Pierre ran along the ledge of the monastery and when he reached the end, he leapt out into the open, toward the armored truck. Genevieve was standing right beneath him and had just finished reloading. She promptly let off a couple of fresh rounds towards Pierre as he flew across the air, closing the gap as the bullets whizzed by him.

Pierre came down with a crash onto the top of the armored truck and skidded along it, nearly rolling off before he was able to barely grasp the side of it with his hand. His legs were dangling freely along the other side as the truck pulled away.

Colette rolled out of the passenger's side door and rested up against the back of the blue Renault as Genevieve turned her attention back towards her ex-husband. She fired off shots until her Glock was empty.

"What do we do now?" Colette asked.

Matthieu opened the chamber of his own pistol. There was only a single bullet left.

"I'll think of something," he said. He glanced over his shoulder at Genevieve.

She tossed her empty Glock to the ground and exchanged it for one of the fallen assault rifles that had been left behind.

"Oh, great," Matthieu mumbled. Semi-automatic rifle fire began pouring into the side of his car and deflated the front tires.

When it finally ceased, he glanced over his shoulder again and saw Genevieve getting into the other black SUV.

"I'm going after her," Matthieu decided.

He leapt out from his covered position and ran over to the wrought iron fence in between his car and the cemetery. When he got to it, he jumped up and reached for the top to try to hoist himself up just as he had seen Pierre do before. The only problem was that he was not nearly the acrobat that Pierre was, and he pathetically failed to lift himself up. He fell back to the ground in defeat.

"Try the gate!" Colette yelled.

"What?" Matthieu called back.

"The gate!" Colette repeated. "Right beside you!"

He glanced to his side and, sure enough, there was a gate in the fence. He blushed in embarrassment and pushed open the gate, just as Genevieve was turning onto the paved road that would lead her straight through to the exit.

Matthieu let the gate slam closed behind him as he ran onto the same paved road that Genevieve was coursing down. He firmly planted both feet in front of her and aimed the barrel of his pistol right at the outline of Genevieve's head that he could make out from a distance through the car's windshield.

"Stop!" He cried.

However, instead, she did the exact opposite and sped up as the SUV drew even closer to him. When she was close enough that Matthieu could see the details of her face through the windshield, he was convinced that he could see her smiling at him like a deranged lunatic on a killing spree that wasn't about to end any time soon.

Matthieu gripped the handle of his pistol tightly as she barreled forward. The woman that he loved was no more. She had been replaced by this murdering sociopath, as Pierre had so eloquently put it.

With his finger on the trigger, he pulled it back just a hair. He was determined to take the shot when she was just a little closer. When Genevieve was no more than a few meters from him, he thought that he could hear her cackling laughter coming from inside of the vehicle.

"Do it!" Colette shouted.

Matthieu pulled the trigger back just another hair. She was in range, but he had frozen. For a moment, it felt like it was just the two of them. They were the only people in this world. Matthieu had a gun pointed at her head and Genevieve had control of the car that was headed straight for him. This wasn't what he had in mind when he had spoken the words, *until death do us part*.

His finger tensed on the trigger as he came back to reality, but then, he released it and dove out of the way at the very last second. The SUV clipped the back of his tweed jacket and blazed past him.

However, Matthieu wasn't done. From his position on the ground, he turned to face his escaping ex-wife and fired off a single bullet towards the SUV, connecting with the back tire. The tire exploded into a dazzling display of pieces and deflated. The sudden change in pressure jerked the SUV in that direction and spun it around wildly. Genevieve lost control and the SUV continued barreling forward until its smashed head on into a tree.

Dark smoke began billowing from the hood of the SUV and Matthieu thought for a moment that the whole car might blow, sending fragments of scorched metal flying in his direction. However, what happened next was much worse than what he had imagined. The driver's side door opened, and Genevieve got out.

Matthieu didn't think that he had ever seen her this angry. She was growling to herself, stumbling a bit after her head had collided with the steering wheel on impact and she was marching directly towards him. Fortunately, she must have lost the assault rifle during the collision because she was coming towards him unarmed.

Matthieu scrambled to his feet and then raised his gun and pointed it towards her. She stopped in her tracks and then started laughing.

"It's over, Genevieve," he said.

She was cackling uncontrollably now. The single stream of blood that was trickling onto her forehead confirmed his suspicion that she probably had a concussion and that she probably wasn't in full control of her actions. Nothing seemed to be driving her now except for pure adrenaline. The only thing more frightening than Genevieve when she was in control, was when she was out of it.

"Give yourself up," Matthieu said. "I don't want to have to shoot you."

"You're not going to shoot me, Martin," Genevieve slurred. "You were never *going* to shoot me!"

She took another step forward as Matthieu's grip of the pistol tightened in his hands. He cocked back the hammer.

"I'm serious," he warned. "Don't make me do it!"

Her laughter continued maniacally as she continued towards him. Matthieu closed his eyes and squeezed the trigger. However, the trigger only answered him with a faint click. It was empty.

Genevieve stopped in her tracks again. She stared at her ex-husband with an accusatory glance.

"You were actually going to do it," she said in disbelief. "I thought that you loved me!"

The fire in her eyes enveloped Matthieu. She was always a passionate woman, but now, all that passion was channeled into her hatred for her ex-husband and she stormed towards him once again.

"Now, wait a minute," Matthieu tried, dropping his empty pistol to the ground and holding his open palms out to her. "We can talk about this!"

She was no more than a meter from him when a woman's voice squeaked out.

"Hold it right there!"

Matthieu and Genevieve both froze and turned towards the direction of the voice.

"Simone St. Clair?!" Matthieu called out in disbelief.

"That's right," Simone answered. "And Genevieve, if you take another step, I'm going to drop you where you stand."

Simone was pointing a pistol towards Genevieve. Genevieve quickly threw her hands in the air in surrender.

"What the hell are you doing here?!" Matthieu asked. "And who gave you a gun?"

"I figured it out!" Simone answered proudly.

"How the hell is everyone figuring this out so easily?" Matthieu mumbled to himself.

"It was really quite simple," she said. "I had my suspicions when Genevieve disappeared from the station yesterday afternoon. Besides that, her theories at the Harquin and Rochefort crime scenes about Pierre's guilt didn't make any sense. Also, there was that streaker at the station yesterday. I wasn't sure who it was at first, but when I saw the peach Peugeot fleeing down the street, I remembered that that was the same car that you had me check the plates on that belonged to Colette Couvrir, Pierre's associate. Then, of course, you called about the Russian Ambassador's flight. Shortly after, Genevieve called. So, I told her that you called, but lied about what I told you. I was trying to bait her out to see what she would do."

"You told her that I called?"

Simone smiled sheepishly, but continued.

"I wanted to see how she would react. When she snapped, I became *very* suspicious. Shortly after, we got the call reporting that there had been shots fired on your street and saw all the bullet holes in your house and the Peugeot in your driveway. When I told her that you called, I didn't think she'd go that berserk, but that solidified her guilt for me. It all came together and I knew it was her. So, I arrived at the airport and then followed the Russian Ambassador's caravan here. I called in backup too, they should be here shortly."

"You called the police?" Matthieu asked.

"Only the people I knew that I could trust," Simone said.

Genevieve was scowling as she held her hands over her head.

"I can hold her here," Simone said.

"I'll stay with you until backup gets here, of course," Matthieu offered.

Simone shook her head.

"You have somebody else who needs you more than I do," she said.

"Who's that?" Matthieu asked before he suddenly remembered Pierre dangling helplessly from the side of the armored truck.

Matthieu raced over to his car and fumbled for his keys. Colette followed him.

"I'm coming with you," she said.

"You're driving," he grunted in response before his eyes shifted to his new tires which had been recently blown to bits by heavy assault rifle fire.

He groaned and then turned to Simone.

"We're going to need to borrow your car," he said.

80

Saturday, the 7th of January, 6:18 a.m.

Pierre's legs dangled helplessly behind him as the armored truck whipped around the corner of the cemetery exit. The truck briefly went onto two wheels before crashing back down on all four. Pierre's fingertips grasped the narrow ledge along the top of the truck for dear life. He looked behind him just in time to see Norman nearly clip the back end of the truck and then continue in the opposite direction.

"Come back!" Pierre called out, but his cries were swallowed in the traffic and the horns that blared from the angry drivers around him.

He glanced over his shoulder and made eye contact in the truck's side view mirror with the Russian who was driving. The Russian grimaced angrily at Pierre and then jerked the steering wheel aggressively, first one way and then the other, to try to shake off his unwanted passenger. Pierre's legs kicked out until he was parallel with the asphalt beneath him and then swung back until his whole body smacked against the side of the truck, knocking the wind out of him.

"That's going to hurt in the morning," Pierre moaned.

With what strength he had left, he scrambled his way up onto the top of the armored truck and then laid there for a minute to catch his breath. The Russian driver glanced in his side view mirror again, and with no sign of Pierre, he assumed that he had shaken him loose. He proceeded like a madman, however, barreling through the Toulouse streets without any intention of slowing down.

As Pierre rested atop the armored truck, he suddenly felt a strong gust of wind, together with the sounds of whirring propellers of helicopter blades.

He looked up curiously just as a helicopter was lowering itself down to the truck.

A figure emerged from the open side panel and jumped down, landing with a loud clunk onto the roof beside him. The helicopter circled around and disappeared behind a row of buildings. Pierre turned his attention to his new adversary, but quickly realized that this was an old foe.

"You!" He stammered. His realization would have been much more dramatic if he had remembered the man's name who was in front of him, but in his surprise it was escaping him. "You're that handsome guy!"

Although, Pierre couldn't help but notice that the man looked slightly less handsome with the fresh bruise on his forehead which had been left behind by his run-in with Colette's two by four.

"François Fouquet," the man reminded him, slightly annoyed. "It's really not that difficult of a name to remember. I don't see why I need to keep telling you every time that I see you."

"Listen, man," Pierre said as he staggered unsteadily to his feet. The truck was swerving beneath him and he struggled to balance himself. "I've had a hell of a week."

François was standing at the front of the truck; Pierre was at the rear. Pierre was facing François and the direction that the truck was heading.

"Whatever, Pierre," François continued. "I suppose it doesn't matter. This time, you aren't getting out of this alive. Let's dance."

Pierre feebly put his hands up to defend himself as François approached him.

François front flipped in front of him following up with a 360-degree spin before finishing off with a swift kick that landed on Pierre's shoulder.

"Ow!" Pierre cried out and stumbled backwards. He reached for his wounded shoulder. "Take it easy, that's where I just got shot!"

François rolled his eyes and rushed toward Pierre again, on the offensive. His fists and feet flew like bullets. Pierre was holding his hands up limply in front of him. He recognized his adversary's fighting style as Shaolin Kung Fu from his various studies of Chinese culture. Pierre had spent countless hours reading about it and knew every way to counter every move that François made. However, reading was a lot different from the real thing, as Pierre learned the hard way, and he failed to deflect even a single blow. Each of François' attacks connected on a different body part until Pierre was lifted off of his feet from a monstrous kick to the chest. Pierre finally landed back on top of the armored truck where his back smacked hard on the metal surface.

As Pierre lay there, holding his chest and gasping for breath, François wasn't content with just injuring him. He intended on killing Pierre. So, he continued to advance on him. Fortunately, Pierre still had barely enough wherewithal to squirm his way over to the very edge of the back of the truck. Fresh blood from his nose trickled its way into his mouth and the bitter taste met his tongue.

François smiled at Pierre but was silent. He grabbed Pierre by the legs and then flipped him over, sending Pierre's legs once again dangling freely off the back end of the truck. Pierre was barely able to grasp at the edge of the metal roof with his fingertips once more. This time, he was in a lot more pain and was barely able to hang on. He could feel his grip beginning to slip. With what remaining strength that he could muster, he hoisted himself up as much as he could with a loud grunt and then rested his chin on his forearms just in time to see François coming in for the final kill.

François stopped just in front of Pierre and then stomped his foot onto Pierre's hand which was barely supporting him. His hand crunched under François' weight, but Pierre barely managed to hang on.

"Any last words from the infamous *Black Lotus*?" François asked.

Pierre glanced over his shoulder at the asphalt below and then behind him at the line of cars that were watching the spectacle and waiting below to swallow him whole. Pierre looked back up at François and his eyes widened.

"Just one," he said. "Well, I guess three if you count those two. Twelve if you count those."

"Out with it already!" François demanded, crushing Pierre's foot even more under his weight.

Pierre let out a cry.

"Duck," he grunted. His eyes shifted suddenly just behind François.

François turned to follow Pierre's gaze just in time to see a traffic light pole overhang that hung across the street fast approaching. The front of the armored truck barely made it under the pole. Before François could even think to react, he stuck his hands up defensively in anticipation as the traffic light pole connected with his gut and yanked him off of his feet. Pierre ducked down just in time to avoid being hit and as he looked back, he could see François dangling helplessly from the pole. François wanted to yell out something threatening toward Pierre, but the blow had knocked the wind out of him, and he could do nothing else but cling to the pole as Pierre and the truck made a clean getaway.

Pierre breathed a sigh of relief and let himself down gently onto the narrow ledge below him that was right in front of the truck's steel lift gate, leading to the inner trunk bed. He undid the latch, lifted the gate and, just like that, he was inside.

Saturday, the 7th of January, 6:33 a.m.

O n the floor of the inner truck bed, rolling carelessly from side to side was the briefcase which contained the *real* Han Sapphire necklace.

Pierre limped over to it, struggling against the force of the truck which was still blazing through the streets and trying to toss him around. He finally reached it and picked it up. This would have seemingly put an end to the events of the past week, but there was still something else to be done.

The briefcase in his hands was a Doettling case, but it wasn't enough for Pierre to simply have the briefcase in his possession. He was after what was inside. After all, from the beginning he'd never intended to cooperate fully with Matthieu's plan, especially since it involved Pierre answering for all of his previous crimes. Pierre had made a plan of his own. He would play along with Matthieu until he had a chance to get the necklace alone and then he could disappear with it forever.

Pierre had overheard Genevieve and the Russian Ambassador discussing the smartphone app that was associated with the case. The Doettling cases had a completely different locking mechanism than the Doettling safes. They were tamper proof, waterproof, fireproof and probably even childproof. So, he couldn't simply crack into the briefcase as he had done with the safe in Boutrel's study.

Guessing the passcode was also out of the question. There were a million different combinations that it could be, and he had overheard Genevieve saying that if he guessed it wrong, the passcode would automatically reset. Guessing the code correctly would be statistically impossible. Pierre's journey seemed otherwise to have reached its unfortunate conclusion, the key word here being *seemed*.

Fortunately for Pierre, he didn't need to guess the passcode, because he'd seen Genevieve entering the numbers as he peered over her shoulder from the monastery window.

He punched in the code as he remembered it. The lock clicked and the latch popped open. There, resting comfortably in the padding was the *real* Han Sapphire necklace. Pierre felt a real tear form in his eye and then stream down his cheek.

He lifted the necklace out and tossed the empty briefcase aside.

"It weighs exactly what I thought it would," he said with delight. "And it's just as sparkly."

Pierre had done it. He had the necklace. Now, all that he needed to do was sell it, and then disappear forever. During this past week, he had been to hell and back, but he would do it all over again if it would bring him to this moment.

His precious moment didn't last, however, as he was rudely interrupted by the sound of something heavy clunking on the roof of the truck. In the next moment, the entire gravity of the truck bed shifted, and Pierre was tossed to the side and slammed against the wall.

"What the hell is it now?" Pierre mumbled. He tucked the necklace into his pocket and then found his way over to the open back of the truck on unsteady feet to look out.

Above him, Pierre could see that the helicopter had returned and had just secured an attachment to the top of the truck bed and had lifted it off the ground.

"Oh, come on," Pierre groaned. "That's not fair!"

"Pierre!" He heard a voice call. He turned to face the street in front of him. There was a police car, driven by Colette, with Detective Matthieu in the passenger's seat, speeding to try to keep up with the truck. "You have to jump, Pierre!" Matthieu shouted.

"Jump?!" Pierre shouted back in disbelief. "Are you crazy?!"

His hand grasped the Han Sapphire necklace in his pocket. If he jumped, he was giving it all away. He would be taken into police custody and then that was the end of it. If he didn't jump, on the other hand, he would be the prisoner of whoever was flying that helicopter, at least until they decided to land. At which point, he would have to run again.

"I'll catch you!" Matthieu shouted.

The truck bed shifted as the helicopter turned suddenly and Pierre was thrown to the side once more. He stared up at the helicopter and then back at the police car where his eyes met Colette's. If he ran, he would be doing so without her. He had an impossible choice to make.

Pierre steadied himself as well as he could and then planted his feet on the ground. He gave one last look up at the helicopter and then glanced back at the police car. Matthieu was flailing his arm out of the passenger side window as the needle of the speedometer was ticking around 85 km/hr. His arm was waving around excitedly and encouraging Pierre that it was now or never.

"If I die because you drop me," Pierre began. "I'm going to kill you!"

He pushed his full weight down against the truck bed and then launched himself into the air with one last desperate leap of faith.

Colette whipped the steering wheel around to try to provide Pierre with a landing pad as Matthieu flailed his arm around wildly in a feeble attempt to catch him.

Pierre floated through the air and then began his descent downwards. He crashed down on the hood of the police car and his momentum continued forward as he tumbled, head over heels.

Colette slammed on the brakes and she and Matthieu could hear Pierre tumbling across the roof overhead. Pierre narrowly grabbed onto the strand of flashing red and blue lights along the top of the police car as the car came to a screeching halt in the middle of the road. Pierre hung on for dear life until it all came to a complete stop and everything settled.

82

Saturday, the 7th of January, 6:42 a.m.

From the roof, Pierre could hear the faint wailing of emergency vehicles off in the distance and he watched as the helicopter escaped with the empty truck bed. Pierre felt a tinge of regret as he watched it disappear, but he felt an even stronger amount of relief. He rolled onto his back and stared up at the Toulouse sky, gasping for breath, everything hurt. Another moment later, he could hear slow laughter coming from the inside of the police car, which eventually developed into full blown hysterics and he couldn't help but to join in and laugh as well.

Colette emerged from the police car first.

"You've both lost your damn minds," she said. Matthieu came out after the laughter had quelled with an enormous smile on his face.

"We did it," he said. "We actually did it!"

Pierre flipped down from the top of the police car.

"I never doubted the plan for a second," he said. "Alright, maybe I did for a second."

"But, it's not over yet," Matthieu said. He stuck out his hand in between him and Pierre and motioned for him to hand it over. "The Han Sapphire."

Pierre hesitated for a moment. However, when he really thought about it, his choice wasn't really a choice at all. It was exactly what it was always going to be. He grinned and reached into his pocket. Colette walked over beside him.

"And I would have gotten away with it, too, if it weren't for you meddling kids," he said and produced the necklace. He slapped it down into Matthieu's hand.

Pierre noticed that Matthieu remained stone faced. It was still almost as if he were immune to the necklace's trance that everyone else seemed to fall victim to.

343

"I misjudged you, Pierre," Matthieu said as he held the necklace up against the morning sunlight.

"So, I guess this is it," Pierre said. "You're going to arrest me now?"

"You know," Matthieu began. "I think I've decided that I'm going to give you a head start."

"A head start?" Colette repeated.

"Really?" Pierre asked in disbelief.

"Really," Matthieu answered. "There's enough of a mess here to clean up already. I don't even think we've got enough holding cells for you anyways, Pierre. Genevieve is in custody and I overheard on the scanner that Norman somehow managed to apprehend the Russian Ambassador and three of his men. The fourth, the one who was driving that truck, is on his way right into a police barricade. It shouldn't be long before we have him as well."

"What about François?" Pierre asked.

"Was that who was dangling from that traffic light overhang just back a little way?"

Pierre nodded.

"Sounds like the description that I've got," he said.

"Don't worry, he's not going anywhere. Last I heard, they were sending a fire truck with a ladder to retrieve him."

"So, you're really letting me go?" Pierre asked.

"I'm not letting you go," Matthieu answered. "I'm just giving you a head start."

Pierre could hear the words that were coming out of Matthieu's mouth, but he could tell that they weren't entirely true. He had earned Matthieu's trust and respect by following through on the mission and now, Matthieu was giving both him and Colette a chance to escape together.

"Alright," Pierre replied. "So, we're just going to go then."

He grabbed Colette by the arm without her even having a chance to argue and they began walking away quickly.

"I'll see you soon, Pierre," Matthieu said with a grin as he stared down at the necklace.

In his hands, he held one of the most priceless artifacts in the world, but he still couldn't see how someone could kill for what essentially amounted to no more than a shiny rock.

Pierre and Colette continued off into the Toulouse sunrise. Colette was too shocked to speak, and her many questions flooded out of her mouth in a waterfall of unintelligible stammering. A sudden urge struck Pierre and he began whistling the tune to Patti LaBelle's "Lady Marmalade" as the lyrics *"Voulez-vous coucher avec moi ce soir?"* filled his head.

As they strolled along further and further away, Pierre couldn't help but think about the words that had been spoken to him long ago. Someone had once said that the difference between a good thief and a great thief was how well they could steal their audience's attention and then deceive them using nothing more than sleight of hand or misdirection. A good thief could steal something from you, but a great thief could make it disappear. A great thief, in a sense, was like a magician.

Pierre didn't know exactly where he and Colette were going to go, but he had an idea. He decided that he was going to find that secret beach with the glistening waterfall in the tropical paradise from the postcard he had pinned up in his room years ago. He could send his brother a Christmas card from there every year and live out the rest of his days in peace.

They quickened their pace away from Detective Matthieu. Pierre had a smug grin on his face and the real Han Sapphire necklace in his pocket.

Epilogue

When Matthieu arrived at the Toulouse Police Department a few hours later, he was greeted by a standing ovation from all the officers on the floor. At first, he tried to quiet them all, but then, he decided to let them continue. After all, he had earned this.

He sat down at his desk and the Chief came over to him.

"Matthieu," the Chief began. "I can't even begin to express how sorry I am about the events of the past week. If we had listened to you from the beginning, maybe we could have solved this thing much sooner."

"It was nothing," Matthieu assured him, but in that casual tone where you try to downplay what you've just accomplished so that other people will continue to commend you.

"No, no," the Chief insisted. "I said some things about you that I'm not proud of. You've been loyal to me for over 25 years and I turned my back on you. I only hope that I can make it up to you somehow."

Matthieu shrugged.

"I'm just glad we figured it out," he said with false modesty.

"To think that it was Genevieve the whole time," the Chief said. "Gives me the chills. Where's the necklace now?"

"I've got it down in forensics, Simone's logging it into evidence as we speak."

"Well, hopefully it stays there," the Chief said. "At least until it's ready to be retrieved. I've got some calls to make to Boutrel's widow and mistress. I'm sure they'll enjoy fighting over it.

Matthieu laughed. Hopefully there would be less slapping involved this time. Although, he seriously doubted it. "Anyways, Matthieu, it's good to have you back," the Chief said. "We'll clean the rest of this mess up and then get back to our normal, day to day. Oh, and I almost forgot. This is for you." The Chief reached into his jacket pocket and pulled out Matthieu's Detective badge. He placed it on the desk in front of him.

"Merry Christmas," he said. "Don't say that I never got you anything."

Matthieu always hated when the Chief made this joke, but he was in good spirits, so it didn't bother him as much this time.

The Chief retired to his office and left Matthieu alone at his desk. Matthieu reached into the cardboard box that rested at his feet and pulled out the mug that read, "World's Best Detective." He placed the mug in front of his computer and then leaned back in his chair and nodded agreeably at it. Suddenly, the phone on his desk rang. He reached over and answered it.

"Detective Matthieu," he said into the phone.

"Detective, it's Simone," squeaked the woman on the other end.

"Simone, to what do I owe the pleasure?"

"Well," she began hesitantly. "It's about the necklace…it's a fake."

Matthieu's eyes sharpened in front of him and his grip tightened on the phone in his hand.

"I'm going to kill him," he mumbled.

Fin

Afterword

Congratulations on making it this far! You've won the secret prize at the end of the book and that's to follow me on Twitter and Instagram @peterjmckenna2 or on at facebook.com/peterjmckenna2 for future titles and updates! Wow! Good for you!

In all seriousness though, I'd like to spend this last page making a few acknowledgements. Those of you who don't care, feel free to leave at any time.

First and foremost, I want to thank Lauren for your amazing cover design and for being patient with me and putting up with all of my frustrating tendencies while I was trying to write, reread and edit. Your check is in the mail.

Thank you to my mom for your help with proofreading. Without you, I'm sure half of the book would have been illegible. Also, for giving birth to me. That was pretty cool.

I also want to thank my friends and my entire family for your support and encouragement to pursue this. Without that push, I don't know if I would have ever finished this project.

Lastly, thank you to you, the reader. It's your support that makes all of this possible. I hope you enjoyed the ride. If you'd like, please leave a review on Amazon, whether positive or negative, to help spread the word. Although, if you made it this far, I hope it was because you enjoyed the book and that it wasn't out of spite.

Until next time,

Peter J. McKenna

Made in the USA
Columbia, SC
11 May 2020